BLOODSUCKERS

ALSO EDITED BY OTTO PENZLER

The Black Lizard Big Book of Pulps

The Vampire Archives

Agents of Treachery

Fangs

BLOODSUCKERS

◆◆◆

The Vampire Archives

VOLUME 1

EDITED AND WITH AN INTRODUCTION BY
OTTO PENZLER

PREFACE BY NEIL GAIMAN

VINTAGE CRIME BLACK LIZARD
VINTAGE BOOKS
A Division of Random House, Inc.
New York

A Vintage Crime/Black Lizard Original, July 2010

The Library of Congress has cataloged *The Vampire Archives* as follows:
The vampire archives / edited by Otto Penzler.
p. cm.
1. Vampires—Fiction. 2. Horror tales, American. I. Penzler, Otto.
PS648.V35V25 2009
813'.0873808375—dc22
2009008864

ISBN: 978-0-307-74184-4

www.vintagebooks.com

Printed in the United States of America
10 9 8 7 6 5 4 3 2 1

Contents

◆◆◆

Introduction

◆◆◆

OTTO PENZLER

Most everything you think you know about vampires is true. Or not. Trying to understand the myth of vampirism is like trying to understand the concept of God. All depends upon the culture, the era, and even an individual's imagination and gullibility, or faith.

In the contemporary Western world, the generally accepted notion of a vampire derives from Bram Stoker's iconic Victorian novel, *Dracula*. To most readers and filmgoers, a vampire is an immortal bloodsucking creature with supernatural powers, able to transform itself into other natural forms, such as a bat, a wolf, or other animal. It sleeps during daylight hours, usually in a coffin or grave, and arises to prey when darkness falls, or when the moon rises, usually by biting a neck and drinking its victim's blood. It cannot be harmed during those waking hours, although it may be repelled with a cross, holy water, or garlic. When it is resting, it may be killed with a wooden (or silver) stake through the heart, or by being decapitated.

The vampire myth actually dates back to ancient times in Eastern as well as Western culture. In ancient Jewish legend, Lilith, Adam's first wife, sucked the blood of men and attacked infants, turning them into Lilam, or children of Lilith, who then grew to feast on blood as well. This myth lasted into the Middle Ages.

In ancient Greece, vampires were the children of

Hecate: beautiful women who seduced and drained the blood of innocents. As often depicted in other parts of the world, they had the power to transform themselves into various kinds of animals. They were able to attack during daylight hours and at night. Also part of ancient Greece's mythological terror was Lamia, a horrible monster with a Gorgon's face, fangs, and snakelike tongue who specialized in killing children for their blood.

Other variations of the myth that date back two millennia are those of American Indian tribes who feared a vampiric creature with a trumpet-shaped mouth designed to suck out the brains of sleeping victims through their ears; the Chinese monster is Kian-si, with blazing green eyes and enormously long talons, causing it great pain when it walks, so it hops from place to place in order to attack its victims, ripping their heads off; in India, Hindu vampires focus on drunk or insane women, though they pale compared to Kali, whose blood lust is so overpowering that, failing to find a victim, she will tear open her own throat to drink blood; in Scotland, the glaistig takes the form of a beautiful young woman and dances with a man until he is exhausted, whereupon she will suck the blood out of him; and the jararaca of Brazil will slip into a house in the dark of night and drink the milk as well as the blood of sleeping women. It seems safe to say that there do not appear to be any cultures in which the myth of a bloodsucking creature with supernatural powers has not existed.

Naturally (or, perhaps more accurately, unnaturally) under these circumstances, with such a universal belief in some variation of the vampire myth, there are numerous examples of real people who exhibited some of the classic symptoms of the vampire, solidifying the legend in the minds of many.

Among the most heinous of real-life vampires was

Countess Elizabeth Bathory, whose family castle was on the border of Hungary, Austria, and the Slovak Republic, where she resided most of the time from 1560 to 1614. She began her life of terror by torturing her servants, any trivial transgression serving as an excuse to visit upon them the most vicious cruelty, including sewing closed the lips of a girl who spoke while performing her duties, submerging another in an icy river in the winter, throwing a naked girl into the snow and pouring ice water over her until she froze to death, and sticking long pins into various parts of their anatomy, including under their fingernails.

On one occasion, when a young girl accidentally pulled her hair while brushing it, she hit her so hard that she drew blood, which fell on her own hand. When she wiped it off, she was certain that her aging skin had acquired the moist freshness of her servant. She immediately had her male servants bring the prettiest young virgins to her and slash their throats and collect the blood in a giant vat in which she bathed. Convinced that this was restoring her youthful beauty, she soon needed more victims and sent emissaries to the nearby village, promising good jobs as maids and servants to beautiful young virgins. It did not take long for the villagers to suspect that the castle was home to vampirism, as bodies drained of blood were found dumped on the ground outside its walls. It also did not take long for the countess to realize that the bloodbaths were not working very well, so her companion, a witch, stated that she needed a better quality of blood, available only from nobility. She was able to attract twenty-five destitute young noblewomen to come to the castle with promises of comfort and instruction in the finer things of life. Within two weeks, all but two had been dispatched. When none of the village girls or noblewomen were ever seen again, convictions increased that they had become the victims of vampires, so complaints by the villagers and the local minister were sent to Parliament. Prime Minister Thurzo of Hungary, a cousin of the countess, attacked her castle and discovered the veritable abattoir with its mutilated victims as well as several caged girls awaiting their fate. He ordered her confined to a single room in the castle, bricking up the doors and windows, leaving only a small slit through which food could be passed. Unrepentant, the countess lived in this manner for three years, having caused the death of as many as 650 young women and girls.

If there can be evidence of a man being an undying vampire, it surely applies to Rasputin, who famously withstood poisoning sufficient to kill ten men, numerous bullets to the chest, and severe bludgeoning. He survived all of it. Only when he was wrapped in a sheet and thrown into a frozen river did he finally succumb. When his corpse was finally pulled from the water, his frozen arms were outstretched, apparently trying to claw through the ice that wouldn't allow him to escape. The cause of death was drowning, although the autopsy showed the presence of the poison and the bullets, either of which should have done the job. Part of the vampire legend is that running water cannot be tolerated, adding to the conviction that Rasputin was killed in one of the few ways in which it was possible to accomplish the deed.

The most famous individual associated with the myth of the vampire is the former ruler of Wallachia, a province on the border of Transylvania (now Romania), Vlad IV, known as the Impaler. Having been involved in the Crusades against the expansionist Ottoman Empire, he led an army against the Turks to drive them from the Danube Valley. A fierce and skilled warrior, he was moderately successful but, badly outnumbered by the powerful

Islamic army, he retreated to his castle, poisoning all the wells and burning his own villages along the way so that the Turks would find neither food nor water as they pursued him. When they approached his castle, they found the heads of twenty thousand Turkish prisoners impaled on spikes along both sides of the road, so frightening that the Turks turned away and refused to continue the pursuit.

No allegations or evidence suggest that Vlad the Impaler was a vampire, but the undoubted cruelty and extremity of his blood-letting, with an estimated thirty to forty thousand victims, including women and children, in addition to the Turkish soldiers, and even animals, have conspired to make him the ideal role model for the ultimate Dracula figure. Stoker recognized this, and enhanced the image by modeling Count Dracula's castle on Vlad's forbidding mountain residence, built on the backs of hundreds of laborers who died during its construction.

You will encounter some pretty nasty characters in this book, but even the most horrific creations of these masterful writers could not conjure villains as loathsome as their real-life predecessors.

Preface

◆◆◆

NEIL GAIMAN

We get the vampires we deserve, after all.

I remember, even as a small boy, growing up, craving vampires. The first vampire fiction I ever read was *Dracula*, on Christopher Harris's dad's bookshelf, and it was a struggle, even if I was a bright eight-year-old. I wanted more. I wanted vampires, like the ones in the opening sequence, not boring vampire hunters writing interminable letters to one another. I wanted to see the fangs come out. I wanted action.

The first horror film I ever watched was *Son of Dracula*, with Lon Chaney Jr. as the count, plotting evil in the Bayou. I watched him transform into a bat, watched him sleep in a coffin, and I loved him even as I feared him. I had believed before that closing a door would keep the monsters out, but Dracula slipped under doors in the form of smoke, and that terrified me. Doors did not work, even when closed.

Seven years later, on East Croydon station, I picked up a copy of Stephen King's novel *Salem's Lot*, its cover a black pressed-out child's face, with one red teardrop at the corner of the mouth. I remember the excitement with which I read it, as I first suspected it was a vampire story, then the delight when my suspicions were confirmed. Indeed, it was a vampire story, a big one, the kind I had wanted to read since I was a boy. And now, looking back,

I do not know how much of my excitement was simply because there *weren't* vampire novels in 1975, or not ones that were crossing my teenage path. The short stories that showed up from time to time in *The Pan Book of Horror Stories* and such had only served to whet my appetite, and I was too young to be allowed into late-night screenings of the breasts-and-blondes Hammer vampire offerings of the time, so I imagined them, and would, in time, be disappointed by how far short of my imaginings the real things would prove.

I wanted vampires. I missed them. A few years later, as a young writer, I would plot vampire stories because I wanted to read them, and because nobody else was writing the stories I wanted to read. (This is a very good reason to write, by the way.) I wrote great reviews of bad movies if they had vampires in them. In the mid-nineties I sold a vampire TV series, and then, when I was told I couldn't control what it looked like, couldn't make sure that it looked and felt grown-up, worried that it might be played for laughs or for camp, I took my vampires and went home. Because I didn't want to sell them short. Because I cared.

And then, one day, they were everywhere. You couldn't move for vampires. There were paranormal vampire romances and junior paranormal vampire romances. There were vampires on TV and vampires in the movies and vampires in the bedrooms and sad, strange, lonely people with their own custom-made teeth in the shadows at conventions. Everywhere vampires, stripped down like a simple metaphor for genitalia-free relationships. Vampires, as Stephen King said, taking Erica Jong's phrase, were the ultimate zipless fuck.

But there's life in the undead yet. You can't kill a vampire, after all, not even with one of those cool, fake-retro

Victorian vampire-killing kits they sell on eBay, with stakes and fresh garlic and perhaps some silver bullets in case you run into a werewolf on the way. They wouldn't be popular if there hadn't been over a hundred years of fine vampire literature as a foundation. Whether as metaphor or as something else—something that stirs the blood, makes you dream of immortality and night, that rustles the counterpanes, or just leaves you glancing nervously at a locked door, because after all, they can move as mist—vampires will always be with us.

So wait until dark, and begin to read . . .

BLOODSUCKERS

GOOD LADY DUCAYNE

⬥⬥⬥

M. E. BRADDON

Bella Rolleston had made up her mind that her only chance of earning her bread and helping her mother to an occasional crust was by going out into the great unknown world as companion to a lady. She was willing to go to any lady rich enough to pay her a salary and so eccentric as to wish for a hired companion. Five shillings told off reluctantly from one of those sovereigns which were so rare with the mother and daughter, and which melted away so quickly, five solid shillings, had been handed to a smartly dressed lady in an office in Harbeck Street, London, W., in the hope that this very Superior Person would find a situation and a salary for Miss Rolleston.

The Superior Person glanced at the two half-crowns as they lay on the table where Bella's hand had placed them, to make sure they were neither of them florins, before she wrote a description of Bella's qualifications and requirements in a formidable-looking ledger.

"Age?" she asked, curtly.

"Eighteen, last July."

"Any accomplishments?"

"No; I am not at all accomplished. If I were I should want to be a governess—a companion seems the lowest stage."

"We have some highly accomplished ladies on our books as companions, or chaperon companions."

"Oh, I know!" babbled Bella, loquacious in her youthful candor. "But that is quite a different thing. Mother hasn't been able to afford a piano since I was twelve years old, so I'm afraid I've forgotten how to play. And I have had to help mother with her needlework, so there hasn't been much time to study."

"Please don't waste time upon explaining what you can't do, but kindly tell me anything you can do," said the Superior Person, crushingly, with her pen poised between delicate fingers waiting to write. "Can you read aloud for two or three hours at a stretch? Are you active and handy, an early riser, a good walker, sweet tempered, and obliging?"

"I can say yes to all those questions except about the sweetness. I think I have a pretty good temper, and I should be anxious to oblige anybody who paid for my services. I should want them to feel that I was really earning my salary."

"The kind of ladies who come to me would not care for a talkative companion," said the Person, severely, having finished writing in her book. "My connection lies chiefly among the aristocracy, and in that class considerable deference is expected."

"Oh, of course," said Bella, "but it's quite different when I'm talking to you. I want to tell you all about myself once and forever."

"I am glad it is to be only once!" said the Person, with the edges of her lips.

The Person was of uncertain age, tightly laced in a black silk gown. She had a powdery complexion and a handsome clump of somebody else's hair on the top of her head. It may be that Bella's girlish freshness and vivacity had an irritating effect upon nerves weakened by an eight-hour day in that overheated second floor in Harbeck

Street. To Bella the official apartment, with its Brussels carpet, velvet curtains and velvet chairs, and French clock, ticking loud on the marble chimney-piece, suggested the luxury of a palace, as compared with another second floor in Walworth where Mrs. Rolleston and her daughter had managed to exist for the last six years.

"Do you think you have anything on your books that would suit me?" faltered Bella, after a pause.

"Oh, dear, no; I have nothing in view at present," answered the Person, who had swept Bella's half-crowns into a drawer, absent-mindedly, with the tips of her fingers. "You see, you are so very unformed—so much too young to be companion to a lady of position. It is a pity you have not enough education for a nursery governess; that would be more in your line."

"And do you think it will be very long before you can get me a situation?" asked Bella, doubtfully.

"I really cannot say. Have you any particular reason for being so impatient—not a love affair, I hope?"

"A love affair!" cried Bella, with flaming cheeks. "What utter nonsense. I want a situation because mother is poor, and I hate being a burden to her. I want a salary that I can share with her."

"There won't be much margin for sharing in the salary you are likely to get at your age—and with your—very—unformed manners," said the Person, who found Bella's peony cheeks, bright eyes, and unbridled vivacity more and more oppressive.

"Perhaps if you'd be kind enough to give me back the fee I could take it to an agency where the connection isn't quite so aristocratic," said Bella, who—as she told her mother in her recital of the interview—was determined not to be sat upon.

"You will find no agency that can do more for you than

mine," replied the Person, whose harpy fingers never relinquished coin. "You will have to wait for your opportunity. Yours is an exceptional case: but I will bear you in mind, and if anything suitable offers I will write to you. I cannot say more than that."

The half-contemptuous bend of the stately head, weighted with borrowed hair, indicated the end of the interview. Bella went back to Walworth—tramped sturdily every inch of the way in the September afternoon—and "took off" the Superior Person for the amusement of her mother and the landlady, who lingered in the shabby little sitting-room after bringing in the tea-tray, to applaud Miss Rolleston's "taking off."

"Dear, dear, what a mimic she is!" said the landlady. "You ought to have let her go on the stage, mum. She might have made her fortune as an actress."

II

Bella waited and hoped, and listened for the postman's knocks which brought such store of letters for the parlors and the first floor, and so few for that humble second floor, where mother and daughter sat sewing with hand and with wheel and treadle, for the greater part of the day. Mrs. Rolleston was a lady by birth and education; but it had been her bad fortune to marry a scoundrel; for the last half-dozen years she had been that worst of widows, a wife whose husband had deserted her. Happily, she was courageous, industrious, and a clever needlewoman; and she had been able just to earn a living for herself and her only child, by making mantles and cloaks for a West-end house. It was not a luxurious living. Cheap lodgings in a shabby street off the Walworth Road, scanty dinners, homely food, well-worn raiment, had been the portion of mother and daughter; but they loved each other so dearly, and Nature had made them both so light-hearted, that they had contrived somehow to be happy.

But now this idea of going out into the world as companion to some fine lady had rooted itself into Bella's mind, and although she idolized her mother, and although the parting of mother and daughter must needs tear two loving hearts into shreds, the girl longed for enterprise and change and excitement, as the pages of old longed to be knights, and to start for the Holy Land to break a lance with the infidel.

She grew tired of racing downstairs every time the postman knocked, only to be told "nothing for you, miss," by the smudgy-faced drudge who picked up the letters from the passage floor. "Nothing for you, miss," grinned the lodging-house drudge, till at last Bella took heart of grace and walked up to Harbeck Street, and asked the Superior Person how it was that no situation had been found for her.

"You are too young," said the Person, "and you want a salary."

"Of course I do," answered Bella. "Don't other people want salaries?"

"Young ladies of your age generally want a comfortable home."

"I don't," snapped Bella. "I want to help mother."

"You can call again this day week," said the Person, "or, if I hear of anything in the meantime, I will write to you."

No letter came from the Person, and in exactly a week Bella put on her nearest hat, the one that had been seldomest caught in the rain, and trudged off to Harbeck Street.

It was a dull October afternoon, and there was a greyness in the air which might turn to fog before night. The Walworth Road shops gleamed brightly through that grey atmosphere, and though to a young lady reared in Mayfair or Belgravia such shop-windows would have been unworthy of a glance, they were a snare and temptation for Bella. There were so many things that she longed for, and would never be able to buy.

Harbeck Street is apt to be empty at this dead season of the year, a long, long street, an endless perspective of eminently respectable houses. The Person's office was at the further end, and Bella looked down that long, grey vista almost despairingly, more tired than usual with the trudge from Walworth. As she looked, a carriage passed her, an old-fashioned, yellow chariot, on cee springs, drawn by a pair of high grey horses, with the stateliest of coachmen driving them, and a tall footman sitting by his side.

"It looks like the fairy godmother's coach," thought Bella. "I shouldn't wonder if it began by being a pumpkin."

It was a surprise when she reached the Person's door to find the yellow chariot standing before it, and the tall footman waiting near the doorstep. She was almost afraid to go in and meet the owner of that splendid carriage. She had caught only a glimpse of its occupant as the chariot rolled by, a plumed bonnet, a patch of ermine.

The Person's smart page ushered her upstairs and knocked at the official door. "Miss Rolleston," he announced, apologetically, while Bella waited outside.

"Show her in," said the Person, quickly; and then Bella heard her murmuring something in a low voice to her client.

Bella went in fresh, blooming, a living image of youth and hope, and before she looked at the Person her gaze was riveted by the owner of the chariot.

Never had she seen anyone as old as the old lady sitting by the Person's fire: a little old figure, wrapped from chin to feet in an ermine mantle; a withered, old face under a plumed bonnet—a face so wasted by age that it seemed only a pair of eyes and a peaked chin. The nose was peaked, too, but between the sharply pointed chin and the great, shining eyes, the small, aquiline nose was hardly visible.

"This is Miss Rolleston, Lady Ducayne."

Claw-like fingers, flashing with jewels, lifted a double eyeglass to Lady Ducayne's shining black eyes, and through the glasses Bella saw those unnaturally bright eyes magnified to a gigantic size, and glaring at her awfully.

"Miss Torpinter has told me all about you," said the old voice that belonged to the eyes. "Have you good health? Are you strong and active, able to eat well, sleep well, walk well, able to enjoy all that there is good in life?"

"I have never known what it is to be ill, or idle," answered Bella.

"Then I think you will do for me."

"Of course, in the event of references being perfectly satisfactory," put in the Person.

"I don't want references. The young woman looks frank and innocent. I'll take her on trust."

"So like you, dear Lady Ducayne," murmured Miss Torpinter.

"I want a strong young woman whose health will give me no trouble."

"You have been so unfortunate in that respect," cooed the Person, whose voice and manner were subdued to a melting sweetness by the old woman's presence.

"Yes, I've been rather unlucky," grunted Lady Ducayne.

"But I am sure Miss Rolleston will not disappoint you, though certainly after your unpleasant experience with Miss Tomson, who looked the picture of health—and

Miss Blandy, who said she had never seen a doctor since she was vaccinated—"

"Lies, no doubt," muttered Lady Ducayne, and then turning to Bella, she asked, curtly, "You don't mind spending the winter in Italy, I suppose?"

In Italy! The very word was magical. Bella's fair young face flushed crimson.

"It has been the dream of my life to see Italy," she gasped.

From Walworth to Italy! How far, how impossible such a journey had seemed to that romantic dreamer.

"Well, your dream will be realized. Get yourself ready to leave Charing Cross by the train deluxe this day week at eleven. Be sure you are at the station a quarter before the hour. My people will look after you and your luggage."

Lady Ducayne rose from her chair, assisted by her crutch-stick, and Miss Torpinter escorted her to the door.

"And with regard to salary?" questioned the Person on the way.

"Salary, oh, the same as usual—and if the young woman wants a quarter's pay in advance you can write to me for a check," Lady Ducayne answered, carelessly.

Miss Torpinter went all the way downstairs with her client, and waited to see her seated in the yellow chariot. When she came upstairs again she was slightly out of breath, and she had resumed that superior manner which Bella had found so crushing.

"You may think yourself uncommonly lucky, Miss Rolleston," she said. "I have dozens of young ladies on my books whom I might have recommended for this situation—but I remembered having told you to call this afternoon—and I thought I would give you a chance. Old Lady Ducayne is one of the best people on my books. She gives her companion a hundred a year, and pays all the travelling expenses. You will live in the lap of luxury."

"A hundred a year! How too lovely! Shall I have to dress very grandly? Does Lady Ducayne keep much company?"

"At her age! No, she lives in seclusion—in her own apartments—her French maid, her footman, her medical attendant, her courier."

"Why did those other companions leave her?" asked Bella.

"Their health broke down!"

"Poor things, and so they had to leave?"

"Yes, they had to leave. I suppose you would like a quarter's salary in advance?"

"Oh, yes, please. I shall have things to buy."

"Very well, I will write for Lady Ducayne's check, and I will send you the balance—after deducting my commission for the year."

"To be sure, I had forgotten the commission."

"You don't suppose I keep this office for pleasure."

"Of course not," murmured Bella, remembering the five shillings entrance fee; but nobody could expect a hundred a year and a winter in Italy for five shillings.

III

From Miss Rolleston, at Cap Ferrino, to Mrs. Rolleston, in Beresford Street, Walworth, London.

How I wish you could see this place, dearest; the blue sky, the olive woods, the orange and lemon orchards between the cliffs and the sea—sheltering in the hollow of the great hills—and with summer waves dancing up to the narrow ridge of pebbles and weeds which is the

Italian idea of a beach! Oh, how I wish you could see it all, mother dear, and bask in this sunshine, that makes it so difficult to believe the date at the head of this paper. November! The air is like an English June—the sun is so hot that I can't walk a few yards without an umbrella. And to think of you at Walworth while I am here! I could cry at the thought that perhaps you will never see this lovely coast, this wonderful sea, these summer flowers that bloom in winter. There is a hedge of pink geraniums under my window, mother—a thick, rank hedge, as if the flowers grew wild—and there are Dijon roses climbing over arches and palisades all along the terrace—a rose garden full of bloom in November! Just picture it all! You could never imagine the luxury of this hotel. It is nearly new, and has been built and decorated regardless of expense. Our rooms are upholstered in pale blue satin, which shows up Lady Ducayne's parchment complexion; but as she sits all day in a corner of the balcony basking in the sun, except when she is in her carriage, and all the evening in her armchair close to the fire, and never sees anyone but her own people, her complexion matters very little.

She has the handsomest suite of rooms in the hotel. My bedroom is inside hers, the sweetest room—all blue satin and white lace—white enamelled furniture, looking-glasses on every wall, till I know my pert little profile as I never knew it before. The room was really meant for Lady Ducayne's dressing-room, but she ordered one of the blue satin couches to be arranged as a bed for me—the prettiest little bed, which I can wheel near the window on sunny mornings, as it is on castors and easily moved about. I feel as if Lady Ducayne were a funny old grandmother, who had suddenly appeared in my life, very, very rich, and very, very kind.

She is not at all exacting. I read aloud to her a good deal, and she dozes and nods while I read. Sometimes I hear her moaning in her sleep—as if she had troublesome dreams. When she is tired of my reading she orders Francine, her maid, to read a French novel to her, and I hear her chuckle and groan now and then, as if she were more interested in those books than in Dickens or Scott. My French is not good enough to follow Francine, who reads very quickly. I have a great deal of liberty, for Lady Ducayne often tells me to run away and amuse myself; I roam about the hills for hours. Everything is so lovely. I lose myself in olive woods, always climbing up and up towards the pine woods above—and above the pines there are the snow mountains that just show their white peaks above the dark hills. Oh, you poor dear, how can I ever make you understand what this place is like—you, whose poor, tired eyes have only the opposite side of Beresford Street? Sometimes I go no farther than the terrace in front of the hotel, which is a favorite lounging-place with everybody. The gardens lie below, and the tennis courts where I sometimes play with a very nice girl, the only person in the hotel with whom I have made friends. She is a year older than I, and has come to Cap Ferrino with her brother, a doctor—or a medical student, who is going to be a doctor. He passed his M.B. exam at Edinburgh just before they left home, Lotta told me. He came to Italy entirely on his sister's account. She had a troublesome chest attack last summer and was ordered to winter abroad. They are orphans, quite alone in the world, and so fond of each other. It is very nice for me to have such a friend as Lotta. She is so thoroughly respectable. I can't help using that word, for some of the girls in this hotel go on in a way that I know you would shudder at. Lotta was brought up by an aunt, deep down in the country, and knows hardly anything about life. Her brother won't allow her to read a novel, French or English, that he has not read and approved.

"He treats me like a child," she told me, "but I don't mind, for it's nice to know somebody loves me, and cares about what I do, and even about my thoughts."

Perhaps this is what makes some girls so eager to marry—the want of someone strong and brave and honest and true to care for them and order them about. I want no one, mother darling, for I have you, and you are all the world to me. No husband could ever come between us two. If I ever were to marry he would have only the second place in my heart. But I don't suppose I ever shall marry, or even know what it is like to have an offer of marriage. No young man can afford to marry a penniless girl nowadays. Life is too expensive.

Mr. Stafford, Lotta's brother, is very clever, and very kind. He thinks it is rather hard for me to have to live with such an old woman as Lady Ducayne, but then he does not know how poor we are—you and I—and what a wonderful life this seems to me in this lovely place. I feel a selfish wretch for enjoying all my luxuries, while you, who want them so much more than I, have none of them—hardly know what they are like—do you, dearest?—for my scamp of a father began to go to the dogs soon after you were married, and since then life has been all trouble and care and struggle for you.

This letter was written when Bella had been less than a month at Cap Ferrino, before the novelty had worn off the landscape, and before the pleasure of luxurious surroundings had begun to cloy. She wrote to her mother every week, such long letters as girls who have lived in closest companionship with a mother alone can write; letters that are like a diary of heart and mind. She wrote gaily always, but when the new year began Mrs. Rolleston thought she detected a note of melancholy under all those lively details about the place and the people.

"My poor girl is getting homesick," she thought. "Her heart is in Beresford Street."

It might be that she missed her new friend and companion, Lotta Stafford, who had gone with her brother for a little tour to Genoa and Spezia, and as far as Pisa. They were to return before February; but in the meantime Bella might naturally feel very solitary among all those strangers, whose manners and doings she described so well.

The mother's instinct had been true. Bella was not so happy as she had been in that first flush of wonder and delight which followed the change from Walworth to the Riviera. Somehow, she knew not how, lassitude had crept upon her. She no longer loved to climb the hills, no longer flourished her orange stick in sheer gladness of heart as her light feet skipped over the rough ground and the coarse grass on the mountain side. The odor of rosemary and thyme, the fresh breath of the sea no longer filled her with rapture. She thought of Beresford Street and her mother's face with a sick longing. They were so far—so far away! And then she thought of Lady Ducayne, sitting by the heaped-up olive logs in the overheated salon—thought of that wizened-nutcracker profile, and those gleaming eyes, with an invincible horror.

Visitors at the hotel had told her that the air of Cap Ferrino was relaxing—better suited to age than to youth, to sickness than to health. No doubt it was so. She was not so well as she had been at Walworth; but she told herself that she was suffering only from the pain of separation from the dear companion of her girlhood, the mother who had been nurse, sister, friend, flatterer, all things in this world to her. She had shed many tears over that parting, had spent many a melancholy hour on the marble terrace with yearning eyes looking westward, and with her heart's desire a thousand miles away.

She was sitting in her favorite spot, an angle at the eastern end of the terrace, a quiet little nook sheltered by orange trees, when she heard a couple of Riviera habitués talking in the garden below. They were sitting on a bench against the terrace wall.

She had no idea of listening to their talk, till the sound of Lady Ducayne's name attracted her, and then she listened without any thought of wrong-doing. They were talking no secrets—just casually discussing a hotel acquaintance.

They were two elderly people whom Bella only knew by sight. An English clergyman who had wintered abroad for half his lifetime; a stout, comfortable, well-to-do spinster, whose chronic bronchitis obliged her to migrate annually.

"I have met her about Italy for the last ten years," said the lady, "but have never found out her real age."

"I put her down at a hundred—not a year less," replied the parson. "Her reminiscences all go back to the Regency. She was evidently then in her zenith; and I have heard her say things that showed she was in Parisian society when the First Empire was at its best—before Josephine was divorced."

"She doesn't talk much now."

"No, there's not much life left in her. She is wise in keeping herself secluded. I only wonder that wicked old quack, her Italian doctor, didn't finish her off years ago."

"I should think it must be the other way, and that he keeps her alive."

"My dear Miss Manders, do you think foreign quackery ever kept anybody alive?"

"Well, there she is—and she never goes anywhere without him. He certainly has an unpleasant countenance."

"Unpleasant," echoed the parson. "I don't believe the foul fiend himself can beat him in ugliness. I pity that poor young woman who has to live between old Lady Ducayne and Dr. Parravicini."

"But the old lady is very good to her companions."

"No doubt. She is very free with her cash; the servants call her good Lady Ducayne. She is a withered old female Croesus, and knows she'll never be able to get through her money, and doesn't relish the idea of other people enjoying it when she's in her coffin. People who live to be as old as she is become slavishly attached to life. I daresay she's generous to those poor girls—but she can't make them happy. They die in her service."

"Don't say 'they,' Mr. Carton; I know that one poor girl died at Mentone last spring."

"Yes, and another poor girl died in Rome three years ago. I was there at the time. Good Lady Ducayne left her there in an English family. The girl had every comfort. The old woman was very liberal to her—but she died. I tell you, Miss Manders, it is not good for any young woman to live with two such horrors as Lady Ducayne and Parravicini."

They talked of other things—but Bella hardly heard them. She sat motionless, and a cold wind seemed to come down upon her from the mountains and to creep up to her from the sea, till she shivered as she sat there in the sunshine, in the shelter of the orange trees in the midst of all that beauty and brightness.

Yes, they were uncanny, certainly, the pair of them—she so like an aristocratic witch in her withered old age; he of no particular age, with a face that was more like a waxen mask than any human countenance Bella had ever seen. What did it matter? Old age is venerable, and worthy of all reverence; and Lady Ducayne had been very kind to her. Dr. Parravicini was a harmless, inoffensive student, who seldom looked up from the book he was reading. He had his private sitting-room, where he made experiments in chemistry and natural science—perhaps in alchemy. What could it matter to Bella? He had always been polite to her, in his far-off way. She could not be more happily placed than she was—in this palatial hotel, with this rich old lady.

No doubt she missed the young English girl who had been so friendly, and it might be that she missed the girl's brother, for Mr. Stafford had talked to her a good deal—had interested himself in the books she was reading, and her manner of amusing herself when she was not on duty.

"You must come to our little salon when you are 'off,' as the hospital nurses call it, and we can have some music. No doubt you play and sing?" Upon which Bella had to own with a blush of shame that she had forgotten how to play the piano ages ago.

"Mother and I used to sing duets sometimes between the lights, without accompaniment," she said, and the tears came into her eyes as she thought of the humble room, the half-hour's respite from work, the sewing machine standing where a piano ought to have been, and her mother's plaintive voice, so sweet, so true, so dear.

Sometimes she found herself wondering whether she would ever see that beloved mother again. Strange forebodings came into her mind. She was angry with herself for giving way to melancholy thoughts.

One day she questioned Lady Ducayne's French maid

about those two companions who had died within three years.

"They were poor, feeble creatures," Francine told her. "They looked fresh and bright enough when they came to Miladi, but they ate too much, and they were lazy. They died of luxury and idleness. Miladi was too kind to them. They had nothing to do, and so they took to fancying things; fancying the air didn't suit them, that they couldn't sleep."

"I sleep well enough, but I have had a strange dream several times since I have been in Italy."

"Ah, you had better not begin to think about dreams, or you will be like those other girls. They were dreamers—and they dreamt themselves into the cemetery."

The dream troubled her a little, not because it was a ghastly or frightening dream, but on account of sensations which she had never felt before in sleep—a whirring of wheels that went round in her brain, a great noise like a whirlwind, but rhythmical like the ticking of a gigantic clock: and then in the midst of this uproar as of winds and waves she seemed to sink into a gulf of unconsciousness, out of sleep into far deeper sleep—total extinction. And then, after that black interval, there had come the sound of voices, and then again the whirr of wheels, louder and louder—and again the black—and then she awoke, feeling languid and oppressed.

She told Dr. Parravicini of her dream one day, on the only occasion when she wanted his professional advice. She had suffered rather severely from the mosquitoes before Christmas—and had been almost frightened at finding a wound upon her arm which she could only attribute to the venomous sting of one of these torturers. Parravicini put on his glasses, and scrutinized the angry mark on the round, white arm, as Bella stood before him and Lady Ducayne with her sleeve rolled up above her elbow.

"Yes, that's rather more than a joke," he said. "He has caught you on the top of a vein. What a vampire! But there's no harm done, signorina, nothing that a little dressing of mine won't heal. You must always show me any bite of this nature. It might be dangerous if neglected. These creatures feed on poison and disseminate it."

"And to think that such tiny creatures can bite like this," said Bella. "My arm looks as if it had been cut by a knife."

"If I were to show you a mosquito's sting under my microscope you wouldn't be surprised at that," replied Parravicini.

Bella had to put up with the mosquito bites, even when they came on the top of a vein, and produced that ugly wound. The wound recurred now and then at longish intervals, and Bella found Dr. Parravicini's dressing a speedy cure. If he were the quack his enemies called him, he had at least a light hand and a delicate touch in performing this small operation.

Bella Rolleston to Mrs. Rolleston—April 14th.

Ever Dearest,

Behold the check for my second quarter's salary—five and twenty pounds. There is no one to pinch off a whole tenner for a year's commission as there was last time, so it is all for you, mother, dear. I have plenty of pocket-money in hand from the cash I brought away with me, when you insisted on my keeping more than I wanted. It isn't possible to spend money here—except on occasional tips to servants, or sous to beggars and children—unless one had lots to spend, for everything one would like to buy—tortoise-shell, coral, lace—is so ridiculously dear that only a millionaire ought to look at it. Italy is a dream of beauty; but for shopping, give me Newington Causeway.

You ask me so earnestly if I am quite well that I fear my letters must have been very dull lately. Yes, dear, I am well—but I am not quite so strong as I was when I used to trudge to the West-end to buy half a pound of tea—just for a constitutional walk—or to Dulwich to look at the pictures. Italy is relaxing, and I feel what the people here call "slack." But I fancy I can see your dear face looking worried as you read this. Indeed, and indeed, I am not ill. I am only a little tired of this lovely scene—as I suppose one might get tired of looking at one of Turner's pictures if it hung on a wall that was always opposite one. I think of you every hour in every day—think of you and our homely little room—our dear little shabby parlor, with the armchairs from the wreck of your old home, and Dick singing in his cage over the sewing machine. Dear, shrill, maddening Dick, who, we flattered ourselves, was so passionately fond of us. Do tell me in your next letter that he is well.

My friend Lotta and her brother never came back after all. They went from Pisa to Rome. Happy mortals! And they are to be on the Italian lakes in May; which lake was not decided when Lotta last wrote to me. She has been a charming correspondent, and has confided all her little flirtations to me. We are all to go to Bellaggio next week—by Genoa and Milan. Isn't that lovely? Lady Ducayne travels by the easiest stages—except when she is bottled up in the train deluxe. We shall stop two days at Genoa and one at Milan. What a bore I shall be to you with my talk about Italy when I come home.

Love and love—and ever more love from your adoring,

Bella.

IV

Herbert Stafford and his sister had often talked of the pretty English girl with her fresh complexion, which made such a pleasant touch of rosy color among all those sallow faces at the Grand Hotel. The young doctor thought of her with a compassionate tenderness—her utter loneliness in that great hotel where there were so many people, her bondage to that old, old woman, where everybody else was free to think of nothing but enjoying life. It was a hard fate, and the poor child was evidently devoted to her mother, and felt the pain of separation—"only two of them, and very poor, and all the world to each other," he thought.

Lotta told him one morning that they were to meet again at Bellaggio. "The old thing and her court are to be there before we are," she said. "I shall be charmed to have Bella again. She is so bright and gay—in spite of an occasional touch of homesickness. I never took to a girl on a short acquaintance as I did to her."

"I like her best when she is homesick," said Herbert, "for then I am sure she has a heart."

"What have you to do with hearts, except for dissection? Don't forget that Bella is an absolute pauper. She told me in confidence that her mother makes mantles for a West-end shop. You can hardly have a lower depth than that."

"I shouldn't think any less of her if her mother made matchboxes."

"Not in the abstract—of course not. Matchboxes are honest labor. But you couldn't marry a girl whose mother makes mantles."

"We haven't come to the consideration of that question yet," answered Herbert, who liked to provoke his sister.

In two years' hospital practice he had seen too much of the grim realities of life to retain any prejudices about rank. Cancer, phthisis, gangrene leave a man with little respect for the humanity. The kernel is always the same—fearfully and wonderfully made—a subject for pity and terror.

Mr. Stafford and his sister arrived at Bellaggio in a fair May evening. The sun was going down as the steamer approached the pier; and all that glory of purple bloom which curtains every wall at this season of the year flushed and deepened in the glowing light. A group of ladies were standing on the pier watching the arrivals, and among them Herbert saw a pale face that startled him out of his wonted composure.

"There she is," murmured Lotta, at his elbow, "but how dreadfully changed. She looks a wreck."

They were shaking hands with her a few minutes later, and a flush had lighted up her poor pinched face in the pleasure of meeting.

"I thought you might come this evening," she said. "We have been here a week."

She did not add that she had been there every evening to watch the boat in, and a good many times during the day. The Grand Bretagne was close by, and it had been easy for her to creep to the pier when the boat bell rang. She felt a joy in meeting these people again; a sense of being with friends; a confidence which Lady Ducayne's goodness had never inspired in her.

"Oh, you poor darling, how awfully ill you must have been," exclaimed Lotta, as the two girls embraced.

Bella tried to answer, but her voice was choked with tears.

"What has been the matter, dear? That horrid influenza, I suppose?"

"No, no, I have not been ill—I have only felt a little weaker than I used to be. I don't think the air of Cap Ferrino quite agreed with me."

"It must have disagreed with you abominably. I never saw such a change in anyone. Do let Herbert doctor you. He is fully qualified, you know. He prescribed for ever so many influenza patients at the Londres. They were glad to get advice from an English doctor in a friendly way."

"I am sure he must be very clever!" faltered Bella. "But there is really nothing the matter. I am not ill, and if I were ill, Lady Ducayne's physician—"

"That dreadful man with the yellow face? I would as soon one of the Borgias prescribed for me. I hope you haven't been taking any of his medicines."

"No, dear, I have taken nothing. I have never complained of being ill."

This was said while they were all three walking to the hotel. The Staffords' rooms had been secured in advance, pretty ground-floor rooms, opening into the garden. Lady Ducayne's statelier apartments were on the floor above.

"I believe these rooms are just under ours," said Bella.

"Then it will be all the easier for you to run down to us," replied Lotta, which was not really the case, as the grand staircase was in the center of the hotel.

"Oh, I shall find it easy enough," said Bella. "I'm afraid you'll have too much of my society. Lady Ducayne sleeps away half the day in this warm weather, so I have a good deal of idle time; and I get awfully moped thinking of mother and home."

Her voice broke upon the last word. She could not have thought of that poor lodging which went by the name of home more tenderly had it been the most beautiful that art and wealth ever created. She moped and pined in this lovely garden, with the sunlit lake and the romantic hills spreading out their beauty before her. She was homesick and she had dreams; or, rather, an occasional recurrence of that one bad dream with all its strange sensations—it was more like a hallucination than dreaming—the whirring of wheels, the sinking into an abyss, the struggling back to consciousness. She had the dream shortly before she left Cap Ferrino, but not since she had come to Bellaggio, and she began to hope the air in this lake district suited her better, and that those strange sensations would never return.

Mr. Stafford wrote a prescription and had it made up at the chemist's near the hotel. It was a powerful tonic, and after two bottles, and a row or two on the lake, and some rambling over the hills and in the meadows where the spring flowers made earth seem paradise, Bella's spirits and looks improved as if by magic.

"It is a wonderful tonic," she said, but perhaps in her heart of hearts she knew that the doctor's kind voice, and the friendly hand that helped her in and out of the boat, and the lake, had something to do with her cure.

"I hope you don't forget that her mother makes mantles," Lotta said warningly.

"Or matchboxes; it is just the same thing, so far as I am concerned."

"You mean that in no circumstances could you think of marrying her?"

"I mean that if ever I love a woman well enough to think of marrying her, riches or rank will count for nothing with me. But I fear—I fear your poor friend may not live to be any man's wife."

"Do you think her so very ill?"

He sighed, and left the question unanswered.

One day, while they were gathering wild hyacinths in an upland meadow, Bella told Mr. Stafford about her bad dream.

"It is curious only because it is hardly like a dream," she said. "I daresay you could find some commonsense reason for it. The position of my head on my pillow, or the atmosphere, or something."

And then she described her sensations: how in the midst of sleep there came a sudden sense of suffocation; and then those whirring wheels, so loud, so terrible; and then a blank; and then a coming back to waking consciousness.

"Have you ever had chloroform given you—by a dentist, for instance?"

"Never—Dr. Parravicini asked me that question one day."

"Lately?"

"No, long ago, when were were in the train deluxe."

"Has Dr. Parravicini prescribed for you since you began to feel weak and ill?"

"Oh, he has given me a tonic from time to time, but I hate medicine, and took very little of the stuff. And then I am not ill, only weaker than I used to be. I was ridiculously strong and well when I lived at Walworth, and used to take long walks every day. Mother made me take those tramps to Dulwich or Norwood, for fear I should suffer from too much sewing machine; sometimes—but very seldom—she went with me. She was generally toiling at home while I was enjoying fresh air and exercise. And she was very careful about our food—that, however plain it was, it should be always nourishing and ample. I owe it to her care that I grew up such a great, strong creature."

"You don't look great or strong now, you poor dear," said Lotta.

"I'm afraid Italy doesn't agree with me."

"Perhaps it is not Italy, but being cooped up with Lady Ducayne that has made you ill."

"But I am never cooped up. Lady Ducayne is absurdly kind, and lets me roam about or sit in the balcony all day if I like. I have read more novels since I have been with her than in all the rest of my life."

"Then she is very different from the average old lady, who is usually a slave driver," said Stafford. "I wonder why she carries a companion about with her if she has so little need of society."

"Oh, I am only part of her state. She is inordinately rich—and the salary she gives me doesn't count. Apropos of Dr. Parravicini, I know he is a clever doctor, for he cures my horrid mosquito bites."

"A little ammonia would do that, in the early stage of the mischief. But there are no mosquitoes to trouble you now."

"Oh, yes, there are; I had a bite just before we left Cap Ferrino." She pushed up her loose lawn sleeve, and exhibited a scar, which he scrutinized intently, with a surprised and puzzled look.

"This is no mosquito bite," he said.

"Oh, yes it is—unless there are snakes or adders at Cap Ferrino."

"It is not a bite at all. You are trifling with me. Miss Rolleston—you have allowed that wretched Italian quack to bleed you. They killed the greatest man in modern Europe that way, remember. How very foolish of you."

"I was never bled in my life, Mr. Stafford."

"Nonsense! Let me look at your other arm. Are there any more mosquito bites?"

"Yes; Dr. Parravicini says I have a bad skin for healing, and that the poison acts more virulently with me than with most people."

Stafford examined both her arms in the broad sunlight, scars new and old.

"You have been very badly bitten, Miss Rolleston," he said, "and if ever I find the mosquito I shall make him smart. But, now tell me, my dear girl, on your word of honor, tell me as you would tell a friend who is sincerely anxious for your health and happiness—as you would tell your mother if she were here to question you—have you no knowledge of any cause for these scars except mosquito bites—no suspicion even?"

"No, indeed! No, upon my honor! I have never seen a mosquito biting my arm. One never does see the horrid little fiends. But I have heard them trumpeting under the curtains and I know that I have often had one of the pestilent wretches buzzing about me."

Later in the day Bella and her friends were sitting at tea in the garden, while Lady Ducayne took her afternoon drive with her doctor.

"How long do you mean to stop with Lady Ducayne, Miss Rolleston?" Herbert Stafford asked, after a thoughtful silence, breaking suddenly upon the trivial talk of the two girls.

"As long as she will go on paying me twenty-five pounds a quarter."

"Even if you feel your health breaking down in her service?"

"It is not the service that has injured my health. You can see that I have really nothing to do—to read aloud for an hour or so once or twice a week; to write a letter once in a while to a London tradesman. I shall never have such an easy time with anybody. And nobody else would give me a hundred a year."

"Then you mean to go on till you break down; to die at your post?"

"Like the other two companions? No! If ever I feel seriously ill—really ill—I shall put myself in a train and go back to Walworth without stopping."

"What about the other two companions?"

"They both died. It was very unlucky for Lady Ducayne. That's why she engaged me; she chose me because I was ruddy and robust. She must feel rather disgusted at my having grown white and weak. By-the-bye, when I told her about the good your tonic had done me, she said she would like to see you and have a little talk with you about her own case."

"And I should like to see Lady Ducayne. When did she say this?"

"The day before yesterday."

"Will you ask her if she will see me this evening?"

"With pleasure! I wonder what you will think of her? She looks rather terrible to a stranger; but Dr. Parravicini says she was once a famous beauty."

It was nearly ten o'clock when Mr. Stafford was summoned by message from Lady Ducayne, whose courier came to conduct him to her ladyship's salon. Bella was reading aloud when the visitor was admitted; and he noticed the languor in the low, sweet tones, the evident effort.

"Shut up the book," said the querulous old voice. "You are beginning to drawl like Miss Blandy."

Stafford saw a small, bent figure crouching over the piled-up olive logs; a shrunken old figure in a gorgeous garment of black and crimson brocade, a skinny throat emerging from a mass of old Venetian lace, clasped with diamonds that flashed like fireflies as the trembling old head turned towards him.

The eyes that looked at him out of the face were almost as bright as the diamonds—the only living feature in that narrow parchment mask. He had seen terrible faces in the hospital—faces on which disease had set dreadful marks—but he had never seen a face that impressed him so painfully as this withered countenance, with its indescribable horror of death outlived, a face that should have been hidden under a coffin-lid years and years ago.

The Italian physician was standing on the other side of the fireplace, smoking a cigarette, and looking down at the little old woman brooding over the hearth as if he were proud of her.

"Good evening, Mr. Stafford; you can go to your room, Bella, and write your everlasting letter to your mother at Walworth," said Lady Ducayne. "I believe she writes a page about every wild flower she discovers in the woods and meadows. I don't know what else she can find to write about," she added, as Bella quietly withdrew to the pretty little bedroom opening out of Lady Ducayne's spacious apartment. Here, as at Cap Ferrino, she slept in a room adjoining the old lady's.

"You are a medical man, I understand, Mr. Stafford."

"I am a qualified practitioner, but I have not begun to practice."

"You have begun upon my companion, she tells me."

"I have prescribed for her, certainly, and I am happy to find my prescription has done her good, but I look upon that improvement as temporary. Her case will require more drastic treatment."

"Never mind her case. There is nothing the matter with the girl—absolutely nothing—except girlish nonsense; too much liberty and not enough work."

"I understand that two of your ladyship's previous companions died of the same disease," said Stafford, looking first at Lady Ducayne, who gave her tremulous old head an impatient jerk, and then at Parravicini, whose yellow complexion had paled a little under Stafford's scrutiny.

"Don't bother me about my companions, sir," said Lady Ducayne. "I sent for you to consult you about myself—not about a parcel of anemic girls. You are young, and medicine is a progressive science, the newspapers tell me. Where have you studied?"

"In Edinburgh—and in Paris."

"Two good schools. And know all the new-fangled theories, the modern discoveries—that remind one of the medieval witchcraft, of Albertus Magnus, and George Ripley; you have studied hypnotism—electricity?"

"And the transfusion of blood," said Stafford, very slowly, looking at Parravicini.

"Have you made any discovery that teaches you to prolong human life—any elixir—any mode of treatment? I want my life prolonged, young man. That man there has been my physician for thirty years. He does all he can to keep me alive—after his lights. He studies all the new theories of all the scientists—but he is old; he gets older every day—his brain-power is going—he is bigoted—prejudiced—can't receive new ideas—can't grapple with new systems. He will let me die if I am not on my guard against him."

"You are of an unbelievable ingratitude, Ecclenza," said Parravicini.

"Oh, you needn't complain. I have paid you thousands to keep me alive. Every year of my life has swollen your hoards; you know there is nothing to come to you when I am gone. My whole fortune is left to endow a home for indigent women of quality who have reached their ninetieth year. Come, Mr. Stafford, I am a rich woman. Give me a few years more in the sunshine, a few years more above ground, and I will give you the price of a fashionable London practice—I will set you up at the West-end."

"How old are you, Lady Ducayne?"

"I was born the day Louis XVI was guillotined."

"Then I think you have had your share of the sunshine and the pleasures of the earth, and that you should spend your few remaining days in repenting your sins and trying to make atonement for the young lives that have been sacrificed to your love of life."

"What do you mean by that, sir?"

"Oh, Lady Ducayne, need I put your wickedness and your physician's still greater wickedness in plain words? The poor girl who is now in your employment has been reduced from robust health to a condition of absolute danger by Dr. Parravicini's experimental surgery; and I have no doubt those other two young women who broke down in your service were treated by him in the same manner. I could take upon myself to demonstrate—by most convincing evidence, to a jury of medical men—that Dr. Parravicini has been bleeding Miss Rolleston after putting her under chloroform, at intervals, ever since she has been in your service. The deterioration in the girl's health speaks for itself; the lancet marks upon the girl's arms are unmistakable; and her description of a series of sensations, which she calls a dream, points unmistakably to the administration of chloroform while she was sleeping. A practice so nefarious, so murderous, must, if exposed, result in a sentence only less severe than the punishment of murder."

"I laugh," said Parravicini, with an airy motion of his skinny fingers. "I laugh at once at your theories and at your threats. I, Parravicini Leopold, have no fear that the law can question anything I have done."

"Take the girl away, and let me hear no more of her," cried Lady Ducayne, in the thin, old voice, which so poorly matched the energy and fire of the wicked old brain that guided its utterances. "Let her go back to her mother—I want no more girls to die in my service. There are girls enough and to spare in the world, God knows."

"If you ever engage another companion—or take another English girl into your service, Lady Ducayne, I will make all England ring with the story of your wickedness."

"I want no more girls. I don't believe in his experiments. They have been full of danger for me as well as for the girl—an air bubble, and I should be gone. I'll have no more of his dangerous quackery. I'll find some new man—a better man than you, sir, a discoverer like Pasteur, or Virchow, a genius—to keep me alive. Take your girl away, young man. Marry her if you like. I'll write a check for a thousand pounds, and let her go and live on beef and beer, and get strong and plump again. I'll have no more such experiments. Do you hear, Parravicini?" she screamed, vindictively, the yellow, wrinkled face distorted with fury, the eyes glaring at him.

The Staffords carried Bella Rolleston off to Varese next day, she very loath to leave Lady Ducayne, whose liberal salary afforded such help for the dear mother. Herbert Stafford insisted, however, treating Bella as coolly as if he had been the family physician, and she had been given over wholly to his care.

"Do you suppose your mother would let you stop here to die?" he asked. "If Mrs. Rolleston knew how ill you are, she would come post haste to fetch you."

"I shall never be well again till I get back to Walworth,"

answered Bella, who was low-spirited and inclined to tears this morning, a reaction after her good spirits of yesterday.

"We'll try a week or two at Varese first," said Stafford. "When you can walk halfway up Monte Generoso without palpitation of the heart, you shall go back to Walworth."

"Poor mother, how glad she will be to see me, and how sorry that I've lost such a good place."

This conversation took place on the boat when they were leaving Bellaggio. Lotta had gone to her friend's room at seven o'clock that morning, long before Lady Ducayne's withered eyelids had opened to the daylight, before even Francine, the French maid, was astir, and had helped to pack a Gladstone bag with essentials, and hustled Bella downstairs and out of doors before she could make any strenuous resistance.

"It's all right," Lotta assured her. "Herbert had a good talk with Lady Ducayne last night, and it was settled for you to leave this morning. She doesn't like invalids, you see."

"No," sighed Bella, "she doesn't like invalids. It was very unlucky that I should break down, just like Miss Tomson and Miss Blandy."

"At any rate, you are not dead, like them," answered Lotta, "and my brother says you are not going to die."

It seemed rather a dreadful thing to be dismissed in that offhand way, without a word of farewell from her employer.

"I wonder what Miss Torpinter will say when I go to her for another situation," Bella speculated, ruefully, while she and her friends were breakfasting on board the steamer.

"Perhaps you may never want another situation," said Stafford.

"You mean that I may never be well enough to be useful to anybody?"

"No, I don't mean anything of the kind."

It was after dinner at Varese, when Bella had been induced to take a whole glass of Chianti, and quite sparkled after that unaccustomed stimulant, that Mr. Stafford produced a letter from his pocket.

"I forgot to give you Lady Ducayne's letter of adieu!" he said.

"What, did she write to me? I am so glad— I hated to leave her in such a cool way; for after all she was very kind to me, and if I didn't like her it was only because she was too dreadfully old."

She tore open the envelope. The letter was short and to the point:—

> *Goodbye, child. Go and marry your doctor. I enclose a farewell gift for your trousseau.*
>
> *—Adeline Ducayne*

"A hundred pounds, a whole year's salary—no—why, it's for a— A check for a thousand!" cried Bella. "What a generous old soul! She really is the dearest old thing."

"She just missed being very dear to you, Bella," said Stafford.

He had dropped into the use of her Christian name while they were on board the boat. It seemed natural now that she was to be in his charge till they all three went back to England.

"I shall take upon myself the privileges of an elder brother till we land at Dover," he said. "After that—well, it must be as you please."

The question of their future relations must have been satisfactorily settled before they crossed the Channel, for

Bella's next letter to her mother communicated three startling facts.

First, that the inclosed check for £1,000 was to be invested in debenture stock in Mrs. Rolleston's name, and was to be her very own, income and principal, for the rest of her life.

Next, that Bella was going home to Walworth immediately.

And last, that she was going to be married to Mr. Herbert Stafford in the following autumn.

"And I am sure you will adore him, mother, as much as I do," wrote Bella.

"It is all good Lady Ducayne's doing. I never could have married if I had not secured that little nest-egg for you. Herbert says we shall be able to add to it as the years go by, and that wherever we live there shall be always a room in our house for you. The word 'mother-in-law' has no terrors for him."

AN AUTHENTICATED VAMPIRE STORY

♦♦♦

FRANZ HARTMANN

On June 10, 1909, there appeared in a prominent Vienna paper (the *Neues Wiener Journal*) a notice (which I herewith enclose) saying that the castle of B—— had been burned by the populace, because there was a great mortality among the peasant children, and it was generally believed that this was due to the invasion of a vampire, supposed to be the last Count B——, who died and acquired that reputation. The castle was situated in a wild and desolate part of the Carpathian Mountains and was formerly a fortification against the Turks. It was not inhabited owing to its being believed to be in the possession of ghosts; only a wing of it was used as a dwelling for the caretaker and his wife.

Now it so happened that when I read the above notice, I was sitting in a coffee-house at Vienna in company with an old friend of mine who is an experienced occultist and editor of a well-known journal and who had spent several months in the neighborhood of the castle. From him I obtained the following account and it appears that the vampire in question was probably not the old Count, but his beautiful daughter, the Countess Elga, whose photograph, taken from the original painting, I obtained. My friend said:—

"Two years ago I was living at Hermannstadt, and being engaged in engineering a road through the hills, I often came within the vicinity of the old castle, where I made the acquaintance of the old castellan, or caretaker, and his wife, who occupied a part of the wing of the house, almost separate from the main body of the building. They were a quiet old couple and rather reticent in giving information or expressing an opinion in regard to the strange noises which were often heard at night in the deserted halls, or of the apparitions which the Wallachian peasants claimed to have seen when they loitered in the surroundings after dark. All I could gather was that the old Count was a widower and had a beautiful daughter, who was one day killed by a fall from her horse, and that soon after the old man died in some mysterious manner, and the bodies were buried in a solitary graveyard belonging to a neighboring village. Not long after their death an unusual mortality was noticed among the inhabitants of the village: several children and even some grown people died without any apparent illness; they merely wasted away; and thus a rumor was started that the old Count had become a vampire after his death. There is no doubt that he was not a saint, as he was addicted to drinking, and some shocking tales were in circulation about his conduct and that of his daughter; but whether or not there was any truth in them, I am not in a position to say.

"Afterwards the property came into possession of ——, a distant relative of the family, who is a young man and officer in a cavalry regiment at Vienna. It appears that the heir enjoyed his life at the capital and did not trouble himself much about the old castle in the wilderness; he did not even come to look at it, but gave his direction by letter to the old janitor, telling him merely to keep things in order and to attend to repairs, if any were necessary. Thus the castellan was actually master of the house and offered its hospitality to me and my friends.

"One evening myself and my two assistants, Dr. E——, a young lawyer, and Mr. W——, a literary man, went to inspect the premises. First we went to the stables. There were no horses, as they had been sold; but what attracted our special attention was an old queer-fashioned coach with gilded ornaments and bearing the emblems of the family. We then inspected the rooms, passing through some halls and gloomy corridors, such as may be found in any old castle. There was nothing remarkable about the furniture; but in one of the halls there hung in a frame an oil-painting, a portrait, representing a lady with a large hat and wearing a fur coat. We all were involuntarily startled on beholding this picture; not so much on account of the beauty of the lady, but on account of the uncanny expression of her eyes, and Dr. E——, after looking at the picture for a short time, suddenly exclaimed—

" 'How strange! The picture closes its eyes and opens them again, and now begins to smile!'

"Now Dr. E——is a very sensitive person and has more than once had some experience in spiritism, and we made up our minds to form a circle for the purpose of investigating this phenomenon. Accordingly, on the same evening we sat around a table in an adjoining room, forming a magnetic chain with our hands. Soon the table began to move and the name *"Elga"* was spelled. We asked who this Elga was, and the answer was rapped out 'The lady, whose picture you have seen.'

" 'Is the lady living?' asked Mr. W——. This question was not answered; but instead it was rapped out: 'If W—— desires it, I will appear to him bodily tonight at two o'clock.' W—— consented, and now the table seemed to be endowed with life and manifested a great affection for W——; it rose on two legs and pressed against his breast, as if it intended to embrace him.

"We inquired of the castellan whom the picture represented; but to our surprise he did not know. He said that it was the copy of a picture painted by the celebrated painter Hans Markart of Vienna, and had been bought by the old Count because its demoniacal look pleased him so much.

"We left the castle, and W—— retired to his room at an inn, a half-hour's journey distant from that place. He was of a somewhat skeptical turn of mind, being neither a firm believer in ghosts and apparitions nor ready to deny their possibility. He was not afraid, but anxious to see what would come out of his agreement, and for the purpose of keeping himself awake he sat down and began to write an article for a journal.

"Towards two o'clock he heard steps on the stairs and the door of the hall opened, there was a rustling of a silk dress and the sound of the feet of a lady walking to and fro in the corridor.

"It may be imagined that he was somewhat startled; but taking courage, he said to himself: 'If this is Elga, let her come in.' Then the door of his room opened and Elga entered. She was most elegantly dressed and appeared still more youthful and seductive than the picture. There was a lounge on the other side of the table where W—— was writing, and there she silently posed herself. She did not speak, but her looks and gestures left no doubt in regard to her desires and intentions.

"Mr. W—— resisted the temptation and remained firm. It is not known whether he did so out of principle or timidity or fear. Be this as it may, he kept on writing, looking from time to time at his visitor and silently wishing that she would leave. At last, after half an hour, which seemed to him much longer, the lady departed in the same manner in which she came.

"This adventure left W—— no peace, and we consequently arranged several sittings at the old castle, where a variety of uncanny phenomena took place. Thus, for instance, once the servant-girl was about to light a fire in the stove, when the door of the apartment opened and Elga stood there. The girl, frightened out of her wits, rushed out of the room, tumbling down the stairs in terror with the petroleum lamp in her hand, which broke and came very near to setting her clothes on fire. Lighted lamps and candles went out when brought near the picture, and many other 'manifestations' took place, which it would be tedious to describe; but the following incident ought not to be omitted.

"Mr. W—— was at that time desirous of obtaining the position as co-editor of a certain journal, and a few days after the above-narrated adventure he received a letter in which a noble lady of high position offered him her patronage for that purpose. The writer requested him to come to a certain place the same evening, where he would meet a gentleman who would give him further particulars. He went and was met by an unknown stranger, who told him that he was requested by the Countess Elga to invite Mr. W—— to a carriage drive and that she would await him at midnight at a certain crossing of two roads, not far from the village. The stranger then suddenly disappeared.

"Now it seems that Mr. W—— had some misgivings about the meeting and drive and he hired a policeman as detective to go at midnight to the appointed place, to see what would happen. The policeman went and reported next morning that he had seen nothing but the well-known, old-fashioned carriage from the castle with two black horses attached to it standing there as if waiting for somebody, and that he had no occasion to interfere and merely waited until the carriage moved on. When the castellan of the castle was asked, he swore that the carriage had not been out that night, and in fact it could not have been out, as there were no horses to draw it.

"But this is not all, for on the following day I met a friend who is a great skeptic and disbeliever in ghosts and always used to laugh at such things. Now, however, he seemed to be very serious and said: 'Last night something very strange happened to me. At about one o'clock this morning I returned from a late visit and as I happened to pass the graveyard of the village, I saw a carriage with gilded ornaments standing at the entrance. I wondered about this taking place at such an unusual hour, and being curious to see what would happen, I waited. Two elegantly dressed ladies issued from the carriage. One of these was young and pretty, but threw at me a devilish and scornful look as they both passed by and entered the cemetery. There they were met by a well-dressed man, who saluted the ladies and spoke to the younger one, saying: "Why, Miss Elga! Are you returned so soon?" Such a queer feeling came over me that I abruptly left and hurried home.'

"This matter has not been explained; but certain experiments which we subsequently made with the picture of Elga brought out some curious facts.

"To look at the picture for a certain time caused me to feel a very disagreeable sensation in the region of the solar plexus. I began to dislike the portrait and proposed to destroy it. We held a sitting in the adjoining room; the table manifested a great aversion against my presence. It was rapped out that I should leave the circle, and that the picture must not be destroyed. I ordered a Bible to be brought in and read the beginning of the first chapter of St. John, whereupon the above-mentioned Mr. E—— (the medium) and another man present claimed that they saw the picture distorting its face. I turned the frame and pricked the back of the picture with my penknife in different places, and Mr. E——, as well as the other man, felt all the pricks, although they had retired to the corridor.

"I made the sign of the pentagram over the picture, and again the two gentlemen claimed that the picture was horribly distorting its face.

"Soon afterwards we were called away and left that country. Of Elga I heard nothing more."

Thus far goes the account of my friend the editor. There are several points in it which call for an explanation. Perhaps the sages of the S.P.R. will find it by investigating the laws of nature ruling the astral plane, unless they prefer to take the easier route, by proclaiming it all to be humbug and fraud.

THE SEA WAS WET AS WET COULD BE

◆◆◆

GAHAN WILSON

I felt we made an embarrassing contrast to the open serenity of the scene around us. The pure blue of the sky was unmarked by a single cloud or bird, and nothing stirred on the vast stretch of beach except ourselves. The sea, sparkling under the freshness of the early morning sun, looked invitingly clean. I wanted to wade into it and wash myself, but I was afraid I would contaminate it.

We are a contamination here, I thought. We're like a group of sticky bugs crawling in an ugly little crowd over polished marble. If I were God and looked down and saw us, lugging our baskets and our silly, bright blankets, I would step on us and squash us with my foot.

We should have been lovers or monks in such a place, but we were only a crowd of bored and boring drunks. You were always drunk when you were with Carl. Good old, mean old Carl was the greatest little drink pourer in the world. He used drinks like other types of sadists used whips. He kept beating you with them until you dropped or sobbed or went mad, and he enjoyed every step of the process.

We'd been drinking all night, and when the morning came, somebody, I think it was Mandie, got the great idea that we should all go out on a picnic. Naturally, we thought it was an inspiration, we were nothing if not real sports, and so we'd packed some goodies, not forgetting the liquor, and we'd piled into the car, and there we were, weaving across the beach, looking for a place to spread our tacky banquet.

We located a broad, low rock, decided it would serve for our table, and loaded it with the latest in plastic chinaware, a haphazard collection of food, and a quantity of bottles.

Someone had packed a tin of Spam among the other offerings and, when I saw it, I was suddenly overwhelmed with an absurd feeling of nostalgia. It reminded me of the war and of myself soldierboying up through Italy. It also reminded me of how long ago the whole thing had been and how little I'd done of what I'd dreamed I'd do back then.

I opened the Spam and sat down to be alone with it and my memories, but it wasn't to be for long. The kind of people who run with people like Carl don't like to be alone, ever, especially with their memories, and they can't imagine anyone else might, at least now and then, have a taste for it.

My rescuer was Irene. Irene was particularly sensitive about seeing people alone because being alone had several times nearly produced fatal results for her. Being alone and taking pills to end the being alone.

"What's wrong, Phil?" she asked.

"Nothing's wrong," I said, holding up a forkful of the pink Spam in the sunlight. "It tastes just like it always did. They haven't lost their touch."

She sat down on the sand beside me, very carefully, so as to avoid spilling the least drop of what must have been her millionth Scotch.

"Phil," she said, "I'm worried about Mandie. I really am. She looks so unhappy!"

I glanced over at Mandie. She had her head thrown

back and she was laughing uproariously at some joke Carl had just made. Carl was smiling at her with his teeth glistening and his eyes deep-down dead as ever.

"Why should Mandie be happy?" I asked. "What, in God's name, has she got to be happy about?"

"Oh, Phil," said Irene. "You pretend to be such an awful cynic. She's *alive*, isn't she?"

I looked at her and wondered what such a statement meant, coming from someone who'd tried to do herself in as earnestly and as frequently as Irene. I decided that I did not know and that I would probably never know. I also decided I didn't want any more of the Spam. I turned to throw it away, doing my bit to litter up the beach, and then I saw them.

They were far away, barely bigger than two dots, but you could tell there was something odd about them even then.

"We've got company," I said.

Irene peered in the direction of my point.

"Look, everybody," she cried, "we've got company!"

Everybody looked, just as she had asked them to.

"What the hell is this?" asked Carl. "Don't they know this is my private property?" And then he laughed.

Carl had fantasies about owning things and having power. Now and then he got drunk enough to have little flashes of believing he was king of the world.

"You tell 'em, Carl!" said Horace.

Horace had sparkling quips like that for almost every occasion. He was tall and bald and he had a huge Adam's apple and, like myself, he worked for Carl. I would have felt sorrier for Horace than I did if I hadn't had a sneaky suspicion that he was really happier when groveling. He lifted one scrawny fist and shook it in the direction of the distant pair.

"You guys better beat it," he shouted. "This is private property!"

"Will you shut up and stop being such an ass?" Mandie asked him. "It's not polite to yell at strangers, dear, and this may damn well be *their* beach for all you know."

Mandie happens to be Horace's wife. Horace's children treat him about the same way. He busied himself with zipping up his windbreaker, because it was getting cold and because he had received an order to be quiet.

I watched the two approaching figures. The one was tall and bulky, and he moved with a peculiar, swaying gait. The other was short and hunched into himself, and he walked in a fretful, zigzag line beside his towering companion.

"They're heading straight for us," I said.

The combination of the cool wind that had come up and the approach of the two strangers had put a damper on our little group. We sat quietly and watched them coming closer. The nearer they got, the odder they looked.

"For heaven's sake!" said Irene. "The little one's wearing a square hat!"

"I think it's made of paper," said Mandie, squinting, "folded newspaper."

"Will you look at the mustache on the big bastard?" asked Carl. "I don't think I've ever seen a bigger bush in my life."

"They remind me of something," I said.

The others turned to look at me.

The Walrus and the Carpenter . . .

"They remind me of the Walrus and the Carpenter," I said.

"The who?" asked Mandie.

"Don't tell me you never heard of the Walrus and the Carpenter?" asked Carl.

"Never once," said Mandie.

"Disgusting," said Carl. "You're an uncultured bitch. The Walrus and the Carpenter are probably two of the most famous characters in literature. They're in a poem by Lewis Carroll in one of the *Alice* books."

"In *Through the Looking Glass*," I said, and then I recited their introduction:

The Walrus and the Carpenter
Were walking close at hand
They wept like anything to see
Such quantities of sand . . .

Mandie shrugged. "Well, you'll just have to excuse my ignorance and concentrate on my charm," she said.

"I don't know how to break this to you all," said Irene, "but the little one *does* have a handkerchief."

We stared at them. The little one did indeed have a handkerchief, a huge handkerchief, and he was using it to dab at his eyes.

"Is the little one supposed to be the Carpenter?" asked Mandie.

"Yes," I said.

"Then it's all right," she said, "because he's the one that's carrying the saw."

"He is, so help me, God," said Carl. "And, to make the whole thing perfect, he's even wearing an apron."

"So the Carpenter in the poem has to wear an apron, right?" asked Mandie.

"Carroll doesn't say whether he does or not," I said, "but the illustrations by Tenniel show him wearing one.

They also show him with the same square jaw and the same big nose this guy's got."

"They're goddamn doubles," said Carl. "The only thing wrong is that the Walrus isn't a walrus, he just looks like one."

"You watch," said Mandie. "Any minute now he's going to sprout fur all over and grow long fangs."

Then, for the first time, the approaching pair noticed us. It seemed to give them quite a start. They stood and gaped at us and the little one furtively stuffed his handkerchief out of sight.

"We can't be as surprising as all that!" whispered Irene.

The big one began moving forward, then, in a hesitant, tentative kind of shuffle. The little one edged ahead, too, but he was careful to keep the bulk of his companion between himself and us.

"First contact with the aliens," said Mandie, and Irene and Horace giggled nervously. I didn't respond. I had come to the decision that I was going to quit working for Carl, that I didn't like any of these people about me, except, maybe, Irene, and that these two strangers gave me the honest creeps.

Then the big one smiled, and everything was changed.

I've worked in the entertainment field, in advertising, and in public relations. This means I have come in contact with some of the prime charm boys and girls in our proud land. I have become, therefore, not only a connoisseur of smiles, I am a being equipped with numerous automatic safeguards against them. When a talcumed smoothie comes at me with his brilliant ivories exposed, it only shows he's got something he can bite me with, that's all.

But the smile of the Walrus was something else.

The smile of the Walrus did what a smile hasn't done for me in years—it melted my heart. I use the corn-ball phrase very much on purpose. When I saw his smile, I knew I could trust him; I felt in my marrow that he was gentle and sweet and had nothing but the best intentions. His resemblance to the Walrus in the poem ceased being vaguely chilling and became warmly comical. I loved him as I had loved the teddy bear of my childhood.

"Oh, I *say*," he said, and his voice was an embarrassed boom, "I *do* hope we're not intruding!"

"I daresay we are," squeaked the Carpenter, peeping out from behind his companion.

"The, uhm, fact is," boomed the Walrus, "we didn't even notice you until just back then, you see."

"We were talking, is what," said the Carpenter.

They wept like anything to see
Such quantities of sand . . .

"About sand?" I asked.

The Walrus looked at me with a startled air.

"We *were*, actually, now you come to mention it."

He lifted one huge foot and shook it so that a little trickle of sand spilled out of his shoe.

"The stuff's impossible," he said. "Gets in your clothes, tracks up the carpet."

"Ought to be swept away, it ought," said the Carpenter.

"If seven maids with seven mops
Swept it for half a year,
Do you suppose," the Walrus said,
"That they could get it clear?"

"It's too much!" said Carl.

"Yes, indeed," said the Walrus, eying the sand around him with vague disapproval, "altogether too much."

Then he turned to us again and we all basked in that smile.

"Permit me to introduce my companion and myself," he said.

"You'll have to excuse George," said the Carpenter, "as he's a bit of a stuffed shirt, don't you know?"

"Be that as it may," said the Walrus, patting the Carpenter on the flat top of his paper hat, "this is Edward Farr, and I am George Tweedy, both at your service. We are, uhm, both a trifle drunk, I'm afraid."

"We are, indeed. We are that."

"As we have just come from a really delightful party, to which we shall soon return."

"Once we've found the fuel, that is," said Farr, waving his saw in the air. By now he had found the courage to come out and face us directly.

"Which brings me to the question," said Tweedy. "Have you seen any *driftwood* lying about the premises? We've been looking high and low and we can't seem to find *any* of the blasted stuff."

"Thought there'd be piles of it," said Farr, "but all there is is sand, don't you see?"

"I would have sworn you were looking for oysters," said Carl.

Again, Tweedy appeared startled.

> *"O Oysters, come and walk with us!"*
> *The Walrus did beseech . . .*

"Oysters?" he asked. "Oh, no, we've *got* the oysters. All we lack is the means to cook 'em."

" 'Course we could always use a few more," said Farr, looking at his companion.

"I suppose we *could*, at that," said Tweedy thoughtfully.

"I'm afraid we can't help you fellows with the driftwood problem," said Carl, "but you're more than welcome to a drink."

There was something unfamiliar about the tone of Carl's voice that made my ears perk up. I turned to look at him, and then had difficulty covering up my astonishment.

It was his eyes. For once, for the first time, they were really friendly.

I'm not saying Carl had fishy eyes, blank eyes—not at all. On the surface, that is. On the surface, with his eyes, with his face, with the handling of his entire body, Carl was a master of animation and expression. From sympathetic, heartfelt warmth, all the way to icy rage, and on every stop in-between, Carl was completely convincing.

But only on the surface. Once you got to know Carl, and it took a while, you realized that none of it was really happening. That was because Carl had died, or been killed, long ago. Possibly in childhood. Possibly he had been born dead. So, under the actor's warmth and rage, the eyes were always the eyes of a corpse.

But now it was different. The friendliness here was genuine, I was sure of it. The smile of Tweedy, of the Walrus, had performed a miracle. Carl had risen from his tomb. I was in honest awe.

"*Delighted*, old chap!" said Tweedy.

They accepted their drinks with obvious pleasure, and we completed the introductions as they sat down to join us. I detected a strong smell of fish when Tweedy sat down beside me but, oddly, I didn't find it offensive in the least. I was glad he'd chosen me to sit by. He turned and smiled at me, and my heart melted a little more.

It soon turned out that the drinking we'd done before

had only scratched the surface. Tweedy and Farr were magnificent boozers, and their gusto encouraged us all to follow suit.

We drank absurd toasts and were delighted to discover that Tweedy was an incredible raconteur. His specialty was outrageous fantasy: wild tales involving incongruous objects, events, and characters. His invention was endless.

> *"The time has come," the Walrus said,*
> *"To talk of many things:*
> *Of shoes—and ships—and sealing-wax—*
> *Of cabbages—and kings—*
> *And why the sea is boiling hot—*
> *And whether pigs have wings."*

We laughed and drank, and drank and laughed, and I began to wonder why in hell I'd spent my life being such a gloomy, moody son of a bitch, been such a distrustful and suspicious bastard, when the whole secret of everything, the whole core secret, was simply to enjoy it, to take it as it came.

I looked around and grinned, and I didn't care if it was a foolish grin. Everybody looked all right, everybody looked swell, everybody looked better than I'd ever seen them look before.

Irene looked happy, honestly and truly happy. She, too, had found the secret. No more pills for Irene, I thought. Now that she knows the secret, now that she's met Tweedy who's given her the secret, she'll have no more need of those goddamn pills.

And I couldn't believe Horace and Mandie. They had their arms around each other, and their bodies were pressed close together, and they rocked as one being when they laughed at Tweedy's wonderful stories. No more nagging for Mandie, I thought, and no more cringing for Horace, now they've learned the secret.

And then I looked at Carl, laughing and relaxed and absolutely free of care, absolutely unchilled, finally, at last, after years of—

And then I looked at Carl again.

And then I looked down at my drink, and then I looked at my knees, and then I looked out at the sea, sparkling, clean, remote and impersonal.

And then I realized it had grown cold, quite cold, and that there wasn't a bird or a cloud in the sky.

The sea was wet as wet could be,
The sands were dry as dry.
You could not see a cloud, because
No cloud was in the sky:
No birds were flying overhead—
There were no birds to fly.

That part of the poem was, after all, a perfect description of a lifeless earth. It sounded beautiful at first, it sounded benign. But then you read it again and you realized that Carroll was describing barrenness and desolation.

Suddenly Carl's voice broke through and I heard him say:

"Hey, that's a hell of an idea, Tweedy! By God, we'd love to! Wouldn't we, gang?"

The others broke out in an affirmative chorus and they all started scrambling to their feet around me. I looked up at them, like someone who's been awakened from sleep in a strange place, and they grinned down at me like loons.

"Come on, Phil!" cried Irene.

Her eyes were bright and shining, but it wasn't with happiness. I could see that now.

> *"It seems a shame," the Walrus said,*
> *"To play them such a trick . . ."*

I blinked my eyes and stared at them, one after the other.

"Old Phil's had a little too much to drink!" cried Mandie, laughing. "Come on, old Phil! Come on and join the party!"

"What party?" I asked.

I couldn't seem to get located. Everything seemed disorientated and grotesque.

"For Christ's sake, Phil," said Carl, "Tweedy and Farr, here, have invited us to join their party. There's no more drinks left, and they've got plenty!"

I set my plastic cup down carefully on the sand. If they would just shut up for a moment, I thought, I might be able to get the fuzz out of my head.

"Come *along,* sir!" boomed Tweedy jovially. "It's only a pleasant walk!"

> *"O oysters come and walk with us,"*
> *The walrus did beseech.*
> *"A pleasant walk, a pleasant talk,*
> *Along the briny beach . . ."*

He was smiling at me, but the smile didn't work anymore.

"You cannot do with more than four," I told him.

"*Uhm?* What's that?"

". . . we cannot do with more than four,
And give a hand to each."

"I said, 'You cannot do with more than four.' "

"He's right, you know," said Farr, the Carpenter.

"Well, uhm, then," said the Walrus, "if you feel you really *can't* come, old chap . . ."

"What, in Christ's name, are you all talking about?" asked Mandie.

"He's hung up on that goddamn poem," said Carl. "Lewis Carroll's got the yellow bastard scared."

"Don't be such a party pooper, Phil!" said Mandie.

"To hell with him," said Carl. And he started off, and all the others followed him. Except Irene.

"Are you sure you really don't want to come, Phil?" she asked.

She looked frail and thin against the sunlight. I realized there really wasn't much of her, and that what there was had taken a terrible beating.

"No," I said. "I don't. Are you sure you want to go?"

"Of course I do, Phil."

I thought of the pills.

"I suppose you do," I said. "I suppose there's really no stopping you."

"No, Phil, there isn't."

And then she stooped and kissed me. Kissed me very gently, and I could feel the dry, chapped surface of her lips and the faint warmth of her breath.

I stood.

"I wish you'd stay," I said.

"I can't," she said.

And then she turned and ran after the others.

I watched them growing smaller and smaller on the beach, following the Walrus and the Carpenter. I watched them come to where the beach curved around the bluff, and watched them disappear behind the bluff.

I looked up at the sky. Pure blue. Impersonal.

"What do you think of this?" I asked it.

Nothing. It hadn't even noticed.

"Now, if you're ready, oysters dear,
We can begin to feed."
"But not on us!" the oysters cried,
Turning a little blue,
"After such kindness, that would be
A dismal thing to do!"

A dismal thing to do.

I began to run up the beach, toward the bluff. I stumbled now and then because I had had too much to drink. Far too much to drink. I heard small shells crack under my shoes, and the sand made whipping noises.

I fell, heavily, and lay there gasping on the beach. My heart pounded in my chest. I was too old for this sort of footwork. I hadn't had any real exercise in years. I smoked too much and I drank too much. I did all the wrong things. I didn't do any of the right things.

I pushed myself up a little and then I let myself down again. My heart was pounding hard enough to frighten me. I could feel it in my chest, frantically pumping, squeezing blood in and spurting blood out.

Like an oyster pulsing in the sea.

"Shall we be trotting home again?"

My heart was like an oyster.

I got up, fell up, and began to run again, weaving widely, my mouth open and the air burning my throat. I was coated with sweat, streaming with it, and it felt icy in the cold wind.

> *"Shall we be trotting home again?"*

I rounded the bluff and then I stopped and stood swaying, and then I dropped to my knees.

The pure blue of the sky was unmarked by a single bird or cloud, and nothing stirred on the whole vast stretch of the beach.

> *But answer came there none—*
> *And this was scarcely odd, because . . .*

Nothing stirred, but they were there. Irene and Mandie and Carl and Horace were there, and four others, too. Just around the bluff.

> *"We cannot do with more than four . . ."*

But the Walrus and the Carpenter had taken two trips.

I began to crawl toward them on my knees. My heart, my oyster heart, was pounding too hard to allow me to stand.

The other four had had a picnic, too, very like our own. They, too, had plastic cups and plates, and they, too, had brought bottles. They had sat and waited for the return of the Walrus and the Carpenter.

Irene was right in front of me. Her eyes were open and stared at, but did not see, the sky. The pure blue uncluttered sky. There were a few grains of sand in her left eye. Her face was almost clear of blood. There were only a few flecks of it on her lower chin. The spray from the huge wound in her chest seemed to have traveled mainly downward and to the right. I stretched out my arm and touched her hand.

"Irene," I said.

But answer came there none—
And this was scarcely odd, because
They'd eaten every one.

I looked up at the others. Like Irene, they were, all of them, dead. The Walrus and the Carpenter had eaten the oysters and left the shells.

The Carpenter never found any firewood, and so they'd eaten them raw. You can eat oysters raw if you want to.

I said her name once more, just for the record, and then I stood and turned from them and walked to the bluff. I rounded the bluff and the beach stretched before me, vast, smooth, empty, and remote.

Even as I ran upon it, away from them, it was remote.

THE MAN UPSTAIRS

◆◆◆

RAY BRADBURY

He remembered how carefully and expertly Grandmother would fondle the cold cut guts of the chicken and withdraw the marvels therein; the wet shining loops of meat-smelling intestine, the muscled lump of heart, the gizzard with the collection of seeds in it. How neatly and nicely Grandma would slit the chicken and push her fat little hand in to deprive it of its medals. These would be segregated, some in pans of water, others in paper to be thrown to the dog later, perhaps. And then the ritual of taxidermy, stuffing the bird with watered, seasoned bread, and performing surgery with a swift, bright needle, stitch after pulled-tight stitch.

This was one of the prime thrills of Douglas's eleven-year-old life span.

Altogether, he counted twenty knives in the various squeaking drawers of the magic kitchen table from which Grandma, a kindly, gentle-faced, white-haired old witch, drew paraphernalia for her miracles.

Douglas was to be quiet. He could stand across the table from Grandma, his freckled nose tucked over the edge, watching, but any loose boy-talk might interfere with the spell. It was a wonder when Grandma brandished silver shakers over the bird, supposedly sprinkling showers of mummy-dust and pulverized Indian bones, muttering mystical verses under her toothless breath.

"Grammy," said Douglas at last, breaking the silence. "Am I like that inside?" He pointed at the chicken.

"Yes," said Grandma. "A little more orderly and presentable, but just about the same. . . ."

"And more *of* it!" added Douglas, proud of his guts.

"Yes," said Grandma. "More of it."

"Grandpa has lots more'n me. His sticks out in front so he can rest his elbows on it."

Grandma laughed and shook her head.

Douglas said, "And Lucie Williams, down the street, she . . ."

"Hush, child!" cried Grandma.

"But she's got . . ."

"Never you mind what she's got! That's different."

"But why is *she* different?"

"A darning-needle dragon-fly is coming by some day and sew up your mouth," said Grandma firmly.

Douglas waited, then asked, "How do you know I've got insides like that, Grandma?"

"Oh, go 'way, now!"

The front doorbell rang.

Through the front-door glass, as he ran down the hall, Douglas saw a straw hat. The bell jangled again and again. Douglas opened the door.

"Good morning, child, is the landlady at home?"

Cold gray eyes in a long, smooth, walnut-colored face gazed upon Douglas. The man was tall, thin, and carried a suitcase, a briefcase, an umbrella under one bent arm, gloves rich and thick and gray on his thin fingers, and wore a horribly new straw hat.

Douglas backed up. "She's busy."

"I wish to rent her upstairs room, as advertised."

"We've got ten boarders, and it's already rented; go away!"

"Douglas!" Grandma was behind him suddenly. "How do you do?" she said to the stranger. "Never mind this child."

Unsmiling, the man stepped stiffly in. Douglas watched them ascend out of sight up the stairs, heard Grandma detailing the conveniences of the upstairs room. Soon she hurried down to pile linens from the linen closet on Douglas and send him scooting up with them.

Douglas paused at the room's threshold. The room was changed oddly, simply because the stranger had been in it a moment. The straw hat lay brittle and terrible upon the bed, the umbrella leaned stiff against one wall like a dead bat with dark wings folded.

Douglas blinked at the umbrella.

The stranger stood in the center of the changed room, tall, tall.

"Here!" Douglas littered the bed with supplies. "We eat at noon sharp, and if you're late coming down the soup'll get cold. Grandma fixes it so it will, every time!"

The tall strange man counted out ten new copper pennies and tinkled them in Douglas's blouse pocket. "We shall be friends," he said, grimly.

It was funny, the man having nothing but pennies. Lots of them. No silver at all, no dimes, no quarters. Just new copper pennies.

Douglas thanked him glumly. "I'll drop these in my dime bank when I get them changed into a dime. I got six dollars and fifty cents in dimes all ready for my camp trip in August."

"I must wash now," said the tall strange man.

Once, at midnight, Douglas had wakened to hear a storm rumbling outside—the cold hard wind shaking the house, the rain driving against the window. And then a lightning bolt had landed outside the window with a silent, terrific concussion. He remembered that fear of looking about at his room, seeing it strange and awful in the instantaneous light.

So it was, now, in this room. He stood looking up at the stranger. This room was no longer the same, but changed indefinably because this man, quick as a lightning bolt, had shed his light about it. Douglas backed up slowly as the stranger advanced.

The door closed in his face.

The wooden fork went up with mashed potatoes, came down empty. Mr. Koberman, for that was his name, had brought the wooden fork and wooden knife and spoon with him when Grandma called lunch.

"Mrs. Spaulding," he said, quietly, "my own cutlery; please use it. I will have lunch today, but from tomorrow on, only breakfast and supper."

Grandma bustled in and out, bearing steaming tureens of soup and beans and mashed potatoes to impress her new boarder, while Douglas sat rattling his silverware on his plate, because he had discovered it irritated Mr. Koberman.

"I know a trick," said Douglas. "Watch." He picked a fork tine with his fingernail. He pointed at various sectors of the table, like a magician. Wherever he pointed, the sound of the vibrating fork-tine emerged, like a metal elfin voice. Simply done, of course. He pressed the fork handle on the tabletop, secretly. The vibration came from the wood like a sounding board. It looked quite magical. "There, there, and *there*!" exclaimed Douglas, happily plucking the fork again. He pointed at Mr. Koberman's soup and the noise came from it.

Mr. Koberman's walnut-colored face became hard and

firm and awful. He pushed the soup bowl away violently, his lips twisting. He fell back in his chair.

Grandma appeared. "Why, what's wrong, Mr. Koberman?"

"I cannot eat this soup."

"Why?"

"Because I am full and can eat no more. Thank you."

Mr. Koberman left the room, glaring.

"What did you do, just then?" asked Grandma at Douglas, sharply.

"Nothing. Grandma, why does he eat with *wooden* spoons?"

"Yours not to question! When do you go back to school, anyway?"

"Seven weeks."

"Oh, my lord!" said Grandma.

Mr. Koberman worked nights. Each morning at eight he arrived mysteriously home, devoured a very small breakfast, and then slept soundlessly in his room all through the dreaming hot daytime, until the huge supper with all the other boarders at night.

Mr. Koberman's sleeping habits made it necessary for Douglas to be quiet. This was unbearable. So, whenever Grandma visited down the street, Douglas stomped up and down stairs beating a drum, bouncing golf balls, or just screaming for three minutes outside Mr. Koberman's door, or flushing the toilet seven times in succession.

Mr. Koberman never moved. His room was silent, dark. He did not complain. There was no sound. He slept on and on. It was very strange.

Douglas felt a pure white flame of hatred burn inside himself with a steady, unflickering beauty. Now that room was Koberman Land. Once it had been flowery bright when Miss Sadlowe lived there. Now it was stark, bare, cold, clean, everything in its place, alien and brittle.

Douglas climbed upstairs on the fourth morning.

Halfway to the second floor was a large sun-filled window, framed by six-inch panes of orange, purple, blue, red, and burgundy glass. In the enchanted early mornings when the sun fell through to strike the landing and slide down the stair banister, Douglas stood entranced at this window peering at the world through the multi-colored panes.

Now a blue world, a blue sky, blue people, blue streetcars, and blue trotting dogs.

He shifted panes. Now—an amber world! Two lemonish women glided by, resembling the daughters of Fu Manchu! Douglas giggled. This pane made even the sunlight more purely golden.

It was eight a.m. Mr. Koberman strolled by below, on the sidewalk, returning from his night's work, his umbrella looped over his elbow, straw hat glued to his head with patent oil.

Douglas shifted panes again. Mr. Koberman was a red man walking through a red world with red trees and red flowers and—something else.

Something about—Mr. Koberman.

Douglas squinted.

The red glass *did* things to Mr. Koberman. His face, his suit, his hands. The clothes seemed to melt away. Douglas almost believed, for one terrible instant, that he could see *inside* Mr. Koberman. And what he saw made him lean wildly against the small red pane, blinking.

Mr. Koberman glanced up just then, saw Douglas, and raised his umbrella angrily, as if to strike. He ran swiftly across the red lawn to the front door.

"Young man!" he cried, running up the stairs. "What were you doing?"

"Just looking," said Douglas, numbly.

"That's all, is it?" cried Mr. Koberman.

"Yes, sir. I look through all the glasses. All kinds of worlds. Blue ones, red ones, yellow ones. All different."

"All kinds of worlds, is it!" Mr. Koberman glanced at the little panes of glass, his face pale. He got hold of himself. He wiped his face with a handkerchief and pretended to laugh. "Yes. All kinds of worlds. All different." He walked to the door of his room. "Go right ahead; play," he said.

The door closed. The hall was empty. Mr. Koberman had gone in.

Douglas shrugged and found a new pane.

"Oh, everything's violet!"

Half an hour later, while playing in his sandbox behind the house, Douglas heard the crash and the shattering tinkle. He leaped up.

A moment later, Grandma appeared on the back porch, the old razor strop trembling in her hand.

"Douglas! I told you time and again never fling your basketball against the house! Oh, I could just cry!"

"I been sitting right here," he protested.

"Come see what you've done, you nasty boy!"

The great colored window panes lay shattered in a rainbow chaos on the upstairs landing. His basketball lay in the ruins.

Before he could even begin telling his innocence, Douglas was struck a dozen stinging blows upon his rump. Wherever he landed, screaming, the razor strop struck again.

Later, hiding his mind in the sandpile like an ostrich, Douglas nursed his dreadful pains. He knew who'd thrown that basketball. A man with a straw hat and a stiff umbrella and a cold, gray room. Yeah, yeah, yeah. He dribbled tears. Just wait. Just *wait.*

He heard Grandma sweeping up the broken glass. She brought it out and threw it in the trash bin. Blue, pink, yellow meteors of glass dropped brightly down.

When she was gone, Douglas dragged himself, whimpering, over to save out three pieces of the incredible glass. Mr. Koberman disliked the colored windows. These—he clinked them in his fingers—would be worth saving.

Grandfather arrived from his newspaper office each night, shortly ahead of the other boarders, at five o'clock. When a slow, heavy tread filled the hall, and a thick mahogany cane thumped in the cane-rack, Douglas ran to embrace the large stomach and sit on Grandpa's knee while he read the evening paper.

"Hi, Grampa!"

"Hello, down there!"

"Grandma cut chickens again today. It's fun watching," said Douglas.

Grandpa kept reading. "That's twice this week, chickens. She's the chickenist woman. You like to watch her cut 'em, eh? Cold-blooded little pepper! Ha!"

"I'm just curious."

"You are," rumbled Grandpa, scowling. "Remember that day when that young lady was killed at the rail station? You just walked over and looked at her, blood and all." He laughed. "Queer duck. Stay that way. Fear nothing, ever in your life. I guess you get it from your father, him being a military man and all, and you so close to him before you came here to live last year." Grandpa returned to his paper.

A long pause. "Gramps?"

"Yes?"

"What if a man didn't have a heart or lungs or stomach but still walked around, alive?"

"That," rumbled Gramps, "would be a miracle."

"I don't mean a—a miracle. I mean, what if he was all *different* inside? Not like me."

"Well, he wouldn't be quite human then, would he, boy?"

"Guess not, Gramps. Gramps, you got a heart and lungs?"

Gramps chuckled. "Well, tell the truth, I don't *know*. Never seen them. Never had an X-ray, never been to a doctor. Might as well be potato-solid for all I know."

"Have *I* got a stomach?"

"You certainly have!" cried Grandma from the parlor entry. " 'Cause I feed it! And you've lungs, you scream loud enough to wake the crumblees. And you've dirty hands, go wash them! Dinner's ready. Grandpa, come on. Douglas, git!"

In the rush of boarders streaming downstairs, Grandpa, if he intended questioning Douglas further about the weird conversation, lost his opportunity. If dinner delayed an instant more, Grandma and the potatoes would develop simultaneous lumps.

The boarders, laughing and talking at the table—Mr. Koberman silent and sullen among them—were silenced when Grandfather cleared his throat. He talked politics a few minutes and then shifted over into the intriguing topic of the recent peculiar deaths in the town.

"It's enough to make an old newspaper editor prick up his ears," he said, eying them all. "That young Miss Larson, lived across the ravine, now. Found her dead three days ago for no reason, just funny kinds of tattoos all over her, and a facial expression that would make Dante cringe. And that other young lady, what was her name? Whitely? She disappeared and *never did* come back."

"Them things happen alla time," said Mr. Britz, the garage mechanic, chewing. "Ever peek inna Missing Peoples Bureau file? It's *that* long." He illustrated. "Can't tell *what* happens to most of 'em."

"Anyone want more dressing?" Grandma ladled liberal portions from the chicken's interior. Douglas watched, thinking about how that chicken had had two kinds of guts—God-made and Man-made.

Well, how about *three* kinds of guts?

Eh?

Why not?

Conversation continued about the mysterious death of so-and-so, and, oh, yes, remember a week ago, Marion Barsumian died of heart failure, but maybe that didn't connect up? or did it? you're crazy! forget it, why talk about it at the dinner table? So.

"Never can tell," said Mr. Britz. "Maybe we got a vampire in town."

Mr. Koberman stopped eating.

"In the year 1927?" said Grandma. "A vampire? Oh go on, now."

"Sure," said Mr. Britz. "Kill 'em with silver bullets. Anything silver for that matter. Vampires *hate* silver. I read it in a book somewhere, once. Sure, I did."

Douglas looked at Mr. Koberman who ate with wooden knives and forks and carried only new copper pennies in his pocket.

"It's poor judgment," said Grandpa, "to call anything by a name. We don't know what a hobgoblin or a vampire or a troll is. Could be lots of things. You can't heave them into categories with labels and say they'll act one way or another. That'd be silly. They're people. People who do things. Yes, that's the way to put it: people who *do* things."

"Excuse me," said Mr. Koberman, who got up and went out for his evening walk to work.

The stars, the moon, the wind, the clock ticking, and the chiming of the hours into dawn, the sun rising, and here it was another morning, another day, and Mr. Koberman coming along the sidewalk from his night's work. Douglas stood off like a small mechanism whirring and watching with carefully microscopic eyes.

At noon, Grandma went to the store to buy groceries.

As was his custom every day when Grandma was gone, Douglas yelled outside Mr. Koberman's door for a full three minutes. As usual, there was no response. The silence was horrible.

He ran downstairs, got the pass-key, a silver fork, and the three pieces of colored glass he had saved from the shattered window. He fitted the key to the lock and swung the door slowly open.

The room was in half light, the shades drawn. Mr. Koberman lay atop his bedcovers, in slumber clothes, breathing gently, up and down. He didn't move. His face was motionless.

"Hello, Mr. Koberman!"

The colorless walls echoed the man's regular breathing.

"Mr. Koberman, hello!"

Bouncing a golf ball, Douglas advanced. He yelled. Still no answer. "Mr. Koberman!"

Bending over Mr. Koberman, Douglas picked the tines of the silver fork in the sleeping man's face.

Mr. Koberman winced. He twisted. He groaned bitterly.

Response. Good. Swell.

Douglas drew a piece of blue glass from his pocket. Looking through the blue glass fragment he found himself in a blue room, in a blue world different from the world he knew. As different as was the red world. Blue furniture, blue bed, blue ceiling and walls, blue wooden eating utensils atop the blue bureau, and the sullen dark blue of Mr. Koberman's face and arms and his blue chest rising, falling. Also . . .

Mr. Koberman's eyes were wide, staring at him with a hungry darkness.

Douglas fell back, pulled the blue glass from his eyes.

Mr. Koberman's eyes were shut.

Blue glass again—open. Blue glass away—shut. Blue glass again—open. Away—shut. Funny. Douglas experimented, trembling. Through the glass the eyes seemed to peer hungrily, avidly, through Mr. Koberman's closed lids. Without the blue glass they seemed tightly shut.

But it was the rest of Mr. Koberman's body . . .

Mr. Koberman's bedclothes dissolved off him. The blue glass had something to do with it. Or perhaps it was the clothes themselves, just being *on* Mr. Koberman. Douglas cried out.

He was looking through the wall of Mr. Koberman's stomach, right *inside* him!

Mr. Koberman was solid.

Or, nearly so, anyway.

There were strange shapes and sizes within him.

Douglas must have stood amazed for five minutes, thinking about the blue worlds, the red worlds, the yellow worlds side by side, living together like glass panes around the big white stair window. Side by side, the colored panes, the different worlds; Mr. Koberman had said so himself.

So this was why the colored window had been broken.

"Mr. Koberman, wake up!"

No answer.

"Mr. Koberman, where do you work at night? Mr. Koberman, where do you work?"

A little breeze stirred the blue window shade.

"In a red world or a green world or a yellow one, Mr. Koberman?"

Over everything was a blue glass silence.

"Wait there," said Douglas.

He walked down to the kitchen, pulled open the great squeaking drawer, and picked out the sharpest, biggest knife.

Very calmly he walked into the hall, climbed back up the stairs again, opened the door to Mr. Koberman's room, went in, and closed it, holding the sharp knife in one hand.

Grandma was busy fingering a piecrust into a pan when Douglas entered the kitchen to place something on the table.

"Grandma, what's this?"

She glanced up briefly, over her glasses. "I don't know."

It was square, like a box, and elastic. It was bright orange in color. It had four square tubes, colored blue, attached to it. It smelled funny.

"Ever see anything like it, Grandma?"

"No."

"That's what *I* thought."

Douglas left it there, went from the kitchen. Five minutes later he returned with something else. "How about *this?*"

He laid down a bright pink linked chain with a purple triangle at one end.

"Don't bother me," said Grandma. "It's only a chain."

Next time he returned with two hands full. A ring, a square, a triangle, a pyramid, a rectangle, and—other shapes. All of them were pliable, resilient, and looked as if they were made of gelatin. "This isn't all," said Douglas, putting them down. "There's more where this came from."

Grandma said, "Yes, yes," in a far-off tone, very busy.

"You were wrong, Grandma."

"About what?"

"About all people being the same inside."

"Stop talking nonsense."

"Where's my piggy-bank?"

"On the mantel, where you left it."

"Thanks."

He tromped into the parlor, reached up for his piggy-bank.

Grandpa came home from the office at five.

"Grandpa, come upstairs."

"Sure, son. Why?"

"Something to show you. It's not nice; but it's interesting."

Grandpa chuckled, following his grandson's feet up to Mr. Koberman's room.

"Grandma mustn't know about this; she wouldn't like it," said Douglas. He pushed the door wide open. "There."

Grandfather gasped.

. . .

Douglas remembered the next few hours all the rest of his life. Standing over Mr. Koberman's naked body, the coroner and his assistants. Grandma, downstairs, asking somebody, "What's going on up there?" and Grandpa saying, shakily, "I'll take Douglas away on a long vacation so he can forget this whole ghastly affair. Ghastly, ghastly affair!"

Douglas said, "Why should it be bad? I don't see anything bad. I don't feel bad."

The coroner shivered and said, "Koberman's dead, all right."

His assistant sweated. "Did you see those *things* in the pans of water and in the wrapping paper?"

"Oh, my God, my God, yes, I saw them."

"Christ."

The coroner bent over Mr. Koberman's body again. "This better be kept secret, boys. It wasn't murder. It was a mercy the boy acted. God knows what might have happened if he hadn't."

"What was Koberman? A vampire? A monster?"

"Maybe. I don't know. Something—not human." The coroner moved his hands deftly over the suture.

Douglas was proud of his work. He'd gone to much trouble. He had watched Grandmother carefully and remembered. Needle and thread and all. All in all, Mr. Koberman was as neat a job as any chicken ever popped into hell by Grandma.

"I heard the boy say that Koberman lived even after all those *things* were taken out of him." The coroner looked at the triangles and chains and pyramids floating in the pans of water. "Kept on *living*. God."

"Did the boy say that?"

"He did."

"Then, what *did* kill Koberman?"

The coroner drew a few strands of sewing thread from their bedding.

"This. . . ." he said.

Sunlight blinked coldly off a half-revealed treasure trove; six dollars and sixty cents' worth of silver dimes inside Mr. Koberman's chest.

"I think Douglas made a wise investment," said the coroner, sewing the flesh back up over the "dressing" quickly.

CHASTEL

♦♦♦

MANLY WADE WELLMAN

"Then you won't let Count Dracula rest in his tomb?" inquired Lee Cobbett, his square face creasing with a grin.

Five of them sat in the parlor of Judge Keith Hilary Pursuivant's hotel suite on Central Park West. The Judge lounged in an armchair, a wineglass in his big old hand. On this, his eighty-seventh birthday, his blue eyes were clear, penetrating. His once tawny hair and mustache had gone blizzard-white, but both grew thick, and his square face showed rosy. In his tailored blue leisure suit, he still looked powerfully deep-chested and broad-shouldered.

Blocky Lee Cobbett wore jacket and slacks almost as brown as his face. Next to him sat Laurel Parcher, small and young and cinnamon-haired. The others were natty Phil Drumm the summer theater producer, and Isobel Arrington from a wire press service. She was blond, expensively dressed, she smoked a dark cigarette with a white tip. Her pen scribbled swiftly.

"Dracula's as much alive as Sherlock Holmes," argued Drumm. "All the revivals of the play, all the films—"

"Your musical should wake the dead, anyway," said Cobbett, drinking. "What's your main number, Phil? 'Garlic Time?' 'Gory, Gory Hallelujah'?"

"Let's have Christian charity here, Lee," Pursuivant came to Drumm's rescue. "Anyway, Miss Arrington came to interview me. Pour her some wine and let me try to answer her questions."

"I'm interested in Mr. Cobbett's remarks," said Isobel Arrington, her voice deliberately throaty. "He's an authority on the supernatural."

"Well, perhaps," admitted Cobbett, "and Miss Parcher has had some experiences. But Judge Pursuivant is the true authority, the author of *Vampiricon.*"

"I've read it, in paperback," said Isobel Arrington. "Phil, it mentions a vampire belief up in Connecticut, where you're having your show. What's that town again?"

"Deslow," he told her. "We're making a wonderful old stone barn into a theater. I've invited Lee and Miss Parcher to visit."

She looked at Drumm. "Is Deslow a resort town?"

"Not yet, but maybe the show will bring tourists. In Deslow, up to now, peace and quiet is the chief business. If you drop your shoe, everybody in town will think somebody's blowing the safe."

"Deslow's not far from Jewett City," observed Pursuivant. "There were vampires there about a century and a quarter ago. A family named Ray was afflicted. And to the east, in Rhode Island, there was a lively vampire folklore in recent years."

"Let's leave Rhode Island to H. P. Lovecraft's imitators," suggested Cobbett. "What do you call your show, Phil?"

"*The Land Beyond the Forest,*" said Drumm. "We're casting it now. Using locals in bit parts. But we have Gonda Chastel to play Dracula's countess."

"I never knew that Dracula had a countess," said Laurel Parcher.

"There was a stage star named Chastel, long ago when

I was young," said Pursuivant. "Just the one name—Chastel."

"Gonda's her daughter, and a year or so ago Gonda came to live in Deslow," Drumm told them. "Her mother's buried there. Gonda has invested in our production."

"Is that why she has a part in it?" asked Isobel Arrington.

"She has a part in it because she's beautiful and gifted," replied Drumm, rather stuffily. "Old people say she's the very picture of her mother. Speaking of pictures, here are some to prove it."

He offered two glossy prints to Isobel Arrington, who murmured "Very sweet," and passed them to Laurel Parcher. Cobbett leaned to see.

One picture seemed copied from an older one. It showed a woman who stood with unconscious stateliness, in a gracefully draped robe with a tiara binding her rich flow of dark hair. The other picture was of a woman in fashionable evening dress, her hair ordered in modern fashion, with a face strikingly like that of the woman in the other photograph.

"Oh, she's lovely," said Laurel. "Isn't she, Lee?"

"Isn't she?" echoed Drumm.

"Magnificent," said Cobbett, handing the pictures to Pursuivant, who studied them gravely.

"Chastel was in Richmond, just after the First World War," he said slowly. "A dazzling Lady Macbeth. I was in love with her. Everyone was."

"Did you tell her you loved her?" asked Laurel.

"Yes. We had supper together, twice. Then she went ahead with her tour, and I sailed to England and studied at Oxford. I never saw her again, but she's more or less why I never married."

Silence a moment. Then: *"The Land Beyond the Forest,"* Laurel repeated. "Isn't there a book called that?"

"There is indeed, my child," said the Judge. "By Emily de Laszowska Gerard. About Transylvania, where Dracula came from."

"That's why we use the title, that's what Transylvania means," put in Drumm. "It's all right, the book's out of copyright. But I'm surprised to find someone who's heard of it."

"I'll protect your guilty secret, Phil," promised Isobel Arrington. "What's over there in your window, Judge?"

Pursuivant turned to look. "Whatever it is," he said, "it's not Peter Pan."

Cobbett sprang up and ran toward the half-draped window. A silhouette with head and shoulders hung in the June night. He had a glimpse of a face, rich-mouthed, with bright eyes. Then it was gone. Laurel had hurried up behind him. He hoisted the window sash and leaned out.

Nothing. The street was fourteen stories down. The lights of moving cars crawled distantly. The wall below was course after course of dull brick, with recesses of other windows to right and left, below, above. Cobbett studied the wall, his hands braced on the sill.

"Be careful, Lee," Laurel's voice besought him.

He came back to face the others. "Nobody out there," he said evenly. "Nobody could have been. It's just a wall—nothing to hang to. Even that sill would be tricky to stand on."

"But I saw something, and so did Judge Pursuivant," said Isobel Arrington, the cigarette trembling in her fingers.

"So did I," said Cobbett. "Didn't you, Laurel?"

"Only a face."

Isobel Arrington was calm again. "If it's a trick, Phil,

you played a good one. But don't expect me to put it in my story."

Drumm shook his head nervously. "I didn't play any trick, I swear."

"Don't try this on old friends," she jabbed at him. "First those pictures, then whatever was up against the glass. I'll use the pictures, but I won't write that a weird vision presided over this birthday party."

"How about a drink all around?" suggested Pursuivant.

He poured for them. Isobel Arrington wrote down answers to more questions, then said she must go. Drumm rose to escort her. "You'll be at Deslow tomorrow, Lee?" he asked.

"And Laurel, too. You said we could find quarters there."

"The Mapletree's a good auto court," said Drumm. "I've already reserved cabins for the two of you."

"On the spur of the moment," said Pursuivant suddenly, "I think I'll come along, if there's space for me."

"I'll check it out for you, Judge," said Drumm.

He departed with Isobel Arrington. Cobbett spoke to Pursuivant. "Isn't that rather offhand?" he asked. "Deciding to come with us?"

"I was thinking about Chastel." Pursuivant smiled gently. "About making a pilgrimage to her grave."

"We'll drive up about nine tomorrow morning."

"I'll be ready, Lee."

Cobbett and Laurel, too, went out. They walked down a flight of stairs to the floor below, where both their rooms were located. "Do you think Phil Drumm rigged up that illusion for us?" asked Cobbett.

"If he did, he used the face of that actress, Chastel."

He glanced keenly at her. "You saw that."

"I thought I did, and so did you."

They kissed good night at the door to her room.

Pursuivant was ready next morning when Cobbett knocked. He had only one suitcase and a thick, brown-blotched malacca cane, banded with silver below its curved handle.

"I'm taking only a few necessaries, I'll buy socks and such things in Deslow if we stay more than a couple of days," he said. "No, don't carry it for me, I'm quite capable."

When they reached the hotel garage, Laurel was putting her luggage in the trunk of Cobbett's black sedan. Judge Pursuivant declined the front seat beside Cobbett, held the door for Laurel to get in, and sat in the rear. They rolled out into bright June sunlight.

Cobbett drove them east on Interstate 95, mile after mile along the Connecticut shore, past service stations, markets, sandwich shops. Now and then they glimpsed Long Island Sound to the right. At toll gates, Cobbett threw quarters into hoppers and drove on.

"New Rochelle to Port Chester," Laurel half chanted, "Norwalk, Bridgeport, Stratford—"

"Where, in 1851, devils plagued a minister's home," put in Pursuivant.

"The names make a poem," said Laurel.

"You can get that effect by reading any timetable," said Cobbett. "We miss a couple of good names—Mystic and Giants Neck, though they aren't far off from our route. And Griswold—that means Gray Woods—where the Judge's book says Horace Ray was born."

"There's no Griswold on the Connecticut map anymore," said the Judge.

"Vanished?" said Laurel. "Maybe it appears at just a certain time of the day, along about sundown."

She laughed, but the Judge was grave.

"Here we'll pass by New Haven," he said. "I was at Yale here, seventy years ago."

They rolled across the Connecticut River between Old Saybrook and Old Lyme. Outside New London, Cobbett turned them north on State Highway 82 and, near Jewett City, took a two-lane road that brought them into Deslow, not long after noon.

There were pleasant clapboard cottages among elm trees and flower beds. Main Street had bright shops with, farther along, the belfry of a sturdy old church. Cobbett drove them to a sign saying MAPLETREE COURT. A row of cabins faced along a cement-floored colonnade, their fronts painted white with blue doors and window frames. In the office, Phil Drumm stood at the desk, talking to the plump proprietress.

"Welcome home," he greeted them. "Judge, I was asking Mrs. Simpson here to reserve you a cabin."

"At the far end of the row, sir," the lady said. "I'd have put you next to your two friends, but so many theater folks have already moved in."

"Long ago I learned to be happy with any shelter," the Judge assured her.

They saw Laurel to her cabin and put her suitcases inside, then walked to the farthest cabin where Pursuivant would stay. Finally Drumm followed Cobbett to the space next to Laurel's. Inside, Cobbett produced a fifth of bourbon from his briefcase. Drumm trotted away to fetch ice. Pursuivant came to join them.

"It's good of you to look after us," Cobbett said to Drumm above his glass.

"Oh, I'll get my own back," Drumm assured him. "The Judge and you, distinguished folklore experts—I'll have you in all the papers."

"Whatever you like," said Cobbett. "Let's have lunch, as soon as Laurel is freshened up."

The four ate crab cakes and flounder at a little restaurant while Drumm talked about *The Land Beyond the Forest*. He had signed the minor film star Caspar Merrick to play Dracula. "He has a fine baritone singing voice," said Drumm. "He'll be at afternoon rehearsal."

"And Gonda Chastel?" inquired Pursuivant, buttering a roll.

"She'll be there tonight." Drumm sounded happy about that. "This afternoon's mostly for bits and chorus numbers. I'm directing as well as producing." They finished their lunch, and Drumm rose. "If you're not tired, come see our theater."

It was only a short walk through town to the converted barn. Cobbett judged it had been built in Colonial times, with a recent roof of composition tile, but with walls of stubborn, brown-gray New England stone. Across a narrow side street stood the old white church, with a hedge-bordered cemetery.

"Quaint, that old burying ground," commented Drumm. "Nobody's spaded under there now, there's a modern cemetery on the far side, but Chastel's tomb is there. Quite a picturesque one."

"I'd like to see it," said Pursuivant, leaning on his silver-banded cane.

The barn's interior was set with rows of folding chairs, enough for several hundred spectators. On a stage at the far end, workmen moved here and there under lights. Drumm led his guests up steps at the side.

High in the loft, catwalks zigzagged and a dark curtain hung like a broad guillotine blade. Drumm pointed out canvas flats, painted to resemble grim castle walls. Pursuivant nodded and questioned.

"I'm no authority on what you might find in Transylvania," he said, "but this looks convincing."

A man walked from the wings toward them. "Hello, Caspar," Drumm greeted him. "I want you to meet Judge Pursuivant and Lee Cobbett. And Miss Laurel Parcher, of course." He gestured the introductions. "This is Mr. Caspar Merrick, our Count Dracula."

Merrick was elegantly tall, handsome, with carefully groomed black hair. Sweepingly he bowed above Laurel's hand and smiled at them all. "Judge Pursuivant's writings I know, of course," he said richly. "I read what I can about vampires, inasmuch as I'm to be one."

"Places for the Delusion number!" called a stage manager.

Cobbett, Pursuivant, and Laurel went down the steps and sat on chairs. Eight men and eight girls hurried into view, dressed in knockabout summer clothes. Someone struck chords on a piano, Drumm gestured importantly, and the chorus sang. Merritt, coming downstage, took solo on a verse. All joined in the refrain. Then Drumm made them sing it over again.

After that, two comedians made much of confusing the words vampire and empire. Cobbett found it tedious. He excused himself to his companions and strolled out and across to the old, tree-crowded churchyard.

The gravestones bore interesting epitaphs: not only the familiar PAUSE O STRANGER PASSING BY / AS YOU ARE NOW SO ONCE WAS I, and A BUD ON EARTH TO BLOOM IN HEAVEN, but several of more originality. One bewailed a man who, since he had been lost at sea, could hardly have been there at all. Another bore, beneath a bat-winged face, the declaration DEATH PAYS ALL DEBTS and the date 1907, which Cobbett associated with a financial panic.

Toward the center of the graveyard, under a drooping willow, stood a shedlike structure of heavy granite blocks. Cobbett picked his way to the door of heavy grillwork, which was fastened with a rusty padlock the size of a sardine can. On the lintel were strongly carved letters: CHASTEL.

Here, then, was the tomb of the stage beauty Pursuivant remembered so romantically. Cobbett peered through the bars.

It was murkily dusty in there. The floor was coarsely flagged, and among sooty shadows at the rear stood a sort of stone chest that must contain the body. Cobbett turned and went back to the theater. Inside, piano music rang wildly and the people of the chorus desperately rehearsed what must be meant for a folk dance.

"Oh, it's exciting," said Laurel as Cobbett sat down beside her. "Where have you been?"

"Visiting the tomb of Chastel."

"Chastel?" echoed Pursuivant. "I must see that tomb."

Songs and dance ensembles went on. In the midst of them, a brisk reporter from Hartford appeared, to interview Pursuivant and Cobbett. At last Drumm resoundingly dismissed the players on stage and joined his guests.

"Principals rehearse at eight o'clock," he announced. "Gonda Chastel will be here, she'll want to meet you. Could I count on you then?"

"Count on me, at least," said Pursuivant. "Just now, I feel like resting before dinner, and so, I think, does Laurel here."

"Yes, I'd like to lie down for a little," said Laurel.

"Why don't we all meet for dinner at the place where we had lunch?" said Cobbett. "You come too, Phil."

"Thanks, I have a date with some backers from New London."

It was half-past five when they went out.

Cobbett went to his quarters, stretched out on the bed, and gave himself to thought.

He hadn't come to Deslow because of this musical interpretation of the Dracula legend. Laurel had come because he was coming, and Pursuivant on a sudden impulse that might have been more than a wish to visit the grave of Chastel. But Cobbett was here because this, he knew, had been vampire country, maybe still was vampire country.

He remembered the story in Pursuivant's book about vampires at Jewett City, as reported in the Norwich *Courier* for 1854. Horace Ray, from the now vanished town of Griswold, had died of a "wasting disease." Thereafter his oldest son, then his second son, had also gone to their graves. When a third son sickened, friends and relatives dug up Horace Ray and the two dead brothers and burned the bodies in a roaring fire. The surviving son got well. And something like that had happened in Exeter, near Providence in Rhode Island. Very well, why organize and present the Dracula musical here in Deslow, so near those places?

Cobbett had met Phil Drumm in the South the year before, knew him for a brilliant if erratic producer, who relished tales of devils and the dead who walk by night. Drumm might have known enough stage magic to have rigged that seeming appearance at Pursuivant's window in New York. That is, if indeed it was only a seeming appearance, not a real face. Might it have been real, a manifestation of the unreal? Cobbett had seen enough of what people dismissed as unreal, impossible, to wonder.

. . .

A soft knock came at the door. It was Laurel. She wore green slacks, a green jacket, and she smiled, as always, at sight of Cobbett's face. They sought Pursuivant's cabin. A note on the door said: MEET ME AT THE CAFÉ.

When they entered there, Pursuivant hailed them from the kitchen door. "Dinner's ready," he hailed them. "I've been supervising in person, and I paid well for the privilege."

A waiter brought a laden tray. He arranged platters of red-drenched spaghetti and bowls of salad on a table. Pursuivant himself sprinkled Parmesan cheese. "No salt or pepper," he warned. "I seasoned it myself, and you can take my word it's exactly right."

Cobbett poured red wine into glasses. Laurel took a forkful of spaghetti. "Delicious," she cried. "What's in it, Judge?"

"Not only ground beef and tomatoes and onions and garlic," replied Pursuivant. "I added marjoram and green pepper and chile and thyme and bay leaf and oregano and parsley and a couple of other important ingredients. And I also minced in some Italian sausage."

Cobbett, too, ate with enthusiastic appetite. "I won't order any dessert," he declared. "I want to keep the taste of this in my mouth."

"There's more in the kitchen for dessert if you want it," the Judge assured him. "But here, I have a couple of keepsakes for you."

He handed each of them a small, silvery object. Cobbett examined his. It was smoothly wrapped in foil. He wondered if it was a nutmeat.

"You have pockets, I perceive," the Judge said. "Put those into them. And don't open them, or my wish for you won't come true."

When they had finished eating, a full moon had begun to rise in the darkening sky. They headed for the theater.

A number of visitors sat in the chairs and the stage lights looked bright. Drumm stood beside the piano, talking to two plump men in summer business suits. As Pursuivant and the others came down the aisle, Drumm eagerly beckoned them and introduced them to his companions, the financial backers with whom he had taken dinner.

"We're very much interested," said one. "This vampire legend intrigues anyone, if you forget that a vampire's motivation is simply nourishment."

"No, something more than that," offered Pursuivant. "A social motivation."

"Social motivation," repeated the other backer.

"A vampire wants company of its own kind. A victim infected becomes a vampire, too, and an associate. Otherwise the original vampire would be a disconsolate loner."

"There's a lot in what you say," said Drumm, impressed.

After that there was financial talk, something in which Cobbett could not intelligently join. Then someone else approached, and both the backers stared.

It was a tall, supremely graceful woman with red-lighted black hair in a bun at her nape, a woman of impressive figure and assurance. She wore a sweeping blue dress, fitted to her slim waist, with a frill-edged neckline. Her arms were bare and white and sweetly turned, with jeweled bracelets on them. Drumm almost ran to bring her close to the group.

"Gonda Chastel," he said, half-prayerfully. "Gonda, you'll want to meet these people."

The two backers stuttered admiringly at her. Pursuivant bowed and Laurel smiled. Gonda Chastel gave Cobbett her slim, cool hand. "You know so much about this thing we're trying to do here," she said, in a voice like cream.

Drumm watched them. His face looked plaintive.

"Judge Pursuivant has taught me a lot, Miss Chastel," said Cobbett. "He'll tell you that once he knew your mother."

"I remember her, not very clearly," said Gonda Chastel. "She died when I was just a little thing, thirty years ago. And I followed her here, now I make my home here."

"You look very like her," said Pursuivant.

"I'm proud to be like my mother in any way," she smiled at them. She could be overwhelming, Cobbett told himself.

"And Miss Parcher," went on Gonda Chastel, turning toward Laurel. "What a little presence she is. She should be in our show—I don't know what part, but she should." She smiled dazzlingly. "Now then, Phil wants me on stage."

"Knock-at-the-door number, Gonda," said Drumm.

Gracefully she mounted the steps. The piano sounded, and she sang. It was the best song, felt Cobbett, that he had heard so far in the rehearsals. "Are they seeking for a shelter from the night?" Gonda Chastel sang richly. Caspar Merritt entered, to join in a recitative. Then the chorus streamed on, singing somewhat shrilly.

Pursuivant and Laurel had sat down. Cobbett strode back up the aisle and out under a moon that rained silver-blue light.

He found his way to the churchyard. The trees that had offered pleasant afternoon shade now made a dubious darkness. He walked underneath branches that seemed to lower like hovering wings as he approached the tomb structure at the center.

The barred door that had been massively locked now stood open. He peered into the gloom within. After a moment he stepped across the threshold upon the flagged floor.

He had to grope, with one hand upon the rough wall. At last he almost stumbled upon the great stone chest at the rear.

It, too, was flung open, its lid heaved back against the wall.

There was, of course, complete darkness within it. He flicked on his cigar lighter. The flame showed him the inside of the stone coffer, solidly made and about ten feet long. Its sides of gray marble were snugly fitted. Inside lay a coffin of rich dark wood with silver fittings and here, yet again, was an open lid.

Bending close to the smudged silk lining, Cobbett seemed to catch an odor of stuffy sharpness, like dried herbs. He snapped off his light and frowned in the dark. Then he groped back to the door, emerged into the open, and headed for the theater again.

"Mr. Cobbett," said the beautiful voice of Gonda Chastel.

She stood at the graveyard's edge, beside a sagging willow. She was almost as tall as he. Her eyes glowed in the moonlight.

"You came to find the truth about my mother," she half-accused.

"I was bound to try," he replied. "Ever since I saw a certain face at a certain window of a certain New York hotel."

She stepped back from him. "You know that she's a—"

"A vampire," Cobbett finished for her. "Yes."

"I beg you to be helpful—merciful." But there was no supplication in her voice. "I already realized, long ago. That's why I live in little Deslow. I want to find a way to give her rest. Night after night, I wonder how."

"I understand that," said Cobbett.

Gonda Chastel breathed deeply. "You know all about these things. I think there's something about you that could daunt a vampire."

"If so, I don't know what it is," said Cobbett truthfully.

"Make me a solemn promise. That you won't return to her tomb, that you won't tell others what you and I know about her. I—I want to think how we two together can do something for her."

"If you wish, I'll say nothing," he promised.

Her hand clutched his.

"The cast took a five-minute break, it must be time to go to work again," she said, suddenly bright. "Let's go back and help the thing along."

They went.

Inside, the performers were gathering on stage. Drumm stared unhappily as Gonda Chastel and Cobbett came down the aisle. Cobbett sat with Laurel and Pursuivant and listened to the rehearsal.

Adaptation from Bram Stoker's novel was free, to say the least. Dracula's eerie plottings were much hampered by his having a countess, a walking dead beauty who strove to become a spirit of good. There were some songs, in interesting minor keys. There was a dance, in which men and women leaped like kangaroos. Finally Drumm called a halt, and the performers trooped wearily to the wings.

Gonda Chastel lingered, talking to Laurel. "I wonder, my dear, if you haven't had acting experience," she said.

"Only in school entertainments down South, when I was little."

"Phil," said Gonda Chastel, "Miss Parcher is a good type, has good presence. There ought to be something for her in the show."

"You're very kind, but I'm afraid that's impossible," said Laurel, smiling.

"You may change your mind, Miss Parcher. Will you and your friends come to my house for a nightcap?"

"Thank you," said Pursuivant. "We have some notes to make, and we must make them together."

"Until tomorrow evening, then, Mr. Cobbett, we'll remember our agreement."

She went away toward the back of the stage. Pursuivant and Laurel walked out. Drumm hurried up the aisle and caught Cobbett's elbow.

"I saw you," he said harshly. "Saw you both as you came in."

"And we saw you, Phil. What's this about?"

"She likes you." It was half an accusation. "Fawns on you, almost."

Cobbett grinned and twitched his arm free. "What's the matter, Phil, are you in love with her?"

"Yes, God damn it, I am. I'm in love with her. She knows it but she won't let me come to her house. And you—the first time she meets you, she invites you."

"Easy does it, Phil," said Cobbett. "If it'll do you any good, I'm in love with someone else, and that takes just about all my spare time."

He hurried out to overtake his companions.

Pursuivant swung his cane almost jauntily as they returned through the moonlight to the auto court.

"What notes are you talking about, Judge?" asked Cobbett.

"I'll tell you at my quarters. What do you think of the show?"

"Perhaps I'll like it better after they've rehearsed more," said Laurel. "I don't follow it at present."

"Here and there, it strikes me as limp," added Cobbett.

They sat down in the Judge's cabin. He poured them drinks. "Now," he said, "there are certain things to recognize here. Things I more or less expected to find."

"A mystery, Judge?" asked Laurel.

"Not so much that, if I expected to find them. How far are we from Jewett City?"

"Twelve or fifteen miles as the crow flies," estimated Cobbett. "And Jewett City is where that vampire family, the Rays, lived and died."

"Died twice, you might say," nodded Pursuivant, stroking his white mustache. "Back about a century and a quarter ago. And here's what might be a matter of Ray family history. I've been thinking about Chastel, whom once I greatly admired. About her full name."

"But she had only one name, didn't she?" asked Laurel.

"On the stage she used one name, yes. So did Bernhardt, so did Duse, so later did Garbo. But all of them had full names. Now, before we went to dinner, I made two telephone calls to theatrical historians I know. To learn Chastel's full name."

"And she had a full name," prompted Cobbett.

"Indeed she did. Her full name was Chastel Ray."

Cobbett and Laurel looked at him in deep silence.

"Not apt to be just coincidence," elaborated Pursuivant. "Now then, I gave you some keepsakes today."

"Here's mine," said Cobbett, pulling the foil-wrapped bit from his shirt pocket.

"And I have mine here," said Laurel, her hand at her throat. "In a little locket I have on this chain."

"Keep it there," Pursuivant urged her. "Wear it around your neck at all times. Lee, have yours always on your person. Those are garlic cloves, and you know what they're good for. You can also guess why I cut up a lot of garlic in our spaghetti for dinner."

"You think there's a vampire here," offered Laurel.

"A specific vampire." The Judge took a deep breath into his broad chest. "Chastel. Chastel Ray."

"I believe it, too," declared Cobbett tonelessly, and Laurel nodded. Cobbett looked at the watch on his wrist.

"It's past one in the morning," he said. "Perhaps we'd all be better off if we had some sleep."

They said their good nights and Laurel and Cobbett walked to where their two doors stood side by side. Laurel put her key into the lock, but did not turn it at once. She peered across the moonlit street.

"Who's that over there?" she whispered. "Maybe I ought to say, what's that?"

Cobbett looked. "Nothing, you're just nervous. Good night, dear."

She went in and shut the door. Cobbett quickly crossed the street.

"Mr. Cobbett," said the voice of Gonda Chastel.

"I wondered what you wanted, so late at night," he said, walking close to her.

She had undone her dark hair and let it flow to her shoulders. She was, Cobbett thought, as beautiful a woman as he had ever seen.

"I wanted to be sure about you," she said. "That you'd respect your promise to me, not to go into the churchyard."

"I keep my promises, Miss Chastel."

He felt a deep, hushed silence all around them. Not even the leaves rustled in the trees.

"I had hoped you wouldn't venture even this far," she went on. "You and your friends are new in town, you might tempt her specially." Her eyes burned at him. "You know I don't mean that as a compliment."

She turned to walk away. He fell into step beside her. "But you're not afraid of her," he said.

"Of my own mother?"

"She was a Ray," said Cobbett. "Each Ray sapped the blood of his kinsmen. Judge Pursuivant told me all about it."

Again the gaze of her dark, brilliant eyes. "Nothing like that has ever happened between my mother and me." She stopped, and so did he. Her slim, strong hand took him by the wrist.

"You're wise and brave," she said. "I think you may have come here for a good purpose, not just about the show."

"I try to have good purposes."

The light of the moon soaked through the overhead branches as they walked on. "Will you come to my house?" she invited.

"I'll walk to the churchyard," replied Cobbett. "I said I wouldn't go into it, but I can stand at the edge."

"Don't go in."

"I've promised that I wouldn't, Miss Chastel."

She walked back the way they had come. He followed the street under silent elms until he reached the border of the churchyard. Moonlight flecked and spattered the tombstones. Deep shadows lay like pools. He had a sense of being watched from within.

As he gazed, he saw movement among the graves. He could not define it, but it was there. He glimpsed, or fancied he glimpsed, a head, indistinct in outline as though swathed in dark fabric. Then another. Another. They huddled in a group, as though to gaze at him.

"I wish you'd go back to your quarters," said Gonda Chastel beside him. She had drifted after him, silent as a shadow herself.

"Miss Chastel," he said, "tell me something if you can. Whatever happened to the town or village of Griswold?"

"Griswold?" she echoed. "What's Griswold? That means gray woods."

"Your ancestor, or your relative, Horace Ray, came from Griswold to die in Jewett City. And I've told you that I knew your mother was born a Ray."

Her shining eyes seemed to flood upon him. "I didn't know that," she said.

He gazed into the churchyard, at those hints of furtive movement.

"The hands of the dead reach out for the living," murmured Gonda Chastel.

"Reach out for me?" he asked.

"Perhaps for both of us. Just now, we may be the only living souls awake in Deslow." She gazed at him again. "But you're able to defend yourself, somehow."

"What makes you think that?" he inquired, aware of the clove of garlic in his shirt pocket.

"Because they—in the churchyard there—they watch, but they hold away from you. You don't invite them."

"Nor do you, apparently," said Cobbett.

"I hope you're not trying to make fun of me," she said, her voice barely audible.

"On my soul, I'm not."

"On your soul," she repeated. "Good night, Mr. Cobbett."

Again she moved away, tall and proud and graceful. He watched her out of sight. Then he headed back toward the motor court.

Nothing moved in the empty street. Only one or two lights shone here and there in closed shops. He thought he heard a soft rustle behind him, but did not look back.

As he reached his own door, he heard Laurel scream behind hers.

Judge Pursuivant sat in his cubicle, his jacket off, studying a worn little brown book. Skinner, said letters on the spine, and *Myths and Legends of Our Own Land.* He had read the passage so often that he could almost repeat it from memory:

"To lay this monster he must be taken up and burned; at least his heart must be; and he must be disinterred in the daytime when he is asleep and unaware."

There were other ways, reflected Pursuivant.

It must be very late by now, rather it must be early. But he had no intention of going to sleep. Not when stirs of motion sounded outside, along the concrete walkway in front of his cabin. Did motion stand still, just beyond the door there? Pursuivant's great, veined hand touched the front of his shirt, beneath which a bag of garlic hung like an amulet. Garlic—was that enough? He himself was fond of garlic, judiciously employed in sauces and salads. But then, he could see himself in the mirror of the bureau yonder, could see his broad old face with its white sweep of mustache like a wreath of snow on a sill. It was a clear image of a face, not a calm face just then, but a determined one. Pursuivant smiled at it, with a glimpse of even teeth that were still his own.

He flicked up his shirt cuff and looked at his watch. Half past one, about. In June, even with daylight savings time, dawn would come early. Dawn sent vampires back to the tombs that were their melancholy refuges, "asleep and unaware," as Skinner had specified.

Putting the book aside, he poured himself a small drink of bourbon, dropped in cubes of ice and a trickle of water, and sipped. He had drunk several times during that day, when on most days he partook of only a single highball, by advice of his doctor; but just now he was grateful for the pungent, walnutty taste of the liquor. It was one of earth's natural things, a good companion when not abused. From the table he took a folder of scribbled notes. He looked at jottings from the works of Montague Summers.

These offered the proposition that a plague of vampires usually stemmed from a single source of infection, a king or queen vampire whose feasts of blood drove victims to their graves, to rise in their turn. If the original vampires were found and destroyed, the others relaxed to rest as normally dead bodies. Bram Stoker had followed the same gospel when he wrote *Dracula*, and doubtless Bram Stoker had known. Pursuivant looked at another page, this time a poem copied from James Grant's curious *Mysteries of All Nations*. It was a ballad in archaic language, that dealt with baleful happenings in "The Towne of Peste"—Budapest?

It was the Corpses that our Churchyardes filled
That did at midnight lumberr up our Stayres;
They suck'd our Bloud, the gorie Banquet swilled,
And harried everie Soule with hydeous Feares . . .

Several verses down:

They barr'd with Boltes of Iron the Churchyard-pale
To keep them out; but all this wold not doe;
For when a Dead-Man has learn'd to draw a naile,
He can also burst an iron Bolte in two.

Many times Pursuivant had tried to trace the author of that verse. He wondered if it was not something quaintly confected not long before 1880, when Grant published his work. At any rate, the Judge felt that he knew what it meant, the experience that it remembered.

He put aside the notes, too, and picked up his spotted walking stick. Clamping the balance of it firmly in his left hand, he twisted the handle with his right and pulled. Out of the hollow shank slid a pale, bright blade, keen and lean and edged on both front and back.

Pursuivant permitted himself a smile above it. This was one of his most cherished possessions, this silver weapon said to have been forged a thousand years ago by St. Dunstan. Bending, he spelled out the runic writing upon it: *Sic pereant omnes inimici tui, Domine.*

That was the end of the fiercely triumphant song of Deborah in the Book of Judges: So perish all thine enemies, O Lord. Whether the work of St. Dunstan or not, the metal was silver, the writing was a warrior's prayer. Silver and writing had proved their strength against evil in the past.

Then, outside, a loud, tremulous cry of mortal terror.

Pursuivant sprang out of his chair on the instant. Blade in hand, he fairly ripped his door open and ran out. He saw Cobbett in front of Laurel's door, wrenching at the knob, and hurried there like a man half his age.

"Open up, Laurel," he heard Cobbett call. "It's Lee out here!"

The door gave inward as Pursuivant reached it, and he and Cobbett pressed into the lighted room.

Laurel half-crouched in the middle of the floor. Her trembling hand pointed to a rear window. "She tried to come in," Laurel stammered.

"There's nothing at that window," said Cobbett, but even as he spoke, there was. A face, pale as tallow, crowded against the glass. They saw wide, staring eyes, a mouth that opened and squirmed. Teeth twinkled sharply.

Cobbett started forward, but Pursuivant caught him by the shoulder. "Let me," he said, advancing toward the window, the point of his blade lifted.

The face at the window writhed convulsively as the silver weapon came against the pane with a clink. The mouth opened as though to shout, but no sound came. The face fell back and vanished from their sight.

"I've seen that face before," said Cobbett hoarsely.

"Yes," said Pursuivant. "At my hotel window. And since."

He dropped the point of the blade to the floor. Outside came a whirring rush of sound, like feet, many of them.

"We ought to wake up the people at the office," said Cobbett.

"I doubt if anyone in this little town could be wakened," Pursuivant told him evenly. "I have it in mind that every living soul, except the three of us, is sound asleep. Entranced."

"But out there—" Laurel gestured at the door, where something seemed to be pressing.

"I said, every living soul," Pursuivant looked from her to Cobbett. "Living," he repeated.

He paced across the floor, and with his point scratched a perpendicular line upon it. Across this he carefully drove a horizontal line, making a cross. The pushing abruptly ceased.

"There it is, at the window again," breathed Laurel.

Pursuivant took long steps back to where the face hovered, with black hair streaming about it. He scraped the glass with his silver blade, up and down, then across, making lines upon it. The face drew away. He moved to mark similar crosses on the other windows.

"You see," he said, quietly triumphant, "the force of old, old charms."

He sat down in a chair, heavily. His face was weary, but he looked at Laurel and smiled.

"It might help if we managed to pity those poor things out there," he said.

"Pity?" she almost cried out.

"Yes," he said, and quoted:

. . . Think how sad it must be
To thirst always for a scorned elixir,
The salt of quotidian blood.

"I know that," volunteered Cobbett. "It's from a poem by Richard Wilbur, a damned unhappy poet."

"Quotidian," repeated Laurel to herself.

"That means something that keeps coming back, that returns daily," Cobbett said.

"It's a term used to refer to a recurrent fever," added Pursuivant.

Laurel and Cobbett sat down together on the bed.

"I would say that for the time being we're safe here," declared Pursuivant. "Not at ease, but at least safe. At dawn, danger will go to sleep and we can open the door."

"But why are we safe, and nobody else?" Laurel cried out. "Why are we awake, with everyone else in this town asleep and helpless?"

"Apparently because we all of us wear garlic," replied Pursuivant patiently, "and because we ate garlic, plenty of it, at dinnertime. And because there are crosses—crude, but unmistakable—wherever something might try to come in. I won't ask you to be calm, but I'll ask you to be resolute."

"I'm resolute," said Cobbett between clenched teeth. "I'm ready to go out there and face them."

"If you did that, even with the garlic," said Pursuivant, "you'd last about as long as a pint of whiskey in a five-handed poker game. No, Lee, relax as much as you can, and let's talk."

They talked, while outside strange presences could be felt rather than heard. Their talk was of anything and everything but where they were and why. Cobbett remembered strange things he had encountered, in towns, among mountains, along desolate roads, and what he had been able to do about them. Pursuivant told of a vampire he had known and defeated in upstate New York, of a werewolf in his own Southern countryside. Laurel, at Cobbett's urging, sang songs, old songs, from her own rustic home place. Her voice was sweet. When she sang "Round Is the Ring," faces came and hung like smudges outside the cross-scored windows. She saw, and sang again, an old Appalachian carol called "Mary She Heared a Knock in the Night." The faces drifted away again. And the hours, too, drifted away, one by one.

"There's a horde of vampires on the night street here, then." Cobbett at last brought up the subject of their problem.

"And they lull the people of Deslow to sleep, to be helpless victims," agreed Pursuivant. "About this show, *The Land Beyond the Forest,* mightn't it be welcomed as a chance to spread the infection? Even a townful of sleepers couldn't feed a growing community of blood drinkers."

"If we could deal with the source, the original infection—" began Cobbett.

"The mistress of them, the queen," said Pursuivant. "Yes. The one whose walking by night rouses them all. If she could be destroyed, they'd all die properly."

He glanced at the front window. The moonlight had a touch of slaty gray.

"Almost morning," he pronounced. "Time for a visit to her tomb."

"I gave my promise I wouldn't go there," said Cobbett.

"But I didn't promise," said Pursuivant, rising. "You stay here with Laurel."

His silver blade in hand, he stepped out into darkness from which the moon had all but dropped away. Overhead, stars were fading out. Dawn was at hand.

He sensed a flutter of movement on the far side of the street, an almost inaudible gibbering of sound. Steadily he walked across. He saw nothing along the sidewalk there, heard nothing. Resolutely he tramped to the churchyard, his weapon poised. More grayness had come to dilute the dark.

He pushed his way through the hedge of shrubs, stepped in upon the grass, and paused at the side of a grave. Above it hung an eddy of soft mist, no larger than the swirl of water draining from a sink. As Pursuivant watched, it seemed to soak into the earth and disappear. That, he said to himself, is what a soul looks like when it seeks to regain its coffin.

On he walked, step by weary, purposeful step, toward the central crypt. A ray of the early sun, stealing between heavily leafed boughs, made his way more visible. In this dawn, he would find what he would find. He knew that.

The crypt's door of open bars was held shut by its heavy padlock. He examined that lock closely. After a moment, he slid the point of his blade into the rusted keyhole and judiciously pressed this way, then that, and back again the first way. The spring creakily relaxed and he dragged the door open. Holding his breath, he entered.

The lid of the great stone vault was closed down. He took hold of the edge and heaved. The lid was heavy, but rose with a complaining grate of the hinges. Inside he saw a dark, closed coffin. He lifted the lid of that, too.

She lay there, calm-faced, the eyes half shut as though dozing.

"Chastel," said Pursuivant to her. "Not Gonda. Chastel."

The eyelids fluttered. That was all, but he knew that she heard what he said.

"Now you can rest," he said. "Rest in peace, really in peace."

He set the point of his silver blade at the swell of her left breast. Leaning both his broad hands upon the curved handle, he drove downward with all his strength.

She made a faint squeak of sound.

Blood sprang up as he cleared his weapon. More light shone in. He could see a dark moisture fading from the blade, like evaporating dew.

In the coffin, Chastel's proud shape shrivelled, darkened. Quickly he slammed the coffin shut, then lowered the lid of the vault into place and went quickly out. He pushed the door shut again and fastened the stubborn old lock. As he walked back through the churchyard among the graves, a bird twittered over his head. More distantly, he heard the hum of a car's motor. The town was waking up.

In the growing radiance, he walked back across the street. By now, his steps were the steps of an old man, old and very tired.

Inside Laurel's cabin, Laurel and Cobbett were stirring instant coffee into hot water in plastic cups. They questioned the Judge with their tired eyes.

"She's finished," he said shortly.

"What will you tell Gonda?" asked Cobbett.

"Chastel was Gonda."

"But—"

"She was Gonda," said Pursuivant again, sitting down. "Chastel died. The infection wakened her out of her tomb, and she told people she was Gonda, and naturally they believed her." He sagged wearily. "Now that she's finished and at rest, those others—the ones she had bled, who also rose at night—will rest, too."

Laurel took a sip of coffee. Above the cup, her face was pale.

"Why do you say Chastel was Gonda?" she asked the Judge. "How can you know that?"

"I wondered from the very beginning. I was utterly sure just now."

"Sure?" said Laurel. "How can you be sure?"

Pursuivant smiled at her, the very faintest of smiles.

"My dear, don't you think a man always recognizes a woman he has loved?"

He seemed to recover his characteristic defiant vigor. He rose and went to the door and put his hand on the knob. "Now, if you'll just excuse me for a while."

"Don't you think we'd better hurry and leave?" Cobbett asked him. "Before people miss her and ask questions?"

"Not at all," said Pursuivant, his voice strong again. "If we're gone, they'll ask questions about us, too, possibly embarrassing questions. No, we'll stay. We'll eat a good breakfast, or at least pretend to eat it. And we'll be as surprised as the rest of them about the disappearance of their leading lady."

"I'll do my best," vowed Laurel.

"I know you will, my child," said Pursuivant, and went out the door.

LA BELLE DAME SANS MERCI

◆◆◆

JOHN KEATS

A BALLAD

O what can ail thee, knight at arms,
Alone and palely loitering?
The sedge has wither'd from the lake,
And no birds sing.

O what can ail thee, knight at arms,
So haggard and so woe-begone?
The squirrel's granary is full,
And the harvest's done.

I see a lily on thy brow
With anguish moist and fever dew,
And on thy cheeks a fading rose
Fast withereth too.

I met a lady in the meads,
Full beautiful, a fairy's child;
Her hair was long; her foot was light,
And her eyes were wild.

I made a garland for her head,
And bracelets too, and fragrant zone;
She look'd at me as she did love,
And made sweet moan.

I set her on my pacing steed,
And nothing else saw all day long,
For sidelong would she bend, and sing
A fairy's song.

She found me roots of relish sweet,
And honey wild, and manna dew,
And sure in language strange she said—
I love thee true.

She took me to her elfin grot,
And there she wept, and sigh'd full sore,
And there I shut her wild wild eyes
With kisses four.

And there she lulled me asleep,
And there I dream'd—Ah! woe betide!
The latest dream I ever dream'd
On the cold hill's side.

I saw pale kings, and princes too,
Pale warriors, death pale were they all;
They cried—"La belle dame sans merci
Hath thee in thrall!"

I saw their starv'd lips in the gloom
With horrid warning gaped wide,
And I awoke and found me here
On the cold hill's side.

And this is why I sojourn here,
Alone and palely loitering,
Though the sedge is wither'd from the lake,
And no birds sing.

AN EPISODE OF CATHEDRAL HISTORY

◆◆◆

M. R. JAMES

There was once a learned gentleman who was deputed to examine and report upon the archives of the Cathedral of Southminster. The examination of these records demanded a very considerable expenditure of time: hence it became advisable for him to engage lodgings in the city: for though the Cathedral body were profuse in their offers of hospitality, Mr. Lake felt that he would prefer to be master of his day. This was recognised as reasonable. The Dean eventually wrote advising Mr. Lake, if he were not already suited, to communicate with Mr. Worby, the principal Verger, who occupied a house convenient to the church and was prepared to take in a quiet lodger for three or four weeks. Such an arrangement was precisely what Mr. Lake desired. Terms were easily agreed upon, and early in December, like another Mr. Datchery (as he remarked to himself), the investigator found himself in the occupation of a very comfortable room in an ancient and "cathedraly" house.

One so familiar with the customs of Cathedral churches, and treated with such obvious consideration by the Dean and Chapter of this Cathedral in particular, could not fail to command the respect of the Head Verger. Mr. Worby even acquiesced in certain modifications of statements he had been accustomed to offer for years to parties of visitors. Mr. Lake, on his part, found the Verger a very cheery companion, and took advantage of any occasion that presented itself for enjoying his conversation when the day's work was over.

One evening, about nine o'clock, Mr. Worby knocked at his lodger's door. "I've occasion," he said, "to go across to the Cathedral, Mr. Lake, and I think I made you a promise when I did so next I would give you the opportunity to see what it looked like at night time. It's quite fine and dry outside, if you care to come."

"To be sure I will; very much obliged to you, Mr. Worby, for thinking of it, but let me get my coat."

"Here it is, sir, and I've another lantern here that you'll find advisable for the steps, as there's no moon."

"Anyone might think we were Jasper and Durdles, over again, mightn't they?" said Lake, as they crossed the Close, for he had ascertained that the Verger had read *Edwin Drood*.

"Well, so they might," said Mr. Worby, with a short laugh, "though I don't know whether we ought to take it as a compliment. Odd ways, I often think, they had at that Cathedral, don't it seem so to you, sir? Full choral matins at seven o'clock in the morning all the year round. Wouldn't suit our boys' voices nowadays, and I think there's one or two of the men would be applying for a rise if the Chapter was to bring it in—particular the altos."

They were now at the south-west door. As Mr. Worby was unlocking it, Lake said, "Did you ever find anybody locked in here by accident?"

"Twice I did. One was a drunk sailor; however he got in I don't know. I s'pose he went to sleep in the service, but by the time I got to him he was praying fit to bring the roof in. Lor'! What a noise that man did make! Said it was the first time he'd been inside a church for ten years, and blest if ever he'd try it again. The other was an old sheep: them boys it was, up to their games. That was the last time they tried it on, though. There, sir, now you see what we look like; our late Dean used now and again to bring parties in, but he preferred a moonlit night, and there was a piece of verse he'd say to 'em, relating to a Scotch cathedral, I understand; but I don't know; I almost think the effect's better when it's all dark-like. Seems to add to the size and height. Now if you won't mind stopping somewhere in the nave while I go up into the choir where my business lays, you'll see what I mean."

Accordingly Lake waited, leaning against a pillar, and watched the light wavering along the length of the church, and up the steps into the choir, until it was intercepted by some screen or other furniture, which only allowed the reflection to be seen on the piers and roof. Not many minutes had passed before Worby reappeared at the door of the choir and by waving his lantern signalled to Lake to rejoin him.

"I suppose it *is* Worby, and not a substitute," thought Lake to himself, as he walked up the nave. There was, in fact, nothing untoward. Worby showed him the papers which he had come to fetch out of the Dean's stall, and asked him what he thought of the spectacle: Lake agreed that it was well worth seeing. "I suppose," he said, as they walked towards the altar-steps together, "that you're too much used to going about here at night to feel nervous—but you must get a start every now and then, don't you, when a book falls down or a door swings to?"

"No, Mr. Lake, I can't say I think much about noises, not nowadays: I'm much more afraid of finding an escape of gas or a burst in the stove pipes than anything else. Still there have been times, years ago. Did you notice that plain altar-tomb there—fifteenth century we say it is, I don't know if you agree to that? Well, if you didn't look at it, just come back and give it a glance, if you'd be so good." It was on the north side of the choir, and rather awkwardly placed: only about three feet from the enclosing stone screen. Quite plain, as the Verger had said, but for some ordinary stone panelling. A metal cross of some size on the northern side (that next to the screen) was the solitary feature of any interest.

Lake agreed that it was not earlier than the Perpendicular period: "But," he said, "unless it's the tomb of some remarkable person, you'll forgive me for saying that I don't think it's particularly noteworthy."

"Well, I can't say as it is the tomb of anybody noted in 'istory," said Worby, who had a dry smile on his face, "for we don't own any record whatsoever of who it was put up to. For all that, if you've half an hour to spare, sir, when we get back to the house, Mr. Lake, I could tell you a tale about that tomb. I won't begin on it now; it strikes cold here, and we don't want to be dawdling about all night."

"Of course I should like to hear it immensely."

"Very well, sir, you shall. Now if I might put a question to you," he went on, as they passed down the choir aisle, "in our little local guide—and not only there, but in the little book on our Cathedral in the series—you'll find it stated that this portion of the building was erected previous to the twelfth century. Now of course I should be glad enough to take that view, but—mind the step, sir—but, I put it to you—does the lay of the stone 'ere in this portion of the wall"—which he tapped with his key—"does it to your eye carry the flavour of what you might call Saxon masonry? No, I thought not; no more it does to me: now, if you'll believe me, I've said as much to those men—one's the librarian of our Free Library here, and the other came down from London on purpose—fifty times, if I have once, but I might just as well have talked to that bit of stonework. But there it is, I suppose everyone's got their opinions."

The discussion of this peculiar trait of human nature occupied Mr. Worby almost up to the moment when he and Lake re-entered the former's house. The condition of the fire in Lake's sitting-room led to a suggestion from Mr. Worby that they should finish the evening in his own parlour. We find them accordingly settled there some short time afterwards.

Mr. Worby made his story a long one, and I will not undertake to tell it wholly in his own words, or in his own order. Lake committed the substance of it to paper immediately after hearing it, together with some few passages of the narrative which had fixed themselves *verbatim* in his mind; I shall probably find it expedient to condense Lake's record to some extent.

Mr. Worby was born, it appeared, about the year 1828. His father before him had been connected with the Cathedral, and likewise his grandfather. One or both had been choristers, and in later life both had done work as mason and carpenter respectively about the fabric. Worby himself, though possessed, as he frankly acknowledged, of an indifferent voice, had been drafted into the choir at about ten years of age.

It was in 1840 that the wave of the Gothic revival smote the Cathedral of Southminster. "There was a lot of lovely stuff went then, sir," said Worby, with a sigh. "My father couldn't hardly believe it when he got his orders to clear out the choir. There was a new dean just come in—Dean Burscough it was—and my father had been 'prenticed to a good firm of joiners in the city, and knew what good work was when he saw it. Crool it was, he used to say: all that beautiful wainscot oak, as good as the day it was put up, and garlands-like of foliage and fruit, and lovely old gilding work on the coats of arms and the organ pipes. All went to the timber yard—every bit except some little pieces worked up in the Lady Chapel, and 'ere in this overmantel. Well—I may be mistook, but I say our choir never looked as well since. Still there was a lot found out about the history of the church, and no doubt but what it did stand in need of repair. There was very few winters passed but what we'd lose a pinnacle." Mr. Lake expressed his concurrence with Worby's views of restoration, but owned to a fear about this point lest the story proper should never be reached. Possibly this was perceptible in his manner.

Worby hastened to reassure him, "Not but what I could carry on about that topic for hours at a time, and do so when I see my opportunity. But Dean Burscough he was very set on the Gothic period, and nothing would serve him but everything must be made agreeable to that. And one morning after service he appointed for my father to meet him in the choir, and he came back after he'd taken off his robes in the vestry, and he'd got a roll of paper with him, and the verger that was then brought in a table, and they begun spreading it out on the table with prayer books to keep it down, and my father helped 'em, and he saw it was a picture of the inside of a choir in a Cathedral; and the Dean—he was a quick-spoken gentleman—he says, 'Well, Worby, what do you think of that?' 'Why,' says my father, 'I don't think I 'ave the pleasure of knowing that view. Would that be Hereford Cathedral, Mr. Dean?' 'No, Worby,' says the Dean, 'that's Southminster Cathedral as we hope to see it before many years.' 'Indeed, sir,' says my father, and that was all he did say—leastways to the Dean—but he used to tell me he felt really faint in himself when he looked round our choir as I can remember it, all comfortable and furnished-like, and then see this nasty little dry picter, as he called it, drawn out by some London architect. Well, there I am again. But you'll see what I mean if you look at this old view."

Worby reached down a framed print from the wall. "Well, the long and the short of it was that the Dean he handed over to my father a copy of an order of the Chapter that he was to clear out every bit of the choir—make a clean sweep—ready for the new work that was being designed up in town, and he was to put it in hand as soon as ever he could get the breakers together. Now then, sir, if you look at that view, you'll see where the pulpit used to stand: that's what I want you to notice, if you please." It was, indeed, easily seen; an unusually large structure of timber with a domed sounding-board, standing at the east end of the stalls on the north side of the choir, facing the bishop's throne. Worby proceeded to explain that during the alterations, services were held in the nave, the members of the choir being thereby disappointed of an anticipated holiday, and the organist in particular incurring the suspicion of having wilfully damaged the mechanism of the temporary organ that was hired at considerable expense from London.

The work of demolition began with the choir screens and organ loft, and proceeded gradually eastwards, disclosing, as Worby said, many interesting features of older work. While this was going on the members of the Chapter were, naturally, in and about the choir a great deal, and it soon became apparent to the elder Worby—who could not help overhearing some of their talk—that, on the part of the senior Canons especially, there must have been a good deal of disagreement before the policy now being carried out had been adopted. Some were of opinion that they should catch their deaths of cold in the return-stalls, unprotected by a screen from the draughts in the nave: others objected to being exposed to the view of persons in the choir aisles, especially, they said, during the sermons, when they found it helpful to listen in a posture which was liable to misconstruction. The strongest opposition, however, came from the oldest of the body, who up to the last moment objected to the removal of the pulpit. "You ought not to touch it, Mr. Dean," he said with great emphasis one morning, when the two were standing before it. "You don't know what mischief you may do." "Mischief? It's not a work of any particular merit, Canon." "Don't call me Canon," said the old man with great asperity, "that is, for thirty years I've been known as Dr. Ayloff, and I shall be obliged, Mr. Dean, if you would kindly humour me in that matter. And as to the pulpit (which I've preached from for thirty years, though I don't insist on that), all I'll say is, I *know* you're doing wrong in moving it." "But what sense could there be, my dear Doctor, in leaving it where it is, when we're fitting up the rest of the choir in a totally different *style*? What reason could be given—apart from the look of the thing?" "Reason! Reason!" said old Dr. Ayloff. "If you young men—if I may say so without any disrespect, Mr. Dean—if you'd only listen to reason a little, and not be always asking for it, we should get on better. But there, I've said my say." The old gentleman hobbled off, and as it proved, never entered the Cathedral again. The season—it was a hot summer—turned sickly on a sudden. Dr. Ayloff was one of the first to go, with some affection of the muscles of the thorax, which took him painfully at night. And at many services the number of choirmen and boys was very thin.

Meanwhile the pulpit had been done away with. In fact, the sounding-board (part of which still exists as a table in a summer-house in the palace garden) was taken down within an hour or two of Dr. Ayloff's protest. The removal of the base—not effected without considerable trouble—disclosed to view, greatly to the exultation of the restoring party, an altar-tomb—the tomb, of course, to which Worby had attracted Lake's attention that same evening. Much fruitless research was expended in attempts to identify the occupant; from that day to this he has never had a name put to him. The structure had been most carefully boxed in under the pulpit-base, so that such slight ornament as it possessed was not defaced; only on the north side of it there was what looked like an injury; a gap between two of the slabs composing the side. It might be two or three inches across. Palmer, the mason, was directed to fill it up in a week's time, when he came to do some other small jobs near that part of the choir.

The season was undoubtedly a very trying one. Whether the church was built on a site that had once been a marsh, as was suggested, or for whatever reason, the residents in its immediate neighbourhood had, many of them, but little enjoyment of the exquisite sunny days and the calm nights of August and September. To several of the older people—Dr. Ayloff, among others, as we have seen—the summer proved downright fatal, but even among the younger, few escaped either a sojourn in bed for a matter of weeks, or at the least, a brooding sense of oppression, accompanied by hateful nightmares. Gradually there formulated itself a suspicion—which grew into a conviction—that the alterations in the Cathedral had something to say in the matter. The widow of a former old verger, a pensioner of the Chapter of Southminster, was visited by dreams, which she retailed to her friends, of a shape that slipped out of the little door of the south transept as the dark fell in, and flitted—taking a fresh direction every night—about the Close, disappearing for a while in house after house, and finally emerging again when the night sky was paling. She could see nothing of it, she said, but that it was a moving form: only she had an impression that when it returned to the church, as it seemed to do in the end of the dream, it turned its head: and then, she could not tell why, but she thought it had red eyes. Worby remembered hearing the old lady tell this dream at a tea-party in the house of the chapter clerk. Its recurrence might, perhaps, he said, be taken as a symptom of approaching illness; at any rate before the end of September the old lady was in her grave.

The interest excited by the restoration of this great church was not confined to its own county. One day that summer an F.S.A., of some celebrity, visited the place. His business was to write an account of the discoveries that had been made, for the Society of Antiquaries, and his wife, who accompanied him, was to make a series of illustrative drawings for his report. In the morning she employed herself in making a general sketch of the choir; in the afternoon she devoted herself to details. She first drew the newly exposed altar-tomb, and when that was finished, she called her husband's attention to a beautiful piece of diaper-ornament on the screen just behind it, which had, like the tomb itself, been completely concealed by the pulpit. Of course, he said, an illustration of that must be made; so she seated herself on the tomb and began a careful drawing which occupied her till dusk.

Her husband had by this time finished his work of measuring and description, and they agreed that it was time to be getting back to their hotel. "You may as well brush my skirt, Frank," said the lady, "it must have got covered with dust, I'm sure." He obeyed dutifully; but, after a moment, he said, "I don't know whether you value this dress particularly, my dear, but I'm inclined to think it's seen its best days. There's a great bit of it gone." "Gone?

Where?" said she. "I don't know where it's gone, but it's off at the bottom edge behind here." She pulled it hastily into sight, and was horrified to find a jagged tear extending some way into the substance of the stuff; very much, she said, as if a dog had rent it away. The dress was, in any case, hopelessly spoilt, to her great vexation, and though they looked everywhere, the missing piece could not be found. There were many ways, they concluded, in which the injury might have come about, for the choir was full of old bits of woodwork with nails sticking out of them. Finally, they could only suppose that one of these had caused the mischief, and that the workmen, who had been about all day, had carried off that particular piece with the fragment of dress still attached to it.

It was about this time, Worby thought, that his little dog began to wear an anxious expression when the hour for it to be put into the shed in the back yard approached. (For his mother had ordained that it must not sleep in the house.) One evening, he said, when he was just going to pick it up and carry it out, it looked at him "like a Christian, and waved its 'and, and, I was going to say—well, you know 'ow they do carry on sometimes, and the end of it was I put it under my coat, and 'uddled it upstairs—and I'm afraid I as good as deceived my poor mother on the subject. After that the dog acted very artful with 'iding itself under the bed for half an hour or more before bedtime came, and we worked it so as my mother never found out what we'd done." Of course Worby was glad of its company anyhow, but more particularly when the nuisance that is still remembered in Southminster as "the crying" set in.

"Night after night," said Worby, "that dog seemed to know it was coming; he'd creep out, he would, and snuggle into the bed and cuddle right up to me shivering, and when the crying come he'd be like a wild thing, shoving his head under my arm, and I was fully near as bad. Six or seven times we'd hear it, not more, and when he'd dror out his 'ed again I'd know it was over for that night. What was it like, sir? Well, I never heard but one thing that seemed to hit it off. I happened to be playing about in the Close, and there was two of the Canons met and said 'Good morning' one to another. 'Sleep well last night?' says one—it was Mr. Henslow that one, and Mr. Lyall was the other. 'Can't say I did,' says Mr. Lyall, 'rather too much of Isaiah xxxiv.14 for me,' 'xxxiv.14,' says Mr. Henslow, 'What's that?' 'You call yourself a Bible reader!' says Mr. Lyall. (Mr. Henslow, you must know, he was one of what used to be termed Simeon's lot—pretty much what we should call the Evangelical party.) 'You go and look it up.' I wanted to know what he was getting at myself, and so off I ran home and got out my own Bible, and there it was: 'the satyr shall cry to his fellow.' Well, I thought, is that what we've been listening to these past nights? And I tell you it made me look over my shoulder a time or two. Of course I'd asked my father and mother about what it could be before that, but they both said it was most likely cats: but they spoke very short, and I could see they was troubled. My word! that was a noise—'ungry-like, as if it was calling after someone that wouldn't come. If ever you felt you wanted company, it would be when you was waiting for it to begin again. I believe two or three nights there was men put on to watch in different parts of the Close; but they all used to get together in one corner, the nearest they could to the High Street, and nothing came of it.

"Well, the next thing was this. Me and another of the boys—he's in business in the city now as a grocer, like his father before him—we'd gone up in the choir after morning service was over, and we heard old Palmer the mason bellowing to some of his men. So we went up nearer, because we knew he was a rusty old chap and there might be some fun going. It appears Palmer'd told this man to stop up the chink in that old tomb. Well, there was this man keeping on saying he'd done it the best he could, and there was Palmer carrying on like all possessed about it. 'Call that making a job of it?' he says. 'If you had your rights you'd get the sack for this. What do you suppose I pay you your wages for? What do you suppose I'm going to say to the Dean and Chapter when they come round, as come they may do any time, and see where you've been bungling about covering the 'ole place with mess and plaster and Lord knows what?' 'Well, master, I done the best I could,' says the man; 'I don't know no more than what you do 'ow it come to fall out this way. I tamped it right in the 'ole,' he says, 'and now it's fell out,' he says, 'I never see.'

" 'Fell out!' says old Palmer. 'Why it's nowhere near the place. Blowed out, you mean'; and he picked up a bit of plaster, and so did I, that was laying up against the screen, three or four feet off, and not dry yet; and old Palmer he looked at it curious-like, and then he turned round on me and he says, 'Now then, you boys, have you been up to some of your games here?' 'No,' I says, 'I haven't, Mr. Palmer; there's none of us been about here till just this minute'; and while I was talking the other boy, Evans, he got looking in through the chink, and I heard him draw in his breath, and he came away sharp and up to us, and says he, 'I believe there's something in there. I saw something shiny.' 'What! I dare say!' says old Palmer. 'Well, I ain't got time to stop about there. You, William, you go off and get some more stuff and make a job of it this time; if not, there'll be trouble in my yard,' he says.

"So the man he went off, and Palmer too, and us boys stopped behind, and I says to Evans, 'Did you really see anything in there?' 'Yes,' he says, 'I did indeed.' So then I says, 'Let's shove something in and stir it up.' And we tried several of the bits of wood that was laying about, but they were all too big. Then Evans he had a sheet of music he'd brought with him, an anthem or a service, I forget which it is now, and he rolled it up small and shoved it in the chink; two or three times he did it, and nothing happened. 'Give it to me, boy,' I said, and I had a try. No, nothing happened. Then, I don't know why I thought of it, I'm sure, but I stooped down just opposite the chink and put my two fingers in my mouth and whistled—you know the way—and at that I seemed to think I heard something stirring, and I says to Evans, 'Come away,' I says; 'I don't like this.' 'Oh, rot,' he says, 'give me that roll,' and he took it and shoved it in. And I don't think ever I see anyone go so pale as he did. 'I say, Worby,' he says, 'it's caught, or else someone's got hold of it.' 'Pull it out or leave it,' I says. 'Come and let's get off.' So he gave a good pull, and it came away. Leastways most of it did, but the end was gone. Torn off it was, and Evans looked at it for a second and then he gave a sort of a croak and let it drop, and we both made off out of there as quick as ever we could. When we got outside Evans says to me, 'Did you see the end of that paper?' 'No,' I says, 'only it was torn.' 'Yes, it was,' he says, 'but it was wet too, and black!' Well, partly because of the fright we had, and partly because that music was wanted in a day or two, and we knew there'd be a set-out about it with the organist, we didn't say nothing to anyone else, and I suppose the workmen they swept up the bit that was left along with the rest of the rubbish. But Evans, if you were to ask him this very day about it, he'd stick to it he saw that paper wet and black at the end where it was torn."

After that the boys gave the choir a wide berth, so that Worby was not sure what was the result of the mason's renewed mending of the tomb. Only he made out from fragments of conversation dropped by the workmen passing through the choir that some difficulty had been met with, and that the governor—Mr. Palmer to wit—had tried his own hand at the job. A little later, he happened to see Mr. Palmer himself knocking at the door of the Deanery and being admitted by the butler. A day or so after that, he gathered from a remark his father let fall at breakfast, that something a little out of the common was to be done in the Cathedral after morning service on the morrow. "And I'd just as soon it was today," his father added. "I don't see the use of running risks." " 'Father,' I says, 'what are you going to do in the Cathedral tomorrow?' And he turned on me as savage as I ever see him—he was a wonderful good-tempered man as a general thing, my poor father was. 'My lad,' he says, 'I'll trouble you not to go picking up your elders' and betters' talk: it's not manners and it's not straight. What I'm going to do or not going to do in the Cathedral tomorrow is none of your business: and if I catch sight of you hanging about the place tomorrow after your work's done, I'll send you home with a flea in your ear. Now you mind that.' Of course I said I was very sorry and that, and equally of course I went off and laid my plans with Evans. We knew there was a stair up in the corner of the transept which you can get up to the triforium, and in them days the door to it was pretty well always open, and even if it wasn't we knew the key usually laid under a bit of matting hard by. So we made up our minds we'd be putting away music and that, next morning while the rest of the boys was clearing off, and then slip up the stairs and watch from the triforium if there was any signs of work going on.

"Well, that same night I dropped off asleep as sound as a boy does, and all of a sudden the dog woke me up, coming into the bed, and thought I, now we're going to get it sharp, for he seemed more frightened than usual. After about five minutes sure enough came this cry. I can't give you no idea what it was like; and so near too—nearer than I'd heard it yet—and a funny thing, Mr. Lake, you know what a place this Close is for an echo, and particular if you stand this side of it. Well, this crying never made no sign of an echo at all. But, as I said, it was dreadful near this night; and on the top of the start I got with hearing it, I got another fright; for I heard something rustling outside in the passage. Now to be sure I thought I was done; but I noticed the dog seemed to perk up a bit, and next there was someone whispered outside the door, and I very near laughed out loud, for I knew it was my father and mother that had got out of bed with the noise. 'Whatever is it?' says my mother. 'Hush! I don't know,' says my father, excited-like. 'Don't disturb the boy. I hope he didn't hear nothing.'

"So, me knowing they were just outside, it made me bolder, and I slippped out of bed across to my little window—giving on the Close—but the dog he bored right down to the bottom of the bed—and I looked out. First go off I couldn't see anything. Then right down in the shadow under a buttress I made out what I shall always say was two spots of red—a dull red it was—nothing like a lamp or a fire, but just so as you could pick 'em out of the black shadow. I hadn't but just sighted 'em when it seemed we wasn't the only people that had been disturbed, because I see a window in a house on the left-hand side become lighted up, and the light moving. I just turned my head to make sure of it, and then looked back into the shadow for those two red things, and they were gone, and for all I peered about and stared, there was not a sign more of them. Then come my last fright that night—something come against my bare leg—but that was all right: that was my little dog had come out of bed, and prancing about making a great to-do, only holding his tongue, and me seeing he was quite in spirits again, I took him back to bed and we slept the night out!

"Next morning I made out to tell my mother I'd had the dog in my room, and I was surprised, after all she'd said about it before, how quiet she took it. 'Did you?' she says. 'Well, by good rights you ought to go without your breakfast for doing such a thing behind my back: but I don't know as there's any great harm done, only another time you ask my permission, do you hear?' A bit after that I said something to my father about having heard cats again. '*Cats*,' he says; and he looked over at my poor mother, and she coughed and he says, 'Oh! Ah! Yes, cats. I believe I heard 'em myself.'

"That was a funny morning altogether: nothing seemed to go right. The organist he stopped in bed, and the minor Canon he forgot it was the 19th day and waited for the *Venite;* and after a bit the deputy set off playing the chant for evensong, which was a minor; and then the Decani boys were laughing so much they couldn't sing, and when it came to the anthem the solo boy he got took with the giggles, and made out his nose was bleeding, and shoved the book at me what hadn't practised the verse and wasn't much of a singer if I had known it. Well, things was rougher, you see, fifty years ago, and I got a nip from the counter-tenor behind me that I remembered.

"So we got through somehow, and neither the men nor the boys weren't by way of waiting to see whether the Canon in residence—Mr. Henslow it was—would come to the vestries and fine 'em, but I don't believe he did: for one thing I fancy he'd read the wrong lesson for the first time in his life, and knew it. Anyhow, Evans and me didn't find no difficulty in slipping up the stairs as I told you, and when we got up we laid ourselves down flat on our stomachs where we could just stretch our heads out over the old tomb, and we hadn't but just done so when we heard the Verger that was then, first shutting the iron porch-gates and locking the south-west door, and then the transept door, so we knew there was something up, and they meant to keep the public out for a bit.

"Next thing was, the Dean and the Canon come in by their door on the north and then I see my father, and old Palmer, and a couple of their best men, and Palmer stood a'talking for a bit with the Dean in the middle of the choir. He had a coil of rope and the men had crows. All of 'em looked a bit nervous. So there they stood talking, and at last I heard the Dean say, 'Well, I've no time to waste, Palmer. If you think this'll satisfy Southminster people, I'll permit it to be done; but I must say this, that never in the whole course of my life have I heard such arrant nonsense from a practical man as I have from you. Don't you agree with me, Henslow?' As far as I could hear Mr. Henslow said something like 'Oh well! We're told, aren't we, Mr. Dean, not to judge others?' And the Dean he gave a kind of sniff, and walked straight up to the tomb, and took his stand behind it with his back to the screen, and the others they come edging up rather gingerly. Henslow, he stopped on the south side and scratched on his chin, he did. Then the Dean spoke up: 'Palmer,' he says, 'which can you do easiest, get the slab off the top, or shift one of the side slabs?'

"Old Palmer and his men they pottered about a bit looking round the edge of the top slab and sounding the sides on the south and east and west and everywhere but the north. Henslow said something about it being better to have a try at the south side, because there was more light and more room to move about in. Then my father, who'd been a'watching of them, went round to the north side, and knelt down and felt the slab by the chink, and he got up and dusted his knees and says to the Dean: 'Beg pardon, Mr. Dean, but I think if Mr. Palmer'll try this here slab he'll find it'll come out easy enough. Seems to me one of the men could prise it out with his crow by means of this chink.' 'Ah! Thank you, Worby,' says the Dean. 'That's a good suggestion. Palmer, let one of your men do that, will you?'

"So the man come round, and put his bar in and bore on it, and just that minute when they were all bending over, and we boys got our heads well over the edge of the triforium, there came a most fearful crash down at the west end of the choir, as if a whole stack of big timber had fallen down a flight of stairs. Well, you can't expect me to tell you everything that happened all in a minute. Of course there was a terrible commotion. I heard the slab fall out, and the crowbar on the floor, and I heard the Dean say, 'Good God!'

"When I looked down again I saw the Dean tumbled over on the floor, the men was making off down the choir, Henslow was just going to help the Dean up, Palmer was going to stop the men (as he said afterwards), and my father was sitting on the altar step with his face in his hands. The Dean he was very cross. 'I wish to goodness you'd look where you're coming to, Henslow,' he says. 'Why you should all take to your heels when a stick of wood tumbles down I cannot imagine'; and all Henslow could do, explaining he was right away on the other side of the tomb, would not satisfy him.

"Then Palmer came back and reported there was nothing to account for this noise and nothing seemingly fallen down, and when the Dean finished feeling of himself they gathered round—except my father, he sat where he was—

and someone lighted up a bit of candle and they looked into the tomb. 'Nothing there,' says the Dean. 'What did I tell you? Stay! Here's something. What's this? A bit of music paper, and a piece of torn stuff—part of a dress it looks like. Both quite modern—no interest whatever. Another time perhaps you'll take the advice of an educated man'—or something like that, and off he went, limping a bit, and out through the north door, only as he went he called back angry to Palmer for leaving the door standing open. Palmer called out, 'Very sorry, sir,' but he shrugged his shoulders, and Henslow says, 'I fancy Mr. Dean's mistaken. I closed the door behind me, but he's a little upset.' Then Palmer says, 'Why, where's Worby?' and they saw him sitting on the step and went up to him. He was recovering himself, it seemed, and wiping his forehead, and Palmer helped him up on to his legs, as I was glad to see.

"They were too far off for me to hear what they said, but my father pointed to the north door in the aisle, and Palmer and Henslow both of them looked very surprised and scared. After a bit, my father and Henslow went out of the church, and the others made what haste they could to put the slab back and plaster it in. And about as the clock struck twelve the Cathedral was opened again and us boys made the best of our way home.

"I was in a great taking to know what it was had given my poor father such a turn, and when I got in and found him sitting in his chair taking a glass of spirits, and my mother standing looking anxious at him, I couldn't keep from bursting out and making confession where I'd been. But he didn't seem to take on, not in the way of losing his temper. 'You was there, was you? Well, did you see it?' 'I saw everything, father,' I said, 'except when the noise came.' 'Did you see what it was knocked the Dean over?'

he says. 'That what come out of the monument? You didn't? Well, that's a mercy.' 'Why, what was it, father?' I said. 'Come, you must have seen it,' he says. '*Didn't* you see? A thing like a man, all over hair, and two great eyes to it?'

"Well, that was all I could get out of him that time, and later on he seemed as if he was ashamed of being so frightened, and he used to put me off when I asked him about it. But years after when I was got to be a grown man, we had more talk now and again on the matter, and he always said the same thing. 'Black it was,' he'd say, 'and a mass of hair, and two legs, and the light caught on its eyes.'

"Well, that's the tale of that tomb, Mr. Lake; it's one we don't tell to our visitors, and I should be obliged to you not to make any use of it till I'm out of the way. I doubt Mr. Evans'll feel the same as I do, if you ask him."

This proved to be the case. But over twenty years have passed by, and the grass is growing over both Worby and Evans; so Mr. Lake felt no difficulty about communicating his notes—taken in 1890—to me. He accompanied them with a sketch of the tomb and a copy of the short inscription on the metal cross which was affixed at the expense of Dr. Lyall to the centre of the northern side. It was from the Vulgate of Isaiah xxiv, and consisted merely of the three words—

IBI CUBAVIT LAMIA.

DRACULA'S GUEST

♦♦♦

BRAM STOKER

When we started for our drive the sun was shining brightly on Munich, and the air was full of the joyousness of early summer. Just as we were about to depart, Herr Delbrück (the maître d'hôtel of the Quatre Saisons, where I was staying) came down, bareheaded, to the carriage and, after wishing me a pleasant drive, said to the coachman, still holding his hand on the handle of the carriage door:

"Remember you are back by nightfall. The sky looks bright but there is a shiver in the north wind that says there may be a sudden storm. But I am sure you will not be late." Here he smiled, and added, "For you know what night it is."

Johann answered with an emphatic, "Ja, mein Herr," and, touching his hat, drove off quickly. When we had cleared the town, I said, after signalling to him to stop:

"Tell me, Johann, what is tonight?"

He crossed himself, as he answered laconically: "Walpurgisnacht." Then he took out his watch, a great, old-fashioned German silver thing as big as a turnip, and looked at it, with his eyebrows gathered together and a little impatient shrug of his shoulders. I realized that this was his way of respectfully protesting against the unnecessary delay, and sank back in the carriage, merely motioning him to proceed. He started off rapidly, as if to make up for lost time. Every now and then the horses seemed to throw up their heads and sniffed the air suspiciously. On such occasions I often looked round in alarm. The road was pretty bleak, for we were traversing a sort of high, windswept plateau. As we drove, I saw a road that looked but little used, and which seemed to dip through a little, winding valley. It looked so inviting that, even at the risk of offending him, I called Johann to stop—and when he had pulled up, I told him I would like to drive down that road. He made all sorts of excuses, and frequently crossed himself as he spoke. This somewhat piqued my curiosity, so I asked him various questions. He answered fencingly, and repeatedly looked at his watch in protest. Finally I said:

"Well, Johann, I want to go down this road. I shall not ask you to come unless you like; but tell me why you do not like to go, that is all I ask." For answer he seemed to throw himself off the box, so quickly did he reach the ground. Then he stretched out his hands appealingly to me, and implored me not to go. There was just enough of English mixed with the German for me to understand the drift of his talk. He seemed always just about to tell me something—the very idea of which evidently frightened him; but each time he pulled himself up, saying, as he crossed himself: "Walpurgisnacht!"

I tried to argue with him, but it was difficult to argue with a man when I did not know his language. The advantage certainly rested with him, for although he began to speak in English, of a very crude and broken kind, he always got excited and broke into his native tongue—and every time he did so, he looked at his watch. Then the horses became restless and sniffed the air. At this he grew very pale, and, looking around in a frightened way, he suddenly jumped forward, took them by the bridles, and led them on some twenty feet. I followed, and asked why he had done this. For answer he crossed himself, pointed to the spot we had left and drew his carriage in the direction of the other road, indicating a cross, and said, first in German, then in English: "Buried him—him what killed themselves."

I remembered the old custom of burying suicides at cross-roads: "Ah! I see, a suicide. How interesting!" But for the life of me I could not make out why the horses were frightened.

While we were talking, we heard a sort of sound between a yelp and a bark. It was far away; but the horses got very restless, and it took Johann all his time to quiet them. He was pale, and said: "It sounds like a wolf—but yet there are no wolves here now."

"No?" I said, questioning him. "Isn't it long since the wolves were so near the city?"

"Long, long," he answered, "in the spring and summer; but with the snow the wolves have been here not so long."

While he was petting the horses and trying to quiet them, dark clouds drifted rapidly across the sky. The sunshine passed away, and a breath of cold wind seemed to drift past us. It was only a breath, however, and more in the nature of a warning than a fact, for the sun came out brightly again. Johann looked under his lifted hand at the horizon and said:

"The storm of snow, he comes before long time." Then he looked at his watch again, and, straightway holding his reins firmly—for the horses were still pawing the ground restlessly and shaking their heads—he climbed to his box as though the time had come for proceeding on our journey.

I felt a little obstinate and did not at once get into the carriage.

"Tell me," I said, "about this place where the road leads," and I pointed down.

Again he crossed himself and mumbled a prayer, before he answered: "It is unholy."

"What is unholy?" I enquired.

"The village."

"Then there is a village?"

"No, no. No one lives there hundreds of years."

My curiosity was piqued: "But you said there was a village."

"There was."

"Where is it now?"

Whereupon he burst out into a long story in German and English, so mixed up that I could not quite understand exactly what he said, but roughly I gathered that long ago, hundreds of years, men had died there and been buried in their graves; and sounds were heard under the clay, and when the graves were opened, men and women were found rosy with life, and their mouths red with blood. And so, in haste to save their lives (aye, and their souls!—and here he crossed himself) those who were left fled away to other places, where the living died, and the dead were dead and not—not something. He was evidently afraid to speak the last words. As he proceeded with his narration, he grew more and more excited. It seemed as if his imagination had got hold of him, and he ended in a perfect paroxysm of fear—white-faced, perspiring, trembling, and looking round him, as if expecting that some dreadful presence would manifest itself there in the bright sunshine on the open plain. Finally, in an agony of desperation, he cried:

"Walpurgisnacht!" and pointed to the carriage for me to get in. All my English blood rose at this, and, standing back, I said:

"You are afraid, Johann—you are afraid. Go home; I shall return alone; the walk will do me good." The carriage door was open. I took from the seat my oak walking stick—which I always carry on my holiday excursions—and closed the door, pointing back to Munich, and said, "Go home, Johann—Walpurgisnacht doesn't concern Englishmen."

The horses were now more restive than ever, and Johann was trying to hold them in while excitedly imploring me not to do anything so foolish. I pitied the poor fellow, he was so deeply in earnest; but all the same I could not help laughing. His English was quite gone now. In his anxiety he had forgotten that his only means of making me understand was to talk my language, so he jabbered away in his native German. It began to be a little tedious. After giving the direction, "Home!" I turned to go down the cross-road into the valley.

With a despairing gesture, Johann turned his horses towards Munich. I leaned on my stick and looked after him. He went slowly along the road for a while; then there came over the crest of the hill a man tall and thin. I could see so much in the distance. When he drew near the horses, they began to jump and kick about, then to scream with terror. Johann could not hold them in; they bolted down the road, running away madly. I watched them out of sight, then looked for the stranger, but I found that he, too, was gone.

With a light heart I turned down the side road through the deepening valley to which Johann had objected. There was not the slightest reason, that I could see, for his objection; and I daresay I tramped for a couple of hours without thinking of time or distance, and certainly without seeing a person or a house. So far as the place was concerned, it was desolation itself. But I did not notice this particularly till, on turning a bend in the road, I came upon a scattered fringe of wood; then I recognized that I had been impressed unconsciously by the desolation of the region through which I had passed.

I sat down to rest myself, and began to look around. It struck me that it was considerably colder than it had been at the commencement of my walk—a sort of sighing sound seemed to be around me, with, now and then, high overhead, a sort of muffled roar. Looking upwards I noticed that great thick clouds were drifting rapidly across the sky from North to South at a great height. There were signs of a coming storm in some lofty stratum of the air. I was a little chilly, and, thinking that it was the sitting still after the exercise of walking, I resumed my journey.

The ground I passed over was now much more picturesque. There were no striking objects that the eye might single out; but in all there was a charm of beauty. I took little heed of time and it was only when the deepening twilight forced itself upon me that I began to think of how I should find my way home. The brightness of the day had gone. The air was cold, and the drifting of clouds high overhead was more marked. They were accompanied by a sort of far-away rushing sound, through which seemed to come at intervals that mysterious cry which the driver had said came from a wolf. For a while I hesitated. I had said I would see the deserted village, so on I went, and presently came on a wide stretch of open country, shut in by hills all around. Their sides were covered with trees which spread down to the plain, dotting, in clumps, the gentler slopes and hollows which showed here and there. I followed with my eye the winding of the road, and saw that it curved close to one of the densest of these clumps and was lost behind it.

As I looked there came a cold shiver in the air, and the

snow began to fall. I thought of the miles and miles of bleak country I had passed, and then hurried on to seek the shelter of the wood in front. Darker and darker grew the sky, and faster and heavier fell the snow, till the earth before and around me was a glistening white carpet the further edge of which was lost in misty vagueness. The road was here but crude, and when on the level its boundaries were not so marked, as when it passed through the cuttings; and in a little while I found that I must have strayed from it, for I missed underfoot the hard surface, and my feet sank deeper in the grass and moss. Then the wind grew stronger and blew with ever increasing force, till I was fain to run before it. The air became icy cold, and in spite of my exercise I began to suffer. The snow was now falling so thickly and whirling around me in such rapid eddies that I could hardly keep my eyes open. Every now and then the heavens were torn asunder by vivid lightning, and in the flashes I could see ahead of me a great mass of trees, chiefly yew and cypress all heavily coated with snow.

I was soon amongst the shelter of the trees, and there in comparative silence, I could hear the rush of the wind high overhead. Presently the blackness of the storm had become merged in the darkness of the night. By-and-by the storm seemed to be passing away: it now only came in fierce puffs and blasts. At such moments the weird sound of the wolf appeared to be echoed by many similar sounds around me.

Now and again, through the black mass of drifting cloud, came a straggling ray of moonlight, which lit up the expanse, and showed me that I was at the edge of a dense mass of cypress and yew trees. As the snow had ceased to fall, I walked out from the shelter and began to investigate more closely. It appeared to me that, amongst so many old foundations as I had passed, there might be still standing a house in which, though in ruins, I could find some sort of shelter for a while. As I skirted the edge of the copse, I found that a low wall encircled it, and following this I presently found an opening. Here the cypresses formed an alley leading up to a square mass of some kind of building. Just as I caught sight of this, however, the drifting clouds obscured the moon, and I passed up the path in darkness. The wind must have grown colder, for I felt myself shiver as I walked; but there was hope of shelter, and I groped my way blindly on.

I stopped, for there was a sudden stillness. The storm had passed; and, perhaps in sympathy with nature's silence, my heart seemed to cease to beat. But this was only momentarily; for suddenly the moonlight broke through the clouds, showing me that I was in a graveyard, and that the square object before me was a great massive tomb of marble, as white as the snow that lay on and all around it. With the moonlight there came a fierce sigh of the storm, which appeared to resume its course with a long, low howl, as of many dogs or wolves. I was awed and shocked, and felt the cold perceptibly grow upon me till it seemed to grip me by the heart. Then while the flood of moonlight still fell on the marble tomb, the storm gave further evidence of renewing, as though it was returning on its track. Impelled by some sort of fascination, I approached the sepulchre to see what it was, and why such a thing stood alone in such a place. I walked around it, and read, over the Doric door, in German—

COUNTESS DOLINGEN OF GRATZ
IN STYRIA SOUGHT AND FOUND DEATH, 1801

On the top of the tomb, seemingly driven through the solid marble—for the structure was composed of a few vast blocks of stone—was a great iron spike or stake. On going to the back I saw, graven in great Russian letters:

THE DEAD TRAVEL FAST

There was something so weird and uncanny about the whole thing that it gave me a turn and made me feel quite faint. I began to wish, for the first time, that I had taken Johann's advice. Here a thought struck me, which came under almost mysterious circumstances and with a terrible shock. This was Walpurgis Night!

Walpurgis Night, when, according to the belief of millions of people, the devil was abroad—when the graves were opened and the dead came forth and walked. When all evil things of earth and air and water held revel. This very place the driver had specially shunned. This was the depopulated village of centuries ago. This was where the suicide lay; and this was the place where I was alone—unmanned, shivering with cold in a shroud of snow with a wild storm gathering again upon me! It took all my philosophy, all the religion I had been taught, all my courage, not to collapse in a paroxysm of fright.

And now a perfect tornado burst upon me. The ground shook as though thousands of horses thundered across it; and this time the storm bore on its icy wings, not snow, but great hailstones which drove with such violence that they might have come from the thongs of Balearic slingers—hailstones that beat down leaf and branch and made the shelter of the cypresses of no more avail than though their stems were standing corn. At the first I had rushed to the nearest tree; but I was soon fain to leave it and seek the only spot that seemed to afford refuge, the deep Doric doorway of the marble tomb. There, crouching against the massive bronze door, I gained a certain amount of protection from the beating of the hailstones, for now they only drove against me as they ricocheted from the ground and the side of the marble.

As I leaned against the door, it moved slightly and opened inwards. The shelter of even a tomb was welcome in that pitiless tempest, and I was about to enter it when there came a flash of forked lightning that lit up the whole expanse of the heavens. In the instant, as I am a living man, I saw, as my eyes were turned into the darkness of the tomb, a beautiful woman, with rounded cheeks and red lips, seemingly sleeping on a bier. As the thunder broke overhead, I was grasped as by the hand of a giant and hurled out into the storm. The whole thing was so sudden that, before I could realize the shock, moral as well as physical, I found the hailstones beating me down. At the same time I had a strange, dominating feeling that I was not alone. I looked towards the tomb. Just then there came another blinding flash, which seemed to strike the iron stake that surmounted the tomb and to pour through to the earth, blasting and crumbling the marble, as in a burst of flame. The dead woman rose for a moment of agony, while she was lapped in the flame, and her bitter scream of pain was drowned in the thundercrash. The last thing I heard was this mingling of dreadful sound, as again I was seized in the giant grasp and dragged away, while the hailstones beat on me, and the air around seemed reverberant with the howling of wolves. The last sight that I remembered was a vague, white, moving mass, as if all the graves around me had sent out the phantoms of their sheeted dead, and that they were closing in on me through the white cloudiness of the driving hail.

. . .

Gradually there came a sort of vague beginning of consciousness; then a sense of weariness that was dreadful. For a time I remembered nothing; but slowly my senses returned. My feet seemed positively racked with pain, yet I could not move them. They seemed to be numbed. There was an icy feeling at the back of my neck and all down my spine, and my ears, like my feet, were dead, yet in torment; but there was in my breast a sense of warmth which was, by comparison, delicious. It was as a nightmare, if one may use such an expression; for some heavy weight on my chest made it difficult for me to breathe.

This period of semi-lethargy seemed to remain a long time, and as it faded away I must have slept or swooned. Then came a sort of loathing, like the first stage of seasickness, and a wild desire to be free from something—I knew not what. A vast stillness enveloped me, as though all the world were asleep or dead—only broken by the low panting as of some animal close to me. I felt a warm rasping at my throat, then came a consciousness of the awful truth, which chilled me to the heart and sent the blood surging up through my brain. Some great animal was lying on me and now licking my throat. I feared to stir, for some instinct of prudence bade me lie still; but the brute seemed to realize that there was now some change in me, for it raised its head. Through my eyelashes I saw above me the two great flaming eyes of a gigantic wolf. Its sharp white teeth gleamed in the gaping red mouth, and I could feel its hot breath fierce and acrid upon me.

For another spell of time I remembered no more. Then I became conscious of a low growl, followed by a yelp, renewed again and again. Then, seemingly very far away,

I heard a "Holloa! Holloa!" as of many voices calling in unison. Cautiously I raised my head and looked in the direction whence the sound came; but the cemetery blocked my view. The wolf still continued to yelp in a strange way, and a red glare began to move round the grove of cypresses, as though following the sound. As the voices drew closer, the wolf yelped faster and louder. I feared to make either sound or motion. Nearer came the red glow, over the white pall which stretched into the darkness around me. Then all at once from beyond the trees there came at a trot a troop of horsemen bearing torches. The wolf rose from my breast and made for the cemetery. I saw one of the horsemen (soldiers by their caps and their long military cloaks) raise his carbine and take aim. A companion knocked up his arm, and I heard the ball whizz over my head. He had evidently taken my body for that of the wolf. Another sighted the animal as it slunk away, and a shot followed. Then, at a gallop, the troop rode forward—some towards me, others following the wolf as it disappeared amongst the snow-clad cypresses.

As they drew nearer I tried to move, but was powerless, although I could see and hear all that went on around me. Two or three of the soldiers jumped from their horses and knelt beside me. One of them raised my head, and placed his hand over my heart.

"Good news, comrades!" he cried. "His heart still beats!"

Then some brandy was poured down my throat; it put vigor into me, and I was able to open my eyes fully and look around. Lights and shadows were moving among the trees, and I heard men call to one another. They drew together, uttering frightened exclamations; and the lights flashed as the others came pouring out of the cemetery pell-mell, like men possessed. When the further ones came close to us, those who were around me asked them eagerly:

"Well, have you found him?"

The reply rang out hurriedly:

"No! No! Come away quick—quick! This is no place to stay, and on this of all nights!"

"What was it?" was the question, asked in all manner of keys. The answer came variously and all indefinitely as though the men were moved by some common impulse to speak, yet were restrained by some common fear from giving their thoughts.

"It—it—indeed!" gibbered one, whose wits had plainly given out for the moment.

"A wolf—and yet not a wolf!" another put in shudderingly.

"No use trying for him without the sacred bullet," a third remarked in a more ordinary manner.

"Serve us right for coming out on this night! Truly we have earned our thousand marks!" were the ejaculations of a fourth.

"There was blood on the broken marble," another said after a pause—"the lightning never brought that there. And for him—is he safe? Look at his throat! See, comrades, the wolf has been lying on him and keeping his blood warm."

The officer looked at my throat and replied:

"He is all right; the skin is not pierced. What does it all mean? We should never have found him but for the yelping of the wolf."

"What became of it?" asked the man who was holding up my head, and who seemed the least panic-stricken of the party, for his hands were steady and without tremor. On his sleeve was the chevron of a petty officer.

"It went to its home," answered the man, whose long face was pallid, and who actually shook with terror as he glanced around him fearfully. "There are graves enough there in which it may lie. Come, comrades—come quickly! Let us leave this cursed spot."

The officer raised me to a sitting posture, as he uttered a word of command; then several men placed me upon a horse. He sprang to the saddle behind me, took me in his arms, gave the word to advance; and, turning our faces away from the cypresses, we rode away in swift, military order.

As yet my tongue refused its office, and I was perforce silent. I must have fallen asleep; for the next thing I remembered was finding myself standing up, supported by a soldier on each side of me. It was almost broad daylight, and to the north a red streak of sunlight was reflected, like a path of blood, over the waste of snow. The officer was telling the men to say nothing of what they had seen, except that they found an English stranger, guarded by a large dog.

"Dog! That was no dog," cut in the man who had exhibited such fear. "I think I know a wolf when I see one."

The young officer answered calmly: "I said a dog."

"Dog!" reiterated the other ironically. It was evident that his courage was rising with the sun; and, pointing to me, he said, "Look at his throat. Is that the work of a dog, master?"

Instinctively I raised my hand to my throat, and as I touched it I cried out in pain. The men crowded round to look, some stooping down from their saddles; and again there came the calm voice of the young officer:

"A dog, as I said. If aught else were said we should only be laughed at."

I was then mounted behind a trooper, and we rode on into the suburbs of Munich. Here we came across a stray carriage, into which I was lifted, and it was driven off to the Quatre Saisons—the young officer accompanying me, while a trooper followed with his horse, and the others rode off to their barracks.

When we arrived, Herr Delbrück rushed so quickly down the steps to meet me that it was apparent he had been watching within. Taking me by both hands he solicitously led me in. The officer saluted me and was turning to withdraw, when I recognized his purpose, and insisted that he should come to my rooms. Over a glass of wine I warmly thanked him and his brave comrades for saving me. He replied simply that he was more than glad, and that Herr Delbrück had at the first taken steps to make all the searching party pleased; at which ambiguous utterance the maître d'hôtel smiled, while the officer pleaded duty and withdrew.

"But Herr Delbrück," I inquired, "how and why was it that the soldiers searched for me?"

He shrugged his shoulders, as if in depreciation of his own deed, as he replied:

"I was so fortunate as to obtain leave from the commander of the regiment in which I served, to ask for volunteers."

"But how did you know I was lost?" I asked.

"The driver came hither with the remains of his carriage, which had been upset when the horses ran away."

"But surely you would not send a search-party of soldiers merely on this account?"

"Oh, no!" he answered. "But even before the coachman arrived, I had this telegram from the Boyar whose guest you are," and he took from his pocket a telegram which he handed to me, and I read:

Bistritz

Be careful of my guest—his safety is most precious to me. Should aught happen to him, or if he be missed, spare nothing to find him and ensure his safety. He is English and therefore adventurous. There are often dangers from snow and wolves and night. Lose not a moment if you suspect harm to him. I answer your zeal with my fortune.

Dracula

As I held the telegram in my hand, the room seemed to whirl around me; and, if the attentive maître d'hôtel had not caught me, I think I should have fallen. There was something so strange in all this, something so weird and impossible to imagine, that there grew on me a sense of my being in some way the sport of opposite forces—the mere vague idea of which seemed in a way to paralyze me. I was certainly under some form of mysterious protection. From a distant country had come, in the very nick of time, a message that took me out of the danger of the snow-sleep and the jaws of the wolf.

THE OLD PORTRAIT

◆◆◆

HUME NISBET

Old-fashioned frames are a hobby of mine. I am always on the prowl amongst the framers and dealers in curiosities for something quaint and unique in picture frames. I don't care much for what is inside them, for being a painter it is my fancy to get the frames first and then paint a picture which I think suits their probable history and design. In this way I get some curious and I think also some original ideas.

One day in December, about a week before Christmas, I picked up a fine but dilapidated specimen of wood-carving in a shop near Soho. The gilding had been worn nearly away, and three of the corners broken off; yet as there was one of the corners still left, I hoped to be able to repair the others from it. As for the canvas inside this frame, it was so smothered with dirt and time stains that I could only distinguish it had been a very badly painted likeness of some sort, of some commonplace person, daubed in by a poor pot-boiling painter to fill the second-hand frame which his patron may have picked up cheaply as I had done after him; but as the frame was alright I took the spoiled canvas along with it, thinking it might come in handy.

For the next few days my hands were full of work of one kind and another, so that it was only on Christmas Eve that I found myself at liberty to examine my purchase, which had been lying with its face to the wall since I had brought into my studio.

Having nothing to do on this night, and not in the mood to go out, I got my picture and frame from the corner, and laying them upon the table, with a sponge, basin of water, and some soap, I began to wash so that I might see them the better. They were in a terrible mess, and I think I used the best part of a packet of soap-powder and had to change the water about a dozen times before the pattern began to show up on the frame, and the portrait within it asserted its awful crudeness, vile drawing, and intense vulgarity. It was the bloated, piggish visage of a publican clearly, with a plentiful supply of jewellery displayed, as is usual with such masterpieces, where the features are not considered of so much importance as a strict fidelity in the depicting of such articles as watch-guard and seals, finger rings, and breast pins; these were all there, as natural and hard as reality.

The frame delighted me, and the picture satisfied me that I had not cheated the dealer with my price, and I was looking at the monstrosity as the gaslight beat full upon it, and wondering how the owner could be pleased with himself as thus depicted, when something about the background attracted my attention—a slight marking underneath the thin coating as if the portrait had been painted over some other subject.

It was not much certainly, yet enough to make me rush over to my cupboard, where I kept my spirits of wine and turpentine, with which, and a plentiful supply of rags, I began to demolish the publican ruthlessly in the vague hope that I might find something worth looking at underneath.

A slow process that was, as well as a delicate one, so that it was close upon midnight before the gold cable rings and vermilion visage disappeared and another picture loomed up before me; then giving it the final wash over, I wiped it dry, and set it in a good light on my easel, while I filled and lit my pipe, and then sat down to look at it.

What had I liberated from that vile prison of crude paint? For I did not require to set it up to know that this bungler of the brush had covered and defiled a work as far beyond his comprehension as the clouds are from the caterpillar.

The bust and head of a young woman of uncertain age, merged within a gloom of rich accessories painted as only a master hand can paint who is above asserting his knowledge, and who has learnt to cover his technique. It was as perfect and natural in its sombre yet quiet dignity as if it had come from the brush of Moroni.

A face and neck perfectly colourless in their pallid whiteness, with the shadows so artfully managed that they could not be seen, and for this quality would have delighted the strong-minded Queen Bess.

At first as I looked I saw in the centre of a vague darkness a dim patch of grey gloom that drifted into the shadow. Then the greyness appeared to grow lighter as I sat from it, and leaned back in my chair until the features stole out softly, and became clear and definite, while the figure stood out from the background as if tangible, although, having washed it, I knew that it had been smoothly painted.

An intent face, with delicate nose, well-shaped, although bloodless, lips, and eyes like dark caverns without a spark of light in them. The hair loosely about the head and oval cheeks, massive, silky-textured, jet black, and lustreless, which hid the upper portion of her brow, with the ears, and fell in straight indefinite waves over the left breast, leaving the right portion of the transparent neck exposed.

The dress and background were symphonies of ebony, yet full of subtle colouring and masterly feeling; a dress of rich brocaded velvet with a background that represented vast receding space, wondrously suggestive and awe-inspiring.

I noticed that the pallid lips were parted slightly, and showed a glimpse of the upper front teeth, which added to the intent expression of the face. A short upper lip, which, curled upward, with the underlip full and sensuous, or rather, if colour had been in it, would have been so.

It was an eerie looking face that I had resurrected on this midnight hour of Christmas Eve; in its passive pallidity it looked as if the blood had been drained from the body, and that I was gazing upon an open-eyed corpse.

The frame, also, I noticed for the first time, in its details appeared to have been designed with the intention of carrying out the idea of life in death; what had before looked like scroll-work of flowers and fruit were loathsome snake-like worms twined amongst charnel-house bones which they half covered in a decorative fashion; a hideous design in spite of its exquisite workmanship, that made me shudder and wish that I had left the cleaning to be done by daylight.

I am not at all of a nervous temperament, and would have laughed had anyone told me that I was afraid, and yet, as I sat here alone, with that portrait opposite to me in this solitary studio, away from all human contact; for none of the other studios were tenanted on this night, and the janitor had gone on his holiday; I wished that I had spent my evening in a more congenial manner, for in spite of a good fire in the stove and the brilliant gas, that intent face and those haunting eyes were exercising a strange influence upon me.

I heard the clocks from the different steeples chime out the last hour of the day, one after the other, like echoes taking up the refrain and dying away in the distance, and still I sat spellbound, looking at that weird picture, with my neglected pipe in my hand, and a strange lassitude creeping over me.

It was the eyes which fixed me now with the unfathomable depths and absorbing intensity. They gave out no light, but seemed to draw my soul into them, and with it my life and strength as I lay inert before them, until overpowered I lost consciousness and dreamt.

I thought that the frame was still on the easel with the canvas, but the woman had stepped from them and was approaching me with a floating motion, leaving behind her a vault filled with coffins, some of them shut down whilst others lay or stood upright and open, showing the grisly contents in their decaying and stained cerements.

I could only see her head and shoulders with the sombre drapery of the upper portion and the inky wealth of hair hanging round.

She was with me now, that pallid face touching my face and those cold bloodless lips glued to mine with a close lingering kiss, while the soft black hair covered me like a cloud and thrilled me through and through with a delicious thrill that, whilst it made me grow faint, intoxicated me with delight.

As I breathed she seemed to absorb it quickly into herself, giving me back nothing, getting stronger as I was becoming weaker, while the warmth of my contact passed into her and made her palpitate with vitality.

And all at once the horror of approaching death seized upon me, and with a frantic effort I flung her from me and started up from my chair, dazed for a moment and uncertain where I was, then consciousness returned and I looked round wildly.

The gas was still blazing brightly, while the fire burned ruddy in the stove. By the timepiece on the mantel I could see that it was half-past twelve.

The picture and frame were still on the easel, only as I looked at them the portrait had changed, a hectic flush was on the cheeks while the eyes glittered with life and the sensuous lips were red and ripe-looking with a drop of blood still upon the nether one. In a frenzy of horror I seized my scraping knife and slashed out the vampire picture, then tearing the mutilated fragments out I crammed them into my stove and watched them frizzle with savage delight.

I have that frame still, but I have not yet had courage to paint a suitable subject for it.

BITE-ME-NOT OR, FLEUR DE FUR

♦♦♦

TANITH LEE

CHAPTER I

In the tradition of young girls and windows, the young girl looks out of this one. It is difficult to see anything. The panes of the window are heavily leaded, and secured by a lattice of iron. The stained glass of lizard-green and storm-purple is several inches thick. There is no red glass in the window. The colour red is forbidden in the castle. Even the sun, behind the glass, is a storm sun, a green-lizard sun.

The young girl wishes she had a gown of palest pastel rose—the nearest affinity to red which is never allowed. Already she has long dark beautiful eyes, a long white neck. Her long dark hair is however hidden in a dusty scarf and she wears rags. She is a scullery maid. As she scours dishes and mops stone floors, she imagines she is a princess floating through the upper corridors, gliding to the dais in the Duke's hall. The Cursed Duke. She is sorry for him. If he had been her father, she would have sympathized and consoled him. His own daughter is dead, as his wife is dead, but these things, being to do with the cursing, are never spoken of. Except, sometimes, obliquely.

"*Rohise!*" dim voices cry now, full of dim scolding soon to be actualized.

The scullery maid turns from the window and runs to have her ears boxed and a broom thrust into her hands.

Meanwhile, the Cursed Duke is prowling his chamber,

high in the East Turret carved with swans and gargoyles. The room is lined with books, swords, lutes, scrolls, and has two eerie portraits, the larger of which represents his wife, and the smaller his daughter. Both ladies look much the same with their pale, egg-shaped faces, polished eyes, clasped hands. They do not really look like his wife or daughter, nor really remind him of them.

There are no windows at all in the turret, they were long ago bricked up and covered with hangings. Candles burn steadily. It is always night in the turret. Save, of course, by night there are particular *sounds* all about it, to which the Duke is accustomed, but which he does not care for. By night, like most of his court, the Cursed Duke closes his ears with softened tallow. However, if he sleeps, he dreams, and hears in the dream the beating of wings. . . . Often, the court holds loud revel all night long.

The Duke does not know Rohise the scullery maid has been thinking of him. Perhaps he does not even know that a scullery maid is capable of thinking at all.

Soon the Duke descends from the turret and goes down, by various stairs and curving passages, into a large, walled garden on the east side of the castle.

It is a very pretty garden, mannered and manicured, which the gardeners keep in perfect order. Over the tops of the high, high walls, where delicate blooms bell the vines, it is just possible to glimpse the tips of sun-baked mountains. But by day the mountains are blue and spiritual to look at, and seem scarcely real. They might only be inked on the sky.

A portion of the Duke's court is wandering about in the garden, playing games or musical instruments, or admiring painted sculptures, or the flora, none of which is red. But the Cursed Duke's court seems vitiated this noon. Nights of revel take their toll.

As the Duke passes down the garden, his courtiers acknowledge him deferentially. He sees them, old and young alike, all doomed as he is, and the weight of his burden increases.

At the furthest, most eastern end of the garden, there is another garden, sunken and rather curious, beyond a wall with an iron door. Only the Duke possesses the key to this door. Now he unlocks it and goes through. His courtiers laugh and play and pretend not to see. He shuts the door behind him.

The sunken garden, which no gardener ever tends, is maintained by other, spontaneous, means. It is small and square, lacking the hedges and the paths of the other, the sundials and statues and little pools. All the sunken garden contains is a broad paved border, and at its center a small plot of humid earth. Growing in the earth is a slender bush with slender velvet leaves.

The Duke stands and looks at the bush only a short while.

He visits it every day. He has visited it every day for years. He is waiting for the bush to flower. Everyone is waiting for this. Even Rohise, the scullery maid, is waiting, though she does not, being only sixteen, born in the castle and uneducated, properly understand why.

The light in the little garden is dull and strange, for the whole of it is roofed over by a dome of thick smoky glass. It makes the atmosphere somewhat depressing, although the bush itself gives off a pleasant smell, rather resembling vanilla.

Something is cut into the stone rim of the earth-plot where the bush grows. The Duke reads it for perhaps the thousandth time. *O, fleur de feu—*

When the Duke returns from the little garden into the

large garden, locking the door behind him, no one seems truly to notice. But their obeisances now are circumspect.

One day, he will perhaps emerge from the sunken garden leaving the door wide, crying out in a great voice. But not yet. Not today.

The ladies bend to the bright fish in the pools, the knights pluck for them blossoms, challenge each other to combat at chess, or wrestling, discuss the menagerie lions; the minstrels sing of unrequited love. The pleasure garden is full of one long and weary sigh.

"Oh flurda fur

"Pourma souffrance—"

Sings Rohise as she scrubs the flags of the pantry floor.

"Ned ormey par,

"May say day mwar—"

"What are you singing, you slut?" someone shouts, and kicks over her bucket.

Rohise does not weep. She tidies her bucket and soaks up the spilled water with her cloths. She does not know what the song, because of which she seems, apparently, to have been chastised, means. She does not understand the words that somehow, somewhere—perhaps from her own dead mother—she learned by rote.

In the hour before sunset, the Duke's hall is lit by flambeaux. In the high windows, the casements of oil-blue and lavender glass and glass like storms and lizards, are fastened tight. The huge window by the dais was long ago obliterated, shut up, and a tapestry hung of gold and silver tissue with all the rubies pulled out and emeralds substituted. It describes the subjugation of a fearsome unicorn by a maiden, and huntsmen.

The court drifts in with its clothes of rainbow from which only the color red is missing.

Music for dancing plays. The lean pale dogs pace about, alert for tidbits as dish on dish comes in. Roast birds in all their plumage glitter and die a second time under the eager knives. Pastry castles fall. Pink and amber fruits, and green fruits and black, glow beside the goblets of fine yellow wine.

The Cursed Duke eats with care and attention, not with enjoyment. Only the very young of the castle still eat in that way, and there are not so many of those.

The murky sun slides through the stained glass. The musicians strike up more wildly. The dances become boisterous. Once the day goes out, the hall will ring to *chanson*, to drum and viol and pipe. The dogs will bark, no language will be uttered except in a bellow. The lions will roar from the menagerie. On some nights the cannons are set off from the battlements, which are now all of them roofed in, fired out through narrow mouths just wide enough to accommodate them, the charge crashing away in thunder down the darkness.

By the time the moon comes up and the castle rocks to its own cacophony, exhausted Rohise has fallen fast asleep in her cupboard bed in the attic. For years, from sunset to rise, nothing has woken her. Once, as a child, when she had been especially badly beaten, the pain woke her and she heard a strange silken scratching, somewhere over her head. But she thought it a rat, or a bird. Yes, a bird, for later it seemed to her there were also wings. . . . But she forgot all this half a decade ago. Now she sleeps deeply and dreams of being a princess, forgetting, too, how the Duke's daughter died. Such a terrible death, it is better to forget.

"The sun shall not smite thee by day, neither the moon by night," intones the priest, eyes rolling, his voice like a bell behind the Duke's shoulder.

"Ne moi mords pas," whispers Rohise in her deep sleep. "Ne mwar mor par, ne par mor mwar. . . ."

And under its impenetrable dome, the slender bush has closed its fur leaves also to sleep. O flower of fire, oh fleur de fur. Its blooms, though it has not bloomed yet, bear the ancient name *Nona Mordica*. In light parlance they call it Bite-Me-Not. There is a reason for that.

CHAPTER II

He is the Prince of a proud and savage people. The pride they acknowledge, perhaps they do not consider themselves to be savages, or at least believe that savagery is the proper order of things.

Feroluce, that is his name. It is one of the customary names his kind give their lords. It has connotations with diabolic royalty and, too, with a royal flower of long petals curved like scimitars. Also the name might be the partial anagram of another name. The bearer of that name was also winged.

For Feroluce and his people are winged beings. They are more like a nest of dark eagles than anything, mounted high among the rocky pilasters and pinnacles of the mountain. Cruel and magnificent, like eagles, the somber sentries motionless as statuary on the ledge-edges, their sable wings folded about them.

They are very alike in appearance (less a race or tribe, more a flock, an unkindness of ravens). Feroluce also, black-winged, black-haired, aquiline of feature, standing on the brink of star-dashed space, his eyes burning through the night like all the eyes along the rocks, depthless red as claret.

They have their own traditions of art and science. They do not make or read books, fashion garments, discuss God or metaphysics or men. Their cries are mostly wordless and always mysterious, flung out like ribbons over the air as they wheel and swoop and hang in wicked cruciform, between the peaks. But they sing, long hours, for whole nights at a time, music that has a language only they know. All their wisdom and theosophy, and all their grasp of beauty, truth, or love, is in the singing.

They look unloving enough, and so they are. Pitiless fallen angels. A traveling people, they roam after sustenance. Their sustenance is blood. Finding a castle, they accepted it, every bastion and wall, as their prey. They have preyed on it and tried to prey on it for years.

In the beginning, their calls, their songs, could lure victims to the feast. In this way, the tribe or unkindness of Feroluce took the Duke's wife, somnambulist, from a midnight balcony. But the Duke's daughter, the first victim, they found seventeen years ago, benighted on the mountain side. Her escort and herself they left to the sunrise, marble figures, the life drunk away.

Now the castle is shut, bolted and barred. They are even more attracted by its recalcitrance (a woman who says "No"). They do not intend to go away until the castle falls to them.

By night, they fly like huge black moths round and round the carved turrets, the dull-lit leaded windows, their wings invoking a cloudy tindery wind, pushing thunder against thundery glass.

They sense they are attributed to some sin, reckoned a punishing curse, a penance, and this amuses them at the level whereon they understand it.

They also sense something of the flower, the *Nona Mordica*. Vampires have their own legends.

But tonight Feroluce launches himself into the air, speeds down the sky on the black sails of his wings, calling, a call like laughter or derision. This morning, in the tween-time before the light began and the sun-to-be drove him away to his shadowed eyrie in the mountain-guts, he saw a chink in the armour of the beloved refusing-woman-prey. A window, high in an old neglected tower, a window with a small eyelet which was cracked.

Feroluce soon reaches the eyelet and breathes on it, as if he would melt it. (His breath is sweet. Vampires do not eat raw flesh, only blood, which is a perfect food and digests perfectly, while their teeth are sound of necessity.) The way the glass mists at breath intrigues Feroluce. But presently he taps at the cranky pane, taps, then claws. A piece breaks away, and now he sees how it should be done.

Over the rims and upthrusts of the castle, which is only really another mountain with caves to Feroluce, the rumble of the Duke's revel drones on.

Feroluce pays no heed. He does not need to reason, he merely knows, *that* noise masks *this*—as he smashes in the window. Its panes were all faulted and the lattice rusty. It is, of course, more than that. The magic of Purpose has protected the castle, and, as in all balances, there must be, or come to be, some balancing contradiction, some flaw. . . .

The people of Feroluce do not notice what he is at. In a way, the dance with their prey has debased to a ritual. They have lived almost two decades on the blood of local mountain beasts, and bird-creatures like themselves brought down on the wing. Patience is not, with them, a virtue. It is a sort of foreplay, and can go on, in pleasure, a long, long while.

Feroluce intrudes himself through the slender window. Muscularly slender himself, and agile, it is no feat. But the wings catch, are a trouble. They follow him because they must, like two separate entities. They have been cut a little on the glass, and bleed.

He stands in a stony small room, shaking bloody feathers from him, snarling, but without sound.

Then he finds the stairway and goes down.

There are dusty landings and neglected chambers. They have no smell of life. But then there comes to be a smell. It is the scent of a nest, a colony of things, wild creatures, in constant proximity. He recognizes it. The light of his crimson eyes precedes him, deciphering blackness. And then other eyes, amber, green, and gold, spring out like stars all across his path.

Somewhere an old torch is burning out. To the human eye, only mounds and glows would be visible, but to Feroluce, the Prince of the vampires, all is suddenly revealed. There is a great stone area, barred with bronze and iron, and things stride and growl behind the bars, or chatter and flee, or only stare. And there, without bars, though bound by ropes of brass to rings of brass, three brazen beasts.

Feroluce, on the steps of the menagerie, looks into the gaze of the Duke's lions. Feroluce smiles, and the lions roar. One is the king, its mane like war-plumes. Feroluce recognizes the king and the king's right to challenge, for this is the lions' domain, their territory.

Feroluce comes down the stair and meets the lion as it leaps the length of its chain. To Feroluce, the chain means nothing, and since he has come close enough, very little either to the lion.

To the vampire Prince the fight is wonderful, exhilarating and meaningful, intellectual even, for it is colored by nuance, yet powerful as sex.

He holds fast with his talons, his strong limbs wrapping

the beast which is almost stronger than he, just as its limbs wrap him in turn. He sinks his teeth in the lion's shoulder, and in fierce rage and bliss begins to draw out the nourishment. The lion kicks and claws at him in turn. Feroluce feels the gouges like fire along his shoulders, thighs, and hugs the lion more nearly as he throttles and drinks from it, loving it, jealous of it, killing it. Gradually the mighty feline body relaxes, still clinging to him, its cat teeth bedded in one beautiful swanlike wing, forgotten by both.

In a welter of feathers, stripped skin, spilled blood, the lion and the angel lie in embrace on the menagerie floor. The lion lifts its head, kisses the assassin, shudders, lets go.

Feroluce glides out from under the magnificent deadweight of the cat. He stands. And pain assaults him. His lover has severely wounded him.

Across the menagerie floor, the two lionesses are crouched. Beyond them, a man stands gaping in simple terror, behind the guttering torch. He had come to feed the beasts, and seen another feeding, and now is paralyzed. He is deaf, the menagerie-keeper, previously an advantage saving him the horror of nocturnal vampire noises.

Feroluce starts toward the human animal swifter than a serpent, and checks. Agony envelops Feroluce and the stone room spins. Involuntarily, confused, he spreads his wings for flight, there in the confined chamber. But only one wing will open. The other, damaged and partly broken, hangs like a snapped fan. Feroluce cries out, a beautiful singing note of despair and anger. He drops fainting at the menagerie-keeper's feet.

The man does not wait for more. He runs away through the castle, screaming invective and prayer, and reaches the Duke's hall and makes the whole hall listen.

All this while, Feroluce lies in the ocean of almost-death that is sleep or swoon, while the smaller beasts in the cages discuss him, or seem to.

And when he is raised, Feroluce does not wake. Only the great drooping bloody wings quiver and are still. Those who carry him are more than ever revolted and frightened, for they have seldom seen blood. Even the food for the menagerie is cooked almost black. Two years ago, a gardener slashed his palm on a thorn. He was banished from the court for a week.

But Feroluce, the center of so much attention, does not rouse. Not until the dregs of the night are stealing out through the walls. Then some nervous instinct invests him. The sun is coming and this is an open place, he struggles through unconsciousness and hurt, through the deepest most bladed waters, to awareness.

And finds himself in a huge bronze cage, the cage of some animal appropriated for the occasion. Bars, bars all about him, and not to be got rid of, for he reaches to tear them away and cannot. Beyond the bars, the Duke's hall, which is only a pointless cold glitter to him in the maze of pain and dying lights. Not an open place, in fact, but too open for his kind. Through the window-spaces of thick glass, muddy sunglare must come in. To Feroluce it will be like swords, acids, and burning fire—

Far off he hears wings beat and voices soaring. His people search for him, call and wheel, and find nothing.

Feroluce cries out, a gravel shriek now, and the persons in the hall rush back from him, calling on God. But Feroluce does not see. He has tried to answer his own. Now he sinks down again under the coverlet of his broken wings, and the wine-red stars of his eyes go out.

CHAPTER III

"And the Angel of Death," the priest intones, "shall surely pass over, but yet like the shadow, not substance—"

The smashed window in the old turret above the menagerie tower has been sealed with mortar and brick. It is a terrible thing that it was for so long overlooked. A miracle that only one of the creatures found and entered by it. God, the Protector, guarded the Cursed Duke and his court. And the magic that surrounds the castle, that too held fast. For from the possibility of a disaster was born a bloom of great value: Now one of the monsters is in their possession. A prize beyond price.

Caged and helpless, the fiend is at their mercy. It is also weak from its battle with the noble lion, which gave its life for the castle's safety (and will be buried with honour in an ornamented grave at the foot of the Ducal family tomb). Just before the dawn came, the Duke's advisers advised him, and the bronze cage was wheeled away into the darkest area of the hall, close by the dais where once the huge window was but is no more. A barricade of great screens was brought, and set around the cage, and the top of it covered. No sunlight now can drip into the prison to harm the specimen. Only the Duke's ladies and gentlemen steal in around the screens and see, by the light of a candle-branch, the demon still lying in its trance of pain and bloodloss. The Duke's alchemist sits on a stool nearby, dictating many notes to a nervous apprentice. The alchemist, and the apothecary for that matter, are convinced the vampire, having drunk the lion almost dry, will recover from its wounds. Even the wings will mend.

The Duke's court painter also came. He was ashamed presently, and went away. The beauty of the demon affected him, making him wish to paint it, not as something wonderfully disgusting, but as a kind of superlative man, vital and innocent, or as Lucifer himself, stricken in the sorrow of his colossal Fall. And all that has caused the painter to pity the fallen one, mere artisan that the painter is, so he slunk away. He knows, since the alchemist and the apothecary told him, what is to be done.

Of course much of the castle knows. Though scarcely anyone has slept or sought sleep, the whole place rings with excitement and vivacity. The Duke has decreed, too, that everyone who wishes shall be a witness. So he is having a progress through the castle, seeking every nook and cranny, while, let it be said, his architect takes the opportunity to check no other windowpane has cracked.

From room to room the Duke and his entourage pass, through corridors, along stairs, through dusty attics and musty storerooms he has never seen, or if seen has forgotten. Here and there some retainer is come on. Some elderly women are discovered spinning like spiders up under the eaves, half-blind and complacent. They curtsy to the Duke from a vague recollection of old habit. The Duke tells them the good news, or rather, his messenger, walking before, announces it. The ancient women sigh and whisper, are left, probably forget. Then again, in a narrow courtyard, a simple boy, who looks after a dovecote, is magnificently told. He has a fit from alarm, grasping nothing; and the doves who love and understand him (by not trying to) fly down and cover him with their soft wings as the Duke goes away. The boy comes to under the doves as if in a heap of warm snow, comforted.

It is on one of the dark staircases above the kitchen that the gleaming entourage sweeps round a bend and comes on Rohise the scullery maid, scrubbing. In these days, when there are so few children and young servants, labor is scarce, and the scullerers are not confined to the scullery.

Rohise stands up, pale with shock, and for a wild instant thinks that, for some heinous crime she has committed in ignorance, the Duke has come in person to behead her.

"Hear then, by the Duke's will," cries the messenger. "One of Satan's night-demons, which do torment us, has been captured and lies penned in the Duke's hall. At sunrise tomorrow, this thing will be taken to that sacred spot where grows the bush of the Flower of the Fire, and here its foul blood shall be shed. Who then can doubt the bush will blossom, and save us all, by the Grace of God."

"And the Angel of Death," intones the priest, on no account to be omitted, "shall surely—"

"Wait," says the Duke. He is as white as Rohise. "Who is this?" he asks. "Is it a ghost?"

The court stare at Rohise, who nearly sinks in dread, her scrubbing rag in her hand.

Gradually, despite the rag, the rags, the rough hands, the court too begins to see.

"Why, it is a marvel."

The Duke moves forward. He looks down at Rohise and starts to cry. Rohise thinks he weeps in compassion at the awful sentence he is here to visit on her, and drops back on her knees.

"No, no," says the Duke tenderly. "Get up. Rise. You are so like my child, my daughter—"

Then Rohise, who knows few prayers, begins in panic to sing her little song as an orison:

"Oh fleur de feu

"Pour ma souffrance—"

"Ah!" says the Duke. "Where did you learn that song?"

"From my mother," says Rohise. And, all instinct now, she sings again:

"O flurda fur,

"Pourma souffrance
"Ned ormey par
"May say day mwar—"

It is the song of the fire-flower bush, the *Nona Mordica*, called Bite-Me-Not. It begins, and continues: *O flower of fire, For my misery's sake, Do not sleep but aid me; wake!* The Duke's daughter sang it very often. In those days the shrub was not needed, being just a rarity of the castle. Invoked as an amulet, on a mountain road, the rhyme itself had besides proved useless.

The Duke takes the dirty scarf from Rohise's hair. She is very, very like his lost daughter, the same pale smooth oval face, the long white neck and long dark polished eyes, and the long dark hair. (Or is it that she is very, very like the painting?)

The Duke gives instructions and Rohise is borne away.

In a beautiful chamber, the door of which has for seventeen years been locked, Rohise is bathed and her hair is washed. Oils and scents are rubbed into her skin. She is dressed in a gown of palest most pastel rose, with a girdle sewn with pearls. Her hair is combed, and on it is set a chaplet of stars and little golden leaves. "Oh, your poor hands," say the maids, as they trim her nails. Rohise has realized she is not to be executed. She has realized the Duke has seen her and wants to love her like his dead daughter. Slowly, an uneasy stir of something, not quite happiness, moves through Rohise. Now she will wear her pink gown, now she will sympathize with and console the Duke. Her daze lifts suddenly.

The dream has come true. She dreamed of it so often it seems quite normal. The scullery was the thing which never seemed real.

She glides down through the castle and the ladies are

astonished by her grace. The carriage of her head under the starry coronet is exquisite. Her voice is quiet and clear and musical, and the foreign tone of her mother, long unremembered, is quite gone from it. Only the roughened hands give her away, but smoothed by unguents, soon they will be soft and white.

"Can it be she is truly the princess returned to flesh?"

"Her life was taken so early—yes, as they believe in the Spice-Lands, by some holy dispensation, she might return."

"She would be about the age to have been conceived the very night the Duke's daughter d— That is, the very night the bane began—"

Theosophical discussion ensues. Songs are composed.

Rohise sits for a while with her adoptive father in the East Turret, and he tells her about the books and swords and lutes and scrolls, but not about the two portraits. Then they walk out together, in the lovely garden in the sunlight. They sit under a peach tree, and discuss many things, or the Duke discusses them. That Rohise is ignorant and uneducated does not matter at this point. She can always be trained. She has the basic requirements: docility, sweetness. There are many royal maidens in many places who know as little as she.

The Duke falls asleep under the peach tree. Rohise listens to the lovesongs her own (her very own) courtiers bring her.

When the monster in the cage is mentioned, she nods as if she knows what they mean. She supposes it is something hideous, a scaring treat to be shown at dinner time, when the sun has gone down.

When the sun moves towards the western line of mountains just visible over the high walls, the court streams into the castle and all the doors are bolted and barred. There is an eagerness tonight in the concourse.

As the light dies out behind the colored windows that have no red in them, covers and screens are dragged away from a bronze cage. It is wheeled out into the center of the great hall.

Cannons begin almost at once to blast and bang from the roof-holes. The cannoneers have had strict instructions to keep up the barrage all night without a second's pause.

Drums pound in the hall. The dogs start to bark. Rohise is not surprised by the noise, for she has often heard it from far up, in her attic, like a sea-wave breaking over and over through the lower house.

She looks at the cage cautiously, wondering what she will see. But she sees only a heap of blackness like ravens, and then a tawny dazzle, torchlight on something like human skin. "You must not go down to look," says the Duke protectively, as his court pours about the cage. Someone pokes between the bars with a gemmed cane, trying to rouse the nightmare which lies quiescent there. But Rohise must be spared this.

So the Duke calls his actors, and a slight, pretty play is put on throughout dinner, before the dais, shutting off from the sight of Rohise the rest of the hall, where the barbaric gloating and goading of the court, unchecked, increases.

CHAPTER IV

The Prince Feroluce becomes aware between one second and the next. It is the sound—heard beyond all others—of the wings of his people beating at the stones of the castle. It is the wings which speak to him, more than their wild orchestral voices. Beside these sensations, the anguish of healing and the sadism of humankind are not much.

Feroluce opens his eyes. His human audience, pleased, but afraid and squeamish, backs away, and asks each other for the two thousandth time if the cage is quite secure. In the torchlight the eyes of Feroluce are more black than red. He stares about. He is, though captive, imperious. If he were a lion or a bull, they would admire this "nobility." But the fact is, he is too much like a man, which serves to point up his supernatural differences unbearably.

Obviously, Feroluce understands the gist of his plight. Enemies have him penned. He is a show for now, but ultimately to be killed, for with the intuition of the raptor he divines everything. He had thought the sunlight would kill him, but that is a distant matter, now. And beyond all, the voices and the voices of the wings of his kindred beat the air outside this room-caved mountain of stone.

And so, Feroluce commences to sing, or at least, this is how it seems to the rabid court and all the people gathered in the hall. It seems he sings. It is the great communing call of his kind, the art and science and religion of the winged vampires, his means of telling them, or attempting to tell them, what they must be told before he dies. So the sire of Feroluce sang, and the grandsire, and each of his ancestors. Generally they died in flight, falling angels spun down the gulches and enormous stairs of distant peaks, singing. Feroluce, immured, believes that his cry is somehow audible.

To the crowd in the Duke's hall the song is merely that, a song, but how glorious. The dark silver voice, turning to bronze or gold, whitening in the higher registers. There seem to be words, but in some other tongue. This is how the planets sing, surely, or mysterious creatures of the sea.

Everyone is bemused. They listen, astonished.

No one now remonstrates with Rohise when she rises and steals down from the dais. There is an enchantment which prevents movement and coherent thought. Of all the roomful, only she is drawn forward. So she comes close, unhindered, and between the bars of the cage, she sees the vampire for the first time.

She has no notion what he can be. She imagined it was a monster or a monstrous beast. But it is neither. Rohise, starved for so long of beauty and always dreaming of it, recognizes Feroluce inevitably as part of the dream-come-true. She loves him instantly. Because she loves him, she is not afraid of him.

She attends while he goes on and on with his glorious song. He does not see her at all, or any of them. They are only things, like mist, or pain. They have no character or personality or worth; abstracts.

Finally, Feroluce stops singing. Beyond the stone and the thick glass of the siege, the wing-beats, too, eddy into silence.

Finding itself mesmerized, silent by night, the court comes to with a terrible joint start, shrilling and shouting, bursting, exploding into a compensation of sound. Music flares again. And the cannons in the roof, which have also fallen quiet, resume with a tremendous roar.

Feroluce shuts his eyes and seems to sleep. It is his preparation for death.

Hands grasp Rohise. "Lady—step back, come away. So close! It may harm you—"

The Duke clasps her in a father's embrace. Rohise, unused to this sort of physical expression, is unmoved. She pats him absently.

"My lord, what will be done?"

"Hush, child. Best you do not know."

Rohise persists.

The Duke persists in not saying.

But she remembers the words of the herald on the stair, and knows they mean to butcher the winged man. She attends thereafter more carefully to snatches of the bizarre talk about the hall, and learns all she needs. At earliest sunrise, as soon as the enemy retreat from the walls, their captive will be taken to the lovely garden with the peach trees. And so to the sunken garden of the magic bush, the fire-flower. And there they will hang him up in the sun through the dome of smoky glass, which will be slow murder to him, but they will cut him, too, so his blood, the stolen blood of the vampire, runs down to water the roots of the fleur de feu. And who can doubt that, from such nourishment, the bush will bloom? The blooms are salvation. Wherever they grow it is a safe place. Whoever wears them is safe from the draining bite of demons. Bite-Me-Not, they call it; vampire-repellent.

Rohise sits the rest of the night on her cushions, with folded hands, resembling the portrait of the princess, which is not like her.

Eventually the sky outside alters. Silence comes down beyond the wall, and so within the wall, and the court lifts its head, a corporate animal scenting day.

At the intimation of sunrise the black plague has lifted and gone away, and might never have been. The Duke, and almost all his castle full of men, women, children, emerge from the doors. The sky is measureless and bluely grey, with one cherry rift in the east that the court refers to as "mauve," since dawns and sunsets are never any sort of red here.

They move through the dimly lightening garden as the last stars melt. The cage is dragged in their midst.

They are too tired, too concentrated now, the Duke's people, to continue baiting their captive. They have had all the long night to do that, and to drink and opine, and now their stamina is sharpened for the final act.

Reaching the sunken garden, the Duke unlocks the iron door. There is no room for everyone within, so mostly they must stand outside, crammed in the gate, or teetering on erections of benches that have been placed around, and peering in over the walls through the glass of the dome. The places in the doorway are the best, of course; no one else will get so good a view. The servants and lower persons must stand back under the trees and only imagine what goes on. But they are used to that.

Into the sunken garden itself there are allowed to go the alchemist and the apothecary, and the priest, and certain sturdy soldiers attendant on the Duke, and the Duke. And Feroluce in the cage.

The east is all "mauve" now. The alchemist has prepared sorcerous safeguards which are being put into operation, and the priest, never to be left out, intones prayers. The bulge-thewed soldiers open the cage and seize the monster before it can stir. But drugged smoke has already been wafted into the prison, and besides, the monster has prepared itself for hopeless death and makes no demur.

Feroluce bangs in the arms of his loathing guards, dimly aware the sun is near. But death is nearer, and already one may hear the alchemist's apprentice sharpening the knife an ultimate time.

The leaves of the *Nona Mordica* are trembling, too, at the commencement of the light, and beginning to unfurl. Although this happens every dawn, the court points to it with optimistic cries. Rohise, who has claimed a position in the doorway, watches it too, but only for an instant. Though she has sung of the fleur de fur since childhood, she had never known what the song was all about. And in just this way, though she has dreamed of being the Duke's daughter most of her life, such an event was never really comprehended either, and so means very little.

As the guards haul the demon forward to the plot of humid earth where the bush is growing, Rohise darts into the sunken garden, and lightning leaps in her hands. Women scream and well they might. Rohise has stolen one of the swords from the East Turret, and now she flourishes it, and now she has swung it and a soldier falls, bleeding red, red, *red*, before them all.

Chaos enters, as in yesterday's play, shaking its tattered sleeves. The men who hold the demon rear back in horror at the dashing blade and the blasphemous gore, and the mad girl in her princess's gown. The Duke makes a pitiful bleating noise, but no one pays him any attention.

The east glows in and like the liquid on the ground.

Meanwhile, the ironically combined sense of impending day and spilled hot blood have penetrated the stunned brain of the vampire. His eyes open and he sees the girl wielding her sword in a spray of crimson as the last guard lets go. Then the girl has run to Feroluce. Though, or because, her face is insane, it communicates her purpose, as she thrusts the sword's hilt into his hands.

No one has dared approach either the demon or the girl. Now they look on in horror and in horror grasp what Feroluce has grasped.

In that moment the vampire springs, and the great swanlike wings are reborn at his back, healed and whole. As the doctors predicted, he has mended perfectly, and prodigiously fast. He takes to the air like an arrow, unhindered, as if gravity does not any more exist. As he does so, the girl grips him about the waist, and slender and light, she is drawn upward too. He does not glance at her. He veers towards the gateway, and tears through it, the sword, his talons, his wings, his very shadow beating men and bricks from his path.

And now he is in the sky above them, a black star which has not been put out. They see the wings flare and beat, and the swirling of a girl's dress and unbound hair, and then the image dives and is gone into the shade under the mountains, as the sun rises.

CHAPTER V

It is fortunate, the mountain shade in the sunrise. Lion's blood and enforced quiescence have worked wonders, but the sun could undo it all. Luckily the shadow, deep and cold as a pool, envelops the vampire, and in it there is a cave, deeper and colder. Here he alights and sinks down, sloughing the girl, whom he has almost forgotten. Certainly he fears no harm from her. She is like a pet animal, maybe, like the hunting dogs or wolves or lammergeyers that occasionally the unkindness of vampires have kept by them for a while. That she helped him is all he needs to know. She will help again. So when, stumbling in the blackness, she brings him in her cupped hands water from a cascade at the poolcave's back, he is not surprised. He drinks the water, which is the only other substance his kind imbibe. Then he smooths her hair, absently, as he would pat or stroke the pet she seems to have become. He is not grateful, as he is not suspicious. The complexities of his intellect are reserved for other things. Since he is exhausted he falls asleep, and since Rohise is exhausted she falls asleep beside him, pressed to his warmth in the freezing dark. Like those of Feroluce, as it turns out, her thoughts are simple. She is sorry for distressing the Cursed Duke. But she has no regrets, for she could no more have left Feroluce to die than she could have refused to leave the scullery for the court.

The day, which had only just begun, passes swiftly in sleep.

Feroluce wakes as the sun sets, without seeing anything of it. He unfolds himself and goes to the cave's entrance, which now looks out on a whole sky of stars above a landscape of mountains. The castle is far below, and to the eyes of Rohise as she follows him, invisible. She does not even look for it, for there is something else to be seen.

The great dark shapes of angels are wheeling against the peaks, the stars. And their song begins, up in the starlit spaces. It is a lament, their mourning, pitiless and strong, for Feroluce, who has died in the stone heart of the thing they prey upon.

The tribe of Feroluce do not laugh, but, like a bird or wild beast, they have a kind of equivalent to laughter. This Feroluce now utters, and like a flung lance he launches himself into the air.

Rohise at the cave mouth, abandoned, forgotten, unnoted even by the mass of vampires, watches the winged man as he flies towards his people. She supposes for a moment that she may be able to climb down the tortuous ways of the mountain, undetected. Where then should she go? She does not spend much time on these ideas. They do not interest or involve her. She watches Feroluce and, because she learned long ago the uselessness of weeping, she does not shed tears, though her heart begins to break.

As Feroluce glides, body held motionless, wings outspread on a downdraught, into the midst of the storm of black wings, the red stars of eyes ignite all about him. The great lament dies. The air is very still.

Feroluce waits then. He waits, for the aura of his people is not as he has always known it. It is as if he had come among emptiness. From the silence, therefore, and from nothing else, he learns it all. In the stone he lay and he sang of his death, as the Prince must, dying. And the ritual was completed, and now there is the threnody, the grief, and thereafter the choosing of a new Prince. And none of this is alterable. He is dead. Dead. It cannot and will not be changed.

There is a moment of protest, then, from Feroluce. Perhaps his brief sojourn among men has taught him some of their futility. But as the cry leaves him, all about the huge wings are raised like swords. Talons and teeth and eyes burn against the stars. To protest is to be torn in shreds. He is not of their people now. They can attack and slaughter him as they would any other intruding thing. *Go,* the talons and the teeth and the eyes say to him. *Go far off.*

He is dead. There is nothing left him but to die.

Feroluce retreats. He soars. Bewildered, he feels the power and energy of his strength and the joy of flight, and cannot understand how this is, if he is dead. Yet he *is* dead. He knows it now.

So he closes his eyelids, and his wings. Spear swift he falls. And something shrieks, interrupting the reverie of nihilism. Disturbed, he opens his wings, shudders, turns like a swimmer, finds a ledge against his side and two hands outstretched, holding him by one shoulder, and by his hair.

"No," says Rohise. (The vampire cloud, wheeling away, have not heard her; she does not think of them.) His eyes stay shut. Holding him, she kisses these eyelids, his forehead, his lips, gently, as she drives her nails into his skin to hold him. The black wings beat, tearing to be free and fall and die. "No," say Rohise. "I love you," she says. "My life is your life." These are the words of the court and of courtly love songs. No matter, she means them. And though he cannot understand her language or her sentiments, yet her passion, purely that, communicates itself, strong and burning as the passions of his kind, who generally love only one thing, which is scarlet. For a second her intensity fills the void which now contains him. But then he dashes himself away from the ledge, to fall again, to seek death again.

Like a ribbon, clinging to him still, Rohise is drawn from the rock and falls with him.

Afraid, she buries her head against his breast, in the shadow of wings and hair. She no longer asks him to reconsider. This is how it must be. *Love* she thinks again, in the instant before they strike the earth. Then that instant comes, and is gone.

Astonished, she finds herself still alive, still in the air. Touching so close feathers have been left on the rocks. Feroluce has swerved away, and upward. Now, conversely, they are whirling towards the very stars. The world seems miles below. Perhaps they will fly into space itself. Perhaps he means to break their bones instead on the cold face of the moon.

He does not attempt to dislodge her, he does not attempt any more to fall and die. But as he flies, he suddenly cries out, terrible lost lunatic cries.

They do not hit the moon. They do not pass through the stars like static rain.

But when the air grows thin and pure there is a peak like a dagger standing in their path. Here, he alights. As Rohise lets go of him, he turns away. He stations himself, sentry-fashion, in the manner of his tribe, at the edge of the pinnacle. But watching for nothing. He has not been able to choose death. His strength and the strong will of another, these have hampered him. His brain has become formless darkness. His eyes glare, seeing nothing.

Rohise, gasping a little in the thin atmosphere, sits at his back, watching for him, in case any harm may come near him.

At last, harm does come. There is a lightening in the east. The frozen, choppy sea of the mountains below and all about grows visible. It is a marvelous sight, but holds no marvel for Rohise. She averts her eyes from the exquisitely penciled shapes, looking thin and translucent as paper, the rivers of mist between, the glimmer of nacreous ice. She searches for a blind hole to hide in.

There is a pale yellow wound in the sky when she returns. She grasps Feroluce by the wrist and tugs at him. "Come," she says. He looks at her vaguely, as if seeing her from the shore of another country. "The sun," she says. "Quickly."

The edge of the light runs along his body like a razor. He moves by instinct now, following her down the slippery dagger of the peak, and so eventually into a shallow cave. It is so small it holds him like a coffin. Rohise closes the entrance with her own body. It is the best she can do. She sits facing the sun as it rises, as if prepared to fight. She hates the sun for his sake. Even as the light warms her chilled body, she curses it. Till light and cold and breathlessness fade together.

When she wakes, she looks up into twilight and endless stars, two of which are red. She is lying on the rock by the cave. Feroluce leans over her, and behind Feroluce his quiescent wings fill the sky.

She has never properly understood his nature: Vampire. Yet her own nature, which tells her so much, tells her some vital part of herself is needful to him, and that he is danger, and death. But she loves him, and is not afraid. She would have fallen to die with him. To help him by her death does not seem wrong to her. Thus, she lies still, and smiles at him to reassure him she will not struggle. From lassitude, not fear, she closes her eyes. Presently she feels the soft weight of hair brush by her cheek, and then his cool mouth rests against her throat. But nothing more happens. For some while, they continue in this fashion, she yielding, he kneeling over her, his lips on her skin. Then he moves a little away. He sits, regarding her. She, knowing the unknown act has not been completed, sits up in turn. She beckons to him mutely, telling him with her gestures and her expression *I consent. Whatever is necessary.* But he does not stir. His eyes blaze, but even of these she has no fear. In the end he looks away from her, out across the spaces of the darkness.

He himself does not understand. It is permissible to drink from the body of a pet, the wolf, the eagle. Even to kill the pet, if need demands. Can it be, outlawed from his people, he has lost their composite soul? Therefore, is he soulless now? It does not seem to him he is. Weakened and famished though he is, the vampire is aware of a wild tingling of life. When he stares at the creature which is his food, he finds he sees her differently. He has borne her through the sky, he has avoided death, by some intuitive process, for her sake, and she has led him to safety, guarded him from the blade of the sun. In the beginning it was she who rescued him from the human things which had taken him. She cannot be human, then. Not pet, and not prey. For no, he could not drain her of blood, as he would not seize upon his own kind, even in combat, to drink and feed. He starts to see her as beautiful, not in the way a man beholds a woman, certainly, but as his kind revere the sheen of water in dusk, or flight, or song. There are no words for this. But the life goes on tingling through him. Though he is dead, life.

In the end, the moon does rise, and across the open face of it something wheels by. Feroluce is less swift than was his wont, yet he starts in pursuit, and catches and brings down, killing on the wing, a great night bird. Turning in the air, Feroluce absorbs its liquors. The heat of life now, as well as its assertion, courses through him. He returns to the rock perch, the glorious flaccid bird dangling from his hand. Carefully, he tears the glory of the bird in pieces, plucks the feathers, splits the bones. He wakes the companion (asleep again from weakness) who is not pet or prey, and feeds her morsels of flesh. At first she is unwilling. But her hunger is so enormous and her nature so untamed that quite soon she accepts the slivers of raw fowl.

Strengthened by blood, Feroluce lifts Rohise and bears her gliding down the moon-slit quill-backed land of the mountains, until there is a rocky cistern full of cold, old rains. Here they drink together. Pale white primroses grow in the fissures where the black moss drips. Rohise makes a garland and throws it about the head of her beloved when he does not expect it. Bewildered but disdainful, he touches at the wreath of primroses to see if it is likely to threaten or hamper him. When it does not, he leaves it in place.

Long before dawn this time, they have found a crevice. Because it is so cold, he folds his wings about her. She speaks of her love to him, but he does not hear, only the murmur of her voice, which is musical and does not displease him. And later, she sings him sleepily the little song of the fleur de fur.

CHAPTER VI

There comes a time then, brief, undated, chartless time, when they are together, these two creatures. Not together in any accepted sense, of course, but together in the strange feeling or emotion, instinct or ritual, that can burst to life in an instant or flow to life gradually across half a century, and which men call *Love*.

They are not alike. No, not at all. Their differences are legion and should be unpalatable. He is a supernatural thing and she a human thing, he was a lord and she a scullery sloven. He can fly, she cannot fly. And he is male, she female. What other items are required to make them enemies? Yet they are bound, not merely by love, they are bound by all they are, the very stumbling blocks. Bound, too, because they are doomed. Because the stumbling blocks have doomed them; everything has. Each has been exiled out of their own kind. Together, they cannot even communicate with each other, save by looks, touches, sometimes by sounds, and by songs neither understands, but which each comes to value since the other appears to value them, and since they give expression to that other. Nevertheless, the binding of the doom, the greatest binding, grows, as it holds them fast to each other, mightier and stronger.

Although they do not know it, or not fully, it is the awareness of doom that keeps them there, among the platforms and steps up and down, and the inner cups, of the mountains.

Here it is possible to pursue the airborne hunt, and Feroluce may now and then bring down a bird to sustain them both. But birds are scarce. The richer lower slopes, pastured with goats, wild sheep, and men—they lie far off and far down from this place as a deep of the sea. And Feroluce does not conduct her there, nor does Rohise ask that he should, or try to lead the way, or even dream of such a plan.

But yes, birds are scarce, and the pastures far away, and winter is coming. There are only two seasons in these mountains. High summer, which dies, and the high cold which already treads over the tips of the air and the rock, numbing the sky, making all brittle, as though the whole landscape might snap in pieces, shatter.

How beautiful it is to wake with the dusk, when the silver webs of night begin to form, frost and ice, on everything. Even the ragged dress—once that of a princess—is tinseled and shining with this magic substance, even the mighty wings—once those of a prince—each feather is drawn glittering with thin rime. And oh, the sky, thick as a daisy-field with the white stars. Up there, when they have fed and have strength, they fly, or, Feroluce flies and Rohise flies in his arms, carried by his wings. Up there in the biting chill like a pane of ghostly vitreous, they have become lovers, true blind lovers, embraced and linked, their bodies a bow, coupling on the wing. By the hour that this first happened the girl had forgotten all she had been, and he had forgotten too that she was anything but the essential mate. Sometimes, borne in this way, by wings and by fire, she cries out as she hangs in the ether. These sounds, transmitted through the flawless silence and amplification of the peaks, scatter over tiny half-buried villages countless miles away, where they are heard in fright and taken for the shrieks of malign invisible devils, tiny as bats, and armed with the barbed stings of scorpions. There are always misunderstandings.

After a while, the icy prologues and the stunning starry fields of winter nights give way to the main argument of winter.

The liquid of the pool, where the flowers made garlands, has clouded and closed to stone. Even the volatile waterfalls are stilled, broken cascades of glass. The wind tears through the skin and hair to gnaw the bones. To weep with cold earns no compassion of the cold.

There is no means to make fire. Besides, the one who was Rohise is an animal now, or a bird, and beasts and birds do not make fire, save for the phoenix in the Duke's bestiary. Also, the sun is fire, and the sun is a foe. Eschew fire.

There begin the calendar months of hibernation. The demon lovers too must prepare for just such a measureless winter sleep, that gives no hunger, asks no action. There is a deep cave they have lined with feathers and withered grass. But there are no more flying things to feed them. Long, long ago, the last warm frugal feast, long, long ago the last flight, joining, ecstasy and song. So, they turn to their cave, to stasis, to sleep. Which each understands, wordlessly, thoughtlessly, is death.

What else? He might drain her of blood, he could persist some while on that, might even escape the mountains, the doom. Or she herself might leave him, attempt to make her way to the places below, and perhaps she could reach them, even now. Others, lost here, have done so. But neither considers these alternatives. The moment for all that is past. Even the death-lament does not need to be voiced again.

Installed, they curl together in their bloodless, icy nest, murmuring a little to each other, but finally still.

Outside, the snow begins to come down. It falls like a curtain. Then the winds take it. Then the night is full of the lashing of whips, and when the sun rises it is white as the snow itself, its flames very distant, giving nothing. The cave mouth is blocked up with snow. In the winter, it seems possible that never again will there be a summer in the world.

Behind the modest door of snow, hidden and secret, sleep is quiet as stars, dense as hardening resin. Feroluce and Rohise turn pure and pale in the amber, in the frigid nest, and the great wings lie like a curious articulated machinery that will not move. And the withered grass and the flowers are crystallized, until the snows shall melt.

At length, the sun deigns to come closer to the earth, and the miracle occurs. The snow shifts, crumbles, crashes off the mountains in rage. The waters hurry after the snow, the air is wrung and racked by splittings and splinterings, by rushes and booms. It is half a year, or it might be a hundred years, later.

Open now, the entry to the cave. Nothing emerges. Then, a flutter, a whisper. Something does emerge. One black feather, and caught in it, the petal of a flower, crumbling like dark charcoal and white, drifting away into the voids below. Gone. Vanished. It might never have been.

But there comes another time (half a year, a hundred years), when an adventurous traveler comes down from the mountains to the pocketed villages the other side of them. He is a swarthy cheerful fellow, you would not take him for herbalist or mystic, but he has in a pot a plant he found high up in the staring crags, which might after all contain anything or nothing. And he shows the plant, which is an unusual one, having slender, dark, and velvety leaves, and giving off a pleasant smell like vanilla. "See, the *Nona Mordica*," he says. "The Bite-Me-Not. The flower that repels vampires."

Then the villagers tell him an odd story, about a castle in another country, besieged by a huge flock, a menace of winged vampires, and how the Duke waited in vain for the magic bush that was in his garden, the Bite-Me-Not, to flower and save them all. But it seems there was a curse on this Duke, who on the very night his daughter was lost, had raped a serving woman, as he had raped others before. But this woman conceived. And bearing the fruit, or flower, of this rape, damaged her, so she lived only a year or two after it. The child grew up unknowing, and in the end betrayed her own father by running away to the vampires, leaving the Duke demoralized. And soon after he went mad, and himself stole out one night, and let the winged fiends into his castle, so all there perished.

"Now if only the bush had flowered in time, as your bush flowers, all would have been well," the villagers cry.

The traveler smiles. He in turn does not tell them of the heap of peculiar bones, like parts of eagles mingled with those of a woman and a man. Out of the bones, from the heart of them, the bush was rising, but the traveler untangled the roots of it with care; it looks sound enough now in its sturdy pot, all of it twining together. It seems as if two separate plants are growing from a single stem, one with blooms almost black, and one pink-flowered, like a young sunset.

"Flur de fur," says the traveler, beaming at the marvel, and his luck.

Fleur de feu. Oh flower of fire. That fire is not hate or fear, which makes flowers come, not terror or anger or lust, it is love that is the fire of the Bite-Me-Not, love which cannot abandon, love which cannot harm. Love which never dies.

THE SILVER COLLAR

◆◆◆

GARRY KILWORTH

The remote Scottish island came into view just as the sun was setting. Outside the natural harbor, the sea was kicking a little in its traces and tossing its white manes in the dying light. My small outboard motor struggled against the ebbing tide, sometimes whining as it raced in the air as a particularly low trough left it without water to push against the blades of its propeller. By the time I reached the jetty, the moon was up and casting its chill light upon the shore and purple-heather hills beyond. There was a smothered atmosphere to this lonely place of rock and thin soil, as if the coarse grass and hardy plants had descended as a complete layer to wrap the ruggedness in a faded cover, hiding the nakedness from mean, inquisitive eyes.

As the agents had promised, he was waiting on the quay, his tall, emaciated figure stark against the gentle upward slope of the hinterland: a splinter of granite from the rock on which he made his home.

"I've brought the provisions," I called, as he took the line and secured it.

"Good. Will you come up to the croft? There's a peat fire going—it's warm, and I have some scotch. Nothing like a dram before an open fire, with the smell of burning peat filling the room."

"I could just make it out with the tide," I said. "Perhaps

I should go now." It was not that I was reluctant to accept the invitation from this eremite, this strange recluse—on the contrary, he interested me—but I had to be sure to get back to the mainland that night, since I was to crew a fishing vessel the next day.

"You have time for a dram," his voice drifted away on the cold wind that had sprung up within minutes, like a breath from the mouth of the icy north. I had to admit to myself that a whisky, by the fire, would set me on my toes for the return trip, and his tone had a faintly insistent quality about it which made the offer difficult to refuse.

"Just a minute then—and thanks. You lead the way."

I followed his lean, lithe figure up through the heather, which scratched at my ankles through my seasocks. The path was obviously not well used and I imagined he spent his time in and around his croft, for even in the moonlight I could discern no other tracks incising the soft shape of the hill.

We reached his dwelling and he opened the wooden door, allowing me to enter first. Then, seating me in front of the fire, he poured me a generous whisky before sitting down himself. I listened to the wind, locked outside the timber and turf croft, and waited for him to speak.

He said, "John, isn't it? They told me on the radio."

"Yes—and you're Samuel."

"Sam. You must call me Sam."

I told him I would and there was a period of silence while we regarded each other. Peat is not a consistent fuel, and tends to spurt and spit colorful plumes of flame as the gases escape, having been held prisoner from the seasons for God knows how long. Nevertheless, I was able to study my host in the brief periods of illumination that the fire afforded. He could have been any age, but I knew he was my senior by a great many years. The same thoughts must have been passing through his own head, for he remarked, "John, how old are you? I would guess at twenty."

"Nearer thirty, Sam. I was twenty-six last birthday." He nodded, saying that those who live a solitary life, away from others, have great difficulty in assessing the ages of people they do meet. Recent events slipped from his memory quite quickly, while the past seemed so close.

He leaned forward, into the hissing fire, as if drawing a breath from the ancient atmospheres it released into the room. Behind him, the earthen walls of the croft, held together by rough timbers and unhewn stones, seemed to move closer to his shoulder, as if ready to support his words with confirmation. I sensed a story coming. I recognized the pose from being in the company of sailors on long voyages and hoped he would finish before I had to leave.

"You're a good-looking boy," he said. "So was I, once upon a time." He paused to stir the flames and a blue-green cough from the peat illuminated his face. The skin was taut over the high cheekbones and there was a wanness to it, no doubt brought about by the inclement weather of the isles—the lack of sunshine and the constant misty rain that comes in as white veils from the north. Yes, he had been handsome—still was. I was surprised by his youthful features and suspected that he was not as old as he implied.

"A long time ago," he began, "when we had horse-drawn vehicles and things were different, in more ways than one . . ."

A sharp whistling note—the wind squeezing through two tightly packed logs in the croft—distracted me. Horse-drawn vehicles? What was this? A second-hand tale, surely? Yet he continued in the first person.

". . . gas lighting in the streets. A different set of values. A different set of beliefs. We were more pagan then. Still had our roots buried in dark thoughts. Machines have changed all that. Those sort of pagan, mystical ideas can't share a world with machines. Unnatural beings can only exist close to the natural world and nature's been displaced.

"Yes, a different world—different things to fear. I was afraid as a young man—the reasons may seem trivial to you, now, in your time. I was afraid of, well, getting into something I couldn't get out of. Woman trouble, for instance—especially one not of my class. You understand?

"I got involved once. Must have been about your age, or maybe a bit younger since I'd only just finished my apprenticeship and was a journeyman at the time. Silversmith. You knew that? No, of course you didn't. A silversmith, and a good one too. My master trusted me with one of his three shops, which puffed my pride a bit, I don't mind telling you. Anyway, it happened that I was working late one evening, when I heard the basement doorbell jangle.

"I had just finished lighting the gas lamps in the workshop at the back, so I hurried to the counter where a customer was waiting. She had left the door open and the sounds from the street were distracting, the basement of course being on a level with the cobbled road. Coaches were rumbling by and the noise of street urchins and flower sellers was fighting for attention with the foghorns from the river. As politely as I could, I went behind the customer and closed the door. Then I turned to her and said, 'Yes madam? Can I be of service?'

"She was wearing one of those large satin cloaks that only ladies of quality could afford and she threw back the hood to reveal one of the most beautiful faces I have ever seen in my life. There was a purity to her complexion that went deeper than her flawless skin, much deeper. And her eyes—how can I describe her eyes?—they were like black mirrors and you felt you could see the reflection of your own soul in them. Her hair was dark—coiled on her head—and it contrasted sharply with that complexion, pale as a winter moon, and soft, soft as the velvet I used for polishing the silver.

" 'Yes,' she replied. 'You may be of service. You are the silversmith, are you not?'

" 'The journeyman, madam. I'm in charge of this shop.'

"She seemed a little agitated, her fingers playing nervously with her reticule.

" 'I . . .' she faltered, then continued. 'I have a rather unusual request. Are you able to keep a secret, silversmith?'

" 'My work is confidential, if the customer wishes it so. Is it some special design you require? Something to surprise a loved one with? I have some very fine filigree work here.' I removed a tray from beneath the counter. 'There's something for both the lady and the gentleman. A cigar case, perhaps? This one has a crest wrought into the case in fine silver wire—an eagle, as you can see. It has been fashioned especially for a particular customer, but I can do something similar if you require . . .'

"I stopped talking because she was shaking her head and seemed to be getting impatient with me.

" 'Nothing like that. Something very personal. I want you to make me a collar—a silver collar. Is that possible?'

" 'All things are possible.' I smiled. 'Given the time of course. A tore of some kind?'

" 'No, you misunderstand me.' A small frown marred

the ivory forehead and she glanced anxiously towards the shop door. 'Perhaps I made a mistake . . . ?'

"Worried, in case I lost her custom, I assured her that whatever was her request I should do my utmost to fulfill it. At the same time I told her that I could be trusted to keep the nature of the work to myself.

" 'No one shall know about this but the craftsman and the customer—you and I.'

"She smiled at me then: a bewitching, spellbinding smile, and my heart melted within me. I would have done anything for her at that moment—I would have robbed my master—and I think she knew it.

" 'I'm sorry,' she said. 'I should have realized I could trust you. You have a kind face. A gentle face. One should learn to trust in faces.

" 'I want you—I want you to make me a collar which will cover my whole neck, especially the throat. I have a picture here, of some savages in Africa. The women have metal bands around their necks which envelop them from shoulder to chin. I want you to encase me in a similar fashion, except with one single piece of silver, do you understand? And I want it to fit tightly, so that not even your . . .' She took my hand in her own small gloved fingers. 'So that not even your little finger will be able to find its way beneath.'

"I was, of course, extremely perturbed at such a request. I tried to explain to her that she would have to take the collar off quite frequently, or the skin beneath would become diseased. Her neck would certainly become very ugly.

" 'In any case, it will chafe and become quite sore. There will be constant irritation . . .'

"She dropped my hand and said, no, I still misunderstood. The collar was to be worn permanently. She had no desire to remove it, once I had fashioned it around her neck. There was to be no locking device or anything of that sort. She wanted me to seal the metal.

" 'But?' I began, but she interrupted me in a firm voice.

" 'Silversmith, I have stated my request, my requirements. Will you carry out my wishes, or do I find another craftsman? I should be loath to do so, for I feel we have reached a level of understanding which might be difficult elsewhere. I'm going to be frank with you. This device, well—its purpose is protective. My husband-to-be is not—not like other men, but I love him just the same. I don't wish to embarrass you with talk that's not proper between strangers, and personal to my situation, but the collar is necessary to ensure my marriage is happy—a limited happiness. Limited to a lifetime. I'm sure you *must* understand now. If you want me to leave your shop, I shall do so, but I am appealing to you because you are young and must know the pain of love—unfulfilled love. You are a handsome man and I don't doubt you have a young lady whom you adore. If she were suffering under some terrible affliction, a disease which you might contract from her, I'm sure it would make no difference to your feelings. You would strive to find a way in which you could live together, yet remain uncontaminated yourself. Am I right?'

"I managed to breathe the word 'Yes,' but at the time I was filled with visions of horror. Visions of this beautiful young woman being wooed by some foul creature of the night—a supernatural beast that had no right to be treading on the same earth, let alone touching that sacred skin, kissing—my mind reeled—kissing those soft, moist lips with his monstrous mouth. How could she? Even the thought of it made me shudder in revulsion.

" 'Ah,' she smiled, knowingly. 'You want to save me

from him. You think he is ugly and that I've been hypnotized, somehow, into believing otherwise? You're quite wrong. He's handsome in a way that you'd surely understand—and sensitive, kind, gentle—those things a woman finds important. He's also very cultured. His blood . . .'

"I winced and took a step backward, but she was lost in some kind of reverie as she listed his attributes and I'm sure was unaware of my presence for some time.

" '. . . his blood is unimpeachable, reaching back through a royal lineage to the most notable of European families. I love him, yet I do not want to become one of his kind, for that would destroy my love . . .'

" 'And—he loves you of course,' I said, daringly.

"For a moment those bright eyes clouded over, but she replied, 'In his way. It's not important that we both feel the same *kind* of love. We want to be together, to share our lives. I prefer him to any man I have ever met and I *will not* be deterred by an obstacle that's neither his fault, nor mine. A barrier that's been placed in our way by the injustice of nature. He can't help the way he is—and I want to go to him. That's all there is to it.'

"For a long time neither of us said anything. My throat felt too dry and constricted for words, and deep inside me I could feel something struggling, like a small creature fighting the folds of a net. The situation was beyond my comprehension: that is, I did not wish to allow it to enter my full understanding or I would have run screaming from the shop and made myself look foolish to my neighbors.

" 'Will you do it, silversmith?'

" 'But,' I said, 'a collar covers only the throat . . .' I left the rest unsaid, but I was concerned that she was not protecting herself fully: the other parts of her anatomy—the wrists, the thighs.

"She became very angry. 'He isn't an *animal.* He's a gentleman. I'm merely guarding against—against moments of high passion. It's not just a matter of survival with him. The act is sensual and spiritual, as well as—as well as—what you're suggesting,' there was a note of loathing in her tone, 'is tantamount to rape.'

"She was so incensed that I did not dare say that her lover must have satisfied his need *somewhere,* and therefore had compromised the manners and morals of a gentleman many times.

" 'Will you help me?' The eyes were pleading now. I tried to look out of the small, half-moon window, at the yellow-lighted streets, at the feet moving by on the pavement above, in an attempt to distract myself, but they were magnetic, those eyes, and they drew me back in less than a moment. I felt helpless—a trapped bird—in its unremitting gaze of anguish, and of course, I submitted.

"I agreed. I just heard myself saying, 'Yes,' and led her into the back of the shop where I began the work. It was not a difficult task to actually fashion the collar, though the sealing of it was somewhat painful to her and had to be carried out in stages, which took us well into the night hours. I must have, subconsciously perhaps, continued to glance through the workshop door at the window, for she said once, very quietly, 'He will not come here.'

"Such a beautiful throat she had too. Very long, and elegant. It seemed a sacrilege to encase such beauty in metal, though I made the collar as attractive as I made any silver ornament which might adorn a pretty woman. On the outside of the metal I engraved centripetal designs and at her request, some representational forms: Christ on the cross, immediately over her jugular vein, but also Zeus and Europa, and Zeus and Leda, with the Greek god in his bestial forms of the bull and the swan. I think she had been seduced by the thought that she was marrying some kind of deity.

"When I had finished, she paid me and left. I watched her walk out, into the early morning mists, with a heavy guilt in my heart. What could I have done? I was just a common craftsman and had no right interfering in the lives of others. Perhaps I should have tried harder to dissuade her, but I doubt she would have listened to my impertinence for more than a few moments. Besides, I had, during those few short hours, fallen in love with her—utterly—and when she realized she had made a mistake, she would have to come back to me again, to have the collar removed.

"I wanted desperately to see her again, though I knew that any chance of romance was impossible, hopeless. She was not of my class—or rather, I was not of hers, and her beauty was more than I could ever aspire to, though I knew myself to be a good-looking young man. Some had called *me* beautiful—it was that kind of handsomeness that I had been blessed with, rather than the rugged sort.

"But despite my physical advantages, I had nothing which would attract a lady of quality from her own kind. The most I could ever hope for—the very most—was perhaps to serve her in some way."

Three weeks later she was back, looking somewhat distraught.

" 'I want it to come off,' she said. 'It must be removed.'

"My fingers trembled as I worked at cutting her free—a much simpler task than the previous one.

" 'You've left him,' I said. 'Won't he follow?'

" 'No, you're quite wrong.' There was a haunted look to her eyes which chilled me to the bone. 'It's not that. I was too mistrustful. I love him too much to withhold from him the very thing he desires. I must give myself to him—wholly and completely. I need him, you see. And he needs me—yet like this I cannot give him the kind of love he has to have. I've been selfish. Very selfish. I must go to him . . .'

" 'Are you mad?' I cried, forgetting my position. 'You'll become like him—you'll become—'

" 'How *dare* you! How dare you preach to *me*? Just do your work, silversmith. Remove the collar!'

"I was weak of course, as most of us are when confronted by a superior being. I cut the collar loose and put it aside. She rubbed her neck and complained loudly that flakes of skin were coming away in her hands.

" 'It's ugly,' she said. 'Scrawny. He'll never want me like this.'

" 'No—thank God!' I cried, gathering my courage.

"At that moment she looked me full in the eyes and a strange expression came over her face.

" 'You're in love with me, aren't you? That's why you're so concerned, silversmith. Oh dear, I am so dreadfully sorry. I thought you were just being meddlesome. It was genuine concern for my welfare and I didn't recognize it at first. Dear man,' she touched my cheek. 'Don't look so sad. It cannot be, you know. You should find some nice girl and try to forget, because you'll never see me again after tonight. And don't worry about me. I know what I'm doing.'

"With that, she gathered up her skirts and was gone again, down towards the river. The sun was just coming up, since she had arrived not long before the dawn, and I thought: At least she will have a few hours more of natural life.

"After that I tried to follow her advice and put her out of my mind. I did my work, something I had always enjoyed, and rarely left the shop. I felt that if I could get over a few months without a change in my normal pattern of existence, I should be safe. There were nightmares of course, to be gone through after sunsets, but those I was able to cope with. I have always managed to keep my dreams at a respectable distance and not let them interfere with my normal activities.

"Then, one day, as I was working on a pendant—a butterfly requested by a banker for his wife—a small boy brought me a message. Though it was unsigned, I knew it was from her and my hands trembled as I read the words.

"They simply said, 'Come. I need you.'

"Underneath this request was scrawled an address, which I knew to be located down by one of the wharves, south of the river.

"She *needed* me—and I knew exactly what for. I touched my throat. I wanted her too, but for different reasons. I did not have the courage that she had—the kind of sacrificial courage that's produced by an overwhelming love. But I was not without strength. If there was a chance, just a chance, that I could meet with her and come away unscathed, then I was prepared to accept the risk.

"But I didn't see how that was possible. Her kind, as she had become, possessed a physical strength which would make any escape fraught with difficulty.

"I had no illusions about her being in love with me—or even fond of me. She wanted to use me for her own purposes, which were as far away from love as earth is from the stars. I remembered seeing deep gouges in the silver collar, the time she had come to have it removed. They were like the claw marks of some beast, incised into the trunk of a tree. No wonder she had asked to have it sealed. Whoever, *what*ever, had made those marks would have had the strength to tear away any hinges or lock. The frenzy to get at what lay beneath the silver must have been appalling to witness—*experience*—yet she had gone back to him, without the collar's protection.

"I wanted her. I dreamed about having her, warm and close to me. That she had become something other than the beautiful woman who had entered my shop was no deterrent. I knew she would be just as lovely in her new form and I desired her above all things. For nights I lay awake, running different schemes over in my mind, trying to find a path which would allow us to make love together, just once, and yet let me walk away safely afterward. Even as I schemed, I saw her beauty laid before me, willingly, and my body and soul ached for her presence.

"One chance. I had this one chance of loving a woman a dozen places above my station: a woman whose refined ways and manner of speech had captivated me from the moment I met her. A woman whose dignity, elegance, and gracefulness were without parallel. Whose form surpassed that of the finest silverwork figurine I had ever known.

"I had to find a way.

"Finally, I came up with a plan which seemed to suit my purposes, and taking my courage in both hands I wrote her a note which said, 'I'm waiting for you. *You* must come to *me*.' I found an urchin to carry it for me and told him to put it through the letter box of the address she had given me.

"That afternoon I visited the church and a purveyor of medical instruments.

"That evening I spent wandering the streets, alternately praising myself for dreaming up such a clever plan and cursing myself for my foolhardiness in carrying it through. As I strolled through the backstreets, stepping around the gin-soaked drunks and tipping my hat to the factory girls as they hurried home from a sixteen-hour day in some garment manufacturer's sweatshop, or a hosiery, I realized that for once I had allowed my emotions to overrule my intellect. I'm not saying I was an intelligent young man—not above the average—but I was wise enough to know that there was great danger in what I proposed to do, yet the force of my feelings was more powerful than fear. I could not deny them their expression. The heart has no reason, but its drive is stronger than sense dictates.

"The barges on the river ploughed slowly against the current as I leaned on the wrought-iron balustrade overlooking the water. I could see the gas lamps reflected on the dark surface and thought about the shadow world that lived alongside our own, where nothing was rigid, set, but could be warped and twisted, like those lights in the water when the ripples from the barges passed through them. Would it take me and twist me into something, not ugly, but insubstantial? Into something that has the appearance of the real thing, but which is evanescent in the daylight and can only make its appearance at night, when vacuous shapes and phantasms take on a semblance of life and mock it with their unreal forms?

"When the smell of the mud below me began to waft upward, as the tide retreated and the river diminished, I made my way homeward. There was a sharpness to the air which cut into my confidence and I was glad to be leaving it behind for the warmth and security of my rooms. Security? I laughed at myself, having voluntarily exposed my vulnerability.

"She came.

"There was a scratching at the casement windowpane in the early hours of the morning and I opened it and let her in. She had not changed. If anything, she was more beautiful than ever, with a paler color to her cheeks and a fuller red to her lips.

"No words were exchanged between us. I lay on the bed naked and she joined me after removing her garments. She stroked my hair and the nape of my neck as I sank into her soft young body. I cannot describe the ecstasy. It was—*unearthly.* She allowed me—encouraged me—and the happiness of those moments was worth all the risks of entering Hell for a taste of Heaven.

"Of course, the moment came when she lowered her head to the base of my throat. I felt the black coils of her hair against my cheek: smelled their sweet fragrance. I could sense the pulse in my neck, throbbing with blood. Her body was warm against mine—deliciously warm. I wanted her to stay there forever. There was just a hint of pain in my throat—a needleprick, no more, and then a feeling of drifting, floating on warm water, as if I had suddenly been transported to tropic seas and lay in the shallows of some sunbleached island's beaches. I felt no fear—only, *bliss.*

"Then, suddenly, she snorted, springing to her feet like no athlete I have ever seen. Her eyes were blazing and she spat and hissed into my face.

" 'What have you done?' she shrieked.

"Then the fear came, rushing to my heart. I cowered at the bedhead, pulling my legs up to my chest in an effort to get as far away from her as possible.

"Again she cried, 'What have you done?'

" 'Holy water,' I said. 'I've injected holy water into my veins.'

"She let out another wail which made my ears sing. Her hands reached for me and I saw those long nails, like talons, ready to slash at an artery, but the fear was gone from me. I just wanted her back in bed with me. I no longer cared for the consequences.

" 'Please?' I said, reaching for her. 'Help me? I want

you to help me.' She withdrew from me then and sprang to the window. It was getting close to dawn: The first rays of the sun were sliding over the horizon.

" 'You fool,' she said, and then she was gone, out into the murk. I jumped up and looked for her through the window, but all I could see was the mist on the river, curling its way around the rotten stumps of an old jetty.

"Once I had recovered my common sense and was out of her influence, I remember thinking to myself that I would have to make a collar—a silver collar . . ."

The fire spat in the grate and I jerked upright. I had no idea how long Sam had been talking but the peat was almost all ashes.

"The tide," I said, alarmed. "I must leave."

"I haven't finished," he complained, but I was already on my feet. I opened the door and began to walk quickly down the narrow path we had made through the heather, to where my boat lay, but even as I approached it, I could see that it was lying on its side in the slick, glinting mud.

Angry, I looked back at the croft on the hillside. He must have known. He must have known. I was about to march back and take Sam to task, when I suddenly saw the croft in a new perspective. It was like most dwellings of its kind—timber framed, with sods of earth filling the cracks, and stones holding down the turf on the roof. But it was a peculiar shape—more of a mound than the normal four walls and a roof—and was without windows.

My mind suddenly ran wild with frightening images of wood, earth, and rocks. The wooden coffin goes inside the earth and the headstone weights it down. A mound—a burial mound. *He hadn't been able to stay away from her. The same trap that had caught her . . .*

I turned back to the boat and tried dragging it across the moonlit mud, toward the distant water, but it was too heavy. I could only inch it along, and rapidly became tired. The muscles in my arms and legs screamed at me. All the time I labored, one side of my mind kept telling me not to be so foolish, while the other was equally insistent regarding the need to get away. I could hear myself repeating the words. "*He couldn't stay away from her. He couldn't stay away.*"

I had covered about six yards when I heard a voice at my shoulder—a soft, dry voice, full of concern.

"Here, John, let me help you . . ."

Sam did help me that day, more than I wished him to. I don't hate him for that, especially now that so many years have passed. Since then I have obtained this job, of night ferryman on the loch, helping young ladies like the one I have in the skiff with me now—a runaway, off to join her lover.

"Don't worry," I try to reassure her, after telling her my story, "we sailors are fond of our tales. Come and join me by the tiller. I'll show you how to manage the boat. Do I frighten you? I don't mean to. I only want to help you . . ."

THE STORY OF CHŪGORŌ

♦♦♦

LAFCADIO HEARN

A long time ago there lived, in the Koishikawa quarter of Yedo, a *batamoto* named Suzuki, whose yashiki was situated on the bank of the Yedogawa, not far from the bridge called Naka-no-hashi. And among the retainers of this Suzuki there was an *ashigaru* named Chūgorō. Chūgorō was a handsome lad, very amiable and clever, and much liked by his comrades.

For several years Chūgorō remained in the service of Suzuki, conducting himself so well that no fault was found with him. But at last the other *ashigaru* discovered that Chūgorō was in the habit of leaving the yashiki every night, by way of the garden, and staying out until a little before dawn. At first they said nothing to him about this strange behavior; for his absences did not interfere with any regular duty, and were supposed to be caused by some love-affair. But after a time he began to look pale and weak; and his comrades, suspecting some serious folly, decided to interfere. Therefore, one evening, just as he was about to steal away from the house, an elderly retainer called him aside, and said:

"Chūgorō, my lad, we know that you go out every night and stay away until early morning, and we have observed that you are looking unwell. We fear that you are keeping bad company and injuring your health. And unless you can give a good reason for your conduct, we shall think that it is our duty to report this matter to the Chief Officer. In any case, since we are your comrades and friends, it is but right that we should know why you go out at night, contrary to the custom of this house."

Chūgorō appeared to be very much embarrassed and alarmed by these words. But after a short silence he passed into the garden, followed by his comrade. When the two found themselves well out of hearing of the rest, Chūgorō stopped, and said:

"I will now tell you everything; but I must entreat you to keep my secret. If you repeat what I tell you, some great misfortune may befall me.

"It was in the early part of last spring—about five months ago—that I first began to go out at night, on account of a love-affair. One evening, when I was returning to the yashiki after a visit to my parents, I saw a woman standing by the riverside, not far from the main gateway. She was dressed like a person of high rank; and I thought it strange that a woman so finely dressed should be standing there alone at such an hour. But I did not think that I had any right to question her; and I was about to pass her by, without speaking, when she stepped forward and pulled me by the sleeve. Then I saw that she was very young and handsome. 'Will you not walk with me as far as the bridge?' she said. 'I have something to tell you.' Her voice was very soft and pleasant; and she smiled as she spoke; and her smile was hard to resist. So I walked with her toward the bridge; and on the way she told me that she had often seen me going in and out of the yashiki, and had taken a fancy to me. 'I wish to have you for my husband,' she said. 'If you can like me, we shall be able to make each other very happy.' I did not know how to answer her; but I thought her very charming. As we neared the bridge, she pulled my sleeve again, and led me down the bank to the very edge of the river. 'Come in with me,' she whispered, and pulled me toward the water. It is deep there, as you know; and I became all at once afraid of her, and tried to turn back. She smiled, and caught me by the wrist, and said, 'Oh, you must never be afraid with me!' And, somehow, at the touch of her hand, I became more helpless than a child. I felt like a person in a dream who tries to run, and cannot move hand or foot. Into the deep water she stepped, and drew me with her; and I neither saw nor heard nor felt anything more until I found myself walking beside her through what seemed to be a great palace, full of light. I was neither wet nor cold: everything around me was dry and warm and beautiful. I could not understand where I was, nor how I had come there. The woman led me by the hand: we passed through room after room—through ever so many rooms, all empty, but very fine—until we entered into a guest-room of a thousand mats. Before a great alcove, at the farther end, lights were burning, and cushions laid as for a feast; but I saw no guests. She led me to the place of honor, by the alcove, and seated herself in front of me, and said; 'This is my home: do you think that you could be happy with me here?' As she asked the question she smiled; and I thought that her smile was more beautiful than anything else in the world; and out of my heart I answered, 'Yes. . . .' In the same moment I remembered the story of Urashima; and I imagined that she might be the daughter of a god; but I feared to ask her any questions. . . . Presently maid-servants came in, bearing rice-wine and many dishes, which they set before us. Then she who sat before me said: 'To-night shall be our bridal night, because you like me; and this is our wedding-feast.' We pledged ourselves to each other for the time of seven existences; and after the banquet we were conducted to a bridal chamber, which had been prepared for us.

"It was yet early in the morning when she awoke me, and said: 'My dear one, you are now indeed my husband. But for reasons which I cannot tell you, and which you must not ask, it is necessary that our marriage remain secret. To keep you here until daybreak would cost both of us our lives. Therefore do not, I beg of you, feel displeased because I must now send you back to the house of your lord. You can come to me tonight again, and every night hereafter, at the same hour that we first met. Wait always for me by the bridge; and you will not have to wait long. But remember, above all things, that our marriage must be a secret, and that, if you talk about it, we shall probably be separated forever.'

"I promised to obey her in all things—remembering the fate of Urashima—and she conducted me through many rooms, all empty and beautiful, to the entrance. There she again took me by the wrist, and everything suddenly became dark, and I knew nothing more until I found myself standing alone on the river bank close to the Naka-no-hashi. When I got back to the yashiki, the temple bells had not yet begun to ring.

"In the evening I went again to the bridge at the hour she had named, and I found her waiting for me. She took me with her, as before into the deep water, and into the wonderful place where we had passed our bridal night. And every night, since then, I have met and parted from her in the same way. To-night she will certainly be waiting for me, and I would rather die than disappoint her: therefore I must go. . . . But let me again entreat you, my friend, never to speak to any one about what I have told you."

. . .

The elder *ashigaru* was surprised and alarmed by this story. He felt that Chūgorō had told him the truth; and the truth suggested unpleasant possibilities. Probably the whole experience was an illusion, and an illusion produced by some evil power for a malevolent end. Nevertheless, if really bewitched, the lad was rather to be pitied than blamed; and any forcible interference would be likely to result in mischief. So the *ashigaru* answered kindly:

"I shall never speak of what you have told me—never, at least, while you remain alive and well. Go and meet the woman; but—beware of her! I fear that you are being deceived by some wicked spirit."

Chūgorō only smiled at the old man's warning, and hastened away. Several hours later he reentered the yashiki, with a strangely dejected look. "Did you meet her?" whispered his comrade. "No," replied Chūgorō, "she was not there. For the first time, she was not there. I think that she will never meet me again. I did wrong to tell you—I was very foolish to break my promise. . . ." The other vainly tried to console him. Chūgorō lay down, and spoke no word more. He was trembling from head to foot, as if he had caught a chill.

When the temple bells announced the hour of dawn, Chūgorō tried to get up, and fell back senseless. He was evidently sick—deathly sick. A Chinese physician was summoned.

"Why, the man has no blood!" exclaimed the doctor, after a careful examination. "There is nothing but water in his veins! It will be very difficult to save him. . . . What maleficence is this?"

. . .

Everything was done that could be done to save Chūgorō's life—but in vain. He died as the sun went down. Then his comrade related the whole story.

"Ah! I might have suspected as much!" exclaimed the doctor. . . . "No power could have saved him. He was not the first whom she destroyed."

"Who is she—or what is she?" the *ashigaru* asked. "A Fox-Woman?"

"No; she had been haunting this river from ancient time. She loves the blood of the young. . . ."

"A Serpent-Woman? A Dragon-Woman?"

"No, no! If you were to see her under that bridge by daylight, she would appear to you a very loathsome creature."

"But what kind of a creature?"

"Simply a Frog—a great and ugly Frog!"

STRAGELLA

♦♦♦

HUGH B. CAVE

Night, black as pitch and filled with the wailing of a dead wind, sank like a shapeless specter into the oily waters of the Indian Ocean, leaving a great gray expanse of sullen sea, empty except for a solitary speck that rose and dropped in the long swell.

The forlorn thing was a ship's boat. For seven days and seven nights it had drifted through the waste, bearing its ghastly burden. Now, groping to his knees, one of the two survivors peered away into the East, where the first glare of a red sun filtered over the rim of the world.

Within arm's reach, in the bottom of the boat, lay a second figure, face down. All night long he had lain there. Even the torrential shower, descending in the dark hours and flooding the dory with life-giving water, had failed to move him.

The first man crawled forward. Scooping water out of the tarpaulin with a battered tin cup, he turned his companion over and forced the stuff through receded lips.

"Miggs!" The voice was a cracked whisper. "Miggs! Good God, you ain't dead, Miggs? I ain't left all alone out here—"

John Miggs opened his eyes feebly.

"What—what's wrong?" he muttered.

"We got water, Miggs! Water!"

"You're dreamin' again, Yancy. It—it ain't water. It's nothin' but sea—"

"It rained!" Yancy screeched. "Last night it rained. I stretched the tarpaulin. All night long I been lyin' face up, lettin' it rain in my mouth!"

Miggs touched the tin cup to his tongue and lapped its contents suspiciously. With a mumbled cry he gulped the water down. Then, gibbering like a monkey, he was crawling toward the tarpaulin.

Yancy flung him back, snarling.

"No you won't!" Yancy rasped. "We got to save it, see? We got to get out of here."

Miggs glowered at him from the opposite end of the dory. Yancy sprawled down beside the tarpaulin and stared once again over the abandoned sea, struggling to reason things out.

They were somewhere in the Bay of Bengal. A week ago they had been on board the *Cardigan*, a tiny tramp freighter carrying its handful of passengers from Maulmain to Georgetown. The *Cardigan* had foundered in the typhoon off the Mergui Archipelago. For twelve hours she had heaved and groaned through an inferno of swirling seas. Then she had gone under.

Yancy's memory of the succeeding events was a twisted, unreal parade of horrors. At first there had been five men in the little boat. Four days of terrific heat, no water, no food, had driven the little Persian priest mad; and he had jumped overboard. The other two had drunk salt water and died in agony. Now he and Miggs were alone.

The sun was incandescent in a white hot sky. The sea was calm, greasy, unbroken except for the slow, patient black fins that had been following the boat for days. But something else, during the night, had joined the sharks in their hellish pursuit. Sea snakes, hydrophiinae, wriggling out of nowhere, had come to haunt the dory, gliding in circles round and round, venomous, vivid, vindictive. And overhead were gulls wheeling, swooping in erratic arcs, cackling fiendishly and watching the two men with relentless eyes.

Yancy glanced up at them. Gulls and snakes could mean only one thing—land! He supposed they had come from the Andamans, the prison isles of India. It didn't much matter. They were here. Hideous, menacing harbingers of hope!

His shirt, filthy and ragged, hung open to the belt, revealing a lean chest tattooed with grotesque figures. A long time ago—too long to remember—he had gone on a drunken binge in Goa. Jap rum had done it. In company with two others of the *Cardigan*'s crew he had shambled into a tattooing establishment and ordered the Jap, in a bloated voice, to "paint anything you damned well like, professor. Anything at all!" And the Jap, being of a religious mind and sentimental, had decorated Yancy's chest with a most beautiful Crucifix, large, ornate, and colorful.

It brought a grim smile to Yancy's lips as he peered down at it. But presently his attention was centered on something else—something unnatural, bewildering, on the horizon. The thing was a narrow bank of fog lying low on the water, as if a distorted cloud had sunk out of the sky and was floating heavily, half submerged in the sea. And the small boat was drifting toward it.

In a little while the fog bank hung dense on all sides. Yancy groped to his feet, gazing about him. John Miggs muttered something beneath his breath and crossed himself.

The thing was shapeless, grayish-white, clammy. It reeked—not with the dank smell of sea fog, but with the sickly, pungent stench of a buried jungle or a subterranean mushroom cellar. The sun seemed unable to penetrate it. Yancy could see the red ball above him, a feeble, smothered eye of crimson fire, blotted by swirling vapor.

"The gulls," mumbled Miggs. "They're gone."

"I know it. The sharks, too—and the snakes. We're all alone, Miggs."

An eternity passed, while the dory drifted deeper and deeper into the cone. And then there was something else—something that came like a moaning voice out of the fog. The muted, irregular, sing-song clangor of a ship's bell!

"Listen!" Miggs cackled. "You hear—"

But Yancy's trembling arm had come up abruptly, pointing ahead.

"By God, Miggs! Look!"

Miggs scrambled up, rocking the boat beneath him. His bony fingers gripped Yancy's arm. They stood there, the two of them, staring at the massive black shape that loomed up, like an ethereal phantom of another world, a hundred feet before them.

"We're saved," Miggs said incoherently. "Thank God, Nels—"

Yancy called out shrilly. His voice rang through the fog with a hoarse jangle, like the scream of a caged tiger. It choked into silence. And there was no answer, no responsive outcry—nothing so much as a whisper.

The dory drifted closer. No sound came from the lips of the two men as they drew alongside. There was nothing—nothing but the intermittent tolling of that mysterious, muted bell.

Then they realized the truth—a truth that brought a moan from Miggs' lips. The thing was a derelict, frowning out of the water, inanimate, sullen, buried in its winding-sheet of unearthly fog. Its stern was high, exposing a propeller red with rust and matted with clinging weeds. Across the bow, nearly obliterated by age, appeared the words: *Golconda—Cardiff.*

"Yancy, it ain't no real ship! It ain't of this world—"

Yancy stooped with a snarl, and picked up the oar in the bottom of the dory. A rope dangled within reach, hanging like a black serpent over the scarred hull. With clumsy strokes he drove the small boat beneath it; then, reaching up, he seized the line and made the boat fast.

"You're—goin' aboard?" Miggs said fearfully.

Yancy hesitated, staring up with bleary eyes. He was afraid, without knowing why. The *Golconda* frightened him. The mist clung to her tenaciously. She rolled heavily, ponderously in the long swell; and the bell was still tolling softly somewhere within the lost vessel.

"Well, why not?" Yancy growled. "There may be food aboard. What's there to be afraid of?"

Miggs was silent. Grasping the ropes, Yancy clambered up them. His body swung like a gibbet-corpse against the side. Clutching the rail, he heaved himself over; then stood there, peering into the layers of thick fog, as Miggs climbed up and dropped down beside him.

"I—don't like it," Miggs whispered. "It ain't—"

Yancy groped forward. The deck planks creaked dismally under him. With Miggs clinging close, he led the way into the waist, then into the bow. The cold fog seemed to have accumulated here in a sluggish mass, as if some magnetic force had drawn it. Through it, with arms outheld in front of him, Yancy moved with shuffling steps, a blind man in a strange world.

Suddenly he stopped—stopped so abruptly that Miggs lurched headlong into him. Yancy's body stiffened. His eyes were wide, glaring at the deck before him. A hollow, unintelligible sound parted his lips.

Miggs cringed back with a livid screech, clawing at his shoulder.

"What—what is it?" he said thickly.

At their feet were bones. Skeletons—lying there in the swirl of vapor. Yancy shuddered as he examined them. Dead things they were, dead and harmless, yet they were given new life by the motion of the mist. They seemed to crawl, to wriggle, to slither toward him and away from him.

He recognized some of them as portions of human frames. Others were weird, unshapely things. A tiger skull grinned up at him with jaws that seemed to widen hungrily. The vertebrae of a huge python lay in disjointed coils on the planks, twisted as if in agony. He discerned the skeletonic remains of tigers, tapirs, and jungle beasts of unknown identity. And human heads, many of them, scattered about like an assembly of mocking, dead-alive faces, leering at him, watching him with hellish anticipation. The place was a morgue—a charnel house!

Yancy fell back, stumbling. His terror had returned with triple intensity. He felt cold perspiration forming on his forehead, on his chest, trickling down the tattooed Crucifix.

Frantically he swung about in his tracks and made for the welcome solitude of the stern deck, only to have Miggs clutch feverishly at his arm.

"I'm goin' to get out of here, Nels! That damned bell—these here things—"

Yancy flung the groping hands away. He tried to control his terror. This ship—this *Golconda*—was nothing but a tramp trader. She'd been carrying a cargo of jungle animals for some expedition. The beasts had got loose, gone amuck, in a storm. There was nothing fantastic about it!

In answer, came the intermittent clang of the hidden

bell below decks and the soft lapping sound of the water swishing through the thick weeds which clung to the ship's bottom.

"Come on," Yancy said grimly. "I'm goin' to have a look around. We need food."

He strode back through the waist of the ship, with Miggs shuffling behind. Feeling his way to the towering stern, he found the fog thinner, less pungent.

The hatch leading down into the stern hold was open. It hung before his face like an uplifted hand, scarred, bloated, as if in mute warning. And out of the aperture at its base straggled a spidery thing that was strangely out of place here on this abandoned derelict—a curious, menacing, crawling vine with mottled triangular leaves and immense orange-hued blossoms. Like a living snake, intertwined about itself, it coiled out of the hold and wormed over the deck.

Yancy stepped closer, hestitantly. Bending down, he reached to grasp one of the blooms, only to turn his face away and fall back with an involuntary mutter. The flowers were sickly sweet, nauseating. They repelled him with their savage odor.

"Somethin'—" Miggs whispered sibilantly, "is watchin' us, Nels! I can feel it."

Yancy peered all about him. He, too, felt a third presence close at hand. Something malignant, evil, unearthly. He could not name it.

"It's your imagination," he snapped. "Shut up, will you?"

"We ain't alone, Nels. This ain't no ship at all!"

"Shut *up*!"

"But the flowers there—they ain't right. Flowers don't grow aboard a Christian ship, Nels!"

"This hulk's been here long enough for trees to grow on

it," Yancy said curtly. "The seeds probably took root in the filth below."

"Well, I don't like it."

"Go forward and see what you can find. I'm goin' below to look around."

Miggs shrugged helplessly and moved away. Alone, Yancy descended to the lower levels. It was dark down here, full of shadows and huge gaunt forms that lost their substance in the coils of thick, sinuous fog. He felt his way along the passage, pawing the wall with both hands. Deeper and deeper into the labyrinth he went, until he found the galley.

The galley was a dungeon, reeking of dead, decayed food, as if the stench had hung there for an eternity without being molested; as if the entire ship lay in an atmosphere of its own—an atmosphere of the grave—through which the clean outer air never broke.

But there was food here; canned food that stared down at him from the rotted shelves. The labels were blurred, illegible. Some of the cans crumbled in Yancy's fingers as he seized them—disintegrated into brown, dry dust and trickled to the floor. Others were in fair condition, airtight. He stuffed four of them into his pockets and turned away.

Eagerly now, he stumbled back along the passage. The prospects of food took some of those other thoughts out of his mind, and he was in better humor when he finally found the captain's cabin.

Here, too, the evident age of the place gripped him. The walls were gray with mold, falling into a broken, warped floor. A single table stood on the far side near the bunk, a blackened, grimy table bearing an upright oil lamp and a single black book.

He picked the lamp up timidly and shook it. The circular base was yet half full of oil, and he set it down carefully. It would come in handy later. Frowning, he peered at the book beside it.

It was a seaman's Bible, a small one, lying there, coated with cracked dust, dismal with age. Around it, as if some crawling slug had examined it on all sides, leaving a trail of excretion, lay a peculiar line of black pitch, irregular but unbroken.

Yancy picked the book up and flipped it open. The pages slid under his fingers, allowing a scrap of loose paper to flutter to the floor. He stooped to retrieve it; then, seeing that it bore a line of penciled script, he peered closely at it.

The writing was an apparently irrevelant scrawl—a meaningless memorandum which said crudely:

It's the bats and the crates. I know it now, but it is too late. God help me!

With a shrug, he replaced it and thrust the Bible into his belt, where it pressed comfortingly against his body. Then he continued his exploration.

In the wall cupboard he found two full bottles of liquor, which proved to be brandy. Leaving them there, he groped out of the cabin and returned to the upper deck in search of Miggs.

Miggs was leaning on the rail, watching something below. Yancy trudged toward him, calling out shrilly:

"Say, I got food, Miggs! Food and brand—"

He did not finish. Mechanically his eyes followed the direction of Miggs' stare, and he recoiled involuntarily as his words clipped into stifled silence. On the surface of the oily water below, huge sea snakes paddled against the ship's side—enormous slithering shapes, banded with streaks of black and red and yellow, vicious and repulsive.

"They're back," Miggs said quickly. "They know this

ain't no proper ship. They come here out of their hell-hole, to wait for us."

Yancy glanced at him curiously. The inflection of Miggs' voice was peculiar—not at all the phlegmatic, guttural tone that usually grumbled through the little man's lips. It was almost eager!

"What did you find?" Yancy faltered.

"Nothin'. All the ship's boats are hangin' in their davits. Never been touched."

"I found food," Yancy said abruptly, gripping his arm. "We'll eat; then we'll feel better. What the hell are we, anyhow—a couple of fools? Soon as we eat, we'll stock the dory and get off this blasted death ship and clear out of this stinkin' fog. We got water in the tarpaulin."

"We'll clear out? Will we, Nels?"

"Yah. Let's eat."

Once again, Yancy led the way below decks to the galley. There, after a twenty-minute effort in building a fire in the rusty stove, he and Miggs prepared a meal, carrying the food into the captain's cabin, where Yancy lighted the lamp.

They ate slowly, sucking the taste hungrily out of every mouthful, reluctant to finish. The lamplight, flickering in their faces, made gaunt masks of features that were already haggard and full of anticipation.

The brandy, which Yancy fetched out of the cupboard, brought back strength and reason—and confidence. It brought back, too, that unnatural sheen to Miggs' twitching eyes.

"We'd be damned fools to clear out of here right off," Miggs said suddenly. "The fog's got to lift sooner or later. I ain't trustin' myself to no small boat again, Nels—not when we don't know where we're at."

Yancy looked at him sharply. The little man turned away with a guilty shrug. Then hesitantly:

"I—I kinda like it here, Nels."

Yancy caught the odd gleam in those small eyes. He bent forward quickly.

"Where'd you go when I left you alone?" he demanded.

"Me? I didn't go nowhere. I—I just looked around a bit, and I picked a couple of them flowers. See."

Miggs groped in his shirt pocket and held up one of the livid, orange-colored blooms. His face took on an unholy brilliance as he held the thing close to his lips and inhaled its deadly aroma. His eyes, glittering across the table, were on fire with sudden fanatic lust.

For an instant Yancy did not move. Then, with a savage oath, he lurched up and snatched the flower out of Miggs' fingers. Whirling, he flung it to the floor and ground it under his boot.

"You damned thick-headed fool!" he screeched. "You—God help you!"

Then he went limp, muttering incoherently. With faltering steps he stumbled out of the cabin and along the black passageway, and up on the abandoned deck. He staggered to the rail and stood there, holding himself erect with nerveless hands.

"God!" he whispered hoarsely. "God—what did I do that for? Am I goin' crazy?"

No answer came out of the silence. But he knew the answer. The thing he had done down there in the skipper's cabin—those mad words that had spewed from his mouth—had been involuntary. Something inside him, some sense of danger that was all about him, had hurled the words out of his mouth before he could control them.

And his nerves were on edge, too; they felt as though they were ready to crack.

But he knew instinctively that Miggs had made a terrible mistake. There was something unearthly and wicked about those sickly sweet flowers. Flowers didn't grow aboard ships. Not real flowers. Real flowers had to take root somewhere, and, besides, they didn't have that drunken, etherish odour. Miggs should have left the vine alone. Clinging at the rail there, Yancy *knew* it, without knowing why.

He stayed there for a long time, trying to think and get his nerves back again. In a little while he began to feel frightened, being alone, and he returned below decks to the cabin.

He stopped in the doorway, and stared.

Miggs was still there, slumped grotesquely over the table. The bottle was empty. Miggs was drunk, unconscious, mercifully oblivious of his surroundings.

For a moment Yancy glared at him morosely. For a moment, too, a new fear tugged at Yancy's heart—fear of being left alone through the coming night. He yanked Miggs' arm and shook him savagely; but there was no response. It would be hours, long, dreary, sinister hours, before Miggs regained his senses.

Bitterly Yancy took the lamp and set about exploring the rest of the ship. If he could find the ship's papers, he considered, they might dispel his terror. He might learn the truth.

With this in mind, he sought the mate's quarters. The papers had not been in the captain's cabin where they belonged; therefore they might be here.

But they were not. There was nothing—nothing but a chronometer, sextant, and other nautical instruments lying in curious positions on the mate's table, rusted beyond repair. And there were flags, signal flags, thrown down as if they had been used at the last moment. And, lying in a distorted heap on the floor, was a human skeleton.

Avoiding this last horror, Yancy searched the room thoroughly. Evidently, he reasoned, the captain had died early in the *Golconda*'s unknown plague. The mate had brought these instruments, these flags, to his own cabin, only to succumb before he could use them.

Only one thing Yancy took with him when he went out: a lantern, rusty and brittle, but still serviceable. It was empty, but he poured oil into it from the lamp. Then, returning the lamp to the captain's quarters where Miggs lay unconscious, he went on deck.

He climbed the bridge and set the lantern beside him. Night was coming. Already the fog was lifting, allowing darkness to creep in beneath it. And so Yancy stood there, alone and helpless, while blackness settled with uncanny quickness over the entire ship.

He was being watched. He felt it. Invisible eyes, hungry and menacing, were keeping check on his movements. On the deck beneath him were those inexplicable flowers, trailing out of the unexplored hold, glowing like phosphorescent faces in the gloom.

"By God," Yancy mumbled, "I'm goin' to get out of here!"

His own voice startled him and caused him to stiffen and peer about him, as if someone else had uttered the words. And then, very suddenly, his eyes became fixed on the far horizon to starboard. His lips twitched open, spitting out a shrill cry.

"Miggs! Miggs! A light! Look, Miggs—"

Frantically he stumbled down from the bridge and clawed his way below decks to the mate's cabin. Feverishly he seized the signal flags. Then, clutching them in his hand, he moaned helplessly and let them fall. He realized that they were no good, no good in the dark. Gibbering to himself, he searched for rockets. There were none.

Suddenly he remembered the lantern. Back again he raced through the passage, on deck, up on the bridge. In another moment, with the lantern dangling from his arm, he was clambering higher and higher into the black spars of the mainmast. Again and again he slipped and caught himself with outflung hands. And at length he stood high above the deck, feet braced, swinging the lantern back and forth. . . .

Below him, the deck was no longer silent, no longer abandoned. From bow to stern it was trembling, creaking, whispering up at him. He peered down fearfully. Blurred shadows seemed to be prowling through the darkness, coming out of nowhere, pacing dolefully back and forth through the gloom. They were watching him with a furtive interest.

He called out feebly. The muted echo of his own voice came back up to him. He was aware that the bell was tolling again, and the swish of the sea was louder, more persistent.

With an effort he caught a grip on himself.

"Damned fool," he rasped. "Drivin' yourself crazy—"

The moon was rising. It blurred the blinking light on the horizon and penetrated the darkness like a livid yellow finger. Yancy lowered the lantern with a sob. It was no good now. In the glare of the moonlight, this puny flame would be invisible to the men aboard that other ship. Slowly, cautiously, he climbed down to the deck.

He tried to think of something to do, to take his mind off the fear. Striding to the rail, he hauled up the water butts from the dory. Then he stretched the tarpaulin to catch the precipitation of the night dew. No telling how long he and Miggs would be forced to remain aboard the hulk.

He turned, then, to explore the forecastle. On his way across the deck, he stopped and held the light over the creeping vine. The curious flowers had become fragrant, heady, with the fumes of an intoxicating drug. He followed the coils to where they vanished into the hold, and he looked down. He saw only a tumbled pile of boxes and crates. Barred boxes which must have been cages at one time.

Again he turned away. The ship was trying to tell him something. He felt it—felt the movements of the deck planks beneath his feet. The moonlight, too, had made hideous white things of the scattered bones in the bow. Yancy stared at them with a shiver. He stared again, and grotesque thoughts obtruded into his consciousness. The bones were moving. Slithering, sliding over the deck, assembling themselves, gathering into definite shapes. He could have sworn it!

Cursing, he wrenched his eyes away. Damned fool, thinking such thoughts! With clenched fists he advanced to the forecastle; but before he reached it, he stopped again.

It was the sound of flapping wings that brought him about. Turning quickly, with a jerk, he was aware that the sound emanated from the open hold. Hesitantly he stepped forward—and stood rigid with an involuntary scream.

Out of the aperture came two horrible shapes—two inhuman things with immense, clapping wings and glittering eyes. Hideous; enormous. *Bats!*

Instinctively he flung his arm up to protect himself. But the creatures did not attack. They hung for an instant, poised over the hatch, eyeing him with something that was fiendishly like intelligence. Then they flapped over the deck, over the rail, and away into the night. As they sped away towards the west, where he had seen the light of that other ship twinkling, they clung together like witches hell-bent on some evil mission. And below them, in the bloated sea, huge snakes weaved smoky, golden patterns—waiting! . . .

He stood fast, squinting after the bats. Like two hellish black eyes they grew smaller and smaller, became pinpoints in the moon-glow, and finally vanished. Still he did not stir. His lips were dry, his body stiff and unnatural. He licked his mouth. Then he was conscious of something more. From somewhere behind him came a thin, throbbing thread of harmony—a lovely, utterly sweet musical note that fascinated him.

He turned slowly. His heart was hammering, surging. His eyes went suddenly wide.

There, not five feet from him, stood a human form. Not his imagination. Real!

But he had never seen a girl like her before. She was too beautiful. She was wild, almost savage, with her great dark eyes boring into him. Her skin was white, smooth as alabaster. Her hair was jet black; and a waving coil of it, like a broken cobweb of pitch strings, framed her face. Grotesque hoops of gold dangled from her ears. In her hair, above them, gleamed two of those sinister flowers from the straggling vine.

He did not speak; he simply gaped. The girl was barefooted, bare-legged. A short, dark skirt covered her slender thighs. A ragged white waist, open at the throat, revealed the full curve of her breast. In one hand she held a long wooden reed, a flute-like instrument fashioned out of crude wood. And about her middle, dangling almost to the deck, twined a scarlet, silken sash, brilliant as the sun, but not so scarlet as her lips, which were parted in a faint, suggestive smile, showing teeth of marble whiteness!

"Who—who are you?" Yancy mumbled.

She shook her head. Yet she smiled with her eyes, and he felt, somehow, that she understood him. He tried again, in such tongues as he knew. Still she shook her head, and still he felt that she was mocking him. Not until he chanced upon a scattered, faltering greeting in Serbian, did she nod her head.

"Dobra!" she replied, in a husky rich voice which sounded, somehow, as if it were rarely used.

He stepped closer then. She was a gipsy evidently. A Tzany of the Serbian hills. She moved very close to him with a floating, almost ethereal movement of her slender body. Peering into his face, flashing her haunting smile at him, she lifted the flute-like instrument and, as if it were nothing at all unnatural or out of place, began to play again the song which had first attracted his attention.

He listened in silence until she had finished. Then, with a cunning smile, she touched her fingers to her lips and whispered softly:

"You—mine. Yes?"

He did not understand. She clutched his arm and glanced fearfully toward the west, out over the sea.

"You—mine!" she said again, fiercely. "Papa Bocito—Seraphino—they no have you. You—not go—to them!"

He thought he understood then. She turned away from him and went silently across the deck. He watched her disappear into the forecastle, and would have followed her, but once again the ship—the whole ship—seemed to be struggling to whisper a warning.

Presently she returned, holding in her white hand a battered silver goblet, very old and very tarnished, brimming with scarlet fluid. He took it silently. It was impossible to refuse her. Her eyes had grown into lakes of night, lit by the burning moon. Her lips were soft, searching, undeniable.

"Who are you?" he whispered.

"Stragella," she smiled.

"Stragella . . . Stragella . . ."

The name itself was compelling. He drank the liquid slowly, without taking his eyes from her lovely face. The stuff had the taste of wine—strong, sweet wine. It was intoxicating, with the same weird effect that was contained in the orange blooms which she wore in her hair and which groveled over the deck behind her.

Yancy's hands groped up weakly. He rubbed his eyes, feeling suddenly weak, powerless, as if the very blood had been drained from his veins. Struggling futilely, he staggered back, moaning half inaudibly.

Stragella's arms went about him, caressing him with sensuous touch. He felt them, and they were powerful, irresistible. The girl's smile maddened him. Her crimson lips hung before his face, drawing nearer, mocking him. Then, all at once, she was seeking his throat. Those warm, passionate, deliriously pleasant lips were searching to touch him.

He sensed his danger. Frantically he strove to lift his arms and push her away. Deep in his mind some struggling intuition, some half-alive idea, warned him that he was in terrible peril. This girl, Stragella, was not of his kind; she was a creature of the darkness, a denizen of a different, frightful world of her own! Those lips, wanting his flesh, were inhuman, too fervid—

Suddenly she shrank away from him, releasing him with a jerk. A snarling animal-like sound surged through her flaming mouth. Her hand lashed out, rigid, pointing to the thing that hung in his belt. Talonic fingers pointed to the Bible that defied her!

But the scarlet fluid had taken its full effect. Yancy slumped down, unable to cry out. In a heap he lay there, paralyzed, powerless to stir.

He knew that she was commanding him to rise. Her lips, moving in pantomime, formed soundless words. Her glittering eyes were fixed upon him, hypnotic. The Bible—she wanted him to cast it over the rail! She wanted him to stand up and go into her arms. Then her lips would find a hold. . . .

But he could not obey. He could not raise his arms to support himself. She, in turn, stood at bay and refused to advance. Then, whirling about, her lips drawn into a diabolical curve, beautiful but bestial, she retreated. He saw her dart back, saw her tapering body whip about, with the crimson sash outflung behind her as she raced across the deck.

Yancy closed his eyes to blot out the sight. When he opened them again, they opened to a new, more intense horror. On the *Golconda*'s deck, Stragella was darting erratically among those piles of gleaming bones. But they were bones no longer. They had gathered into shapes, taken on flesh, blood. Before his very eyes they assumed substance, men and beasts alike. And then began an orgy such as Nels Yancy had never before looked upon—an orgy of the undead.

Monkeys, giant apes, lunged about the deck. A huge python reared its sinuous head to glare. On the hatch cover a snow-leopard, snarling furiously, crouched to spring. Tigers, tapirs, crocodiles—fought together in the bow. A great brown bear, of the type found in the lofty plateaus of the Pamirs, clawed at the rail.

And the men! Most of them were dark-skinned—dark enough to have come from the same region, from Madras. With them crouched Chinamen, and some Anglo-Saxons. Starved, all of them. Lean, gaunt, mad!

Pandemonium raged then. Animals and men alike were insane with hunger. In a little struggling knot, the men were gathered about the number-two hatch, defending themselves. They were wielding firearms—firing point-blank with desperation into the writhing mass that confronted them. And always, between them and around them and among, darted the girl who called herself Stragella.

They cast no shadows, those ghost shapes. Not even the girl, whose arms he had felt about him only a moment ago. There was nothing real in the scene, nothing human. Even the sounds of the shots and the screams of the cornered men, even the roaring growls of the big cats, were smothered as if they came to him through heavy glass windows, from a sealed chamber.

He was powerless to move. He lay in a cataleptic condition, conscious of the entire pantomime, yet unable to flee from it. And his senses were horribly acute—so acute that he turned his eyes upward with an abrupt twitch, instinctively; and then shrank into himself with a new fear as he discerned the two huge bats which had winged their way across the sea. . . .

They were returning now. Circling above him, they flapped down one after the other and settled with heavy, sullen thuds upon the hatch, close to that weird vine of flowers. They seemed to have lost their shape, these nocturnal monstrosities, to have become fantastic blurs, enveloped in an unearthly bluish radiance. Even as he stared at them, they vanished altogether for a moment;

and then the strange vapor cleared to reveal the two creatures who stood there!

Not bats! Humans! Inhumans! They were gipsies, attired in moldy, decayed garments which stamped them as Balkans. Man and woman. Lean, emaciated, ancient man with fierce white mustache; plump old woman with black, rat-like eyes that seemed unused to the light of day. And they spoke to Stragella—spoke to her eagerly. She, in turn, swung about with enraged face and pointed to the Bible in Yancy's belt.

But the pantomime was not finished. On the deck the men and animals lay moaning, sobbing. Stragella turned noiselessly, calling the old man and woman after her. Calling them by name.

"Come—Papa Bocito, Seraphino!"

The tragedy of the ghost-ship was being reenacted. Yancy knew it, and shuddered at the thought. Starvation, cholera had driven the *Golconda*'s crew mad. The jungle beasts, unfed, hideously savage, had escaped out of their confinement. And now—now that the final conflict was over—Stragella and Papa Bocito and Seraphino were proceeding about their ghastly work.

Stragella was leading them. Her charm, her beauty, gave her a hold on the men. They were in love with her. She had *made* them love her, madly and without reason. Now she was moving from one to another, loving them and holding them close to her. And as she stepped away from each man, he went limp, faint, while she laughed terribly and passed on to the next. Her lips were parted. She licked them hungrily—licked the blood from them with a sharp, crimson tongue.

How long it lasted, Yancy did not know. Hours, hours on end. He was aware, suddenly, that a high wind was screeching and wailing in the upper reaches of the ship; and, peering up, he saw that the spars were no longer bare and rotten with age. Great gray sails stood out against the black sky—fantastic things without any definite form or outline. And the moon above them had vanished utterly. The howling wind was bringing a storm with it, filling the sails to bulging proportions. Beneath the decks the ship was groaning like a creature in agony. The seas were lashing her, slashing her, carrying her forward with amazing speed.

Of a sudden came a mighty grinding sound. The *Golconda* hurtled back, as if a huge, jagged reef of submerged rock had bored into her bottom. She listed. Her stern rose high in the air. And Stragella with her two fellow fiends, was standing in the bow, screaming in mad laughter in the teeth of the wind. The other two laughed with her.

Yancy saw them turn toward him, but they did not stop. Somehow, he did not expect them to stop. This scene, this mad pantomime, was not the present; it was the past. He was not here at all. All this had happened years ago! Forgotten, buried in the past!

But he heard them talking, in a mongrel dialect full of Serbian words.

"It is done. Papa Bocito! We shall stay here forever now. There is land within an hour's flight, where fresh blood abounds and will always abound. And here, on this wretched hulk, they will never find our graves to destroy us!"

The horrible trio passed close. Stragella turned, to stare out across the water, and raised her hand in silent warning. Yancy, turning wearily to stare in the same direction, saw that the first streaks of daylight were beginning to filter over the sea.

With a curious floating, drifting movement the three undead creatures moved toward the open hatch. They descended out of sight. Yancy, jerking himself erect and surprised to find that the effects of the drug had worn off with the coming of dawn, crept to the hatch and peered down—in time to see those fiendish forms enter their coffins. He knew then what the crates were. In the dim light, now that he was staring directly into the aperture, he saw what he had not noticed before. Three of those oblong boxes were filled with dank grave-earth!

He knew then the secret of the unnatural flowers. They *had* roots! They were rooted in the soil which harbored those undead bodies!

Then, like a groping finger, the dawn came out of the sea. Yancy walked to the rail, dazed. It was over now—all over. They orgy was ended. The *Golconda* was once more an abandoned, rotted hulk.

For an hour he stood at the rail, sucking in the warmth and glory of the sunlight. Once again that wall of unsightly mist was rising out of the water on all sides. Presently it would bury the ship, and Yancy shuddered.

He thought of Miggs. With quick steps he paced to the companionway and descended to the lower passage. Hesitantly he prowled through the thickening layers of dank fog. A queer sense of foreboding crept over him.

He called out even before he reached the door. There was no answer. Thrusting the barrier open, he stepped across the sill—and then he stood still while a sudden harsh cry broke from his lips.

Miggs was lying there, half across the table, his arms flung out, his head turned grotesquely on its side, staring up at the ceiling.

"Miggs! Miggs!" The sound came choking through Yancy's lips. "Oh, God, Miggs—what's happened?"

He reeled forward. Miggs was cold and stiff, and quite dead. All the blood was gone out of his face and arms. His eyes were glassy, wide open. He was as white as marble, shrunken horribly. In his throat were two parallel marks, as if a sharp-pointed staple had been hammered into the flesh and then withdrawn. The marks of the vampire.

For a long time Yancy did not retreat. The room swayed and lurched before him. He was alone. Alone! The whole ghastly thing was too sudden, too unexpected.

Then he stumbled forward and went down on his knees, clawing at Miggs' dangling arm.

"Oh God, Miggs," he mumbled incoherently. "You got to help me. I can't stand it!"

He clung there, white-faced, staring, sobbing thickly—and presently slumped in a pitiful heap, dragging Miggs over on top of him.

It was later afternoon when he regained consciousness. He stood up, fighting away the fear that overwhelmed him. He had to get away, get away! The thought hammered into his head with monotonous force. Get away!

He found his way to the upper deck. There was nothing he could do for Miggs. He would have to leave him here. Stumbling, he moved along the rail and reached down to draw the small boat closer, where he could provision it and make it ready for his departure.

His fingers clutched emptiness. The ropes were gone. The dory was gone. He hung limp, staring down at a flat expanse of oily sea.

For an hour he did not move. He fought to throw off his fear long enough to think of a way out. Then he stiffened with a sudden jerk and pushed himself away from the rail.

The ship's boats offered the only chance. He groped to the nearest one and labored feverishly over it.

But the task was hopeless. The life boats were of metal, rusted through and through, wedged in their davits. The wire cables were knotted and immovable. He tore his hands on them, wringing blood from his scarred fingers. Even while he worked, he knew that the boats would not float. They were rotten, through and through.

He had to stop, at last, from exhaustion.

After that, knowing that there was no escape, he had to do something, anything, to keep sane. First he would clear those horrible bones from the deck, then explore the rest of the ship. . . .

It was a repulsive task, but he drove himself to it. If he could get rid of the bones, perhaps Stragella and the other two creatures would not return. He did not know. It was merely a faint hope, something to cling to.

With grim, tight-pressed lips he dragged the bleached skeletons over the deck and kicked them over the side, and stood watching them as they sank from sight. Then he went to the hold, smothering his terror, and descended into the gloomy belly of the vessel. He avoided the crates with a shudder of revulsion. Ripping up that evil vine-thing by the roots, he carried it to the rail and flung it away, with the mold of grave-earth still clinging to it.

After that he went over the entire ship, end to end, but found nothing.

He slipped the anchor chains then, in the hopes that the ship would drift away from that vindictive bank of fog. Then he paced back and forth, muttering to himself and trying to force courage for the most hideous task of all.

The sea was growing dark, and with dusk came increasing terror. He knew the *Golconda* was drifting. Knew, too, that the undead inhabitants of the vessel were furious with him for allowing the boat to drift away from their source of food. Or they *would* be furious when they came alive again after their interim of forced sleep.

And there was only one method of defeating them. It was a horrible method, and he was already frightened. Nevertheless he searched the deck for a marlin spike and found one; and, turning sluggishly, he went back to the hold.

A stake, driven through the heart of each of the horrible trio . . .

The rickety stairs were deep in shadow. Already the dying sun, buried behind its wreath of evil fog, was a ring of bloody mist. He glanced at it and realized that he must hurry. He cursed himself for having waited so long.

It was hard, lowering himself into the pitch-black hold when he could only feel his footing and trust to fate. His boots scraped ominously on the steps. He held his hands above him, gripping the deck timbers.

And suddenly he slipped.

His foot caught on the edge of a lower step, twisted abruptly, and pitched him forward. He cried out. The marlin spike dropped from his hands and clattered on one of the crates below. He tumbled in a heap, clawing for support. The impact knocked something out of his belt. And he realized, even as his head came in sharp contact with the foremost oblong box, that the Bible, which had heretofore protected him, was no longer a part of him.

He did not lose complete control of his senses. Frantically he sought to regain his knees and grope for the black book in the gloom of the hold. A sobbing, choking sound came pitifully from his lips.

A soft, triumphant laugh came out of the darkness close

to him. He swung about heavily—so heavily that the movement sent him sprawling again in an inert heap.

He was too late. She was already there on her knees, glaring at him hungrily. A peculiar bluish glow welled about her face. She was ghastly beautiful as she reached behind her into the oblong crate and began to trace a circle about the Bible with a chunk of soft, tarry, pitch-like substance clutched in her white fingers.

Yancy stumbled toward her, finding strength in desperation. She straightened to meet him. Her lips, curled back, exposed white teeth. Her arms coiled out, enveloping him, stifling his struggles. God, they were strong. He could not resist them. The same languid, resigned feeling came over him. He would have fallen, but she held him erect.

She did not touch him with her lips. Behind her he saw two other shapes take form in the darkness. The savage features of Papa Bocito glowered at him; and Seraphino's ratty, smoldering eyes, full of hunger, bored into him. Stragella was obviously afraid of them.

Yancy was lifted from his feet. He was carried out on deck and borne swiftly, easily, down the companionway, along the lower passage, through a swirling blanket of hellish fog and darkness, to the cabin where Miggs lay dead. And he lost consciousness while they carried him.

He could not tell, when he opened his eyes, how long he had been asleep. It seemed a long, long interlude. Stragella was sitting beside him. He lay on the bunk in the cabin, and the lamp was burning on the table, revealing Miggs' limp body in full detail.

Yancy reached up fearfully to touch his throat. There were no marks there; not yet.

He was aware of voices, then. Papa Bocito and the

ferret-faced woman were arguing with the girl beside him. The savage old man in particular was being angered by her cool, possessive smile.

"We are drifting away from the prison isles," Papa Bocito snarled, glancing at Yancy with unmasked hate. "It is his work, lifting the anchor. Unless you share him with us until we drift ashore, we shall perish!"

"He is mine," Stragella shrugged, modulating her voice to a persuasive whisper. "You had the other. This one is mine. I shall have him!"

"He belongs to us all!"

"Why?" Stragella smiled. "Because he has looked upon the resurrection night? Ah, he is the first to learn our secret."

Seraphino's eyes narrowed at that, almost to pinpoints. She jerked forward, clutching the girl's shoulder.

"We have quarreled enough," she hissed. "Soon it will be daylight. He belongs to us all because he has taken us away from the isles and learned our secrets."

The words drilled their way into Yancy's brain. "The resurrection night!" There was an ominous significance in it, and he thought he knew its meaning. His eyes, or his face, must have revealed his thoughts, for Papa Bocito drew near to him and pointed into his face with a long, bony forefinger, muttering triumphantly.

"You have seen what no other eyes have seen," the ancient man growled bitterly. "Now, for that, you shall become one of us. Stragella wants you. She shall have you for eternity—for a life without death. Do you know what that means?"

Yancy shook his head dumbly, fearfully.

"We are the undead," Bocito leered. "Our victims become creatures of the blood, like us. At night we are free. During the day we must return to our graves. That is why"—he cast his arm toward the upper deck in a hideous gesture—"those other victims of ours have not yet become like us. They were never buried; they have no graves to return to. Each night we give them life for our own amusement, but they are not of the brotherhood—yet."

Yancy licked his lips and said nothing. He understood then. Every night it happened. A nightly pantomime, when the dead become alive again, reenacting the events of the night when the *Golconda* had become a ship of hell.

"We are gipsies," the old man gloated. "Once we were human, living in our pleasant little camp in the shadow of the Pobyezdin Potok's crusty peaks, in the Morava Valley of Serbia. That was in the time of Milutin, six hundreds of years ago. Then the vampires of the hills came for us and took us to them. We lived the undead life, until there was no more blood in the valley. So we went to the coast, we three, transporting our grave-earth with us. And we lived there, alive by night and dead by day, in the coastal villages of the Black Sea, until the time came when we wished to go to the far places."

Seraphino's guttural voice interrupted him, saying harshly:

"Hurry. It is nearly dawn!"

"And we obtained passage on this *Golconda*, arranging to have our crates of grave-earth carried secretly to the hold. And the ship fell into cholera and starvation and storm. She went aground. And—here we are. Ah, but there is blood upon the islands, my pretty one, and so we anchored the *Golconda* on the reef, where life was close at hand!"

Yancy closed his eyes with a shudder. He did not understand all of the words; they were in a jargon of gipsy tongue. But he knew enough to horrify him.

Then the old man ceased gloating. He fell back, glowering at Stragella. And the girl laughed, a mad, cackling, triumphant laugh of possession. She leaned forward, and the movement brought her out of the line of the lamplight, so that the feeble glow fell full over Yancy's prostrate body.

At that, with an angry snarl, she recoiled. Her eyes went wide with abhorrence. Upon his chest gleamed the Crucifix—the tattooed Cross and Savior which had been indelibly printed there. Stragella held her face away, shielding her eyes. She cursed him horribly. Backing away, she seized the arms of her companions and pointed with trembling finger to the thing which had repulsed her.

The fog seemed to seep deeper and deeper into the cabin during the ensuing silence. Yancy struggled to a sitting posture and cringed back against the wall, waiting for them to attack him. It would be finished in a moment, he knew. Then he would join Miggs, with those awful marks on his throat and Stragella's lips crimson with his sucked blood.

But they held their distance. The fog enveloped them, made them almost indistinct. He could see only three pairs of glaring, staring, phosphorescent eyes that grew larger and wider and more intensely terrible.

He buried his face in his hands, waiting. They did not come. He heard them mumbling, whispering. Vaguely he was conscious of another sound, far off and barely audible. The howl of wolves.

Beneath him the bunk was swaying from side to side with the movement of the ship. The *Golconda* was drifting swiftly. A storm had risen out of nowhere, and the wind was singing its dead dirge in the rotten spars high above decks. He could hear it moaning, wheezing, like a human being in torment.

Then the three pairs of glittering orbs moved nearer. The whispered voices ceased, and a cunning smile passed over Stragella's features. Yancy screamed, and flattened against the wall. He watched her in fascination as she crept upon him. One arm was flung across her eyes to protect them from the sight of the Crucifix. In the other hand, outstretched, groping ever nearer, she clutched that hellish chunk of pitch-like substance with which she had encircled the Bible!

He knew what she would do. The thought struck him like an icy blast, full of fear and madness. She would slink closer, closer, until her hand touched his flesh. Then she would place the black substance around the tattooed cross and kill its powers. His defense would be gone. Then—those cruel lips on his throat . . .

There was no avenue of escape. Papa Bocito and the plump old woman, grinning malignantly, had slid to one side, between him and the doorway. And Stragella writhed forward with one alabaster arm feeling . . . feeling. . . .

He was conscious of the roar of surf, very close, very loud, outside the walls of the fog-filled enclosure. The ship was lurching, reeling heavily, pitching in the swell. Hours must have passed. Hours and hours of darkness and horror.

Then she touched him. The sticky stuff was hot on his chest, moving in a slow circle. He hurled himself back, stumbled, went down, and she fell upon him.

Under his tormented body the floor of the cabin split asunder. The ship buckled from top to bottom with a grinding, roaring impact. A terrific shock burst through the ancient hulk, shattering its rotted timbers.

The lamp caromed off the table, plunging the cabin in semidarkness. Through the port-holes filtered a gray glare. Stragella's face, thrust into Yancy's, became a mask of beautiful fury. She whirled back. She stood rigid, screaming lividly to Papa Bocito and the old hag.

"Go back! Go back!" she railed. "We have waited too long! It is dawn!"

She ran across the floor, grappling with them. Her lips were distorted. Her body trembled. She hurled her companions to the door. Then, as she followed them into the gloom of the passage, she turned upon Yancy with a last unholy snarl of defeated rage. And she was gone.

Yancy lay limp. When he struggled to his feet at last and went on deck, the sun was high in the sky, bloated and crimson, struggling to penetrate the cone of fog which swirled about the ship.

The ship lay far over, careened on her side. A hundred yards distant over the port rail lay the heaven-sent sight of land—a bleak, vacant expanse of jungle-rimmed shore line.

He went deliberately to work—a task that had to be finished quickly, lest he be discovered by the inhabitants of the shore and be considered stark mad. Returning to the cabin, he took the oil lamp and carried it to the open hold. There, sprinkling the liquid over the ancient wood, he set fire to it.

Turning, he stepped to the rail. A scream of agony, unearthly and prolonged, rose up behind him. Then he was over the rail, battling in the surf.

When he staggered up on the beach, twenty minutes later, the *Golconda* was a roaring furnace. On all sides of her the flames snarled skyward, spewing through that hellish cone of vapor. Grimly Yancy turned away and trudged along the beach.

He looked back after an hour of steady plodding. The

lagoon was empty. The fog had vanished. The sun gleamed down with warm brilliance on a broad, empty expanse of sea.

Hours later he reached a settlement. Men came and talked to him, and asked curious questions. They pointed to his hair which was stark white. They told him he had reached Port Blair, on the southern island of the Andamans. After that, noticing the peculiar gleam of his blood-shot eyes, they took him to the home of the governor.

There he told his story—told hesitantly, because he expected to be disbelieved, mocked.

The governor looked at him cryptically.

"You don't expect me to understand?" the governor said. "I am not so sure, sir. This is a penal colony, a prison isle. During the past few years, more than two hundred of our convicts have died in the most curious way. Two tiny punctures in the throat. Loss of blood."

"You—you must destroy the graves," Yancy muttered.

The governor nodded silently, significantly.

After that, Yancy returned to the world, alone. Always alone. Men peered into his face and shrank away from the haunted stare of his eyes. They saw the Crucifix upon his chest and wondered why, day and night, he wore his shirt flapping open, so that the brilliant design glared forth.

But their curiosity was never appeased. Only Yancy knew; and Yancy was silent.

POPSY

◆◆◆

STEPHEN KING

Sheridan was cruising slowly down the long blank length of the shopping mall when he saw the little kid push out through the main doors under the lighted sign which read COUSINTOWN. It was a boy-child, perhaps a big three and surely no more than five. On his face was an expression to which Sheridan had become exquisitely attuned. He was trying not to cry but soon would.

Sheridan paused for a moment, feeling the familiar soft wave of self-disgust . . . though every time he took a child, that feeling grew a little less urgent. The first time he hadn't slept for a week. He kept thinking about that big greasy Turk who called himself Mr. Wizard, kept wondering what he did with the children.

"They go on a boat ride, Mr. Sheridan," the Turk told him, only it came out *Dey goo on a botrahd, Messtair Shurdunn.* The Turk smiled. *And if you know what's good for you, you won't ask any more about it,* that smile said, and it said it loud and clear, without an accent.

Sheridan *hadn't* asked anymore, but that didn't mean he hadn't kept wondering. Especially afterward. Tossing and turning, wishing he had the whole thing to do over again so he could turn it around, so he could walk away from temptation. The second time had been almost as bad . . . the third time a little less . . . and by the fourth time he had almost stopped wondering about the botrahd, and what might be at the end of it for the little kids.

Sheridan pulled his van into one of the handicap parking spaces right in front of the mall. He had one of the special license plates the state gave to crips on the back of his van. That plate was worth its weight in gold, because it kept any mall security cop from getting suspicious, and those spaces were so convenient and almost always empty.

You always pretend you're not going out looking, but you always lift a crip plate a day or two before.

Never mind all that bullshit; he was in a jam and that kid over there could solve some very big problems.

He got out and walked toward the kid, who was looking around with increasing panic. Yes, Sheridan thought, he was five all right, maybe even six—just very frail. In the harsh fluorescent glare thrown through the glass doors the boy looked parchment-white, not just scared but perhaps physically ill. Sheridan reckoned it was just big fear, however. Sheridan usually recognized that look when he saw it, because he'd seen a lot of big fear in his own mirror over the last year and a half or so.

The kid looked up hopefully at the people passing around him, people going into the mall eager to buy, coming out laden with packages, their faces dazed, almost drugged, with something they probably thought was satisfaction.

The kid, dressed in Tuffskin jeans and a Pittsburgh Penguins tee-shirt, looked for help, looked for somebody to look at him and see something was wrong, looked for someone to ask the right question—*You get separated from your dad, son?* would do—looking for a friend.

Here I am, Sheridan thought, approaching. *Here I am, sonny—I'll be your friend.*

He had almost reached the kid when he saw a mall rent-a-cop ambling slowly up the concourse toward the doors. He was reaching in his pocket, probably for a pack of cigarettes. He would come out, see the boy, and, there would go Sheridan's sure thing.

Shit, he thought, but at least he wouldn't be seen talking to the kid when the cop came out. That would have been worse.

Sheridan drew back a little and made a business of feeling in his own pockets, as if to make sure he still had his keys. His glance flicked from the boy to the security cop and back to the boy. The boy had started to cry. Not all-out bawling, not yet, but great big tears that looked pinkish in the reflected glow of the red COUSINTOWN sign as they tracked down his smooth cheeks.

The girl in the information booth flagged down the cop and said something to him. She was pretty, dark-haired, about twenty-five; he was sandy-blond with a moustache. As the cop leaned on his elbows, smiling at her, Sheridan thought they looked like the cigarette ads you saw on the backs of magazines. Salem Spirit. Light My Lucky. He was dying out here and they were in there making chit-chat—whatcha doin after work, ya wanna go and get a drink at that new place, and blah-blah-blah. Now she was also batting her eyes at him. How cute.

Sheridan abruptly decided to take the chance. The kid's chest was hitching, and as soon as he started to bawl out loud, someone would notice him. Sheridan didn't like moving in with a cop less than sixty feet away, but if he didn't cover his markers at Mr. Reggie's within the next twenty-four hours, he thought a couple of very large men would pay him a visit and perform impromptu surgery on his arms, adding several elbow-bends to each.

He walked up to the kid, a big man dressed in an ordinary Van Heusen shirt and khaki pants, a man with a broad, ordinary face that looked kind at first glance. He bent over the little boy, hands on his legs just above the knees, and the boy turned his pale, scared face up to Sheridan's. His eyes were as green as emeralds, their color accentuated by the light-reflecting tears that washed them.

"You get separated from your dad, son?" Sheridan asked.

"My *Popsy*," the kid said, wiping his eyes. "I . . . I can't find my P-P-Popsy!"

Now the kid *did* begin to sob, and a woman headed in glanced around with some vague concern.

"It's all right," Sheridan said to her, and she went on. Sheridan put a comforting arm around the boy's shoulders and drew him a little to the right . . . in the direction of the van. Then he looked back inside.

The rent-a-cop had his face right down next to the information girl's now. Looked like maybe more than that little girl's Lucky was going to get lit tonight. Sheridan relaxed. At this point there could be a stick-up going on at the bank just up the concourse and the cop wouldn't notice a thing. This was starting to look like a cinch.

"I want my Popsy!" the boy wept.

"Sure you do, of course you do," Sheridan said. "And we're going to find him. Don't you worry."

He drew him a little more to the right.

The boy looked up at him, suddenly hopeful.

"Can you? Can you, mister?"

"Sure!" Sheridan said, and grinned heartily. "Finding lost Popsys . . . well, you might say it's kind of a specialty of mine."

"It is?" The kid actually smiled a little, although his eyes were still leaking.

"It sure is," Sheridan said, glancing inside again to

make sure the cop, whom he could now barely see (and who would barely be able to see Sheridan and the boy, should he happen to look up), was still enthralled. He was. "What was your Popsy wearing, son?"

"He was wearing his suit," the boy said. "He almost always wears his suit. I only saw him once in jeans." He spoke as if Sheridan should know all these things about his Popsy.

"I bet it was a black suit," Sheridan said.

The boy's eyes lit up. "You *saw* him! Where?"

He started eagerly back toward the doors, tears forgotten, and Sheridan had to restrain himself from grabbing the pale-faced little brat right then and there. That type of thing was no good. Couldn't cause a scene. Couldn't do anything people would remember later. Had to get him in the van. The van had sun-filter glass everywhere except in the windshield; it was almost impossible to see inside unless you had your face smashed right up against it.

Had to get him in the van first.

He touched the boy on the arm. "I didn't see him inside, son. I saw him right over there."

He pointed across the huge parking lot with its endless platoons of cars. There was an access road at the far end of it, and beyond that were the double yellow arches of McDonald's.

"Why would Popsy go over *there?*" the boy asked, as if either Sheridan or Popsy—or maybe both of them—had gone utterly mad.

"I don't know," Sheridan said. His mind was working fast, clicking along like an express train as it always did when it got right down to the point where you had to stop shitting and either do it up right or fuck it up righteously. Popsy. Not Dad or Daddy but Popsy. The kid had corrected him on it. Maybe Popsy meant Granddad,

Sheridan decided. "But I'm pretty sure that was him. Older guy in a black suit. White hair . . . green tie . . ."

"Popsy had his blue tie on," the boy said. "He knows I like it the best."

"Yeah, it could have been blue," Sheridan said. "Under these lights, who can tell? Come on, hop in the van, I'll run you over there to him."

"Are you *sure* it was Popsy? Because I don't know why he'd go to a place where they—"

Sheridan shrugged. "Look, kid, if you're sure that wasn't him, maybe you better look for him on your own. You might even find him." And he started brusquely away, heading back toward the van.

The kid wasn't biting. He thought about going back, trying again, but it had already gone on too long—you either kept observable contact to a minimum or you were asking for twenty years in Hammerton Bay. He'd better go on to another mall. Scoterville, maybe. Or—

"Wait, mister!" It was the kid, with panic in his voice. There was the light thud of running sneakers. "Wait up! I told him I was thirsty, he must have thought he had to go way over there to get me a drink. Wait!"

Sheridan turned around, smiling. "I wasn't really going to leave you anyway, son."

He led the boy to the van, which was four years old and painted a nondescript blue. He opened the door and smiled at the kid, who looked up at him doubtfully, his green eyes swimming in that pallid little face, as huge as the eyes of a waif in a velvet painting, the kind advertised in the cheap weekly tabloids like *The National Enquirer* and *Inside View*.

"Step into my parlor, little buddy," Sheridan said, and produced a grin which looked almost entirely natural. It was really sort of creepy, how good he'd gotten at this.

The kid did, and although he didn't know it, his ass belonged to Briggs Sheridan the minute the passenger door swung shut.

There was only one problem in his life. It wasn't broads, although he liked to hear the swish of a skirt or feel the smooth smoke of silken hose as well as any man, and it wasn't booze, although he had been known to take a drink or three of an evening. Sheridan's problem—his fatal flaw, you might even say—was cards. Any kind of cards, as long as it was the kind of game where wagers were allowed. He had lost jobs, credit cards, the home his mother had left him. He had never, at least so far, been in jail, but the first time he got in trouble with Mr. Reggie, he'd thought jail would be a rest-cure by comparison.

He had gone a little crazy that night. It was better, he had found, when you lost right away. When you lost right away you got discouraged, went home, watched Letterman on the tube, and then went to sleep. When you won a little bit at first, you chased. Sheridan had chased that night and had ended up owing seventeen thousand dollars. He could hardly believe it; he went home dazed, almost elated, by the enormity of it. He kept telling himself in the car on the way home that he owed Mr. Reggie not seven hundred, not seven *thousand*, but *seventeen thousand* iron men. Every time he tried to think about it he giggled and turned up the volume on the radio.

But he wasn't giggling the next night when the two gorillas—the ones who would make sure his arms bent in all sorts of new and interesting ways if he didn't pay up—brought him into Mr. Reggie's office.

"I'll pay," Sheridan began babbling at once. "I'll pay,

listen, it's no problem, couple of days, a week at the most, two weeks at the outside—"

"You bore me, Sheridan," Mr. Reggie said.

"I—"

"Shut up. If I give you a week, don't you think I know what you'll do? You'll tap a friend for a couple of hundred if you've got a friend left to tap. If you can't find a friend, you'll hit a liquor store . . . if you've got the guts. I doubt if you do, but anything is possible." Mr. Reggie leaned forward, propped his chin on his hands, and smiled. He smelled of Ted Lapidus cologne. "And if you do come up with two hundred dollars, what will you do with it?"

"Give it to you," Sheridan had babbled. By then he was very close to tears. "I'll give it to you, right away!"

"No you won't," Mr. Reggie said. "You'll take it to the track and try to make it grow. What you'll give me is a bunch of shiny excuses. You're in over your head this time, my friend. Way over your head."

Sheridan could hold back the tears no longer; he began to blubber.

"These guys could put you in the hospital for a long time," Mr. Reggie said reflectively. "You would have a tube in each arm and another one coming out of your nose."

Sheridan began to blubber louder.

"I'll give you this much," Mr. Reggie said, and pushed a folded sheet of paper across his desk to Sheridan. "You might get along with this guy. He calls himself Mr. Wizard, but he's a shitbag just like you. Now get out of here. I'm gonna have you back in here in a week, though, and I'll have your markers on this desk. You either buy them back or I'm going to have my friends tool up on you. And like Booker T. says, once they start, they do it until they're satisfied."

The Turk's real name was written on the folded sheet of paper. Sheridan went to see him, and heard about the kids and the botrahds. Mr. Wizard also named a figure which was a fairish bit larger than the markers Mr. Reggie was holding. That was when Sheridan started cruising the malls.

He pulled out of the Cousintown Mall's main parking lot, looked for traffic, then drove across the access road and into the McDonald's in-lane. The kid was sitting all the way forward on the passenger seat, hands on the knees of his Tuffskins, eyes agonizingly alert. Sheridan drove toward the building, swung wide to avoid the drive-thru lane, and kept on going.

"Why are you going around the back?" the kid asked.

"You have to go around to the other doors," Sheridan said. "Keep your shirt on, kid. I think I saw him in there."

"You did? You really did?"

"I'm pretty sure, yeah."

Sublime relief washed over the kid's face, and for a moment Sheridan felt sorry for him—hell, he wasn't a monster or a maniac, for Christ's sake. But his markers had gotten a little deeper each time, and that bastard Mr. Reggie had no compunctions at all about letting him hang himself. It wasn't seventeen thousand this time, or twenty thousand, or even twenty-five thousand. This time it was thirty-five grand, a whole damn marching battalion of iron men, if he didn't want a few new sets of elbows by next Saturday.

He stopped in the back by the trash-compactor. Nobody was parked back here. Good. There was an elasticized pouch on the side of the door for maps and things. Sheridan reached into it with his left hand and brought out a pair of blued-steel Kreig handcuffs. The loop-jaws were open.

"Why are we stopping here, mister?" the kid asked. The fear was back in his voice, but the quality of it had changed; he had suddenly realized that maybe getting separated from good old Popsy in the busy mall wasn't the worst thing that could happen to him, after all.

"We're not, not really," Sheridan said easily. He had learned the second time he'd done this that you didn't want to underestimate even a six-year-old once he had his wind up. The second kid had kicked him in the balls and had damn near gotten away. "I just remembered I forgot to put my glasses on when I started driving. I could lose my license. They're in that glasses-case on the floor there. They slid over to your side. Hand 'em to me, would you?"

The kid bent over to get the glasses-case, which was empty. Sheridan leaned over and snapped one of the cuffs on the kid's reaching hand as neat as you please. And then the trouble started. Hadn't he just been thinking it was a bad mistake to underestimate even a six-year-old? The brat fought like a timberwolf pup, twisting with a powerful muscularity Sheridan would not have credited had he not been experiencing it. He bucked and fought and lunged for the door, panting and uttering weird birdlike cries. He got the handle. The door swung open, but no domelight came on—Sheridan had broken it after that second outing.

Sheridan got the kid by the round collar of his Penguins tee-shirt and hauled him back in. He tried to clamp the other cuff on the special strut beside the passenger seat and missed. The kid bit his hand twice, bringing blood. God, his teeth were like razors. The pain went deep and sent a steely ache all the way up his arm. He punched the kid in the mouth. The kid fell back into the seat, dazed, Sheridan's blood on his lips and chin and dripping onto the ribbed neck of the tee-shirt. Sheridan locked the other cuff on to the strut and then fell back into his own seat, sucking the back of his right hand.

The pain was really bad. He pulled his hand away from his mouth and looked at it in the weak glow of the dash-lights. Two shallow, ragged tears, each maybe two inches long, ran up toward his wrist from just above the knuckles. Blood pulsed in weak little rills. Still, he felt no urge to pop the kid again, and that had nothing to do with damaging the Turk's merchandise, in spite of the almost fussy way the Turk had warned him against that—*demmege the goots end you demmege the velue,* the Turk had said in his greasy accent.

No, he didn't blame the kid for fighting—he would have done the same. He would have to disinfect the wound as soon as he could, though, might even have to have a shot; he had read somewhere that human bites were the worst kind. Still, he couldn't help but admire the kid's guts.

He dropped the transmission into drive and pulled around the hamburger stand, past the drive-thru window, and back onto the access road. He turned left. The Turk had a big ranch-style house in Taluda Heights, on the edge of the city. Sheridan would go there by secondary roads, just to be safe. Thirty miles. Maybe forty-five minutes, maybe an hour.

He passed a sign which read THANK YOU FOR SHOPPING THE BEAUTIFUL COUSINTOWN MALL, turned left, and let the van creep up to a perfectly legal forty miles an hour. He fished a handkerchief out of his back pocket, folded it over the back of his right hand, and concentrated on following his headlights to the forty grand the Turk had promised for a boy-child.

. . .

"You'll be sorry," the kid said.

Sheridan looked impatiently around at him, pulled from a dream in which he had just won twenty straight hands and had Mr. Reggie grovelling at *his* feet for a change, sweating bullets and begging him to stop, what did he want to do, break him?

The kid was crying again, and his tears still had that odd pinkish cast, even though they were now well away from the bright lights of the mall. Sheridan wondered for the first time if the kid might have some sort of communicable disease. He supposed it was a little late to start worrying about such things, so he put it out of his mind.

"When my *Popsy* finds you you'll be sorry," the kid elaborated.

"Yeah," Sheridan said, and lit a cigarette. He turned off State Road 28 and onto an unmarked stretch of two-lane blacktop. There was a long marshy area on the left, unbroken woods on the right.

The kid pulled at the handcuffs and made a sobbing noise.

"Quit it. Won't do you any good."

Nevertheless, the kid pulled again. And this time there was a groaning, protesting sound Sheridan didn't like at *all.* He looked around and was amazed to see that the metal strut on the side of the seat—a strut he had welded in place himself—was twisted out of shape. *Shit!* he thought. *He's got teeth like razors and now I find out he's also strong as a fucking ox. If this is what he's like when he's sick, God forbid I should have grabbed him on a day when he was feeling well.*

He pulled over onto the soft shoulder and said, "Stop it!"

"I *won't!*"

The kid yanked at the handcuff again, and Sheridan saw the metal strut bend a little more. Christ, how could *any* kid do that?

It's panic, he answered himself. *That's how he can do it.*

But none of the others had been able to do it, and many of them had been a lot more terrified than this kid by this stage of the game.

He opened the glove compartment in the center of the dash. He brought out a hypodermic needle. The Turk had given it to him, and cautioned him not to use it unless he absolutely had to. Drugs, the Turk said (pronouncing it *drocks*), could *demmege* the merchandise.

"See this?"

The kid gave the hypo a glimmering sideways glance and nodded.

"You want me to use it?"

The kid shook his head at once. Strong or not, he had any kid's instant terror of the needle, Sheridan was happy to see.

"That's very smart. It would put out your lights." He paused. He didn't want to say it—hell, he was a nice guy, really, when he didn't have his ass in a sling—but he had to. "Might even kill you."

The kid stared at him, lips trembling, cheeks papery with fear.

"You stop yanking the cuff, I put away the needle. Deal?"

"Deal," the kid whispered.

"You promise?"

"Yes." The kid lifted his lip, showing white teeth. One of them was spotted with Sheridan's blood.

"You promise on your mother's name?"

"I never had a mother."

"Shit," Sheridan said, disgusted, and got the van rolling

again. He moved a little faster now, and not only because he was finally off the main road. The kid was a spook. Sheridan wanted to turn him over to the Turk, get his money, and split.

"My Popsy's really strong, mister."

"Yeah?" Sheridan asked and thought: *I bet he is, kid. Only guy in the old folks' home who can bench-press his own truss, right?*

"He'll find me."

"Uh-huh."

"He can smell me."

Sheridan believed it. *He* could smell the kid. That fear had an odor was something he had learned on his previous expeditions, but this was unreal—the kid smelled like a mixture of sweat, mud, and slowly cooking battery acid. Sheridan was becoming more and more sure that something was seriously wrong with the kid . . . but soon that would be Mr. Wizard's problem, not his, and *caveat emptor*, as those old fellows in the togas used to say, *caveat* fucking *emptor.*

Sheridan cracked his window. On the left, the marsh went on and on. Broken slivers of moonlight glimmered in the stagnant water.

"Popsy can fly."

"Yeah," Sheridan said, "after a couple of bottles of Night Train, I bet he flies like a sonofabitchin eagle."

"Popsy—"

"Enough of the Popsy shit, kid—okay?"

The kid shut up.

Four miles farther on, the marsh on the left broadened into a wide empty pond. Sheridan made a turn onto a stretch of hardpan dirt that skirted the pond's north side.

Five miles west of here he would turn right onto Highway 41, and from there it would be a straight shot into Taluda Heights.

He glanced toward the pond, a flat silver sheet in the moonlight . . . and then the moonlight was gone. Blotted out.

Overhead there was a flapping sound like big sheets on a clothesline.

"Popsy!" the kid cried.

"Shut up. It was only a bird."

But suddenly he was spooked, very spooked. He looked at the kid. The kid's lip was drawn back from his teeth again. His teeth were very white, very big.

No . . . not big. Big wasn't the right word. *Long* was the right word. Especially the two at the top at each side. The . . . what did you call them? The canines.

His mind suddenly started to fly again, clicking along as if he were on speed.

I told him I was thirsty.

Why would Popsy go to a place where they—

(?eat was he going to say eat?)

He'll find me.

He can smell me.

Popsy can fly.

Something landed on the roof of the van with a heavy clumsy thump.

"Popsy!" the kid screamed again, almost delirious with delight, and suddenly Sheridan could not see the road anymore—a huge membranous wing, pulsing with veins, covered the windshield from side to side.

Popsy can fly.

Sheridan screamed and jumped on the brake, hoping to tumble the thing on the roof off the front. There was that groaning, protesting sound of metal under stress from his right again, this time followed by a short bitter snap. A moment later the kid's fingers were clawing into his face, pulling open his cheek.

"He stole me, Popsy!" the kid was screeching at the roof of the van in that birdlike voice. *"He stole me, he stole me, the bad man stole me!"*

You don't understand, kid, Sheridan thought. He groped for the hypo and found it. *I'm not a bad guy, I just got in a jam.*

Then a hand, more like a talon than a real hand, smashed through the side window and ripped the hypo from Sheridan's grasp—along with two of his fingers. A moment later Popsy peeled the entire driver's-side door out of its frame, the hinges now bright twists of meaningless metal. Sheridan saw a billowing cape, black on the outside, lined with red silk on the inside, and the creature's tie . . . and although it was actually a cravat, it was blue all right—just as the boy had said.

Popsy yanked Sheridan out of the car, talons sinking through his jacket and shirt and deep into the meat of his shoulders; Popsy's green eyes suddenly turned as red as blood-roses.

"We came to the mall because my grandson wanted some Ninja Turtle figures," Popsy whispered, and his breath was like flyblown meat. "The ones they show on TV. All the children want them. You should have left him alone. You should have left *us* alone."

Sheridan was shaken like a rag doll. He shrieked and was shaken again. He heard Popsy asking solicitously if the kid was still thirsty; heard the kid saying yes, very, the bad man had scared him and his throat was *so* dry. He saw Popsy's thumbnail for just a second before it disappeared under the shelf of his chin, the nail ragged and thick. His throat was cut with that nail before he realized what was happening, and the last things he saw before his sight dimmed to black were the kid, cupping his hands to catch the flow the way Sheridan himself had cupped his hands under the backyard faucet for a drink on a hot summer day when he was a kid, and Popsy, stroking the boy's hair gently, with grandfatherly love.

BLOOD

◆◆◆

FREDRIC BROWN

In their time machine, Vron and Dreena, last two survivors of the race of vampires, fled into the future to escape annihilation. They held hands and consoled one another in their terror and their hunger.

In the twenty-second century mankind had found them out, had discovered that the legend of vampires living secretly among humans was not a legend at all, but fact. There had been a pogrom that had found and killed every vampire but these two, who had already been working on a time machine and who had finished in time to escape in it. Into the future, far enough into the future that the very word *vampire* would be forgotten so they could again live unsuspected—and from their loins regenerate their race.

"I'm hungry, Vron. Awfully hungry."

"I too, Dreena dear. We'll stop again soon."

They had stopped four times already and had narrowly escaped dying each time. They had *not* been forgotten. The last stop, half a million years back, had shown them a world gone to the dogs—quite literally: human beings were extinct and dogs had become civilized and manlike. Still they had been recognized for what they were. They'd managed to feed once, on the blood of a tender young bitch, but then they'd been hounded back to their time machine and into flight again.

"Thanks for stopping," Dreena said. She sighed.

"Don't thank me," said Vron grimly. "This is the end of the line. We're out of fuel and we'll find none here—by now all radioactives will have turned to lead. We live here—or else."

They went out to scout. "Look," said Dreena excitedly, pointing to something walking toward them. "A new creature! The dogs are gone and something else has taken over. And surely we're forgotten."

The approaching creature was telepathic. "I have heard your thoughts," said a voice inside their brains. "You wonder whether we know 'vampires,' whatever they are. We do not."

Dreena clutched Vron's arm in ecstasy. "Freedom!" she murmured hungrily. "And *food*!"

"You also wonder," said the voice, "about my origin and evolution. All life today is vegetable. I—" He bowed low to them. "I, a member of the dominant race, was once what you called a turnip."

REVELATIONS IN BLACK

◆◆◆

CARL JACOBI

It was a dreary, forlorn establishment way down on Harbor Street. An old sign announced the legend: "Giovanni Larla—Antiques," and a dingy window revealed a display half masked in dust.

Even as I crossed the threshold that cheerless September afternoon, driven from the sidewalk by a gust of rain and perhaps a fascination for all antiques, the gloominess fell upon me like a material pall. Inside was half darkness, piled boxes and a monstrous tapestry, frayed with the warp showing in worn places. An Italian Renaissance wine cabinet shrank despondently in its corner and seemed to frown at me as I passed.

"Good afternoon, *Signor.* There is something you wish to buy? A picture, a ring, a vase perhaps?"

I peered at the squat, pudgy bulk of the Italian proprietor there in the shadows and hesitated.

"Just looking around," I said, turning my eyes to the jumble about me. "Nothing in particular . . ."

The man's oily face moved in a smile as though he had heard the remark a thousand times before. He sighed, stood there in thought a moment, the rain drumming and swishing against the outer pane. Then very deliberately he stepped to the shelves and glanced up and down them, considering. I moved to his side, letting my eyes sweep across the stacked array of ancient oddities. At length he drew forth an object which I perceived to be a painted chalice.

"An authentic sixteenth-century Tandart," he murmured. "A work of art, *Signor.*"

I shook my head. "No pottery," I said. "Books perhaps, but no pottery."

He frowned slowly. "I have books too," he replied, "rare books which nobody sells but me, Giovanni Larla. But you must look at my other treasures too."

There was, I found, no hurrying the man. A quarter of an hour passed, during which I had to see a Glycon cameo brooch, a carved chair of some indeterminate style and period, and a muddle of yellowed statuettes, small oils, and one or two dreary Portland vases. Several times I glanced at my watch impatiently, wondering how I might break away from this Italian and his gloomy shop. Already the fascination of its dust and shadows had begun to wear off, and I was anxious to reach the street.

But when he had conducted me well towards the rear of the shop, something caught my fancy. I drew then from the shelf the first book of horror. If I had but known the terrible events that were to follow, if I could only have had a foresight into the future that September day, I swear I would have avoided the book like a leprous thing, would have shunned that wretched antique store and the very street it stood on like places accursed. A thousand times I have wished my eyes had never rested on that cover in black. What writhings of the soul, what terrors, what unrest, what madness would have been spared me!

But never dreaming the hideous secret of its pages I fondled it casually and remarked:

"An unusual book. What is it?"

Larla glanced up and scowled.

"That is not for sale," he said quietly. "I don't know how it got on these shelves. It was my poor brother's."

The volume in my hand was indeed unusual in appearance. Measuring but four inches across and five inches in length and bound in black velvet with each outside corner protected with a triangle of ivory, it was the most beautiful piece of bookbinding I had ever seen. In the centre of the cover was mounted a tiny piece of ivory intricately cut in the shape of a skull. But it was the title of the book that excited my interest. Embroidered in gold braid, the title read:

"*Five Unicorns and a Pearl.*"

I looked at Larla. "How much?" I asked and reached for my wallet.

He shook his head. "No, it is not for sale. It is . . . it is the last work of my brother. He wrote it just before he died in the institution."

"The institution?" I queried.

Larla made no reply but stood staring at the book, his mind obviously drifting away in deep thought. A moment of silence dragged by. There was a strange gleam in his eyes when finally he spoke. And I thought I saw his fingers tremble slightly.

"My brother, Alessandro, was a fine man before he wrote that book," he said slowly. "He wrote beautifully, *Signor,* and he was strong and healthy. For hours I could sit while he read to me his poems. He was a dreamer, Alessandro; he loved everything beautiful, and the two of us were very happy.

"All . . . until that terrible night. Then he . . . but no . . . a year has passed now. It is best to forget." He passed his hand before his eyes and drew in his breath sharply.

"What happened?" I asked sympathetically, his words arousing my curiosity.

"Happened, *Signor*? I do not really know. It was all so confusing. He became suddenly ill, ill without reason. The flush of sunny Italy, which was always on his cheek, faded, and he grew white and drawn. His strength left him day by day. Doctors prescribed, gave medicines, but nothing helped. He grew steadily weaker until . . . until that night."

I looked at him curiously, impressed by his perturbation.

"And then?" I urged.

Hands opening and closing, Larla seemed to sway unsteadily; his liquid eyes opened wide to the brows, and his voice was strained and tense as he continued:

"And then . . . oh, if I could but forget! It was horrible. Poor Alessandro came home screaming, sobbing, tearing his hair. He was . . . he was stark, raving mad!

"They took him to the institution for the insane and said he needed a complete rest, that he had suffered from some terrific mental shock. He . . . died three weeks later with the crucifix on his lips."

For a moment I stood there in silence, staring out at the falling rain. Then I said:

"He wrote this book while confined to the institution?"

Larla nodded absently.

"Three books," he replied. "Two others exactly like the one you have in your hand. The bindings he made, of course, when he was quite well. It was his original intention, I believe, to pen in them by hand the verses of Marini. He was very clever at such work. But the wanderings of his mind which filled the pages now, I have never read. Nor do I intend to. I want to keep with me the memory of him when he was happy. This book has come on these shelves by mistake. I shall put it with his other possessions."

My desire to read the few pages bound in velvet increased a thousandfold when I found they were unobtainable. I have always had an interest in abnormal psychology and have gone through a number of books on the subject. Here was the work of a man confined in the asylum for the insane. Here was the unexpurgated writing of an educated brain gone mad. And unless my intuition failed me, here was a suggestion of some deep mystery. My mind was made up. I must have it.

I turned to Larla and chose my words carefully.

"I can well appreciate your wish to keep the book," I said, "and since you refuse to sell, may I ask if you would consider lending it to me for just one night? If I promised to return it in the morning? . . ."

The Italian hesitated. He toyed undecidedly with a heavy gold watch chain.

"No, I am sorry. . ."

"Ten dollars and back tomorrow unharmed."

Larla studied his shoe.

"Very well, *Signor,* I will trust you. But please, I ask you, please be sure and return it."

That night in the quiet of my apartment I opened the book. Immediately my attention was drawn to three lines scrawled in a feminine hand across the inside of the front cover, lines written in a faded red solution that looked more like blood than ink. They read:

"Revelations meant to destroy but only binding without the stake. Read, fool, and enter my field, for we are chained to the spot. Oh, woe unto Larla!"

I mused over these undecipherable sentences for some

time without solving their meaning. At last, shrugging my shoulders, I turned to the first page and began the last work of Alessandro Larla, the strangest story I had ever, in my years of browsing through old books, come upon.

"On the evening of the fifteenth of October I turned my steps into the cold and walked until I was tired. The roar of the present was in the distance when I came to twenty-six blue-jays silently contemplating the ruins. Passing in the midst of them I wandered by the skeleton trees and seated myself where I could watch the leering fish. A child worshipped. Glass threw the moon at me. Grass sang a litany at my feet. And the pointed shadow moved slowly to the left.

"I walked along the silver gravel until I came to five unicorns galloping beside water of the past. Here I found a pearl, a magnificent pearl, a pearl beautiful but black. Like a flower it carried a rich perfume, and once I thought the odour was but a mask, but why should such a perfect creation need a mask?

"I sat between the leering fish and the five galloping unicorns, and I fell madly in love with the pearl. The past lost itself in drabness and—"

I laid the book down and sat watching the smoke-curls from my pipe eddy ceilingward. There was much more, but I could make no sense to any of it. All was in that strange style and completely incomprehensible. And yet it seemed the story was more than the mere wanderings of a madman. Behind it all seemed to lie a narrative cloaked in symbolism.

Something about the few sentences—just what I cannot say—had cast an immediate spell of depression over me. The vague lines weighed upon my mind, hung before my eyes like a design, and I felt myself slowly seized by a deep feeling of uneasiness.

The air of the room grew heavy and close. The open

casement and the out-of-doors seemed to beckon to me. I walked to the window, thrust the curtain aside, stood there, smoking furiously. Let me say that regular habits have long been a part of my make-up. I am not addicted to nocturnal strolls or late meanderings before seeking my bed; yet now, curiously enough, with the pages of the book still in my mind I suddenly experienced an indefinable urge to leave my apartment and walk the darkened streets.

I paced the room nervously, irritated that the sensation did not pass. The clock on the mantel pushed its ticks slowly through the quiet. And at length with a shrug I threw my pipe to the table, reached for my hat and coat and made for the door.

Ridiculous as it may sound, upon reaching the street I found that urge had increased to a distinct attraction: I felt that under no circumstances must I turn any direction but northward, and although this way led into a district quite unknown to me, I was in a moment pacing forward, choosing streets deliberately and heading without knowing why towards the outskirts of the city. It was a brilliant moonlight night in September. Summer had passed and already there was the smell of frosted vegetation in the air. The great chimes in Capitol tower were sounding midnight, and the buildings and shops and later the private houses were dark and silent as I passed.

Try as I would to erase from my memory the queer book which I had just read, the mystery of its pages hammered at me, arousing my curiosity, dampening my spirits. "Five Unicorns and a Pearl!" What did it all mean?

More and more I realized as I went on that a power other than my own will was leading my steps. It was absurd, and I tried to resist, to turn back. Yet once I did momentarily come to a halt that attraction swept upon me as inexorably as the desire for a narcotic.

It was far out on Easterly Street that I came upon a high stone wall flanking the sidewalk. Over its ornamented top I could see the shadows of a dark building set well back in the grounds. A wrought-iron gate in the wall opened upon a view of wild desertion and neglect. Swathed in the light of the moon, an old courtyard strewn with fountains, stone benches and statues lay tangled in rank weeds and undergrowth. The windows of the building, which evidently had once been a private dwelling, were boarded up, all except those on a little tower or cupola rising to a point in the front. And here the glass caught the blue-grey light and refracted it into the shadows.

Before that gate my feet stopped like dead things. The psychic power which had been leading me had now become a reality. Directly from the courtyard it emanated, drawing me towards it with an intensity that smothered all reluctance.

Strangely enough, the gate was unlocked; and feeling like a man in a trance I swung the creaking hinges and entered, making my way along a grass-grown path to one of the benches. It seemed that once inside the court the distant sounds of the city died away, leaving a hollow silence broken only by the wind rustling through the tall dead weeds. Rearing up before me, the building with its dark wings, cupola and façade oddly resembled a colossal hound, crouched and ready to spring.

There were several fountains, weather-beaten and ornamented with curious figures, to which at the time I paid only casual attention. Farther on, half hidden by the underbrush, was the life-size statue of a little child kneeling in position of prayer. Erosion on the soft stone had disfigured the face, and in the half-light the carved features presented an expression strangely grotesque and repelling.

How long I sat there in the quiet, I don't know. The surroundings under the moonlight blended harmoniously with my mood. But more than that I seemed physically unable to rouse myself and pass on.

It was with a suddenness that brought me electrified to my feet that I became aware of the real significance of the objects about me. Held motionless, I stood there running my eyes wildly from place to place, refusing to believe. Surely I must be dreaming. In the name of all that was unusual this . . . this absolutely couldn't be. And yet—

It was the fountain at my side that had caught my attention first. Across the top of the water basin were *five stone unicorns,* all identically carved, each seeming to follow the other in galloping procession. Looking farther, prompted now by a madly rising recollection, I saw that the cupola, towering high above the house, eclipsed the rays of the moon and threw *a long pointed shadow* across the ground *at my left.* The other fountain some distance away was ornamented with the figure of a stone fish, *a fish* whose empty eye-sockets *were leering* straight in my direction. And the climax of it all—the wall! At intervals of every three feet on top of the street expanse were mounted crude carven stone shapes of birds. And counting them I saw *that those birds were twenty-six blue-jays.*

Unquestionably—startling and impossible as it seemed—I was in the same setting as described in Larla's book! It was a staggering revelation, and my mind reeled at the thought of it. How strange, how odd that I should be drawn to a portion of the city I had never before frequented and thrown into the midst of a narrative written almost a year before!

I saw now that Alessandro Larla, writing as a patient in the institution for the insane, had seized isolated details but neglected to explain them. Here was a problem for the psychologist, the mad, the symbolic, the incredible story of the dead Italian. I was bewildered, confused, and I pondered for an answer.

As if to soothe my perturbation there stole into the court then a faint odour of perfume. Pleasantly it touched my nostrils, seemed to blend with the moonlight. I breathed it in deeply as I stood there by the curious fountain. But slowly that odour became more noticeable, grew stronger, a sickish sweet smell that began to creep down my lungs like smoke. And absently I recognized it. Heliotrope! The honeyed aroma blanketed the garden, thickened the air, seemed to fall upon me like a drug.

And then came my second surprise of the evening. Looking about to discover the source of the irritating fragrance I saw opposite me, seated on another stone bench, a woman. She was dressed entirely in black, and her face was hidden by a veil. She seemed unaware of my presence. Her head was slightly bowed, and her whole position suggested a person deep in contemplation.

I noticed also the thing that crouched by her side. It was a dog, a tremendous brute with a head strangely out of proportion and eyes as large as the ends of big spoons. For several moments I stood staring at the two of them. Although the air was quite chilly, the woman wore no over-jacket, only the black dress relieved solely by the whiteness of her throat.

With a sigh of regret at having my pleasant solitude thus disturbed I moved across the court until I stood at her side. Still she showed no recognition of my presence, and clearing my throat I said hesitatingly:

"I suppose you are the owner here. I . . . I really didn't know the place was occupied, and the gate . . . well, the gate was unlocked. I'm sorry I trespassed."

She made no reply to that, and the dog merely gazed at

me in dumb silence. No graceful words of polite departure came to my lips, and I moved hesitatingly towards the gate.

"Please don't go," she said suddenly, looking up. "I'm lonely. Oh, if you but knew how lonely I am!" She moved to one side of the bench and motioned that I sit beside her. The dog continued to examine me with its big eyes.

Whether it was the nearness of that odour of heliotrope, the suddenness of it all, or perhaps the moonlight, I did not know, but at her words a thrill of pleasure ran through me, and I accepted the proffered seat.

There followed an interval of silence, during which I puzzled my brain for a means to start conversation. But abruptly she turned to the beast and said in German:

"*Fort mit dir, Johann!*"

The dog rose obediently to its feet and stole slowly off into the shadows. I watched it for a moment until it disappeared in the direction of the house. Then the woman said to me in English, which was slightly stilted and marked with an accent:

"It has been ages since I have spoken to anyone . . . We are strangers. I do not know you, and you do not know me. Yet . . . strangers sometimes find in each other a bond of interest. Supposing . . . supposing we forget customs and formality of introduction? Shall we?"

For some reason I felt my pulse quicken as she said that. "Please do," I replied. "A spot like this is enough introduction in itself. Tell me, do you live here?"

She made no answer for a moment, and I began to fear I had taken her suggestion too quickly. Then she began slowly:

"My name is Perle von Mauren, and I am really a stranger to your country, though I have been here now more than a year. My home is in Austria near what is now the Czechoslovakian frontier. You see, it was to find my only brother that I came to the United States. During the war he was a lieutenant under General Makensen,* but in 1916, in April I believe it was, he . . . he was reported missing.

"War is a cruel thing. It took our money; it took our castle on the Danube, and then—my brother. Those following years were horrible. We lived always in doubt, hoping against hope that he was still living.

"Then after the Armistice a fellow officer claimed to have served next to him on grave-digging detail at a French prison camp near Monpré. And later came a thin rumour that he was in the United States. I gathered together as much money as I could and came here in search of him."

Her voice dwindled off, and she sat in silence staring at the brown weeds. When she resumed, her voice was low and wavering.

"I . . . found him . . . but would to God I hadn't! He . . . he was no longer living."

I stared at her. "Dead?" I asked.

The veil trembled as though moved by a shudder, as though her thoughts had exhumed some terrible event of the past. Unconscious of my interruption she went on:

"Tonight I came here—I don't know why—merely because the gate was unlocked, and there was a place of quiet within. Now have I bored you with my confidences and personal history?"

"Not at all," I replied. "I came here by chance myself. Probably the beauty of the place attracted me. I dabble in

*Properly Field-Marshal August von Makensen of the famous Death's Head Hussars in World War I. He served under the Kaiser and the Führer with distinction.

amateur photography occasionally and react strongly to unusual scenes. Tonight I went for a midnight stroll to relieve my mind from the bad effect of a book I was reading."

She made a strange reply to that, a reply away from our line of thought and which seemed an interjection that escaped her involuntarily.

"Books," she said, "are powerful things. They can fetter one more than the walls of a prison."

She caught my puzzled stare at the remark and added hastily: "It is odd that we should meet here."

For a moment I didn't answer. I was thinking of her heliotrope perfume, which for a woman of her apparent culture was applied in far too great a quantity to manifest good taste. The impression stole upon me that the perfume cloaked some secret, that if it were removed I should find . . . but what? It was ridiculous, and I tried to cast the feeling aside.

The hours passed, and still we sat there talking, enjoying each other's companionship. She did not remove her veil, and though I was burning with a desire to see her features, I had not dared ask her to. A strange nervousness had slowly seized me. The woman was a charming conversationalist, but there was about her an indefinable something which produced in me a distinct feeling of unease.

It was, I should judge, but a few moments before the first streaks of dawn when it happened. As I look back now, even with mundane objects and thoughts on every side, it is not difficult to realize the dire significance, the absolute baseness of that vision. But at the time my brain was too much in a whirl to understand.

A thin shadow moving across the garden attracted my gaze once again into the night about me. I looked up over the spire of the deserted house and started as if struck by a blow. For a moment I thought I had seen a curious cloud formation racing low directly above me, a cloud black and impenetrable with two winglike ends strangely in the shape of a monstrous flying bat.

I blinked my eyes hard and looked again.

"That cloud!" I exclaimed. "That strange cloud! . . . Did you see—"

I stopped and stared dumbly.

The bench at my side was empty. The woman had disappeared.

During the next day I went about my professional duties in the law office with only half interest, and my business partner looked at me queerly several times when he came upon me mumbling to myself. The incidents of the evening before were rushing through my mind in grand turmoil. Questions unanswerable hammered at me. That I should have come upon the very details described by mad Larla in his strange book: the leering fish, the praying child, the twenty-six blue-jays, the pointed shadow of the cupola—it was unexplainable; it was weird.

Five Unicorns and a Pearl. The unicorns were the stone statues ornamenting the old fountain, yes—but the pearl? With a start I suddenly recalled the name of the woman in black: *Perle* von Mauren. The revelation climaxed my train of thought. What did it all mean?

Dinner had little attraction for me that evening. Earlier I had gone to the antique-dealer and begged him to loan me the sequel, the second volume of his brother Alessandro. When he had refused, objected because I had not yet returned the first book, my nerves had suddenly jumped on edge. I felt like a narcotic fiend faced with the realization that he could not procure the desired drug. In desperation, yet hardly knowing why, I offered the man money, more money, until at length I had come away, my powers of persuasion and my pocket book successful.

The second volume was identical in outward respects to its predecessor except that it bore no title. But if I was expecting more disclosures in symbolism I was doomed to disappointment. Vague as *Five Unicorns and a Pearl* had been, the text of the sequel was even more wandering and was obviously only the ramblings of a mad brain. By watching the sentences closely I did gather that Alessandro Larla had made a second trip to his court of the twenty-six blue-jays and met there again his "pearl."

"Can it possibly be? I pray that it is not. And yet I have seen it and heard it snarl. Oh, the loathsome creature! I will not, I will not believe it."

I closed the book with a snap and tried to divert my attention elsewhere by polishing the lens of my newest portable camera. But again, as before, that same urge stole upon me, that same desire to visit the garden. I confess that I had watched the intervening hours until I would meet the woman in black again; for strangely enough, in spite of her abrupt exit before, I never doubted but that she would be there waiting for me. I wanted her to lift the veil. I wanted to talk with her. I wanted to throw myself once again into the narrative of Larla's book.

Yet the whole thing seemed preposterous, and I fought the sensation with every ounce of willpower I could call to mind. Then it suddenly occured to me what a remarkable picture she would make, sitting there on the stone bench, clothed in black, with the classic background of the old courtyard. If I could but catch the scene on a photographic plate . . .

I halted my polishing and mused a moment. With a new electric flash-lamp, that handy invention which has supplanted the old mussy flash-powder, I could illuminate the garden and snap the picture with ease. And if the result were satisfactory it would make a worthy contribution to the international Camera Contest at Geneva next month.

The idea appealed to me, and gathering together the necessary equipment I drew on an ulster (for it was a wet, chilly night) and slipped out of my rooms and headed northward. Mad, unseeing fool that I was! If only I had stopped then and there, returned the book to the antique dealer and closed the incident! But the strange magnetic attraction had gripped me in earnest, and I rushed headlong into the horror. A fall rain was drumming the pavement, and the streets were deserted. Off to the east, however, the heavy blanket of clouds glowed with a soft radiance where the moon was trying to break through, and a strong wind from the south gave promise of clearing the skies before long. With my collar turned well up at the throat I passed once again into the older section of the town and down forgotten Easterly Street. I found the gate to the grounds unlocked as before, and the garden a dripping place masked in shadow.

The woman was not there. Still the hour was early, and I did not for a moment doubt that she would appear later. Gripped now with the enthusiasm of my plan, I set the camera carefully on the stone fountain, training the lens as well as I could on the bench where we had sat the previous evening. The flash-lamp with its battery handle I laid within easy reach.

Scarcely had I finished my arrangements when the crunch of gravel on the path caused me to turn. She was approaching the stone bench, heavily veiled as before and with the same sweeping black dress.

"You have come again," she said as I took my place beside her.

"Yes," I replied. "I could not stay away."

Our conversation that night gradually centred about her dead brother, although I thought several times that the woman tried to avoid the subject. He had been, it seemed, the black sheep of the family, had led more or less of a dissolute life and had been expelled from the University of Vienna not only because of his lack of respect for the pedagogues of the various sciences but also because of his queer unorthodox papers on philosophy. His sufferings in the war prison camp must have been intense. With a kind of grim delight she dwelt on his horrible experiences in the grave-digging detail which had been related to her by the fellow officer. But of the manner in which he had met his death she would say absolutely nothing.

Stronger than on the night before was the sweet smell of heliotrope. And again as the fumes crept nauseatingly down my lungs there came that same sense of nervousness, that same feeling that the perfume was hiding something I should know. The desire to see beneath the veil had become maddening by this time, but still I lacked the boldness to ask her to lift it.

Towards midnight the heavens cleared and the moon in splendid contrast shone high in the sky. The time had come for my picture.

"Sit where you are," I said. "I'll be back in a moment."

Stepping quickly to the fountain I grasped the flashlamp, held it aloft for an instant and placed my finger on the shutter lever of the camera. The woman remained motionless on the bench, evidently puzzled as to the meaning of my movements. The range was perfect. A click, and a dazzling white light enveloped the courtyard about us. For a brief second she was outlined there against the old wall. Then the blue moonlight returned, and I was smiling in satisfaction.

"It ought to make a beautiful picture," I said.

She leaped to her feet.

"Fool!" she cried hoarsely. "Blundering fool! What have you done?"

Even though the veil was there to hide her face I got the instant impression that her eyes were glaring at me, smouldering with hatred. I gazed at her curiously as she stood erect, head thrown back, body apparently taut as wire, and a slow shudder crept down my spine. Then without warning she gathered up her dress and ran down the path towards the deserted house. A moment later she had disappeared somewhere in the shadows of the giant bushes.

I stood there by the fountain, staring after her in a daze. Suddenly, off in the umbra of the house's façade there rose a low animal snarl.

And then before I could move, a huge grey shape came hurtling through the long weeds, bounding in great leaps straight towards me. It was the woman's dog, which I had seen with her the night before. But no longer was it a beast passive and silent. Its face was contorted in diabolic fury, and its jaws were dripping slaver. Even in that moment of terror as I stood frozen before it, the sight of those white nostrils and those black hyalescent eyes emblazoned itself on my mind, never to be forgotten.

Then with a lunge it was upon me. I had only time to thrust the flash-lamp upward in half protection and throw my weight to the side. My arm jumped in recoil. The bulb exploded, and I could feel those teeth clamp down hard on the handle. Backwards I fell, a scream gurgling to my lips, a terrific heaviness surging upon my body.

I struck out frantically, beat my fists into that growling face. My fingers groped blindly for its throat, sank deep into the hairy flesh. I could feel its breath mingling with my own now, but desperately I hung on.

The pressure of my hands told. The dog coughed and fell back. And seizing that instant I struggled to my feet, jumped forward and planted a terrific kick straight into the brute's middle.

"*Fort mit dir, Johann!*" I cried, remembering the woman's German command.

It leaped back and, fangs bared, glared at me motionless for a moment. Then abruptly it turned and slunk off through the weeds.

Weak and trembling, I drew myself together, picked up my camera, and passed through the gate towards home.

Three days passed. Those endless hours I spent confined to my apartment suffering the tortures of the damned.

On the day following the night of my terrible experience with the dog I realized I was in no condition to go to work. I drank two cups of strong black coffee and then forced myself to sit quietly in a chair, hoping to soothe my nerves. But the sight of the camera there on the table excited me to action. Five minutes later I was in the dark room arranged as my studio, developing the picture I had taken the night before. I worked feverishly, urged on by the thought of what an unusual contribution it would make for the amateur contest next month at Geneva, should the result be successful.

An exclamation burst from my lips as I stared at the still-wet print. There was the old garden clear and sharp with the bushes, the statue of the child, the fountain and the wall in the background, but the bench—the stone bench was empty. There was no sign, not even a blur of the woman in black.

My brain in a whirl, I rushed the negative through a saturated solution of mercuric chloride in water, then treated it with ferrous oxalate. But even after this intensifying process the second print was like the first, focused in every detail, the bench standing in the foreground in sharp relief, but no trace of the woman.

I stared incredulously. She had been in plain view when I snapped the shutter. Of that I was positive. And my camera was in perfect condition. What then was wrong? Not until I had looked at the print hard in the daylight would I believe my eyes. No explanation offered itself, none at all; at length, confused unto weakness, I returned to my bed and fell into a heavy sleep.

Straight through the day I slept. Hours later I seemed to wake from a vague nightmare, and had not strength to rise from my pillow. A great physical faintness had overwhelmed me. My arms, my legs, lay like dead things. My heart was fluttering weakly. All was quiet, so still that the clock on my bureau ticked distinctly each passing second. The curtain billowed in the night breeze, though I was positive I had closed the casement when I entered the room.

And then suddenly I threw back my head and screamed from the bottomest depths of my soul! For slowly, slowly creeping down my lungs was that detestable odour of heliotrope.

Morning, and I found all was not a dream. My head was ringing, my hands trembling, and I was so weak I could hardly stand. The doctor I called in looked grave as he felt my pulse.

"You are on the verge of a complete collapse," he said. "If you do not allow yourself a rest it may permanently affect your mind. Take things easy for a while. And if you don't mind I'll cauterize those two little cuts on your neck. They're rather raw wounds. What caused them?"

I moved my fingers to my throat and drew them away again tipped with blood.

"I . . . I don't know," I faltered.

He busied himself with his medicines, and a few minutes later reached for his hat.

"I advise that you don't leave your bed for a week at least," he said. "I'll give you a thorough examination then and see if there are any signs of anaemia." But as he went out the door I thought I saw a puzzled look on his face.

Those subsequent hours allowed my thoughts to run wild once more. I vowed I would forget it all, go back to my work and never look upon the books again. But I knew I could not. The woman in black persisted in my mind, and each minute away from her became a torture. But more than that, if there had been a decided urge to continue my reading in the second book, the desire to see the third book, the last of the trilogy, was slowly increasing to an obsession. It gripped me, etched itself deep into my thoughts.

At length I could stand it no longer, and on the morning of the third day I took a cab to the antique store and tried to persuade Larla to give me the third volume of his brother. But the Italian was firm. I had already taken two books, neither of which I had returned. Until I brought them back he would not listen. Vainly I tried to explain that one was of no value without the sequel and that I wanted to read the entire narrative as a unit. He merely shrugged his shoulders and toyed with his watch chain.

Cold perspiration broke out on my forehead as I heard my desire disregarded. Like the blows of a bludgeon the thought beat upon me that I must have that book. I argued. I pleaded. But to no avail.

At length when Larla had turned the other way I gave in to desperation, seized the third book as I saw it lying on the shelf, slid it into my pocket, and walked guiltily out. I make no apologies for my action. In the light of what developed later it may be considered a temptation inspired, for my will at the time was a conquered thing blanketed by that strange lure.

Back in my apartment I dropped into a chair and hastened to open the velvet cover. Here was the last chronicle of that strange series of events which had so completely become a part of my life during the last five days. Larla's volume three. Would all be explained in its pages? If so, what secret would be revealed?

With the light from a reading lamp glaring full over my shoulder I opened the book, thumbed through it slowly, marvelling at the exquisite hand-printing. It seemed then as I sat there that an almost palpable cloud of intense quiet settled over me, a mental miasma muffling the distant sounds of the street. I was vaguely aware of an atmosphere, heavy and dense, in which objects other than the book lost their focus and became blurred in proportion.

For a moment I hesitated. Something psychic, something indefinable seemed to forbid me to read farther. Conscience, curiosity, that queer urge told me to go on. Slowly, like a man in a hypnotic trance wavering between two wills, I began to turn the pages, one at a time, from back to front.

Symbolism again. Vague wanderings with no sane meaning.

But suddenly my fingers stopped! My eyes had caught

sight of the last paragraph on the last page, the final pennings of Alessandro Larla. I started downwards as a terrific shock ripped through me from head to foot. I read, reread, and read again those words, those blasphemous words. I brought the book closer. I traced each word in the lamplight, slowly, carefully, letter for letter. I opened and closed my eyes. Then the horror of it burst like a bomb within me.

In blood-red ink the lines read:

"What shall I do? She has drained my blood and rotted my soul. My pearl is black, black as all evil. The curse be upon her brother, for it is he who made her thus. I pray the truth in these pages will destroy them for ever.

"But my brain is hammering itself apart. Heaven help me, Perle von Mauren and her brother, Johann, are vampires!"

With a scream I leaped to my feet.

"Vampires!" I shrieked. "Vampires! Oh, my God!"

I clutched at the edge of the table and stood there swaying, the realization of it surging upon me like the blast of a furnace. Vampires! Those horrible creatures with a lust for human blood, fiends of hell, taking the shape of men, of bats, of dogs. I saw it all now, and my brain reeled at the horror of it.

Oh, why had I been such a fool? Why had I not looked beneath the surface, taken away the veil, gone farther than the perfume? That damnable heliotrope was a mask, a mask hiding all the unspeakable foulness of the grave.

My emotions burst out of control then. With a cry I swept the water-glass, the books, the vase from the table, smote my fist down upon the flat surface again and again until a thousand little pains were stabbing the flesh.

"Vampires!" I screamed. "No, no—oh God, it isn't true!"

But I knew that it was. The events of the past few days rose before me in all their horror now, and I could see the black significance of every detail.

The brother, Johann—some time since the war he had become a vampire. When the woman sought him out years later he had forced this terrible existence upon her too. Yes, that was it.

With the garden as their lair the two of them had entangled poor Alessandro Larla in their serpentine coils a year before. He had loved the woman, had worshipped her madly. And then he had found the truth, the awful truth that had sent him stumbling home, stark, raving mad.

Mad, yes, but not mad enough to keep him from writing the facts in his three velvet-bound books for the world to see. He had hoped the disclosures would dispatch the woman and her brother for ever. But it was not enough.

Following my thoughts, I whipped the first book from the table stand and opened the front cover. There again I saw those scratched lines which had meant nothing to me before.

"Revelations meant to destroy but only binding without the stake. Read, fool, and enter my field, for we are chained to the spot. Oh, woe unto Larla!"

Perle von Mauren had written that. Fool that I was, unseeing fool! The books had not put an end to the evil of her or her brother. No, only one thing could do that. Yet the exposures had not been written in vain. They were recorded for mortal posterity to see.

Those books bound the two vampires, Perle von Mauren and her brother, Johann, to the old garden, kept them from roaming the night streets in search of victims. Only he who had once passed through the gate could they pursue and attack.

It was the old metaphysical law: evil shrinking in the face of truth.

Yet if the books had bound their power in chains they had also opened a new avenue for their attacks. Once immersed in the pages of the trilogy, the reader fell helplessly into their clutches. Those printed lines had become the outer reaches of their web. They were an entrapping net within which the power of the vampires always crouched.

That was why my life had blended so strangely with the story of Larla. The moment I had cast my eyes on the opening paragraph I had fallen into their coils to do with as they had done with Larla a year before. I had been lured, drawn relentlessly into the tentacles of the woman in black. Once I was past the garden gate the binding spell of the books was gone, and they were free to pursue me and to—

A giddy sensation rose within me. Now I saw why the scientific doctor had been puzzled. Now I saw the reason for my physical weakness. Oh, the foulness of it! She had been—feasting on my blood!

With a sobbing cry I flung the book to a far corner, turned and began madly pacing up and down the room. Cold perspiration oozed from every pore. My heart pounded like a runner's. My brain ran wild.

Was I to end as Larla had ended, another victim of this loathsome being's power? Was she to gorge herself further on my life and live on? Were others to be preyed upon and go down into the pits of despair? No, and again no! If Larla had been ignorant of the one and only way in which to dispose of such a creature, I was not. I had not vacationed in southern Europe without learning something of these ancient evils.

Frantically I looked about the room, took in the objects

about me. A chair, a table, a taboret, one of my cameras with its long tripod. I stared at the latter as in my terror-stricken mind a plan leaped into action. With a lunge I was across the floor, had seized one of the wooden legs of the tripod in my hands. I snapped it across my knee. Then, grasping the two broken pieces, both now with sharp splintered ends, I rushed hatless out of the door to the street.

A moment later I was racing northward in a cab bound for Easterly Street.

"Hurry!" I cried to the driver as I glanced at the westering sun. "Faster, do you hear?"

We shot along the cross-streets, into the old suburbs and towards the outskirts of town. Every traffic halt found me fuming at the delay. But at length we drew up before the wall of the garden.

Tossing the driver a bill, I swung the wrought-iron gate open and with the wooden pieces of the tripod still under my arm, rushed in. The courtyard was a place of reality in the daylight, but the mouldering masonry and tangled weeds were steeped in silence as before.

Straight for the house I made, climbing the rotten steps to the front entrance. The door was boarded up and locked. Smothering an impulse to scream, I retraced my steps at a run and began to circle the south wall of the building. It was this direction I had seen the woman take when she had fled after I had tried to snap her picture. The twenty-six blue-jays on the wall leered at me like a flock of harpies.

Well towards the rear of the building I reached a small half-open door leading to the cellar. For a moment I hesitated there, sick with the dread of what I knew lay before me. Then, clenching hard the two wooden tripod stakes, I entered.

Inside, cloaked in gloom, a narrow corridor stretched before me. The floor was littered with rubble and fallen masonry, the ceiling interlaced with a thousand cobwebs.

I stumbled forward, my eyes quickly accustoming themselves to the half-light from the almost opaque windows. A maddening urge to leave it all and flee back to the sunlight was welling up within me now. I fought it back. Failure would mean a continuation of the horrors—a lingering death—would leave the gate open for others.

At the end of the corridor a second door barred my passage. I thrust it open—and stood swaying there on the sill staring inward. A great loathing crept over me, a stifling sense of utter repulsion. Hot blood rushed to my head. The air seemed to move upward in palpable swirls.

Beyond was a small room, barely ten feet square, with a low-raftered ceiling. And by the light of the open door I saw side by side in the centre of the floor—two white wood coffins.

How long I stood there leaning weakly against the stone wall I don't know. There was a silence so profound the beating of my heart pulsed through the passage like the blows of a mallet. And there was a slow penetrating odour drifting from out of that chamber that entered my nostrils and claimed instant recognition. Heliotrope! But heliotrope defiled by the rotting smell of an ancient grave.

Then suddenly with a determination born of despair I leaped forward, rushed to the nearest coffin, seized its cover, and ripped it open.

Would to heaven I could forget the sight that met my eyes. There lay Perle von Mauren, the woman in black—unveiled.

That face—how can I describe it? It was divinely beautiful, the hair black as sable, the cheeks a classic white. But the lips—oh God! Those lips! I grew suddenly sick as

I looked upon them. They were scarlet, crimson . . . and sticky with human blood.

I moved like an automaton then. With a low sob I reached for one of the tripod stakes, seized a flagstone from the floor and with the pointed end of the wood resting directly over the woman's heart, struck a crashing blow. The stake jumped downward. A sickening crunch—and a violent contortion shook the coffin. Up to my face rushed a warm, nauseating breath of rot and decay.

I wheeled and hurled open the lid of her brother's coffin. With only a flashing glance at the young masculine Teutonic face I raised the other stake high in the air and brought it stabbing down with all the strength in my right arm. Red blood suddenly began to form a thick pool on the floor.

For an instant I stood rooted to the spot, the utter obscenity of it all searing its way into my brain like a hot sword. Even in that moment of stark horror I realized that not even the most subtle erasures of Time would be able to remove that blasphemous sight from my inner eye.

It was a scene so abysmally corrupt—I pray heaven my dreams will never find it and re-vision its unholy tableau. There before me, focused in the shaft of light that filtered through the open door like the miasma from a fever swamp, lay the two white caskets.

And within them now, staring up at me from eyeless sockets—two grey and mouldering skeletons, each with its hideous leering head of death.

The rest is but a vague dream. I seem to remember rushing madly outside, along the path to the gate and down the street, down Easterly, away from that accursed garden of the jays.

At length, utterly exhausted, I reached my apartment, burst open the door, and staggered in. Those mundane surroundings that confronted me were like balm to my burning eyes. But as if in mocking irony there centred into my gaze three objects lying where I had left them, the three volumes of Larla.

I moved across to them, picked them up, and stared down vacantly upon their black sides. These were the hellish works that had caused it all. These were the pages that were responsible . . .

With a low cry I turned to the grate on the other side of the room and flung the three of them on to the still glowing coals.

There was an instant hiss, and a line of yellow flame streaked upward and began eating into the velvet. I watched the fire grow higher . . . higher . . . and diminish slowly.

And as the last glowing spark died into a blackened ash there swept over me a mighty feeling of quiet and relief.

THE DEATH OF ILALOTHA

◆◆◆

CLARK ASHTON SMITH

Black Lord of bale and fear, master of all confusion!
By thee, thy prophet saith,
New power is given to wizards after death,
And witches in corruption draw forbidden breath,
And weave such wild enchantment and illusion
As none but lamiae may use;
And through thy grace the charnelled corpses lose
Their horror, and nefarious loves are lighted
In noisome vaults long nighted
And vampires make their sacrifice to thee—
Disgorging blood as if great urns had poured
Their bright vermilion hoard
About the washed and weltering sarcophagi.

—LUDAR'S LITANY TO THASAIDON

According to the custom in old Tasuun, the obsequies of Ilalotha, lady-in-waiting to the self-widowed Queen Xantlicha, had formed an occasion of much merry-making and prolonged festivity. For three days, on a bier of diverse-coloured silks from the Orient, under a rose-hued canopy that might well have domed some nuptial couch, she had lain clad with gala garments amid the great feasting hall of the royal palace in Miraab. About her, from morning dusk to sunset, from cool even to torridly glaring dawn, the feverish tide of the funeral orgies had surged and eddied without slackening. Nobles, court officials, guardsmen, scullions, astrologers, eunuchs, and all the high ladies, waiting women, and female slaves of Xantlicha had taken part in that prodigal debauchery which was believed to honour most fitly the deceased. Mad songs and obscene ditties were sung, and dancers whirled in vertiginous frenzy to the lascivious pleading of untirable lutes. Wines and liquors were poured torrentially from monstrous amphoras; the tables fumed with spicy meats piled in huge hummocks and forever replenished. The drinkers offered libation to Ilalotha, till the fabrics of her bier were stained to darker hues by the spilt vintages. On all sides around her, in attitudes of disorder or prone abandonment, lay those who had yielded to amorous licence or the fullness of their potations. With half-shut eyes and lips slightly parted, in the rosy shadow cast by the catafalque, she bore no aspect of death but seemed a sleeping empress who ruled impartially over the living and the dead. This appearance, together with a strange heightening of her natural beauty, was remarked by many: and some said that she seemed to await a lover's kiss rather than the kisses of the worm.

On the third evening, when the many-tongued brazen lamps were lit and the rites drew to their end, there returned to court the Lord Thulos, acknowledged lover of Queen Xantlicha, who had gone a week previous to visit his domain on the western border and had heard nothing of Ilalotha's death. Still unaware, he came into the hall at that hour when the saturnalia began to flag and the fallen revellers to outnumber those who still moved and drank and made riot.

He viewed the disordered hall with little surprise, for such scenes were familiar to him from childhood. Then, approaching the bier, he recognized its occupant with a certain startlement. Among the numerous ladies of Miraab who had drawn his libertine affections, Ilalotha had held sway longer than most; and, it was said, she had grieved more passionately over his defection than any other. She had been superseded a month before by Xantlicha, who had shown favour to Thulos in no ambiguous manner; and Thulos, perhaps, had abandoned her not without regret: for the role of lover to the queen, though advantageous and not wholly disagreeable, was somewhat precarious. Xantlicha, it was universally believed, had rid herself of the late King Archain by means of a tomb-discovered vial of poison that owed its peculiar subtlety and virulence to the art of ancient sorcerers. Following this act of disposal, she had taken many lovers, and those who failed to please her came invariably to ends no less violent than that of Archain. She was exigent, exorbitant, demanding a strict fidelity somewhat irksome to Thulos; who, pleading urgent affairs on his remote estate, had been glad enough of a week away from court.

Now, as he stood beside the dead woman, Thulos forgot the queen and bethought him of certain summer nights that had been honeyed by the fragrance of jasmine and the jasmine-white beauty of Ilalotha. Even less than the others could he believe her dead: for her present aspect differed in no wise from that which she had often assumed during their old intercourse. To please his whim she had feigned the inertness and complaisance of slumber or death; and at such times he had loved her with an ardour undismayed by the pantherine vehemence with which, at other whiles, she was wont to reciprocate or invite his caresses.

Moment by moment, as if through the working of some

powerful necromancy, there grew upon him a curious hallucination, and it seemed that he was again the lover of those lost nights, and had entered that bower in the palace gardens where Ilalotha awaited him on a couch strewn with over-blown petals, lying with bosom quiet as her face and hands. No longer was he aware of the crowded hall: the highflaring lights, the wine-flushed faces had become a moon-bright parterre of drowsily nodding blossoms, and the voices of the courtiers were no more than a faint suspiration of wind amid cypress and jasmine. The warm, aphrodisiac perfumes of the June night welled about him; and again, as of old, it seemed that they arose from the person of Ilalotha no less than from the flowers. Prompted by intense desire, he stooped over and felt her cool arm stir involuntarily beneath his kiss.

Then, with the bewilderment of a sleepwalker awakened rudely, he heard a voice that hissed in his ear with soft venom. "Hast forgotten thyself, my Lord Thulos? Indeed, I wonder little, for many of my bawcocks deem that she is fairer in death than in life." And, turning from Ilalotha, while the weird spell dissolved from his senses, he found Xantlicha at his side. Her garments were disarrayed, her hair was unbound and dishevelled, and she reeled slightly, clutching him by the shoulder with sharp-nailed fingers. Her full, poppy-crimson lips were curled by a vixenish fury, and in her long-lidded yellow eyes there blazed the jealousy of an amorous cat.

Thulos, overwhelmed by a strange confusion, remembered but partially the enchantment to which he had succumbed; and he was unsure whether or not he had actually kissed Ilalotha and had felt her flesh quiver to his mouth. Verily, he thought, this thing could not have been, and a waking dream had momentarily seized him. But he was troubled by the words of Xantlicha and her anger, and by the half-furtive drunken laughters and ribald whispers that he heard passing among the people about the hall.

"Beware, my Thulos," the queen murmured, her strange anger seeming to subside, "for men say that she was a witch . . ."

"How did she die?" queried Thulos.

"From no other fever than that of love, it is rumoured."

"Then, surely, she was no witch," Thulos argued with a lightness that was far from his thoughts and feelings, "for true sorcery should have found the cure."

"It was from love of thee," said Xantlicha darkly, "and, as all women know, thy heart is blacker and harder than black adamant. No witchcraft, however potent, could prevail thereon." Her mood, as she spoke, appeared to soften suddenly. "Thy absence has been over-long, my lord. Come to me at midnight: I will wait for thee in the south pavilion." Then, eyeing him sultrily for an instant from under drooped lids, and pinching his arm in such manner that her nails pierced through cloth and skin like a cat's talons, she turned from Thulos to hail certain of the harem eunuchs.

Thulos, when the queen's attention was disengaged from him, ventured to look again at Ilalotha; pondering, meanwhile, the curious remarks of Xantlicha. He knew that Ilalotha, like many of the court ladies, had dabbled in spells and philtres; but her witchcraft had never concerned him, since he felt no interest in other charms or enchantments than those with which nature had endowed the bodies of women. And it was quite impossible for him to believe that Ilalotha had died from a fatal passion: since, in his experience, passion was never fatal.

Indeed, as he regarded her with confused emotions, he

was again beset by the impression that she had not died at all. There was no repetition of the weird, half-remembered hallucination of other time and place; but it seemed to him that she had stirred from her former position on the wine-stained bier, turning her face towards him a little, as a woman turns to an expected lover; that the arm he had kissed (either in dream or reality) was outstretched a little farther from her side.

Thulos bent nearer, fascinated by the mystery and drawn by a stronger attraction that he could not have named. Again, surely, he had dreamt or had been mistaken. But even as the doubt grew, it seemed that the bosom of Ilalotha stirred in faint respiration and he heard an almost inaudible but thrilling whisper: "Come to me at midnight. I will wait for thee . . . in the tomb."

At this instant there appeared beside the catafalque certain people in the sober and rusty raiment of sextons, who had entered the hall silently, unperceived by Thulos or by any of the company. They carried among them a thin-walled sarcophagus of newly welded and burnished bronze. It was their office to remove the dead woman and bear her to the sepulchral vaults of her family, which were situated in the old necropolis lying somewhat to northward of the palace gardens.

Thulos would have cried out to restrain them from their purpose; but his tongue clove tightly; nor could he move any of his members. Not knowing whether he slept or woke, he watched the people of the cemetery as they placed Ilalotha in the sarcophagus and bore her quickly from the hall, unfollowed and still unheeded by the drowsy bacchanalians. Only when the sombre cortège had departed was he able to stir from his position by the empty bier. His thoughts were sluggish, and full of darkness and indecision. Smitten by an immense fatigue that was not unnatural after his daylong journey, he withdrew to his apartments and fell instantly into death-deep slumber.

Freeing itself gradually from the cypress-boughs, as if from the long, stretched fingers of witches, a waning and misshapen moon glared horizontally through the eastern window when Thulos awoke. By this token, he knew that the hour drew towards midnight, and recalled the assignation which Queen Xantlicha had made with him: an assignation which he could hardly break without incurring the queen's deadly displeasure. Also, with singular clearness, he recalled another rendezvous . . . at the same time but in a different place. Those incidents and impressions of Ilalotha's funeral, which, at the time, had seemed so dubitable and dreamlike, returned to him with a profound conviction of reality, as if etched on his mind by some mordant chemistry of sleep . . . or the strengthening of some sorcerous charm. He felt that Ilalotha had indeed stirred on her bier and spoken to him; that the sextons had borne her still living to the tomb. Perhaps her supposed demise had been merely a sort of catalepsy; or else she had deliberately feigned death in a last effort to revive his passion. These thoughts awoke within him a raging fever of curiosity and desire; and he saw before him her pale, inert, luxurious beauty, presented as if by enchantment.

Direly distraught, he went down by the lampless stairs and hallways to the moonlit labyrinth of the gardens. He cursed the untimely exigence of Xantlicha. However, as he told himself, it was more than likely that the queen, continuing to imbibe the liquors of Tasuun, had long since reached a condition in which she would neither keep nor recall her appointment. This thought reassured him: in his queerly bemused mind, it soon became a certainty; and he did not hasten towards the south pavilion but strolled vaguely amid the wan and sombre boscage.

More and more it seemed unlikely that any but himself was abroad: for the long unlit wings of the palace sprawled as in vacant stupor; and in the gardens there were only dead shadows, and pools of still fragrance in which the winds had drowned. And over all, like a pale, monstrous poppy, the moon distilled her death-white slumber.

Thulos, no longer mindful of his rendezvous with Xantlicha, yielded without further reluctation to the urgence that drove him towards another goal. Truly, it was no less than obligatory that he should visit the vaults and learn whether or not he had been deceived in his belief concerning Ilalotha. Perhaps, if he did not go, she would stifle in the shut sarcophagus, and her pretended death would quickly become an actuality. Again, as if spoken in the moonlight before him, he heard the words she had whispered, or seemed to whisper, from the bier. "Come to me at midnight . . . I will wait for thee . . . in the tomb."

With the quickening steps and pulses of one who fares to the warm, petal-sweet couch of an adored mistress, he left the palace grounds by an unguarded northern postern and crossed the weedy common between the royal gardens and the old cemetery. Unchilled and undismayed, he entered those always-open portals of death, where ghoulheaded monsters of black marble, glaring with hideously pitted eyes, maintained their charnel postures before the crumbling pylons.

The very stillness of the low-bosomed graves, the rigour and pallor of the tall shafts, the deepness of bedded cypress shadows, the inviolacy of death by which all things were invested, served to heighten the singular excitement that had fired Thulos' blood. It was as if he had drunk a philtre spiced with mummia. All around him the mortuary silence seemed to burn and quiver with a thousand memories of Ilalotha, together with those expectations to which he had given as yet no formal image . . .

Once, with Ilalotha, he had visited the subterranean tomb of her ancestors; and recalling its situation clearly, he came without indirection to the low-arched and cedar-darkened entrance. Rank nettles and fetid fumitories, growing thickly about the seldom-used adit, were crushed down by the tread of those who had entered there before Thulos; and the rusty, iron-wrought door sagged heavily inward on its loose hinges. At his feet there lay an extinguished flambeau, dropped, no doubt, by one of the departing sextons. Seeing it, he realized that he had brought with him neither candle nor lanthorn for the exploration of the vaults, and found in that providential torch an auspicious omen.

Bearing the lit flambeau, he began his investigation. He gave no heed to the piled and dusty sarcophagi in the first reaches of the subterrane: for during their past visit, Ilalotha had shown to him a niche at the innermost extreme, where, in due time, she herself would find sepulture among the members of that decaying line. Strangely, insidiously, like the breath of some vernal garden, the languid and luscious odour of jasmine swam to meet him through the musty air, amid the tiered presence of the dead; and it drew him to the sarcophagus that stood open between others tightly lidded. There he beheld Ilalotha, lying in the gay garments of her funeral, with half-shut eyes and half-parted lips; and upon her was the same weird and radiant beauty, the same voluptuous pallor and stillness, that had drawn Thulos with a necromantic charm.

"I knew that thou wouldst come, O Thulos," she murmured, stirring a little, as if involuntarily, beneath the deepening ardour of his kisses that passed quickly from throat to bosom . . .

The torch that had fallen from Thulos' hand expired in the thick dust . . .

Xantlicha, retiring to her chamber betimes, had slept illy. Perhaps she had drunk too much or too little of the dark ardent vintages; perhaps her blood was fevered by the return of Thulos, and her jealousy still troubled by the hot kiss which he had laid on Ilalotha's arm during the obsequies. A restlessness was upon her; and she rose well before the hour of her meeting with Thulos, and stood at her chamber window seeking such coolness as the night air might afford.

The air, however, seemed heated as by the burning of hidden furnaces; her heart appeared to swell in her bosom and stifle her; and her unrest and agitation were increased rather than diminished by the spectacle of the moon-lulled gardens. She would have hurried forth to the tryst in the pavilion; but despite her impatience, she thought it well to keep Thulos waiting. Leaning thus from her sill, she beheld Thulos when he passed amid the parterres and arbors below. She was struck by the unusual haste and intentness of his steps; and she wondered at their direction, which could only bring him to places remote from the rendezvous she had named. He disappeared from her sight in the cypress-lined alley that led to the north garden gate; and her wonderment was soon mingled with alarm and anger when he did not return.

It was incomprehensible to Xantlicha that Thulos, or any man, would dare to forget the tryst in his normal senses; and seeking an explanation, she surmised that the working of some baleful and potent sorcery was probably involved. Nor, in the light of certain incidents that she had observed, and much else that had been rumoured, was it hard for her to identify the sorceress. Ilalotha, the queen knew, had loved Thulos to the point of frenzy, and had grieved inconsolably after his desertion of her. People said that she had wrought various ineffectual spells to bring him back; that she had vainly invoked demons and sacrificed to them, and had made futile invultuations and death-charms against Xantlicha. In the end, she had died of sheer chagrin and despair, or perhaps had slain herself with some undetected poison . . . But, as was commonly believed in Tasuun, a witch dying thus, with unslaked desires and frustrate cantrips, could turn herself into a lamia or vampire and procure thereby the consummation of all her sorceries . . .

The queen shuddered, remembering these things; and remembering also the hideous and malign transformation that was said to accompany the achievement of such ends: for those who used in this manner the power of hell must take on the very character and the actual semblance of infernal beings. Too well she surmised the destination of Thulos, and the danger to which he had gone forth if her suspicions were true. And, knowing that she might face an equal danger, Xantlicha determined to follow him.

She made little preparation, for there was no time to waste; but took from beneath her silken bedcushions a small, straight-bladed dagger that she kept always within reach. The dagger had been anointed from point to hilt with such venom as was believed efficacious against either the living or the dead. Bearing it in her right hand, and carrying in the other a slot-eyed lanthorn that she might require later, Xantlicha stole swiftly from the palace.

The last lees of the evening's wine ebbed wholly from her brain, and dim, ghastly fears awoke, warning her like the voices of ancestral phantoms. But, firm in her determination, she followed the path taken by Thulos; the path taken earlier by those sextons who had borne Ilalotha to her place of sepulture. Hovering from tree to tree, the moon accompanied her like a worm-hollowed visage. The soft, quick patter of her cothurns, breaking the white silence, seemed to tear the filmy cobweb pall that withheld from her a world of spectral abominations. And more and more she recalled of those legendries that concerned such beings as Ilalotha; and her heart was shaken within her: for she knew that she would meet no mortal woman but a thing raised up and inspirited by the seventh hell. But amid the chill of these horrors, the thought of Thulos in the lamia's arms was like a red brand that seared her bosom.

Now the necropolis yawned before Xantlicha, and her path entered the cavernous gloom of far-vaulted funeral trees, as if passing into monstrous and shadowy mouths that were tusked with white monuments. The air grew dank and noisome, as if filled with the breathings of open crypts. Here the queen faltered, for it seemed that black, unseen cacodemons rose all about her from the graveyard ground, towering higher than the shafts and boles, and standing in readiness to assail her if she went farther. Nevertheless, she came anon to the dark adit that she sought. Tremulously she lit the wick of the slot-eyed lanthorn; and, piercing the gross underground darkness before her with its bladed beam, she passed with ill-subdued terror and repugnance into that abode of the dead . . . and perchance of the Undead.

However, as she followed the first turnings of the catacomb, it seemed that she was to encounter nothing more abhorrent than charnel mould and century-sifted dust; nothing more formidable than the serried sarcophagi that lined the deeply hewn shelves of stone: sarcophagi that had stood silent and undisturbed ever since the time of their deposition. Here, surely, the slumber of all the dead was unbroken, and the nullity of death was inviolate.

Almost the queen doubted that Thulos had preceded her there; till, turning her light on the ground, she discerned the print of his poulaines, long-tipped and slender in the deep dust amid those footmarks left by the rudely shod sextons. And she saw that the footprints of Thulos pointed only in one direction, while those of the others plainly went and returned.

Then, at an undetermined distance in the shadows ahead, Xantlicha heard a sound in which the sick moaning of some amorous woman was blent with a snarling as of jackals over the meat. Her blood returned frozen upon her heart as she went onward step by slow step, clutching her dagger in a hand drawn sharply back, and holding the light high in advance. The sound grew louder and more distinct; and there came to her now a perfume as of flowers in some warm June night; but, as she still advanced, the perfume was mixed with more and more of a smothering foulness such as she had never heretofore known, and was touched with the hot reeking of blood.

A few paces more, and Xantlicha stood as if a demon's arm had arrested her: for her lanthorn's light had found the inverted face and upper body of Thulos, hanging from the end of a burnished, new-wrought sarcophagus that occupied a scant interval between others green with rust. One of Thulos' hands clutched rigidly the rim of the sarcophagus, while the other hand, moving feebly, seemed to caress a dim shape that leaned above him with arms showing jasmine-white in the narrow beam, and dark fingers plunging into his bosom. His head and body seemed but an empty hull, and his hand hung skeleton-thin on the bronze rim, and his whole aspect was vein-drawn, as if he had lost more blood than was evident on his torn throat and face, and in his sodden raiment and dripping hair.

From the thing stooping above Thulos, there came ceaselessly that sound which was half moan and half snarl. And as Xantlicha stood in petrific fear and loathing, she seemed to hear from Thulos' lips an indistinct murmur, more of ecstasy than pain. The murmur ceased, and his head hung slacklier than before, so that the queen deemed him verily dead. At this she found such wrathful courage as enabled her to step nearer and raise the lanthorn higher: for, even amid her extreme panic, it came to her that by means of the wizard-poisoned dagger she might still haply slay the thing that had slain Thulos.

Waveringly the light crept aloft, disclosing inch by inch that infamy which Thulos had caressed in the darkness. . . . It crept even to the crimson-smeared wattles, and the fanged and ruddled orifice that was half mouth and half beak . . . till Xantlicha knew why the body of Thulos was a mere shrunken hull . . . In what the queen saw, there remained nothing of Ilalotha except the white, voluptuous arms, and a vague outline of human breasts melting momently into breasts that were not human, like clay moulded by a demon sculptor. The arms too began to change and darken; and, as they changed, the dying hand of Thulos stirred again and fumbled with a caressing movement towards the horror. And the thing seemed to heed him not but withdrew its fingers from his bosom, and reached across him with members stretching enormously, as if to claw the queen or fondle her with its dribbling talons.

It was then that Xantlicha let fall the lanthorn and the dagger, and ran with shrill, endless shriekings and laughters of immitigable madness from the vault.

WHEN GRETCHEN WAS HUMAN

✦✦✦

MARY A. TURZILLO

"You're only human," said Nick Scuroforno, fanning the pages of a tattered first edition of *Image of the Beast.*

The conversation had degenerated from half-hearted sales pitch, Gretchen trying to sell Nick Scuroforno an early Pang-born imprint. Now they sat cross-legged on the scarred wooden floor of Miss Trilby's Tomes, watching dust motes dance in August four o'clock sun. Gretchen was wallowing in self-disclosure and voluptuous self-pity.

"Sometimes I don't even feel human." Gretchen settled her back against the soft, dusty-smelling spines of a leather-bound 1910 imprint *Book of Knowledge.*

"I can identify."

"And given the choice, who'd really want to be?" asked Gretchen, tracing the grain of the wooden floor with chapped fingers.

"You have a choice?" asked Scuroforno.

"See, after Ashley was diagnosed, my ex got custody of her. Just as well." She rummaged her smock for a tissue. "I didn't have hospitalization after we split. And his would cover her, but only if she goes to a hospital way off in Seattle." Unbidden, a memory rose: Ashley's warm little body, wriggly as a puppy's, settling in her lap, opening *Where the Wild Things Are,* striking the page with her tiny pink index finger. *Mommy, read!*

Scuroforno nodded. “But can’t they cure leukaemia now?”

“Sometimes. She’s in remission at the moment. But how long will that last?” Gretchen kept sneaking looks at Scuroforno. Amazingly, she found him attractive. She thought depression had killed the sexual impulse in her. He was a big man, chunky but not actually fat, with evasive amber eyes and shaggy hair. Not bad looking, but not handsome either, in gray sweatpants, a brown T-shirt and beach sandals. He had a habit of twisting the band of his watch, revealing a strip of pale skin from which the fine hairs of his wrist had been worn.

“And yet cancer itself is immortal,” he mused. “Why can’t it make its host immortal too?”

“Cancer is immortal?” But of course cancer would be immortal. It was the ultimate predator. Why shouldn’t it hold all the high cards?

“The cells are. There’s some pancreatic cancer cells that have been growing in a lab fifty years since the man with the cancer died. And yet, cancer cells are not even as intelligent as a virus. A virus knows not to kill its host.”

“But viruses do kill!”

He smiled. “That’s true, lots do kill. Bacteria, too. But there are bacteria that millennia ago decided to infect every cell in our bodies. Turned into—let me think of the word. Organelles? Like the mitochondrion.”

“What’s a mitochondrion?”

He shrugged, slyly basking in his superior knowledge. “It’s an energy-converting organ in animal cells. Different DNA from the host. You’d think you could design a mitochondrion that would make the host live for ever.”

She stared at him. “No. I certainly wouldn’t think that.”

"Why not?"

"It would be horrible. A zombie. A vampire."

He was silent, a smile playing around his eyes.

She shuddered. "You get these ideas from Miss Trilby's Tomes?"

"The wisdom of the ages." He gestured at the high shelves, then stood. "And of course the world wide web. Here comes Madame Trilby herself. Does she like you lounging on the floor with customers?"

Gretchen flushed. "Oh, she never minds anything. My grandpa was friends with her father, and I've worked here off and on since I was little." She took Scuroforno's proffered hand and pulled herself to her feet.

Miss Trilby, frail and spry, wafting a fragrance of face powder and mouldy paper, lugged in a milk crate of pamphlets. She frowned at Gretchen. Strange, thought Gretchen. Yesterday she said I should find a new man, but now she's glaring at me. For sitting on the floor? I sit on the floor to do paperwork all the time. There's no room for chairs. It has to be for schmoozing with a male customer.

Miss Trilby dumped the mail on the counter and swept into the back room.

"Cheerful today, hmm?" said Scuroforno.

"Really, she's so good to me. She lends me money to go to Seattle and see my daughter. She's just nervous today."

"Ah. By the way, before I leave, do you have a cold, or were you crying?"

Gretchen reddened. "I have a chronic sinus infection." She suddenly saw herself objectively: stringy hair, bad posture, skinny. How could she be flirting with this man?

He touched her wrist. "Take care." And strode through the door into the street.

"Him you don't need," said Miss Trilby, bustling back in and firing up the shop's ancient Kaypro computer.

"Did I say I did?"

"Your face says you think you do. Did he buy anything?"

"I'm sorry. I can never predict what he'll be interested in."

"I'll die in the poorhouse. Sell him antique medical texts. Or detective novels. He stands reading historical novels right off the shelf and laughs. Pretends to be an expert, finds all the mistakes."

"What have you got against him, besides reading and not buying?"

"Oh, he buys. But Gretchen, lambkin, a man like that you don't need. Loner. Crazy."

"But he listens. He's so understanding."

"Like the butcher with the calf. What's this immortal cancer stuff he's feeding you?"

"Nothing. We were talking about Ashley."

"Sorry, lambkin. Life hasn't been kind to you. But be a little wise. This man has delusions he's a vampire."

Gretchen smoothed the dust jacket of *Euryanthe and Oberon at Covent Garden*. "Maybe he is."

Miss Trilby rounded her lips in mock horror. "Perhaps! Doesn't look much like Frank Langella, though, does he?"

No, he didn't, thought Gretchen, as she sorted orders for reprints of Kadensho's *Book of the Flowery Tradition* and de Honnecourt's *Fervor of Buenos Aires*.

But there was something appealing about Nick Scuroforno, something besides his empathy for a homely divorcée with a terminally ill child. His spare, dark humour, maybe that was it. Miss Trilby did not understand everything.

Why not make a play for him?

Even to herself, her efforts seemed pathetic. She got Keesha, the single mother across the hall in her apartment, to help her frost her hair. She bought a cheap cardigan trimmed with angora and dug out an old padded bra.

"Lambkin," said Miss Trilby dryly one afternoon when Gretchen came in dolled up in her desperate finery, "the man is not exactly a fashion plate himself."

But Scuroforno seemed flattered, if not impressed, by Gretchen's efforts, and took her out for coffee, then a late dinner. Mostly, however, he came into the bookstore an hour before closing and let her pretend to sell him some white elephant like the Reverend Wood's *Trespassers: How Inhabitants of Earth, Air, and Water Are Enabled to Trespass on Domains Not Their Own.* She would fiddle with the silver chain on her neck, and they would slide to the floor where she would pour out her troubles to him. Other customers seldom came in so late.

"You trust him with private details of your life," said Miss Trilby, "but what do you know of his?"

He did talk. He did. Philosophy, history, details of Gretchen's daughter's illness. One day, she asked, "What do you do?"

"I steal souls. Photographer."

Oh.

"Can't make much money on that artsy stuff," Miss Trilby commented when she heard this. "Rumor says he's got a private source of income."

"Illegal, you mean?"

"What a romantic you are, Gretchen. Ask him."

Gambling luck and investments, he told her.

One day, leaving for the shop, Gretchen opened her mail and found a letter—not even a phone call—that

Ashley's remission was over. Her little girl was in the hospital again.

The grief was surreal, physical. She was afraid to go back into her apartment. She had bought a copy of Jan Pienkowski's *Haunted House*, full of diabolically funny pop-ups, for Ashley's birthday. She couldn't bear to look at it now, waiting like a poisoned bait on the counter.

She went straight to the shop, began alphabetizing the new stock. Nothing made sense, she couldn't remember if O came after N. Miss Trilby had to drag her away, make her stop.

"What's wrong? Is it Ashley?"

Gretchen handed her the letter.

Miss Trilby read it through her thick lorgnette. Then, "Look at yourself. Your cheeks are flushed. Eyes bright. Disaster becomes you. Or is it the nearness of death bids us breed, like romance in a concentration camp?"

Gretchen shuddered. "Maybe my body is tricking me into reproducing again."

"To replace Ashley. Not funny, lambkin. But possibly true. I ask again, why this man? Doesn't madness frighten you?"

Next day, Gretchen followed him to his car. It seemed natural to get in, uninvited, ride home with him, follow him up two flights of stairs covered with cracked treads.

He let her perch on a stool in his kitchen darkroom while he printed peculiar old architectural photographs. The room smelled of chemicals, vinegary. An old Commodore 64 propped the pantry door open. She had seen a new computer in his living-room, running a screen saver of Giger babies holding grenades, and wraiths dancing an agony dance.

"I never eat here," he said. "As a kitchen, it's useless."

He emptied trays, washed solutions down the drain, rinsed. Her heart beat hard under the sleazy angora. His body, sleek as a lion's, gave off a male scent, faintly predatory.

While his back was turned, she undid her cardigan. The buttons too easily slipped out of the cheap fuzzy fabric, conspiring with lust.

She slipped it off as he turned around. And felt the draught of the cold kitchen and the surprise of his gaze on her inadequate chest.

He turned away, dried his hands on the kitchen towel. "Don't fall in love with me."

"Not at all arrogant, are you?" She wouldn't, wouldn't fall in love. No. That wasn't quite it.

"Not arrogance. A warning. I'm territorial; predators have to be. For a while, yes, I'd keep you around. But sooner or later, you'd interfere with my hunting. I'd kill you or drive you away to prevent myself from killing you."

"I won't fall in love with you." Level. Convincing.

"All right." He threw the towel into the sink, came to her. Covered her mouth with his.

She responded clumsily, overreacting after the long dry spell, clawing his back.

The kiss ended. He stroked her hair. "Don't worry. I won't draw blood. I can control the impulse."

She half pretended to play along with him. Half of her did believe. "It doesn't matter. I want to be like you." A joke?

He sat on the kitchen chair, pulled her to him, and put his cheek against her breasts. "It doesn't work that way. You have to have the right genes to be susceptible."

"It really is an infection?" Still half pretending to believe, still almost joking.

"A virus that gives you cancer. All I know is that of all

the thousands I've preyed upon, only a few have got the fever and lived to become—like me."

"Vampire?"

"As good a word as any. One who I infected and who lived on was my son. He got the fever and turned. That's why I think it's genetic." He pulled her nearer, as if for warmth.

"What happens if the prey doesn't have the genes?"

"Nothing. Nothing happens. I never take enough to kill. I haven't killed a human in over a hundred years. You're safe."

She slid to her knees, wrapping her arms around his waist. He held her head to him, stroking her bare arms and shoulders. "Silk," he said finally, pulling her up, touching her breast. She had nursed Ashley, but it hadn't stopped her from getting leukemia. Fire and ice sizzled across her breasts, as if her milk were letting down.

"Are you lonely?"

"God, yes. That's the only reason I was even tempted to let you do this. You know, I have the instincts of a predator, it does that. But I was born human."

"How did you infect your son?"

"Accident. I was infected soon after I was married. Pietra, my wife, is long dead."

"Pietra. Strange name."

"Not so strange in thirteenth-century Florence. I turned shortly after I was married. I was very ill. I knew I needed blood, but no knowledge of why or how to control my thirst. I took blood from a priest who came to give me last rites. My thirst was so voracious, I killed him. Not murder, Gretchen. I was no more guilty than a baby suckling at breast. The first thirst is overpowering. I took too much, and when I saw that he was dead, I put on my clothes and ran away."

"Leaving your wife."

"Never saw her again. But years later I encountered this young man at a gambling table. Pretended to befriend him. Overpowered him in a narrow dark street. Drank to slake my thirst. Later I encountered him, changed. As a rival for the blood of the neighbourhood. I had infected him, he had got the fever, developed into—what I am. Later I put the pieces together; I had left Pietra pregnant, this was our son, you see. He had the right genes. If he hadn't, he would have never even noticed that modest blood loss." His hand stroked her naked shoulder.

"Where is he now?"

"I often wonder. I drove him off soon after he finished the change. Vampires can't stand one another. They interfere with each other's hunting."

"Why have you chosen to tell me this?" She tried to control her voice, but heard it thicken.

"I tell people all the time what I am. Nobody ever believes it." He stood, pulling her to her feet, kissed her again, pressing his hips to her body. She ran her hands over his shoulders and loosened his shirt. "You don't believe me, either."

And then she smiled. "I want to believe you. I told you once, I don't want to be human."

He raised his eyebrows and smiled down at her. "I doubt you have the right genes to be anything else."

His bedroom was neat, sparsely furnished. She recognized books from Miss Trilby's Tomes, *Red Dragon*, *Confessions of an English Opium Eater* on a low shelf near the bed. Unexpectedly, he lifted her off her feet and laid her on the quilt. They kissed again, a long, complicated kiss. He took her slowly. He didn't close the door, and from the bed she could see his computer screen in the living room. The Giger wraiths in his screen saver danced slowly to their passion. And then she closed her eyes, and the wraiths danced behind her lids.

When they were finished, she knew that she had lied; if she did not feel love, then it was something as strong and as dangerous.

She traced a vein on the back of his hand. "You were born in Italy?"

He kissed the hand with which she had been tracing his veins. "Hundreds of years ago, yes. Before my flesh became numb."

"Then why don't you speak with an accent?"

He rolled on to his back, hands behind his head, and grinned. "I've been an American longer than you have. I made it a point to get rid of my accent. Aren't you going to ask me about the sun and garlic and silver bullets?"

"All just superstition?"

"It would seem." He smiled wryly. "But there is the gradual loss of feeling."

"You say you can't love."

He groped in the bedside table for a pen. He drove the tip into his arm. "You see?" Blood welled up slowly.

"Stop! My god, must you hurt yourself?"

"Just demonstrating. The flesh has been consumed by the—by the cancer, if that's what it is. It starts in the coldest parts of the body. No nerves. I don't *feel*. It has nothing to do with emotion."

"And because you are territorial—"

"Yes. But the emotions don't die, exactly. There's this horrible conflict. And physically, the metastasis continues, very slowly. I heard of a very old vampire whose brain had turned. He was worse than a shark, a feeding machine."

She pulled the sheets around her. The room seemed cold now that they were no longer entwined. "You seemed human enough, when you—"

"You didn't feel it when I kissed you?"

"Feel . . ."

He guided her index finger into his mouth, under the tongue. A bony little organ there, tiny spikes, retracted under the root of the tongue.

She jerked her hand away, suddenly afraid. He caught it and kissed it again, almost mockingly.

She shuddered, tenderness confounded with terror, and buried her face in the pillow. But wasn't this what she had secretly imagined, hoped for?

"Next time," she said, turning her face up to him, like a daisy to the sun, "draw blood, do."

The wraiths in his screen saver danced.

The idea of a bus trip to Seattle filled her with dread, and she put it off, as if somehow by staying in Warren she could stop the progress of reality. But a second letter, this from her ex-sister-in-law Miriam, forced her to face facts. The chemotherapy, Miriam wrote, was not working this time. Ashley was "fading."

"Fading!"

The same mail brought a postcard from Scuroforno. *Out of town on business, seeing to investments. Be well, human,* he wrote.

She told Miss Trilby she needed time off to see Ashley.

"Lambkin, you look awful. Don't go on the bus. I'll lend you the money for the plane, and you can pay me back when you marry some rich lawyer."

"No, Miss Trilby. I have a cold, that's all." Her skin itched, her throat and mouth were sore, her head throbbed.

They dusted books that afternoon. When Gretchen

came down from the stepladder, she was so exhausted she curled up on the settee in the back room with a copy of *As You Desire*. The words swam before her eyes, but they might stop her from thinking, thinking about Ashley, about cancer, immortal cells killing their mortal host. Thinking, *immortal*. It might have worked. A different cancer. And then she stopped thinking.

And awoke in All Souls' Hospital, in pain and confusion.

"Drink. You're dehydrated," the nurse said. The room smelled of bleach and dead flowers.

Who had brought her in?

"I don't know. Your employer? An elderly woman. Doctor will be in to talk to you. Try to drink at least a glass every hour."

In lucid moments, Gretchen rejoiced. It was the change, surely it was the change. If she lived, she would be released from all the degrading baggage that being human hung upon her.

The tests showed nothing. Of course, the virus would not culture in agar, Gretchen thought. If it was a virus.

She awoke nights thinking of human blood. She whimpered when they took away her roommate, an anorexic widow, nearly dry, but an alluring source of a few delicious drops, if only she could get to her while the nurses were away.

Miss Trilby visited, and only by iron will did Gretchen avoid leaping upon her. Gretchen screamed, "Get away from me! I'll kill you!" The doctors, unable to identify her illness, must have worried about her outburst; she didn't get another roommate. And they didn't release her, though she had no insurance.

Miss Trilby did not come back.

They never thought of cancer. Cancer does not bring a fever and thirst, and bright, bright eyes, and a numbness in the fingers.

Finally, she realized she had waited too long. The few moments of each day that delirium left her, she was too weak to overpower anybody.

Scuroforno came in when she was almost gone. She was awake, floating, relishing death's sweet breath, the smell of disinfectants.

"I'm under quarantine," she whispered. This was not true, but nobody had come to see her since she had turned on Miss Trilby.

He waved that aside and unwrapped a large syringe. "What you need is blood. They wouldn't think of that, though."

"Where did you get that?" Blood was so beautiful. She wanted to press Scuroforno's wrists against the delicate itching structure under her tongue, to faint in the heat from his veins.

"You're too weak to drink. Ideally, you should have several quarts of human blood. But mine will do."

She watched, sick with hunger, as he tourniqueted his arm, slipped the needle into the vein inside his elbow, and drew blood.

She reached for the syringe. He held it away from her. She lunged with death-strength. He put the syringe on the table behind him, caught her wrists, held them together.

"You're stronger than I expected." He squeezed until the distant pain quelled her. She pretended to relax, still fixated on the sip of blood, so near. She darted at his throat, but he held her easily.

"Stop it! There isn't enough blood in the syringe to help you if you drink it! If I inject it, you'll get some relief. But my blood is forbidden."

Yes, she would have killed him, anybody, for blood. She sank back, shaking with desire. The needle entered her vein and she never felt the prick. She shuddered with pleasure as the blood trickled in. She could taste it. Old blood, sour with a hunger of its own, but the echo of satiety radiated from her arm.

"Here are some clothes. You should be just strong enough to walk to the car. I'll carry you from there."

She fumbled for his wrists. "No. Any more vampire blood would kill you. Or"—he laughed grimly—"you might be strong enough to kill me. On your feet." He lifted her like a child.

In his apartment, he carried her to the bedroom and laid her on the bed. She smelled blood. Next to her was an unconscious girl, perhaps twenty, very blonde, dressed in white suede jeans, boots, a black lace bra.

Ineptly, she went for the girl's jugular. The girl was wearing strong jasmine perfume, a cheap knock-off scent insistent and sexy.

"Wait. Don't slash her and waste it all. Be neat." He leaned over, pressed his mouth to the girl's neck.

Gretchen lunged.

She thrilled to sink her new blood-sucking organ into the girl's neck, but discovered it was at the wrong place. Hissing with anger, she broke away and tried a third time. Salty, thick comfort seeped into her body like hot whisky.

In an instant, Gretchen felt Scuroforno slip his finger into her mouth, breaking the suction. She came away giddy with frustration. Scuroforno held her arms, hurting her. The pain was in another universe. She tried to twist away.

"You're going to kill her," he warned.

"Who is she?" She shook herself into self-control, gazed longingly at the girl, who seemed comatose.

"Nobody. A girl. I take her out now and then. I never take enough blood to harm her. I don't actually enjoy hurting people."

"She's drugged?"

"No, no. I—we have immunity to bacteria and so on, but drugs are bad. I hypnotized her."

"You hypnotized—she sleeps through all this?"

"She thinks she's dead drunk. Here, help me get her sweater back on."

"She thinks you made love to her?"

Scuroforno smiled.

"You did make love to her?"

He busied himself with adjusting the girl's clothes.

Gretchen lay back against the headboard. "I need more, God, I need more."

"I know. But you'll have to find your own from now on."

"How do I get them to submit?"

Scuroforno yawned. "That's your problem. Rescuing you was hard work. Now you'll have to find your own way. You're cleverer and stronger than humans now. Did you notice your sinus infection is gone?"

"Nick, help."

He did not look at her. "It would be better if you left town now."

"But you saved me."

"You're my competitor now. Leave before the rage for blood takes you, before we go after the same prey."

She held the hunger down inside her, remembering human emotions. "It makes no difference that I love you?" And suddenly, she did love him.

"Tomorrow you'll know what hate is, too."

On the way out, she noticed he had a new screen saver: red blood cells floating on black, swelling, bursting apart.

. . .

On the bus to Seattle, she wept. Yes, she had loved him, and she had learned what hate was, too. She played with a sewing needle, stabbed her fingers. Numb. But her feelings were not numb, not yet. Would that happen? Was Nick emotionally dead?

Would the physical numbness spread? If her body was immortal, why would she need nerves, pain, to warn of danger?

Maybe she would regret the bargain she had made.

The numbness did spread. Her fingers and hands were immune to pain. But she still felt thirst. The cancer metastasized into her tongue and nerves, wanted to be fed.

Her seatmate was a Mormon missionary, separated from his partner because the bus was crowded. In Chicago, he asked her to change seats, so he could sit with his partner. But she refused. It didn't fit her plan.

She stroked his cheek, held the back of his neck in a vice grip, all the while smiling, cat-like. Scarcely feeling her own skin, but vividly feeling the nourishment under his. He tried to repel her, laughing uneasily, taking it for an erotic game. A forward, sluttish gentile woman. Then he was fighting, uselessly. He twisted her thumb back, childish self-defence. She felt no pain. Then he was weeping, softening, falling into a trance. She kissed his throat with her open mouth. Drank from him. Drank again and again. Had he fought, she could have broken his neck. She was completely changed.

In Seattle, the floor nurse in Pediatrics challenged her. Sniffing phenol and the sweet, sick urine that could never quite be cleaned up, Gretchen glanced at her reflection in a dead computer screen behind the nurse. She did look predatory now. Like a wax manikin, but also like a cougar. Powerful. Not like anybody's mother. Two other nurses drifted up, as if sensing trouble.

She showed the nurse her driver's license. They almost believed her, then. Let her go down the hall, to room 409. But still the nurses' eyes followed her. She had changed.

She opened the door. The floor nurse drifted in behind her. This balding, emaciated tyke, tangled in tubing, could not be her Ashley.

Ashley had changed, too. From a less benign cancer.

The nurse sniffed. "I'm sorry. She's gone downhill a lot in the last few weeks." The nurse clearly did not approve of noncustodial mothers. Maybe still did not believe this quiet, strong woman *was* the mother.

When Gretchen had been human, she would have been humiliated, would have tried to explain that Ashley had been taken from her by legal tricks. Now, she considered the nurse simply as a convenient beverage container from which, under suitable conditions, she might sip. She smiled, a cat smile, and the nurse could not hold her gaze.

"Ashley," said Gretchen, when they were alone. She had brought the Jan Pienkowski book, wrapped in red velvet paper with black cats on it. Ashley liked cats. She would love the scary haunted house pop-ups. They would read them together. Gretchen put the gift on the chair, because first she must tend to more important things. "Ashley, it's Mommy. Wake up, darling."

But the little girl only opened her eyes, huge and bruised in the pinched face, and sobbed feebly.

Gretchen lowered the rail on the bed and slid her arm under Ashley. The child was frighteningly light.

Gretchen felt the warmth of her feverish child, smelled the antiseptic of the room, the sweet girl-smell of her daughter's skin. But those were all at a distance. Gretchen was being subsumed by something immortal.

We are very territorial. Isn't that what Nick had said? *It's not an emotional numbness; it's physical.* And the memory of him jabbing the pen into his arm, the needle into his vein, her own numb fingers, how everything, even her daughter's warmth and the smell of the child and the room were all receding, distant. Immortal. Numb. Strong beyond human strength. Alone.

She touched her new, predatory mouth to her child's throat. Would Ashley thank her for this?

Now she must decide.

REPLACEMENTS

♦♦♦

LISA TUTTLE

Walking through gray north London to the tube station, feeling guilty that he hadn't let Jenny drive him to work and yet relieved to have escaped another pointless argument, Stuart Holder glanced down at a pavement covered in a leaf-fall of fast-food cartons and white paper bags and saw, amid the dog turds, beer cans, and dead cigarettes, something horrible.

It was about the size of a cat, naked-looking, with leathery, hairless skin and thin, spiky limbs that seemed too frail to support the bulbous, ill-proportioned body. The face, with tiny bright eyes and a wet slit of a mouth, was like an evil monkey's. It saw him and moved in a crippled, spasmodic way. Reaching up, it made a clotted, strangled noise. The sound touched a nerve, like metal between the teeth, and the sight of it, mewling and choking and scrabbling, scaly claws flexing and wriggling, made him feel sick and terrified. He had no phobias, he found insects fascinating, not frightening, and regularly removed, unharmed, the spiders, wasps, and mayflies which made Jenny squeal or shudder helplessly.

But this was different. This wasn't some rare species of wingless bat escaped from a zoo, it wasn't something he would find pictured in any reference book. It was something that should not exist, a mistake, something alien. It did not belong in his world.

A little snarl escaped him and he took a step forward and brought his foot down hard.

The small, shrill scream lanced through him as he crushed it beneath his shoe and ground it into the road.

Afterward, as he scraped the sole of his shoe against the curb to clean it, nausea overwhelmed him. He leaned over and vomited helplessly into a red-and-white-striped box of chicken bones and crumpled paper.

He straightened up, shaking, and wiped his mouth again and again with his pocket handkerchief. He wondered if anyone had seen, and had a furtive look around. Cars passed at a steady crawl. Across the road a cluster of schoolgirls dawdled near a man smoking in front of a newsagent's, but on this side of the road the fried chicken franchise and bathroom suppliers had yet to open for the day and the nearest pedestrians were more than a hundred yards away.

Until that moment, Stuart had never killed anything in his life. Mosquitoes and flies of course, other insects probably, a nest of hornets once, that was all. He had never liked the idea of hunting, never lived in the country. He remembered his father putting out poisoned bait for rats, and he remembered shying bricks at those same vermin on a bit of waste ground where he had played as a boy. But rats weren't like other animals; they elicited no sympathy. Some things had to be killed if they would not be driven away.

He made himself look to make sure the thing was not still alive. Nothing should be left to suffer. But his heel had crushed the thing's face out of recognition, and it was unmistakably dead. He felt a cool tide of relief and satisfaction, followed at once, as he walked away, by a nagging uncertainty, the imminence of guilt. Was he right to have killed it, to have acted on violent, irrational impulse? He didn't even know what it was. It might have been somebody's pet.

He went hot and cold with shame and self-disgust. At the corner he stopped with five or six others waiting to cross the road and because he didn't want to look at them he looked down.

And there it was, alive again.

He stifled a scream. No, of course it was not the same one, but another. His leg twitched; he felt frantic with the desire to kill it, and the terror of his desire. The thin wet mouth was moving as if it wanted to speak.

As the crossing-signal began its nagging blare he tore his eyes away from the creature squirming at his feet. Everyone else had started to cross the street, their eyes, like their thoughts, directed ahead. All except one. A woman in a smart business suit was standing still on the pavement, looking down, a sick fascination on her face. As he looked at her looking at it, the idea crossed his mind that he should kill it for her, as a chivalric, protective act. But she wouldn't see it that way. She would be repulsed by his violence. He didn't want her to think he was a monster. He didn't want to be the monster who had exulted in the crunch of fragile bones, the flesh and viscera merging pulpily beneath his shoe.

He forced himself to look away, to cross the road, to spare the alien life. But he wondered, as he did so, if he had been right to spare it.

Stuart Holder worked as an editor for a publishing company with offices an easy walk from St. Paul's. Jenny had worked there, too, as a secretary, when they met five years ago. Now, though, she had quite a senior position with another publishing house, south of the river, and recently they had given her a car. He had been supportive of her ambitions, supportive of her learning to drive, and proud of her on all fronts when she succeeded, yet he was aware, although he never spoke of it, that something about her success made him uneasy. One small, niggling, insecure part of himself was afraid that one day she would realize she didn't need him anymore. That was why he picked at her, and second-guessed her decisions when she was behind the wheel and he was in the passenger seat. He recognized this as he walked briskly through more crowded streets toward his office, and he told himself he would do better. He would have to. If anything drove them apart it was more likely to be his behavior than her career. He wished he had accepted her offer of a ride today. Better any amount of petty irritation between husband and wife than to be haunted by the memory of that tiny face, distorted in the death he had inflicted. Entering the building, he surreptitiously scraped the sole of his shoe against the carpet.

Upstairs two editors and one of the publicity girls were in a huddle around his secretary's desk; they turned on him the guilty-defensive faces of women who have been discussing secrets men aren't supposed to know.

He felt his own defensiveness rising to meet theirs as he smiled. "Can I get any of you chaps a cup of coffee?"

"I'm sorry, Stuart, did you want . . . ?" As the others faded away, his secretary removed a stiff white paper bag with the NEXT logo, printed on it from her desktop.

"Joke, Frankie, joke." He always got his own coffee because he liked the excuse to wander, and he was always having to reassure her that she was not failing in her secretarial duties. He wondered if Next sold sexy underwear, decided it would be unkind to tease her further.

He felt a strong urge to call Jenny and tell her what had

happened, although he knew he wouldn't be able to explain, especially not over the phone. Just hearing her voice, the sound of sanity, would be a comfort, but he restrained himself until just after noon, when he made the call he made every day.

Her secretary told him she was in a meeting. "Tell her Stuart rang," he said, knowing she would call him back as always.

But that day she didn't. Finally, at five minutes to five, Stuart rang his wife's office and was told she had left for the day.

It was unthinkable for Jenny to leave work early, as unthinkable as for her not to return his call. He wondered if she was ill. Although he usually stayed in the office until well after six, now he shoved a manuscript in his briefcase and went out to brave the rush hour.

He wondered if she was mad at him. But Jenny didn't sulk. If she was angry she said so. They didn't lie or play those sorts of games with each other, pretending not to be in, "forgetting" to return calls.

As he emerged from his local underground station Stuart felt apprehensive. His eyes scanned the pavement and the gutters, and once or twice the flutter of paper made him jump, but of the creatures he had seen that morning there were no signs. The body of the one he had killed was gone, perhaps eaten by a passing dog, perhaps returned to whatever strange dimension had spawned it. He noticed, before he turned off the high street, that other pedestrians were also taking a keener than usual interest in the pavement and the edge of the road, and that made him feel vindicated somehow.

London traffic being what it was, he was home before Jenny. While he waited for the sound of her key in the lock he made himself a cup of tea, cursed, poured it down the sink, and had a stiff whiskey instead. He had just finished it and was feeling much better when he heard the street door open.

"Oh!" The look on her face reminded him unpleasantly of those women in the office this morning, making him feel like an intruder in his own place. Now Jenny smiled, but it was too late. "I didn't expect you to be here so early."

"Nor me. I tried to call you, but they said you'd left already. I wondered if you were feeling all right."

"I'm fine!"

"You look fine." The familiar sight of her melted away his irritation. He loved the way she looked: her slender, boyish figure, her close-cropped, curly hair, her pale complexion and bright blue eyes.

Her cheeks now had a slight hectic flush. She caught her bottom lip between her teeth and gave him an assessing look before coming straight out with it. "How would you feel about keeping a pet?"

Stuart felt a horrible conviction that she was not talking about a dog or a cat. He wondered if it was the whiskey on an empty stomach which made him feel dizzy.

"It was under my car. If I hadn't happened to notice something moving down there I could have run over it." She lifted her shoulders in a delicate shudder.

"Oh, God, Jenny, you haven't brought it home!"

She looked indignant. "Well, of course I did! I couldn't just leave it in the street—somebody else might have run it over."

Or stepped on it, he thought, realizing now that he could never tell Jenny what he had done. That made him feel even worse, but maybe he was wrong. Maybe it was just a cat she'd rescued. "What is it?"

She gave a strange, excited laugh. "I don't know.

Something very rare, I think. Here, look." She slipped the large, woven bag off her shoulder, opening it, holding it out to him. "Look. Isn't it the sweetest thing?"

How could two people who were so close, so alike in so many ways, see something so differently? He only wanted to kill it, even now, while she had obviously fallen in love. He kept his face carefully neutral although he couldn't help flinching from her description. "*Sweet?*"

It gave him a pang to see how she pulled back, holding the bag protectively close as she said, "Well, I know it's not pretty, but so what? I thought it was horrible, too, at first sight. . . ." Her face clouded, as if she found her first impression difficult to remember, or to credit, and her voice faltered a little. "But then, then I realized how *helpless* it was. It needed me. It can't help how it looks. Anyway, doesn't it kind of remind you of the Psammead?"

"The what?"

"Psammead. You know, *The Five Children and It?*"

He recognized the title but her passion for old-fashioned children's books was something he didn't share. He shook his head impatiently. "That thing didn't come out of a book, Jen. You found it in the street and you don't know what it is or where it came from. It could be dangerous, it could be diseased."

"Dangerous," she said in a withering tone.

"You don't know."

"I've been with him all day and he hasn't hurt me, or anybody else at the office, he's perfectly happy being held, and he likes being scratched behind the ears."

He did not miss the pronoun shift. "It might have rabies."

"Don't be silly."

"Don't *you* be silly; it's not exactly native, is it? It might be carrying all sorts of foul parasites from South America or Africa or wherever."

"Now you're being racist. I'm not going to listen to you. *And* you've been drinking." She flounced out of the room.

If he'd been holding his glass still he might have thrown it. He closed his eyes and concentrated on breathing in and out slowly. This was worse than any argument they'd ever had, the only crucial disagreement of their marriage. Jenny had stronger views about many things than he did, so her wishes usually prevailed. He didn't mind that. But this was different. He wasn't having that creature in his home. He had to make her agree.

Necessity cooled his blood. He had his temper under control when his wife returned. "I'm sorry," he said, although she was the one who should have apologized. Still looking prickly, she shrugged and would not meet his eyes. "Want to go out to dinner tonight?"

She shook her head. "I'd rather not. I've got some work to do."

"Can I get you something to drink? I'm only one whiskey ahead of you, honest."

Her shoulders relaxed. "I'm sorry. Low blow. Yeah, pour me one. And one for yourself." She sat down on the couch, her bag by her feet. Leaning over, reaching inside, she cooed, "Who's my little sweetheart, then?"

Normally he would have taken a seat beside her. Now, though, he eyed the pale, misshapen bundle on her lap and, after handing her a glass, retreated across the room. "Don't get mad, but isn't having a pet one of those things we discuss and agree on beforehand?"

He saw the tension come back into her shoulders, but she went on stroking the thing, keeping herself calm. "Normally, yes. But this is special. I didn't plan it. It happened, and now I've got a responsibility to him. Or her." She giggled. "We don't even know what sex you are, do we, my precious?"

He said carefully, "I can see that you had to do something when you found it, but keeping it might not be the best thing."

"I'm not going to put it out in the street."

"No, no, but . . . don't you think it would make sense to let a professional have a look at it? Take it to a vet, get it checked out . . . maybe it needs shots or something."

She gave him a withering look and for a moment he faltered, but then he rallied. "Come on, Jenny, be reasonable! You can't just drag some strange animal in off the street and keep it, just like that. You don't even know what it eats."

"I gave it some fruit at lunch. It ate that. Well, it sucked out the juice. I don't think it can chew."

"But you don't know, do you? Maybe the fruit juice was just an aperitif, maybe it needs half its weight in live insects every day, or a couple of small, live mammals. Do you really think you could cope with feeding it mice or rabbits fresh from the pet shop every week?"

"Oh, Stuart."

"Well? Will you just take it to a vet? Make sure it's healthy? Will you do that much?"

"And then I can keep it? If the vet says there's nothing wrong with it, and it doesn't need to eat anything too impossible?"

"Then we can talk about it. Hey, don't pout at me; I'm not your father, I'm not telling you what to do. We're partners, and partners don't make unilateral decisions about things that affect them both; partners discuss things and reach compromises and . . ."

"There can't be any compromise about this."

He felt as if she'd doused him with ice water. "What?"

"Either I win and I keep him or you win and I give him up. Where's the compromise?"

This was why wars were fought, thought Stuart, but he didn't say it. He was the picture of sweet reason, explaining as if he meant it. "The compromise is that we each try to see the other person's point. You get the animal checked out, make sure it's healthy and I, I'll keep an open mind about having a pet, and see if I might start liking . . . him. Does he have a name yet?"

Her eyes flickered. "No . . . we can choose one later, together. If we keep him."

He still felt cold and, although he could think of no reason for it, he was certain she was lying to him.

In bed that night as he groped for sleep Stuart kept seeing the tiny, hideous face of the thing screaming as his foot came down on it. That moment of blind, killing rage was not like him. He couldn't deny he had done it, or how he had felt, but now, as Jenny slept innocently beside him, as the creature she had rescued, a twin to his victim, crouched alive in the bathroom, he tried to remember it differently.

In fantasy, he stopped his foot, he controlled his rage, and, staring at the memory of the alien animal, he struggled to see past his anger and his fear, to see through those fiercer masculine emotions and find his way to Jenny's feminine pity. Maybe his intuition had been wrong and hers was right. Maybe, if he had waited a little longer, instead of lashing out, he would have seen how unnecessary his fear was.

Poor little thing, poor little thing. It's helpless, it needs me, it's harmless so I won't harm it.

Slowly, in imagination, he worked toward that feeling, *her* feeling, and then, suddenly, he was there, through the anger, through the fear, through the hate to . . . not love, he couldn't say that, but compassion. Glowing and warm, compassion filled his heart and flooded his veins, melting the ice there and washing him out into the sea of sleep, and dreams where Jenny smiled and loved him and there was no space between them for misunderstanding.

He woke in the middle of the night with a desperate urge to pee. He was out of bed in the dark hallway when he remembered what was waiting in the bathroom. He couldn't go back to bed with the need unsatisfied, but he stood outside the bathroom door, hand hovering over the light switch on this side, afraid to turn it on, open the door, go in.

It wasn't, he realized, that he was afraid of a creature no bigger than a football and less likely to hurt him; rather, he was afraid that he might hurt it. It was a stronger variant of that reckless vertigo he had felt sometimes in high places, the fear, not of falling, but of throwing oneself off, of losing control and giving in to self-destructive urges. He didn't *want* to kill the thing—had his own feelings not undergone a sea change, Jenny's love for it would have been enough to stop him—but something, some dark urge stronger than himself, might make him.

Finally he went down to the end of the hall and outside to the weedy, muddy little area which passed for the communal front garden and in which the rubbish bins, of necessity, were kept, and, shivering in his thin cotton pajamas in the damp, chilly air, he watered the sickly forsythia, or whatever it was, that Jenny had planted so optimistically last winter.

When he went back inside, more uncomfortable than

when he had gone out, he saw the light was on in the bathroom, and as he approached the half-open door, he heard Jenny's voice, low and soothing. "There, there. Nobody's going to hurt you, I promise. You're safe here. Go to sleep now. Go to sleep."

He went past without pausing, knowing he would be viewed as an intruder, and got back into bed. He fell asleep, lulled by the meaningless murmur of her voice, still waiting for her to join him.

Stuart was not used to doubting Jenny, but when she told him she had visited a veterinarian who had given her new pet a clean bill of health, he did not believe her.

In a neutral tone he asked, "Did he say what kind of animal it was?"

"He didn't know."

"He didn't know what it was, but he was sure it was perfectly healthy."

"God, Stuart, what do you want? It's obvious to everybody but you that my little friend is healthy and happy. What do you want, a birth certificate?"

He looked at her "friend," held close against her side, looking squashed and miserable. "What do you mean, 'everybody'?"

She shrugged. "Everybody at work. They're all jealous as anything." She planted a kiss on the thing's pointy head. Then she looked at him, and he realized that she had not kissed him, as she usually did, when he came in. She'd been clutching that thing the whole time. "I'm going to keep him," she said quietly. "If you don't like it, then . . ." Her pause seemed to pile up in solid, transparent blocks between them. "Then, I'm sorry, but that's how it is."

So much for an equal relationship, he thought. So much for sharing. Mortally wounded, he decided to pretend it hadn't happened.

"Want to go out for Indian tonight?"

She shook her head, turning away. "I want to stay in. There's something on telly. You go on. You could bring me something back, if you wouldn't mind. A spinach bahjee and a couple of nans would do me."

"And what about . . . something for your little friend?"

She smiled a private smile. "He's all right. I've fed him already."

Then she raised her eyes to his and acknowledged his effort. "Thanks."

He went out and got take-away for them both, and stopped at the off-license for the Mexican beer Jenny favored. A radio in the off-license was playing a sentimental song about love that Stuart remembered from his earliest childhood: his mother used to sing it. He was shocked to realize he had tears in his eyes.

That night Jenny made up the sofa bed in the spare room, explaining, "He can't stay in the bathroom; it's just not satisfactory, you know it's not."

"He needs the bed?"

"I do. He's confused, everything is new and different, I'm the one thing he can count on. I have to stay with him. He needs me."

"He needs you? What about me?"

"Oh, Stuart," she said impatiently. "You're a grown man. You can sleep by yourself for a night or two."

"And that thing can't?"

"Don't call him a thing."

"What am I supposed to call it? Look, you're not its mother—it doesn't need you as much as you'd like to think. It was perfectly all right in the bathroom last night—it'll be fine in here on its own."

"Oh? And what do you know about it? You'd like to kill him, wouldn't you? Admit it."

"No," he said, terrified that she had guessed the truth. If she knew how he had killed one of those things she would never forgive him. "It's not true, I don't—I couldn't hurt it any more than I could hurt you."

Her face softened. She believed him. It didn't matter how he felt about the creature. Hurting it, knowing how she felt, would be like committing an act of violence against her, and they both knew he wouldn't do that. "Just for a few nights, Stuart. Just until he settles in."

He had to accept that. All he could do was hang on, hope that she still loved him and that this wouldn't be forever.

The days passed. Jenny no longer offered to drive him to work. When he asked her, she said it was out of her way and with traffic so bad a detour would make her late. She said it was silly to take him the short distance to the station, especially as there was nowhere she could safely stop to let him out, and anyway, the walk would do him good. They were all good reasons, which he had used in the old days himself, but her excuses struck him painfully when he remembered how eager she had once been for his company, how ready to make any detour for his sake. Her new pet accompanied her everywhere, even to work, snug in the little nest she had made for it in a woven carrier bag.

"Of course things are different now. But I haven't stopped loving you," she said when he tried to talk to her about the breakdown of their marriage. "It's not like I've found another man. This is something completely different. It doesn't threaten you; you're still my husband."

But it was obvious to him that a husband was no longer something she particularly valued. He began to have fantasies about killing it. Not, this time, in a blind rage, but as part of a carefully thought-out plan. He might poison it, or spirit it away somehow and pretend it had run away. Once it was gone he hoped Jenny would forget it and be his again.

But he never had a chance. Jenny was quite obsessive about the thing, as if it were too valuable to be left unguarded for a single minute. Even when she took a bath, or went to the toilet, the creature was with her, behind the locked door of the bathroom. When he offered to look after it for her for a few minutes she just smiled, as if the idea was manifestly ridiculous, and he didn't dare insist.

So he went to work, and went out for drinks with colleagues, and spent what time he could with Jenny, although they were never alone. He didn't argue with her, although he wasn't above trying to move her to pity if he could. He made seemingly casual comments designed to convince her of his change of heart so that eventually, weeks or months from now, she would trust him and leave the creature with him—and then, later, perhaps, they could put their marriage back together.

One afternoon, after an extended lunch break, Stuart returned to the office to find one of the senior editors crouched on the floor beside his secretary's empty desk, whispering and chuckling to herself.

He cleared his throat nervously. "Linda?"

She lurched back on her heels and got up awkwardly. She blushed and ducked her head as she turned, looking very unlike her usual high-powered self. "Oh, uh, Stuart, I was just—"

Frankie came in with a pile of photocopying. "Uh-huh," she said loudly.

Linda's face got even redder. "Just going," she mumbled, and fled.

Before he could ask, Stuart saw the creature, another crippled bat-without-wings, on the floor beside the open bottom drawer of Frankie's desk. It looked up at him, opened its slit of a mouth and gave a sad little hiss. Around one matchstick-thin leg it wore a fine golden chain which was fastened at the other end to the drawer.

"Some people would steal anything that's not chained down," said Frankie darkly. "People you wouldn't suspect."

He stared at her, letting her see his disapproval, his annoyance, disgust, even. "Animals in the office aren't part of the contract, Frankie."

"It's not an animal."

"What is it, then?"

"I don't know. You tell me."

"It doesn't matter what it is, you can't have it here."

"I can't leave it at home."

"Why not?"

She turned away from him, busying herself with her stacks of paper. "I can't leave it alone. It might get hurt. It might escape."

"Chance would be a fine thing."

She shot him a look, and he was certain she knew he wasn't talking about *her* pet. He said, "What does your boyfriend think about it?"

"I don't have a boyfriend." She sounded angry but then, abruptly, the anger dissipated, and she smirked. "I don't have to have one, do I?"

"You can't have that animal here. Whatever it is. You'll have to take it home."

She raised her fuzzy eyebrows. "Right now?"

He was tempted to say yes, but thought of the manuscripts that wouldn't be sent out, the letters that wouldn't be typed, the delays and confusions, and he sighed. "Just don't bring it back again. All right?"

"Yowza."

He felt very tired. He could tell her what to do but she would no more obey than would his wife. She would bring it back the next day and keep bringing it back, maybe keeping it hidden, maybe not, until he either gave in or was forced into firing her. He went into his office, closed the door, and put his head down on his desk.

That evening he walked in on his wife feeding the creature with her blood.

It was immediately obvious that it was that way round. The creature might be a vampire—it obviously was—but his wife was no helpless victim. She was wide-awake and in control, holding the creature firmly, letting it feed from a vein in her arm.

She flinched as if anticipating a shout, but he couldn't speak. He watched what was happening without attempting to interfere and gradually she relaxed again, as if he wasn't there.

When the creature, sated, fell off, she kept it cradled on her lap and reached with her other hand for the surgical spirit and cotton wool on the table, moistened a piece of cotton wool and tamped it to the tiny wound. Then, finally, she met her husband's eyes.

"He has to eat," she said reasonably. "He can't chew. He needs blood. Not very much, but . . ."

"And he needs it from you? You can't . . . ?"

"I can't hold down some poor scared rabbit or dog for

him, no." She made a shuddering face. "Well, really, think about it. You know how squeamish I am. This is so much easier. It doesn't hurt."

It hurts me, he thought, but couldn't say it. "Jenny . . ."

"Oh, don't start," she said crossly. "I'm not going to get any disease from it, and he doesn't take enough to make any difference. Actually, I like it. We both do."

"Jenny, please don't. Please. For me. Give it up."

"No." She held the scraggy, ugly thing close and gazed at Stuart like a dispassionate executioner. "I'm sorry, Stuart, I really am, but this is nonnegotiable. If you can't accept that you'd better leave."

This was the showdown he had been avoiding, the end of it all. He tried to rally his arguments and then he realized he had none. She had said it. She had made her choice, and it was nonnegotiable. And he realized, looking at her now, that although she reminded him of the woman he loved, he didn't want to live with what she had become.

He could have refused to leave. After all, he had done nothing wrong. Why should he give up his home, this flat which was half his? But he could not force Jenny out onto the streets with nowhere to go; he still felt responsible for her.

"I'll pack a bag, and make a few phone calls," he said quietly. He knew someone from work who was looking for a lodger, and if all else failed, his brother had a spare room. Already, in his thoughts, he had left.

He ended up, once they'd sorted out their finances and formally separated, in a flat just off the Holloway Road, near Archway. It was not too far to walk if Jenny cared to visit, which she never did. Sometimes he called on her, but it was painful to feel himself an unwelcome visitor in the home they once had shared.

He never had to fire Frankie; she handed in her notice a week later, telling him she'd been offered an editorial job at The Women's Press. He wondered if pets in the office were part of the contract over there.

He never learned if the creatures had names. He never knew where they had come from, or how many there were. Had they fallen only in Islington? (Frankie had a flat somewhere off Upper Street.) He never saw anything on the news about them, or read any official confirmation of their existence, but he was aware of occasional oblique references to them in other contexts, occasional glimpses.

One evening, coming home on the tube, he found himself looking at the woman sitting opposite. She was about his own age, probably in her early thirties, with strawberry-blond hair, greenish eyes, and an almost translucent complexion. She was strikingly dressed in high, soft-leather boots, a long black woolen skirt, and an enveloping cashmere cloak of cranberry red. High on the cloak, below and to the right of the fastening at the neck, was a simple, gold circle brooch. Attached to it he noticed a very fine golden chain which vanished inside the cloak, like the end of a watch fob.

He looked at it idly, certain he had seen something like it before, on other women, knowing it reminded him of something. The train arrived at Archway, and as he rose to leave the train, so did the attractive woman. Her stride matched his. They might well leave the station together. He tried to think of something to say to her, some pretext for striking up a conversation. He was, after all, a single man again now, and she might be a single woman. He had forgotten how single people in London contrived to meet.

He looked at her again, sidelong, hoping she would

turn her head and look at him. With one slender hand she toyed with her gold chain. Her cloak fell open slightly as she walked, and he caught a glimpse of the creature she carried beneath it, close to her body, attached by a slender golden chain.

He stopped walking and let her get away from him. He had to rest for a little while before he felt able to climb the stairs to the street.

By then he was wondering if he had really seen what he thought he had seen. The glimpse had been so brief. But he had been deeply shaken by what he saw or imagined, and he turned the wrong way outside the station. When he finally realized, he was at the corner of Jenny's road, which had once also been his. Rather than retrace his steps, he decided to take the turning and walk past her house.

Lights were on in the front room, the curtains drawn against the early winter dark. His footsteps slowed as he drew nearer. He felt such a longing to be inside, back home, belonging. He wondered if she would be pleased at all to see him. He wondered if she ever felt lonely, as he did.

Then he saw the tiny, dark figure between the curtains and the window. It was spread-eagled against the glass, scrabbling uselessly; inside, longing to be out.

As he stared, feeling its pain as his own, the curtains swayed and opened slightly as a human figure moved between them. He saw the woman reach out and pull the creature away from the glass, back into the warm, lighted room with her, and the curtains fell again, shutting him out.

CARRION COMFORT

♦♦♦

DAN SIMMONS

Nina was going to take credit for the death of the Beatle, John. I thought that was in very bad taste. She had her scrapbook laid out on my mahogany coffee table, newspaper clippings neatly arranged in chronological order, the bald statements of death recording all of her Feedings. Nina Drayton's smile was radiant, but her pale-blue eyes showed no hint of warmth.

"We should wait for Willi," I said.

"Of course, Melanie. You're right, as always. How silly of me. I know the rules." Nina stood and began walking around the room, idly touching the furnishings or exclaiming softly over a ceramic statuette or piece of needlepoint. This part of the house had once been the conservatory, but now I used it as my sewing room. Green plants still caught the morning light. The light made it a warm, cozy place in the daytime, but now that winter had come the room was too chilly to use at night. Nor did I like the sense of darkness closing in against all those panes of glass.

"I love this house," said Nina.

She turned and smiled at me. "I can't tell you how much I look forward to coming back to Charleston. We should hold all of our reunions here."

I knew how much Nina loathed this city and this house.

"Willi would be hurt," I said. "You know how he likes to show off his place in Beverly Hills—and his new girlfriends."

"And boyfriends," Nina said, laughing. Of all the changes and darkenings in Nina, her laugh has been least affected. It was still the husky but childish laugh that I had first heard so long ago. It had drawn me to her then—one lonely, adolescent girl responding to the warmth of another as a moth to a flame. Now it served only to chill me and put me even more on guard. Enough moths had been drawn to Nina's flame over the many decades.

"I'll send for tea," I said.

Mr. Thorne brought the tea in my best Wedgwood china. Nina and I sat in the slowly moving squares of sunlight and spoke softly of nothing important: mutually ignorant comments on the economy, references to books that the other had not gotten around to reading, and sympathetic murmurs about the low class of persons one meets while flying these days. Someone peering in from the garden might have thought he was seeing an aging but attractive niece visiting her favorite aunt. (I drew the line at suggesting that anyone would mistake us for mother and daughter.) People usually consider me a well-dressed if not stylish person. Heaven knows I have paid enough to have the wool skirts and silk blouses mailed from Scotland and France. But next to Nina I've always felt dowdy.

This day she wore an elegant, light-blue dress that must have cost several thousand dollars. The color made her complexion seem even more perfect than usual and brought out the blue of her eyes. Her hair had gone as gray as mine, but somehow she managed to get away with wearing it long and tied back with a single barrette. It looked youthful and chic on Nina and made me feel that my short artificial curls were glowing with a blue rinse.

Few would suspect that I was four years younger than Nina. Time had been kind to her. And she had Fed more often.

She set down her cup and saucer and moved aimlessly around the room again. It was not like Nina to show such signs of nervousness. She stopped in front of the glass display case. Her gaze passed over the Hummels and the pewter pieces and then stopped in surprise.

"Good heavens, Melanie. A pistol! What an odd place to put an old pistol."

"It's an heirloom," I said. "A Colt Peacemaker from right after the War Between the States. Quite expensive. And you're right, it *is* a silly place to keep it. But it's the only case I have in the house with a lock on it and Mrs. Hodges often brings her grandchildren when she visits—"

"You mean it's *loaded*?"

"No, of course not," I lied. "But children should not play with such things . . ." I trailed off lamely. Nina nodded but did not bother to conceal the condescension in her smile. She went to look out the south window into the garden.

Damn her. It said volumes about Nina that she did not recognize that pistol.

On the day he was killed, Charles Edgar Larchmont had been my beau for precisely five months and two days. There had been no formal announcement, but we were to be married. Those five months had been a microcosm of the era itself—naive, flirtatious, formal to the point of preciosity, and romantic. Most of all, romantic. Romantic in the worst sense of the word: dedicated to saccharine or insipid ideals that only an adolescent—or an adolescent society—would strive to maintain. We were children playing with loaded weapons.

Nina, she was Nina Hawkins then, had her own beau—a tall, awkward, but well-meaning Englishman named Roger Harrison. Mr. Harrison had met Nina in London a year earlier, during the first stages of the Hawkinses' Grand Tour. Declaring himself smitten—another absurdity of those times—the tall Englishman had followed her from one European capital to another until, after being firmly reprimanded by Nina's father (an unimaginative little milliner who was constantly on the defensive about his doubtful social status), Harrison returned to London to "settle his affairs." Some months later he showed up in New York just as Nina was being packed off to her aunt's home in Charleston in order to terminate yet another flirtation. Still undaunted, the clumsy Englishman followed her south, ever mindful of the protocols and restrictions of the day.

We were a gay group. The day after I met Nina at Cousin Celia's June ball, the four of us were taking a hired boat up the Cooper River for a picnic on Daniel Island. Roger Harrison, serious and solemn on every topic, was a perfect foil for Charles's irreverent sense of humor. Nor did Roger seem to mind the good-natured jesting, since he was soon joining in the laughter with his peculiar *haw-haw-haw*.

Nina loved it all. Both gentlemen showered attention on her, and although Charles never failed to show the primacy of his affection for me, it was understood by all that Nina Hawkins was one of those young women who invariably becomes the center of male gallantry and attention in any gathering. Nor were the social strata of Charleston blind to the combined charm of our foursome. For two months of that now-distant summer, no party was complete, no excursion adequately planned, and no occasion considered a success unless we four were invited and had chosen to attend. Our happy dominance of the youthful social scene was so pronounced that Cousins Celia and Loraine wheedled their parents into leaving two weeks early for their annual August sojourn in Maine.

I am not sure when Nina and I came up with the idea of the duel. Perhaps it was during one of the long, hot nights when the other "slept over"—creeping into the other's bed, whispering and giggling, stifling our laughter when the rustling of starched uniforms betrayed the presence of our colored maids moving through the darkened halls. In any case, the idea was the natural outgrowth of the romantic pretensions of the time. The picture of Charles and Roger actually dueling over some abstract point of honor relating to *us* thrilled both of us in a physical way that I recognize now as a simple form of sexual titillation.

It would have been harmless except for the Ability. We had been so successful in our manipulation of male behavior—a manipulation that was both expected and encouraged in those days—that neither of us had yet suspected that there was anything beyond the ordinary in the way we could translate our whims into other people's actions. The field of parapsychology did not exist then; or rather, it existed only in the rappings and knockings of parlor-game séances. At any rate, we amused ourselves for several weeks with whispered fantasies, and then one of us—or perhaps both of us—used the Ability to translate the fantasy into reality.

In a sense, it was our first Feeding.

I do not remember the purported cause of the quarrel, perhaps some deliberate misinterpretation of one of

Charles's jokes. I cannot recall who Charles and Roger arranged to have serve as seconds on that illegal outing. I do remember the hurt and confused expression on Roger Harrison's face during those few days. It was a caricature of ponderous dullness, the confusion of a man who finds himself in a situation not of his making and from which he cannot escape. I remember Charles and his mercurial swings of mood—the bouts of humor, periods of black anger, and the tears and kisses the night before the duel.

I remember with great clarity the beauty of that morning. Mists were floating up from the river and diffusing the rays of the rising sun as we rode out to the dueling field. I remember Nina reaching over and squeezing my hand with an impetuous excitement that was communicated through my body like an electric shock.

Much of the rest of that morning is missing. Perhaps in the intensity of that first, subconscious Feeding, I literally lost consciousness as I was engulfed in the waves of fear, excitement, pride—of *maleness*—emanating from our two beaus as they faced death on that lovely morning. I remember experiencing the shock of realizing, *this is really happening,* as I shared the tread of high boots through the grass. Someone was calling off the paces. I dimly recall the weight of the pistol in my hand—Charles's hand, I think; I will never know for sure—and a second of cold clarity before an explosion broke the connection, and the acrid smell of gunpowder brought me back to myself.

It was Charles who died. I have never been able to forget the incredible quantities of blood that poured from the small, round hole in his breast. His white shirt was crimson by the time I reached him. There had been no blood in our fantasies. Nor had there been the sight of Charles with his head lolling, mouth dribbling saliva onto his bloodied chest while his eyes rolled back to show the whites like two eggs embedded in his skull.

Roger Harrison was sobbing as Charles breathed his final, shuddering gasps on that field of innocence.

I remember nothing at all about the confused hours that followed. The next morning I opened my cloth bag to find Charles's pistol lying with my things. Why would I have kept that revolver? If I had wished to take something from my fallen lover as a sign of remembrance, why that alien piece of metal? Why pry from his dead fingers the symbol of our thoughtless sin?

It said volumes about Nina that she did not recognize that pistol.

"Willi's here," announced Nina's amanuensis, the loathsome Miss Barrett Kramer. Kramer's appearance was as unisex as her name: short-cropped, black hair, powerful shoulders, and a blank, aggressive gaze that I associated with lesbians and criminals. She looked to be in her mid-thirties.

"Thank you, Barrett dear," said Nina.

Both of us went out to greet Willi, but Mr. Thorne had already let him in, and we met in the hallway.

"Melanie! You look marvelous! You grow younger each time I see you. Nina!" The change in Willi's voice was evident. Men continued to be overpowered by their first sight of Nina after an absence. There were hugs and kisses. Willi himself looked more dissolute than ever. His alpaca sport coat was exquisitely tailored, his turtleneck sweater successfully concealed the eroded lines of his wattled neck, but when he swept off his jaunty sports-car cap the long strands of white hair he had brushed forward to hide his encroaching baldness were knocked into disarray.

Willi's face was flushed with excitement, but there was also the telltale capillary redness about the nose and cheeks that spoke of too much liquor, too many drugs.

"Ladies, I think you've met my associates, Tom Luhar and Jenson Reynolds?" The two men added to the crowd in my narrow hall. Mr. Luhar was thin and blond, smiling with perfectly capped teeth. Mr. Reynolds was a gigantic Negro, hulking forward with a sullen, bruised look on his coarse face. I was sure that neither Nina nor I had encountered these specific cat's-paws of Willi's before. It did not matter.

"Why don't we go into the parlor?" I suggested. It was an awkward procession ending with the three of us seated on the heavily upholstered chairs surrounding the Georgian tea table that had been my grandmother's. "More tea, please, Mr. Thorne." Miss Kramer took that as her cue to leave, but Willi's two pawns stood uncertainly by the door, shifting from foot to foot and glancing at the crystal on display as if their mere proximity could break something. I would not have been surprised if that had proved to be the case.

"Jense!" Willi snapped his fingers. The Negro hesitated and then brought forward an expensive leather attaché case. Willi set it on the tea table and clicked the catches open with his short, broad fingers. "Why don't you two see Mrs. Fuller's man about getting something to drink?"

When they were gone Willi shook his head and smiled apologetically at Nina. "Sorry about that, Love."

Nina put her hand on Willi's sleeve. She leaned forward with an air of expectancy. "Melanie wouldn't let me begin the Game without you. Wasn't that *awful* of me to want to start without you, Willi dear?"

Willi frowned. After fifty years he still bridled at being called Willi. In Los Angeles he was Big Bill Borden.

When he returned to his native Germany—which was not often because of the dangers involved—he was once again Wilhelm von Borchert, lord of dark manor, forest, and hunt. But Nina had called him Willi when they had first met in 1931 in Vienna, and Willi he had remained.

"You begin, Willi dear," said Nina. "You go first."

I could remember the time when we would have spent the first few days of our reunion in conversation and catching up with one another's lives. Now there was not even time for small talk.

Willi showed his teeth and removed news clippings, notebooks, and a stack of cassettes from his briefcase. No sooner had he covered the small table with his material than Mr. Thorne arrived with the tea and Nina's scrapbook from the sewing room. Willi brusquely cleared a small space.

At first glance one might see certain similarities between Willi Borchert and Mr. Thorne. One would be mistaken. Both men tended to the florid, but Willi's complexion was the result of excess and emotion; Mr. Thorne had known neither of these for many years. Willi's balding was a patchy, self-consciously concealed thing—a weasel with mange; Mr. Thorne's bare head was smooth and unwrinkled. One could not imagine Mr. Thorne ever having *had* hair. Both men had gray eyes—what a novelist would call cold, gray eyes—but Mr. Thorne's eyes were cold with indifference, cold with a clarity coming from an absolute absence of troublesome emotion or thought. Willi's eyes were the cold of a blustery North Sea winter and were often clouded with shifting curtains of the emotions that controlled him—pride, hatred, love of pain, the pleasures of destruction.

Willi never referred to his use of the Ability as *Feedings*—I was evidently the only one who thought in those terms—but Willi sometimes talked of The Hunt. Perhaps it was the dark forests of his homeland that he thought of as he stalked his human quarry through the sterile streets of Los Angeles. Did Willi dream of the forest, I wondered. Did he look back to green wool hunting jackets, the applause of retainers, the gouts of blood from the dying boar? Or did Willi remember the slam of jackboots on cobblestones and the pounding of his lieutenants' fists on doors? Perhaps Willi still associated his Hunt with the dark European night of the ovens that he had helped to oversee.

I called it Feeding. Willi called it The Hunt. I had never heard Nina call it anything.

"Where is your VCR?" Willi asked. "I have put them all on tape."

"Oh, Willi," said Nina in an exasperated tone. "You know Melanie. She's *so* old-fashioned. You know she wouldn't have a video player."

"I don't even have a television," I said. Nina laughed.

"Goddamn it," muttered Willi. "It doesn't matter. I have other records here." He snapped rubber bands from around the small, black notebooks. "It just would have been better on tape. The Los Angeles stations gave much coverage to the Hollywood Strangler, and I edited in the . . . Ach! Never mind."

He tossed the videocassettes into his briefcase and slammed the lid shut.

"Twenty-three," he said. "Twenty-three since we met twelve months ago. It doesn't seem that long, does it?"

"Show us," said Nina. She was leaning forward, and her blue eyes seemed very bright. "I've been wondering since I saw the Strangler interviewed on *Sixty Minutes*. He *was* yours, Willi? He seemed so—"

"*Ja, ja*, he was mine. A nobody. A timid little man. He

was the gardener of a neighbor of mine. I left him alive so that the police could question him, erase any doubts. He will hang himself in his cell next month after the press loses interest. But this is more interesting. Look at this." Willi slid across several glossy black-and-white photographs. The NBC executive had murdered the five members of his family and drowned a visiting soap-opera actress in his pool. He had then stabbed himself repeatedly and written *50 share* in blood on the wall of the bathhouse.

"Reliving old glories, Willi?" asked Nina. "*Death to the pigs* and all that?"

"No, goddamn it. I think it should receive points for irony. The girl had been scheduled to drown on the program. It was already in the script outline."

"Was he hard to Use?" It was my question. I was curious despite myself.

Willi lifted one eyebrow. "Not really. He was an alcoholic and heavily into cocaine. There was not much left. And he hated his family. Most people do."

"Most people in California, perhaps," said Nina primly. It was an odd comment from Nina. Years ago her father had committed suicide by throwing himself in front of a trolley car.

"Where did you make contact?" I asked.

"A party. The usual place. He bought the coke from a director who had ruined one of my—"

"Did you have to repeat the contact?"

Willi frowned at me. He kept his anger under control, but his face grew redder. "*Ja, ja.* I saw him twice more. Once I just watched from my car as he played tennis."

"Points for irony," said Nina. "But you lose points for repeated contact. If he were as empty as you say, you should have been able to Use him after only one touch. What else do you have?"

He had his usual assortment. Pathetic skid-row murders. Two domestic slayings. A highway collision that turned into a fatal shooting. "I was in the crowd," said Willi. "I made contact. He had a gun in the glove compartment."

"Two points," said Nina.

Willi had saved a good one for last. A once-famous child star had suffered a bizarre accident. He had left his Bel Air apartment while it filled with gas and then returned to light a match. Two others had died in the ensuing fire.

"You get credit only for him," said Nina.

"*Ja, ja.*"

"Are you absolutely sure about this one? It *could* have been an accident."

"Don't be ridiculous," snapped Willi. He turned toward me. "*This* one was very hard to Use. Very strong. I blocked his memory of turning on the gas. Had to hold it away for two hours. Then forced him into the room. He struggled not to strike the match."

"You should have had him use his lighter," said Nina.

"He didn't smoke," growled Willi. "He gave it up last year."

"Yes," smiled Nina. "I seem to remember him saying that to Johnny Carson." I could not tell whether Nina was jesting.

The three of us went through the ritual of assigning points. Nina did most of the talking. Willi went from being sullen to expansive to sullen again. At one point he reached over and patted my knee as he laughingly asked for my support. I said nothing. Finally he gave up, crossed the parlor to the liquor cabinet, and poured himself a tall glass of bourbon from father's decanter. The evening light was sending its final horizontal rays through the stained-glass panels of the bay windows, and it cast a red hue on Willi as he stood next to the oak cupboard. His eyes were small, red embers in a bloody mask.

"Forty-one," said Nina at last.

She looked up brightly and showed the calculator as if it verified some objective fact. "I count forty-one points. What do you have, Melanie?"

"*Ja*," interrupted Willi. "That is fine. Now let us see your claims, Nina." His voice was flat and empty. Even Willi had lost some interest in the Game.

Before Nina could begin, Mr. Thorne entered and motioned that dinner was served. We adjourned to the dining room—Willi pouring himself another glass of bourbon and Nina fluttering her hands in mock frustration at the interruption of the Game. Once seated at the long mahogany table, I worked at being a hostess. From decades of tradition, talk of the Game was banned from the dinner table. Over soup we discussed Willi's new movie and the purchase of another store for Nina's line of boutiques. It seemed that Nina's monthly column in *Vogue* was to be discontinued but that a newspaper syndicate was interested in picking it up.

Both of my guests exclaimed over the perfection of the baked ham, but I thought that Mr. Thorne had made the gravy a trifle too sweet. Darkness had filled the windows before we finished our chocolate mousse. The refracted light from the chandelier made Nina's hair dance with highlights while I feared that mine glowed more bluely than ever.

Suddenly there was a sound from the kitchen. The huge Negro's face appeared at the swinging door. His shoulder was hunched against white hands and his expression was that of a querulous child.

". . . the hell you think we are sittin' here like goddamned—" The white hands pulled him out of sight.

"Excuse me, ladies." Willi dabbed linen at his lips and stood up. He still moved gracefully for all of his years.

Nina poked at her chocolate. There was one sharp, barked command from the kitchen and the sound of a slap. It was the slap of a man's hand—hard and flat as a small-caliber-rifle shot. I looked up and Mr. Thorne was at my elbow, clearing away the dessert dishes.

"Coffee, please, Mr. Thorne. For all of us." He nodded and his smile was gentle.

Franz Anton Mesmer had known of it even if he had not understood it. I suspect that Mesmer must have had some small touch of the Ability. Modern pseudosciences have studied it and renamed it, removed most of its power, confused its uses and origins, but it remains the shadow of what Mesmer discovered. They have no idea of what it is like to Feed.

I despair at the rise of modern violence. I truly give in to despair at times, that deep, futureless pit of despair that poet Gerard Manley Hopkins called carrion comfort. I watch the American slaughterhouse, the casual attacks on popes, presidents, and uncounted others, and I wonder whether there are many more out there with the Ability or whether butchery has simply become the modern way of life.

All humans feed on violence, on the small exercises of power over another. Bur few have tasted—as we have—the ultimate power. And without the Ability, few know the unequaled pleasure of taking a human life. Without the Ability, even those who do feed on life cannot savor the flow of emotions in stalker and victim, the total exhilaration of the attacker who has moved beyond all rules and punishments, the strange, almost sexual submission of the victim in that final second of truth when all options are canceled, all futures denied, all possibilities erased in an exercise of absolute power over another.

I despair at modern violence. I despair at the impersonal nature of it and the casual quality that has made it accessible to so many. I had a television set until I sold it at the height of the Vietnam War. Those sanitized snippets of death—made distant by the camera's lens—meant nothing to me. But I believe it meant something to these cattle that surround me. When the war and the nightly televised body counts ended, they demanded more, *more*, and the movie screens and streets of this sweet and dying nation have provided it in mediocre mob abundance. It is an addiction I know well.

They miss the point. Merely observed, violent death is a sad and sullied tapestry of confusion. But to those of us who have Fed, death can be a *sacrament*.

"My turn! My turn!" Nina's voice still resembled that of the visiting belle who had just filled her dance card at Cousin Celia's June ball.

We had returned to the parlor. Willi had finished his coffee and requested a brandy from Mr. Thorne. I was embarrassed for Willi. To have one's closest associates show any hint of unplanned behavior was certainly a sign of weakening Ability. Nina did not appear to have noticed.

"I have them all in order," said Nina. She opened the scrapbook on the now-empty tea table. Willi went through them carefully, sometimes asking a question, more often grunting assent. I murmured occasional agreement although I had heard of none of them. Except for the Beatle, of course. Nina saved that for near the end.

"Good God, Nina, that was you?" Willi seemed near anger. Nina's Feedings had always run to Park Avenue suicides and matrimonial disagreements ending in shots fired from expensive, small-caliber ladies' guns. This type of thing was more in Willi's crude style. Perhaps he felt that his territory was being invaded. "I mean . . . you were risking a lot, weren't you? It's so . . . damn it . . . so *public.*"

Nina laughed and set down the calculator. "Willi *dear,* that's what the Game is *about*, is it not?"

Willi strode to the liquor cabinet and refilled his brandy snifter. The wind tossed bare branches against the leaded glass of the bay window. I do not like winter. Even in the South it takes its toll on the spirit.

"Didn't this guy . . . what's his name . . . buy the gun in Hawaii or someplace?" asked Willi from across the room. "That sounds like his initiative to me. I mean, if he was *already* stalking the fellow—"

"Willi dear." Nina's voice had gone as cold as the wind that raked the branches. "No one said he was *stable*. How many of yours are stable, Willi? But I made it *happen*, darling. I chose the place and the time. Don't you see the irony of the *place*, Willi? After that little prank on the director of that witchcraft movie a few years ago? It was straight from the script—"

"I don't know," said Willi. He sat heavily on the divan, spilling brandy on his expensive sport coat. He did not notice. The lamplight reflected from his balding skull. The mottles of age were more visible at night, and his neck, where it disappeared into his turtleneck, was all ropes and tendons. "I don't know." He looked up at me and smiled suddenly, as if we shared a conspiracy. "It could be like that writer fellow, eh, Melanie? It could be like that."

Nina looked down at the hands in her lap. They were clenched and the well-manicured fingers were white at the tips.

The Mind Vampires. That's what the writer was going to call his book.

I sometimes wonder if he really would have written anything. What was his name? Something Russian.

Willi and I received telegrams from Nina: COME QUICKLY YOU ARE NEEDED. That was enough. I was on the next morning's flight to New York. The plane was a noisy, propeller-driven Constellation, and I spent much of the flight assuring the overly solicitous stewardess that I needed nothing, that, indeed, I felt fine. She obviously had decided that I was someone's grandmother, who was flying for the first time.

Willi managed to arrive twenty minutes before me. Nina was distraught and as close to hysteria as I had ever seen her. She had been at a party in lower Manhattan two days before—she was not so distraught that she forgot to tell us what important names had been there—when she found herself sharing a corner, a fondue pot, and confidences with a young writer. Or rather, the writer was sharing confidences. Nina described him as a scruffy sort with a wispy little beard, thick glasses, a corduroy sport coat worn over an old plaid shirt—one of the type invariably sprinkled around successful parties of that era, according to Nina. She knew enough not to call him a beatnik, for that term had just become passé, but no one had yet heard the term *hippie*, and it wouldn't have applied to him anyway. He was a writer of the sort that barely ekes out a living, these days at least, by selling blood and doing novelizations of television series. Alexander something.

His idea for a book—he told Nina that he had been working on it for some time—was that many of the murders then being committed were actually the result of a small group of psychic killers, he called them *mind vampires,* who used others to carry out their grisly deeds.

He said that a paperback publisher had already shown interest in his outline and would offer him a contract tomorrow if he would change the title to *The Zombie Factor* and put in more sex.

"So what?" Willi had said to Nina in disgust. "You have me fly across the continent for this? I might buy the idea myself."

That turned out to be the excuse we used to interrogate this Alexander somebody during an impromptu party given by Nina the next evening. I did not attend. The party was not overly successful according to Nina but it gave Willi the chance to have a long chat with the young would-be novelist. In the writer's almost pitiable eagerness to do business with Bill Borden, producer of *Paris Memories, Three on a Swing,* and at least two other completely forgettable Technicolor features touring the drive-ins that summer, he revealed that the book consisted of a well-worn outline and a dozen pages of notes.

He was sure, however, that he could do a treatment for Mr. Borden in five weeks, perhaps even as fast as three weeks if he were flown out to Hollywood to get the proper creative stimulation.

Later that evening we discussed the possibility of Willi simply buying an option on the treatment, but Willi was short on cash at the time and Nina was insistent. In the end the young writer opened his femoral artery with a

Gillette blade and ran screaming into a narrow Greenwich Village side street to die. I don't believe that anyone ever bothered to sort through the clutter and debris of his remaining notes.

"It could be like that writer, *ja*, Melanie?" Willi patted my knee. I nodded. "He was mine," continued Willi, "and Nina tried to take credit. Remember?"

Again I nodded. Actually he had been neither Nina's nor Willi's. I had avoided the party so that I could make contact later without the young man noticing he was being followed. I did so easily. I remember sitting in an overheated little delicatessen across the street from the apartment building. It was over so quickly that there was almost no sense of Feeding. Then I was aware once again of the sputtering radiators and the smell of salami as people rushed to the door to see what the screaming was about. I remember finishing my tea slowly so that I did not have to leave before the ambulance was gone.

"Nonsense," said Nina. She busied herself with her little calculator. "How many points?" She looked at me. I looked at Willi.

"Six," he said with a shrug. Nina made a small show of totaling the numbers.

"Thirty-eight," she said and sighed theatrically. "You win again, Willi. Or rather, you beat *me* again. We must hear from Melanie. You've been so quiet, dear. You must have some surprise for us."

"Yes," said Willi, "it is your turn to win. It has been several years."

"None," I said. I had expected an explosion of questions, but the silence was broken only by the ticking of the clock on the mantelpiece. Nina was looking away from me, at something hidden by the shadows in the corner.

"None?" echoed Willi.

"There was . . . one," I said at last. "But it was by accident. I came across them robbing an old man behind . . . but it was completely by accident."

Willi was agitated. He stood up, walked to the window, turned an old straight-back chair around, and straddled it, arms folded. "What does this mean?"

"You're quitting the Game?" Nina asked as she turned to look at me. I let the question serve as the answer.

"Why?" snapped Willi. In his excitement it came out with a hard *v*.

If I had been raised in an era when young ladies were allowed to shrug, I would have done so. As it was, I contented myself with running my fingers along an imaginary seam on my skirt. Willi had asked the question, but I stared straight into Nina's eyes when I finally answered, "I'm tired. It's been too long. I guess I'm getting old."

"You'll get a lot *older* if you do not Hunt," said Willi. His body, his voice, the red mask of his face, everything signaled great anger just kept in check. "My God, Melanie, you *already* look older! You look terrible. This is *why* we hunt, woman. Look at yourself in the mirror! Do you want to die an old woman just because you're tired of using *them*?" Willi stood and turned his back.

"Nonsense!" Nina's voice was strong, confident, in command once more. "Melanie's *tired*, Willi. Be nice. We all have times like that. I remember how *you* were after the war. Like a whipped puppy. You wouldn't even go outside your miserable little flat in Baden. Even after we helped you get to New Jersey you just sulked around feeling sorry for yourself. Melanie *made up* the Game to help you feel better. So quiet! *Never* tell a lady who feels tired and depressed that she looks terrible. Honestly, Willi, you're such a *Schwachsinniger* sometimes. And a crashing boor to boot."

I had anticipated many reactions to my announcement, but this was the one I feared most. It meant that Nina had also tired of the Game. It meant that she was ready to move to another level of play.

It had to mean that.

"Thank you, Nina darling," I said. "I knew you would understand."

She reached across and touched my knee reassuringly. Even through my wool skirt, I could feel the cold of her fingers.

My guests would not stay the night. I implored. I remonstrated. I pointed out that their rooms were ready, that Mr. Thorne had already turned down the quilts.

"Next time," said Willi. "Next time, Melanie, my little love. We'll make a weekend of it as we used to. A week!" Willi was in a much better mood since he had been paid his thousand-dollar prize by each of us. He had sulked, but I had insisted. It soothed his ego when Mr. Thorne brought in a check already made out to *William D. Borden*.

Again I asked him to stay, but he protested that he had a midnight flight to Chicago. He had to see a prizewinning author about a screenplay. Then he was hugging me good-bye, his companions were in the hall behind me, and I had a brief moment of terror.

But they left. The blond young man showed his white smile, and the Negro bobbed his head in what I took as a farewell. Then we were alone.

Nina and I were alone.

Not quite alone. Miss Kramer was standing next to Nina at the end of the hall. Mr. Thorne was out of sight behind the swinging door to the kitchen. I left him there.

Miss Kramer took three steps forward. I felt my breath stop for an instant. Mr. Thorne put his hand on the swinging door. Then the husky little brunette opened the door to the hall closet, removed Nina's coat, and stepped back to help her into it.

"Are you sure you won't stay?"

"No, thank you, darling. I've promised Barrett that we would drive to Hilton Head tonight."

"But it's late—"

"We have reservations. Thank you anyway, Melanie. I *will* be in touch."

"Yes."

"I mean it, dear. We must talk. I understand *exactly* how you feel, but you have to remember that the Game is still important to Willi. We'll have to find a way to end it without hurting his feelings. Perhaps we could visit him next spring in Karinhall or whatever he calls that gloomy old Bavarian place of his. A trip to the Continent would do wonders for you, dear."

"Yes."

"I *will* be in touch. After this deal with the new store is settled. We need to spend some time together, Melanie . . . just the two of us . . . like old times." Her lips kissed the air next to my cheek. She held my forearms tightly. "Good-bye, darling."

"Good-bye, Nina."

I carried the brandy glass to the kitchen. Mr. Thorne took it in silence.

"Make sure the house is secure," I said. He nodded and

went to check the locks and alarm system. It was only nine forty-five, but I was very tired. *Age,* I thought. I went up the wide staircase, perhaps the finest feature of the house, and dressed for bed. It had begun to storm, and the sound of the cold raindrops on the window carried a sad rhythm to it.

Mr. Thorne looked in as I was brushing my hair and wishing it were longer. I turned to him. He reached into the pocket of his dark vest. When his hand emerged a slim blade flicked out. I nodded. He palmed the blade shut and closed the door behind him. I listened to his footsteps recede down the stairs to the chair in the front hall, where he would spend the night.

I believe I dreamed of vampires that night. Or perhaps I was thinking about them just prior to falling asleep, and a fragment had stayed with me until morning. Of all mankind's self-inflicted terrors, of all its pathetic little monsters, only the myth of the vampire had any vestige of dignity. Like the humans it feeds on, the vampire must respond to its own dark compulsions. But unlike its petty human prey, the vampire carries out its sordid means to the only possible ends that could justify such actions—the goal of literal immortality. There is a nobility there. And a sadness.

Before sleeping I thought of that summer long ago in Vienna. I saw Willi young again—blond, flushed with youth, and filled with pride at escorting two such independent American ladies.

I remembered Willi's high, stiff collars and the short dresses that Nina helped to bring into style that summer. I remembered the friendly sounds of crowded *Biergartens* and the shadowy dance of leaves in front of gas lamps.

I remembered the footsteps on wet cobblestones, the shouts, the distant whistles, and the silences.

Willi was right; I had aged. The past year had taken a greater toll than the preceding decade. But I had not Fed. Despite the hunger, despite the aging reflection in the mirror, *I had not Fed.*

I fell asleep trying to think of that writer's last name. I fell asleep hungry.

Morning. Bright sunlight through bare branches. It was one of those crystalline, warming winter days that make living in the South so much less depressing than merely surviving a Yankee winter. I had Mr. Thorne open the window a crack when he brought in my breakfast tray. As I sipped my coffee I could hear children playing in the courtyard. Once Mr. Thorne would have brought the morning paper with the tray, but I had long since learned that to read about the follies and scandals of the world was to desecrate the morning. I was growing less and less interested in the affairs of men. I had done without a newspaper, telephone, or television for twelve years and had suffered no ill effects unless one were to count a growing self-contentment as an ill thing. I smiled as I remembered Willi's disappointment at not being able to play his video cassettes. He was such a child.

"It is Saturday, is it not, Mr. Thorne?" At his nod I gestured for the tray to be taken away. "We will go out today," I said. "A walk. Perhaps a trip to the fort. Then dinner at Henry's and home. I have arrangements to make."

Mr. Thorne hesitated and half-stumbled as he was leaving the room. I paused in the act of belting my robe. It was not like Mr. Thorne to commit an ungraceful movement. I realized that he too was getting old. He straightened the tray and dishes, nodded his head, and left for the kitchen.

I would not let thoughts of aging disturb me on such a

beautiful morning. I felt charged with a new energy and resolve. The reunion the night before had not gone well but neither had it gone as badly as it might have. I had been honest with Nina and Willi about my intention of quitting the Game. In the weeks and months to come, they—or at least Nina—would begin to brood over the ramifications of that, but by the time they chose to react, separately or together, I would be long gone. Already I had new (and old) identities waiting for me in Florida, Michigan, London, southern France, and even in New Delhi. Michigan was out for the time being. I had grown unused to the harsh climate. New Delhi was no longer the hospitable place for foreigners it had been when I resided there briefly before the war.

Nina had been right about one thing—a return to Europe would be good for me. Already I longed for the rich light and cordial *savoir vivre* of the villagers near my old summer house outside of Toulon.

The air outside was bracing. I wore a simple print dress and my spring coat. The trace of arthritis in my right leg had bothered me coming down the stairs, but I used my father's old walking stick as a cane. A young Negro servant had cut it for father the summer we moved from Greenville to Charleston. I smiled as we emerged into the warm air of the courtyard.

Mrs. Hodges came out of her doorway into the light. It was her grandchildren and their friends who were playing around the dry fountain. For two centuries the courtyard had been shared by the three brick buildings. Only my home had not been parceled into expensive town houses or fancy apartments.

"Good morning, Miz Fuller."

"Good morning, Mrs. Hodges. A beautiful day, isn't it?"

"It is that. Are you off shopping?"

"Just for a walk, Mrs. Hodges. I'm surprised that Mr. Hodges isn't out today. He always seems to be working in the yard on Saturdays."

Mrs. Hodges frowned as one of the little girls ran between us. Her friend came squealing after her, sweater flying. "Oh, George is at the marina already."

"In the daytime?" I had often been amused by Mr. Hodges's departure for work in the evening, his security-guard uniform neatly pressed, gray hair jutting out from under his cap, black lunch pail gripped firmly under his arm.

Mr. Hodges was as leathery and bowlegged as an aged cowboy. He was one of those men who were always on the verge of retiring but who probably realized that to be suddenly inactive would be a form of death sentence.

"Oh, yes. One of those colored men on the day shift down at the storage building quit, and they asked George to fill in. I told him that he was too old to work four nights a week and then go back on the weekend, but you know George. He'll never retire."

"Well, give him my best," I said.

The girls running around the fountain made me nervous.

Mrs. Hodges followed me to the wrought-iron gate. "Will you be going away for the holidays, Miz Fuller?"

"Probably, Mrs. Hodges. Most probably." Then Mr. Thorne and I were out on the sidewalk and strolling toward the Battery. A few cars drove slowly down the narrow streets, some tourists stared at the houses of our Old Section, but the day was serene and quiet.

I saw the masts of the yachts and sailboats before we came in sight of the water as we emerged onto Broad Street.

"Please acquire tickets for us, Mr. Thorne," I said. "I believe I would like to see the fort."

As is typical of most people who live in close proximity to a popular tourist attraction, I had not taken notice of it for many years. It was an act of sentimentality to visit the fort now. An act brought on by my increasing acceptance of the fact that I would have to leave these parts forever. It is one thing to plan a move; it is something altogether different to be faced with the imperative reality of it.

There were few tourists. The ferry moved away from the marina and into the placid waters of the harbor. The combination of warm sunlight and the steady throb of the diesel caused me to doze briefly. I awoke as we were putting in at the dark hulk of the island fort.

For a while I moved with the tour group, enjoying the catacomb silences of the lower levels and the mindless singsong of the young woman from the Park Service. But as we came back to the museum, with its dusty dioramas and tawdry little trays of slides, I climbed the stairs back to the outer walls. I motioned for Mr. Thorne to stay at the top of the stairs and moved out onto the ramparts.

Only one other couple—a young pair with a cheap camera and a baby in an uncomfortable-looking papoose carrier—were in sight along the wall.

It was a pleasant moment. A midday storm was approaching from the west and it set a dark backdrop to the still-sunlit church spires, brick towers, and bare branches of the city.

Even from two miles away I could see the movement of people strolling along the Battery walkway. The wind was blowing in ahead of the dark clouds and tossing whitecaps against the rocking ferry and wooden dock. The air smelled of river and winter and rain by nightfall.

It was not hard to imagine that day long ago. The shells had dropped onto the fort until the upper layers were little more than protective piles of rubble. People had cheered from the rooftops behind the Battery. The bright colors of dresses and silk parasols must have been maddening to the Yankee gunners. Finally one had fired a shot above the crowded rooftops. The ensuing confusion must have been amusing from this vantage point.

A movement down below caught my attention. Something dark was sliding through the gray water—something dark and shark silent. I was jolted out of thoughts of the past as I recognized it as a Polaris submarine, old but obviously still operational, slipping through the dark water without a sound. Waves curled and rippled over the porpoise-smooth hull, sliding to either side in a white wake. There were several men on the tower. They were muffled in heavy coats, their hats pulled low. An improbably large pair of binoculars hung from the neck of one man, whom I assumed to be the captain. He pointed at something beyond Sullivan's Island. I stared. The periphery of my vision began to fade as I made contact. Sounds and sensations came to me as from a distance.

Tension. The pleasure of salt spray, breeze from the north, northwest. Anxiety of the sealed orders below. Awareness of the sandy shallows just coming into sight on the port side.

I was startled as someone came up behind me. The dots flickering at the edge of my vision fled as I turned.

Mr. Thorne was there. At my elbow. Unbidden. I had opened my mouth to command him back to the top of the stairs when I saw the cause of his approach. The youth who had been taking pictures of his pale wife was now walking toward me. Mr. Thorne moved to intercept him.

"Hey, excuse me, ma'am. Would you or your husband mind taking our picture?"

I nodded and Mr. Thorne took the proffered camera. It looked minuscule in his long-fingered hands. Two snaps and the couple were satisfied that their presence there was documented for posterity. The young man grinned idiotically and bobbed his head. Their baby began to cry as the cold wind blew in.

I looked back to the submarine, but already it had passed on, its gray tower a thin stripe connecting the sea and sky.

We were almost back to town, the ferry was swinging in toward the ship, when a stranger told me of Willi's death.

"It's awful, isn't it?" The garrulous old woman had followed me out onto the exposed section of deck. Even though the wind had grown chilly and I had moved twice to escape her mindless chatter, the woman had obviously chosen me as her conversational target for the final stages of the tour. Neither my reticence nor Mr. Thorne's glowering presence had discouraged her. "It must have been terrible," she continued. "In the dark and all."

"What was that?" A dark premonition prompted my question.

"Why, the airplane crash. Haven't you heard about it? It must have been awful, falling into the swamp and all. I told my daugher this morning—"

"What airplane crash? When?" The old woman cringed a bit at the sharpness of my tone, but the vacuous smile stayed on her face.

"Why last night. This morning I told my daughter—"

"Where? What aircraft are you talking about?" Mr. Thorne came closer as he heard the tone of my voice.

"The one last night," she quavered. "The one from Charleston. The paper in the lounge told all about it. Isn't it terrible? Eighty-five people. I told my daughter—"

I left her standing there by the railing. There was a

crumpled newspaper near the snack bar, and under the four-word headline were the sparse details of Willi's death. Flight 417, bound for Chicago, had left Charleston International Airport at twelve-eighteen a.m. Twenty minutes later the aircraft had exploded in midair not far from the city of Columbia. Fragments of fuselage and parts of bodies had fallen into Congaree Swamp, where fishermen had found them. There had been no survivors. The FAA and FBI were investigating.

There was a loud rushing in my ears, and I had to sit down or faint. My hands were clammy against the green-vinyl upholstery. People moved past me on their way to the exits.

Willi was dead. Murdered. Nina had killed him. For a few dizzy seconds I considered the possibility of a conspiracy—an elaborate ploy by Nina and Willi to confuse me into thinking that only one threat remained. But no. There would be no reason. If Nina had included Willi in her plans, there would be no need for such absurd machinations.

Willi was dead. His remains were spread over a smelly, obscure marshland. I could imagine his last moments. He would have been leaning back in first-class comfort, a drink in his hand, perhaps whispering to one of his loutish companions.

Then the explosion. Screams. Sudden darkness. A brutal tilting and the final fall to oblivion. I shuddered and gripped the metal arm of the chair.

How had Nina done it? Almost certainly not one of Willi's entourage. It was not beyond Nina's powers to Use Willi's own cat's-paws, especially in light of his failing Ability, but there would have been no reason to do so. She could have Used anyone on that flight. It *would* have been difficult. The elaborate step of preparing the bomb. The supreme effort of blocking all memory of it, and the almost unbelievable feat of Using someone even as we sat together drinking coffee and brandy.

But Nina could have done it. Yes, she *could* have. And the timing. The timing could mean only one thing.

The last of the tourists had filed out of the cabin. I felt the slight bump that meant we had tied up to the dock. Mr. Thorne stood by the door.

Nina's timing meant that she was attempting to deal with both of us at once. She obviously had planned it long before the reunion and my timorous announcement of withdrawal. How amused Nina must have been. No wonder she had reacted so generously! Yet, she had made one great mistake. By dealing with Willi first, Nina had banked everything on my not hearing the news before she could turn on me. She knew that I had no access to daily news and only rarely left the house anymore. Still, it was unlike Nina to leave anything to chance. Was it possible that she thought I had lost the Ability completely and that Willi was the greater threat?

I shook my head as we emerged from the cabin into the gray afternoon light. The wind sliced at me through my thin coat. The view of the gangplank was blurry, and I realized that tears had filled my eyes. For Willi? He had been a pompous, weak old fool. For Nina's betrayal? Perhaps it was only the cold wind.

The streets of the Old Section were almost empty of pedestrians. Bare branches clicked together in front of the windows of fine homes. Mr. Thorne stayed by my side. The cold air sent needles of arthritic pain up my right leg to my hip. I leaned more heavily upon father's walking stick.

What would her next move be? I stopped. A fragment

of newspaper, caught by the wind, wrapped itself around my ankle and then blew on.

How would she come at me? Not from a distance. She was somewhere in town. I knew that. While it is possible to Use someone from a great distance, it would involve great rapport, an almost intimate knowledge of that person. And if contact were lost, it would be difficult if not impossible to reestablish at a distance. None of us had known why this was so. It did not matter now. But the thought of Nina still here, nearby, made my heart begin to race.

Not from a distance. I would see my assailant. If I knew Nina at all, I knew that. Certainly Willi's death had been the least personal Feeding imaginable, but that had been a mere technical operation. Nina obviously had decided to settle old scores with *me*, and Willi had become an obstacle to her, a minor but measurable threat that had to be eliminated before she could proceed. I could easily imagine that in Nina's own mind her choice of death for Willi would be interpreted as an act of compassion, almost a sign of affection. Not so with me. I felt that Nina would want me to know, however briefly, that she was behind the attack. In a sense, her own vanity would be my warning. Or so I hoped.

I was tempted to leave immediately. I could have Mr. Thorne get the Audi out of storage, and we could be beyond Nina's influence in an hour—away to a new life within a few more hours. There were important items in the house, of course, but the funds that I had stored elsewhere would replace most of them. It would be almost welcome to leave everything behind with the discarded identity that had accumulated them.

No. I could not leave. Not yet.

From across the street the house looked dark and malevolent. Had *I* closed those blinds on the second floor? There was a shadowy movement in the courtyard, and I saw Mrs. Hodges's granddaughter and a friend scamper from one doorway to another. I stood irresolutely on the curb and tapped father's stick against the black-barked tree. It was foolish to dither so—I knew it was—but it had been a long time since I had been forced to make a decision under stress.

"Mr. Thorne, please check the house. Look in each room. Return quickly."

A cold wind came up as I watched Mr. Thorne's black coat blend into the gloom of the courtyard. I felt terribly exposed standing there alone. I found myself glancing up and down the street, looking for Miss Kramer's dark hair, but the only sign of movement was a young woman pushing a perambulator far down the street.

The blinds on the second floor shot up, and Mr. Thorne's face stared out whitely for a minute. Then he turned away, and I remained staring at the dark rectangle of window. A shout from the courtyard startled me, but it was only the little girl—what was her name?—calling to her friend. Kathleen, that was it. The two sat on the edge of the fountain and opened a box of animal crackers. I stared intently at them and then relaxed. I even managed to smile a little at the extent of my paranoia. For a second I considered using Mr. Thorne directly, but the thought of being helpless on the street dissuaded me. When one is in complete contact, the senses still function but are a distant thing at best.

Hurry. The thought was sent almost without volition. Two bearded men were walking down the sidewalk on my side of the street. I crossed to stand in front of my own gate. The men were laughing and gesturing at each other. One looked over at me. *Hurry*.

Mr. Thorne came out of the house, locked the door behind him, and crossed the courtyard toward me. One of the girls said something to him and held out the box of crackers, but he ignored her. Across the street the two men continued walking. Mr. Thorne handed me the large front-door key. I dropped it in my coat pocket and looked sharply at him. He nodded. His placid smile unconsciously mocked my consternation.

"You're sure?" I asked. Again the nod. "You checked all of the rooms?" Nod. "The alarms?" Nod. "You looked in the basement?" Nod. "No sign of disturbance?" Mr. Thorne shook his head.

My hand went to the metal of the gate, but I hesitated. Anxiety filled my throat like bile. I was a silly old woman, tired and aching from the chill, but I could not bring myself to open that gate.

"Come." I crossed the street and walked briskly away from the house. "We will have dinner at Henry's and return later." Only I was not walking toward the old restaurant. I was heading away from the house in what I knew was a blind, directionless panic. It was not until we reached the waterfront and were walking along the Battery wall that I began to calm down.

No one else was in sight. A few cars moved along the street, but to approach us someone would have to cross a wide, empty space. The gray clouds were quite low and blended with the choppy, white-crested waves in the bay.

The open air and fading evening light served to revive me, and I began to think more clearly. Whatever Nina's plans had been, they certainly had been thrown into disarray by my day-long absence. I doubted that Nina would stay if there were the slightest risk to herself. No, she would be returning to New York by plane even as I stood shivering on the Battery walk. In the morning I would receive a telegram, I could see it. MELANIE ISN'T IT TERRIBLE ABOUT WILLI? TERRIBLY SAD. CAN YOU TRAVEL WITH ME TO THE FUNERAL? LOVE, NINA.

I began to realize that my reluctance to leave immediately had come from a desire to return to the warmth and comfort of my home. I simply had been afraid to shuck off this old cocoon. I could do so now. I would wait in a safe place while Mr. Thorne returned to the house to pick up the one thing I could not leave behind. Then he would get the car out of storage, and by the time Nina's telegram arrived I would be far away. It would be *Nina* who would be starting at shadows in the months and years to come. I smiled and began to frame the necessary commands.

"Melanie."

My head snapped around. Mr. Thorne had not spoken in twenty-eight years. He spoke now.

"Melanie." His face was distorted in a rictus that showed his back teeth. The knife was in his right hand. The blade flicked out as I stared. I looked into his empty, gray eyes, and I knew.

"Melanie."

The long blade came around in a powerful arc. I could do nothing to stop it. It cut through the fabric of my coat sleeve and continued into my side. But in the act of turning, my purse had swung with me. The knife tore through the leather, ripped through the jumbled contents, pierced my coat, and drew blood above my lowest left rib. The purse had saved my life.

I raised father's heavy walking stick and struck Mr. Thorne squarely in his left eye. He reeled but did not make a sound. Again he swept the air with the knife, but I had taken two steps back and his vision was clouded. I took a two-handed grip on the cane and swung sideways again, bringing the stick around in an awkward chop. Incredibly, it again found the eye socket. I took three more steps back.

Blood streamed down the left side of Mr. Thorne's face, and the damaged eye protruded onto his cheek. The rictal grin remained. His head came up, he raised his left hand slowly, plucked out the eye with a soft snapping of a gray cord, and thew it into the water of the bay. He came toward me. I turned and ran.

I *tried* to run. The ache in my right leg slowed me to a walk after twenty paces. Fifteen more hurried steps and my lungs were out of air, my heart threatening to burst. I could feel a wetness seeping down my left side and there was a tingling—like an ice cube held against the skin—where the knife blade had touched me. One glance back showed me that Mr. Thorne was striding toward me faster than I was moving. Normally he could have overtaken me in four strides. But it is hard to make someone run when you are Using him. Especially when that person's body is reacting to shock and trauma. I glanced back again, almost slipping on the slick pavement. Mr. Thorne was grinning widely. Blood poured from the empty socket and stained his teeth. No one else was in sight.

Down the stairs, clutching at the rail so as not to fall. Down the twisting walk and up the asphalt path to the street. Pole lamps flickered and went on as I passed. Behind me Mr. Thorne took the steps in two jumps. As I hurried up the path, I thanked God that I had worn low-heel shoes for the boat ride. What would an observer think seeing this bizarre, slow-motion chase between two old people? There were no observers.

I turned onto a side street. Closed shops, empty warehouses. Going left would take me to Broad Street, but to the right, half a block away, a lone figure had emerged from a dark storefront. I moved that way, no longer able to run, close to fainting. The arthritic cramps in my leg hurt more than I could ever have imagined and threatened to collapse me on the sidewalk. Mr. Thorne was twenty paces behind me and quickly closing the distance.

The man I was approaching was a tall, thin Negro wearing a brown nylon jacket. He was carrying a box of what looked like framed sepia photographs.

He glanced at me as I approached and then looked over my shoulder at the apparition ten steps behind.

"Hey!" The man had time to shout the single syllable and then I reached out with my mind and *shoved.* He twitched like a poorly handled marionette. His jaw dropped, and his eyes glazed over, and he lurched past me just as Mr. Thorne reached for the back of my coat.

The box flew into the air, and glass shattered on the brick sidewalk. Long, brown fingers reached for a white throat. Mr. Thorne backhanded him away, but the Negro clung tenaciously, and the two swung around like awkward dance partners. I reached the opening to an alley and leaned my face against the cold brick to revive myself. The effort of concentration while Using this stranger did not afford me the luxury of resting even for a second.

I watched the clumsy stumblings of the two tall men for a while and resisted an absurd impulse to laugh.

Mr. Thorne plunged the knife into the other's stomach, withdrew it, plunged it in again. The Negro's fingernails were clawing at Mr. Thorne's good eye now. Strong teeth were snapping in search of the blade for a third time, but the heart was still beating and he was still usable. The man jumped, scissoring his legs around Mr. Thorne's middle while his jaws closed on the muscular throat. Fingernails raked bloody streaks across white skin. The two went down in a tumble.

Kill him. Fingers groped for an eye, but Mr. Thorne reached up with his left hand and snapped the thin wrist. Limp fingers continued to flail. With a tremendous exertion, Mr. Thorne lodged his forearm against the other's chest and lifted him bodily as a reclining father tosses a child above him. Teeth tore away a piece of flesh, but there was no vital damage. Mr. Thorne brought the knife between them, up, left, then right. He severed half the Negro's throat with the second swing, and blood fountained over both of them. The smaller man's legs spasmed twice, Mr. Thorne threw him to one side, and I turned and walked quickly down the alley.

Out into the light again, the fading evening light, and I realized that I had run myself into a dead end. Backs of warehouses and the windowless, metal side of the Battery Marina pushed right up against the waters of the bay. A street wound away to the left, but it was dark, deserted, and far too long to try.

I looked back in time to see the black silhouette enter the alley behind me.

I tried to make contact, but there was nothing there. Nothing. Mr. Thorne might as well have been a hole in the air. I would worry later how Nina had done this thing.

The side door to the marina was locked. The main door was almost a hundred yards away and would also be locked. Mr. Thorne emerged from the alley and swung his head left and right in search of me. In the dim light his heavily streaked face looked almost black. He began lurching toward me.

I raised father's walking stick, broke the lower pane of the window, and reached in through the jagged shards. If there was a bottom or top bolt I was dead. There was a simple doorknob lock and crossbolt. My fingers slipped on the cold metal, but the bolt slid back as Mr. Thorne stepped up on the walk behind me. Then I was inside and throwing the bolt.

It was very dark. Cold seeped up from the concrete floor and there was a sound of many small boats rising and falling at their moorings. Fifty yards away light spilled out of the office windows. I had hoped there would be an alarm system, but the building was too old and the marina too cheap to have one. I walked toward the light as Mr. Thorne's forearm shattered the remaining glass in the door behind me. The arm withdrew. A great kick broke off the top hinge and splintered wood around the bolt. I glanced at the office, but only the sound of a radio talk show came out of the impossibly distant door. Another kick.

I turned to my right and stepped to the bow of a bobbing inboard cruiser. Five steps and I was in the small, covered space that passed for a forward cabin. I closed the flimsy access panel behind me and peered out through the Plexiglas.

Mr. Thorne's third kick sent the door flying inward, dangling from long strips of splintered wood. His dark form filled the doorway. Light from a distant streetlight glinted off the blade in his right hand.

Please. Please hear the noise. But there was no movement from the office, only the metallic voices from the radio. Mr. Thorne took four paces, paused, and stepped down onto the first boat in line. It was an open outboard, and he was back up on the concrete in six seconds. The second boat had a small cabin. There was a ripping sound as Mr. Thorne kicked open the tiny hatch door, and then he was back up on the walkway. My boat was the eighth in line. I wondered why he couldn't just hear the wild hammering of my heart.

I shifted position and looked through the starboard port. The murky Plexiglas threw the light into streaks and patterns. I caught a brief glimpse of white hair through the window, and the radio was switched to another station. Loud music echoed in the long room. I slid back to the other porthole. Mr. Thorne was stepping off the fourth boat.

I closed my eyes, forced my ragged breathing to slow, and tried to remember countless evenings watching a bowlegged old figure shuffle down the street. Mr. Thorne finished his inspection of the fifth boat, a longer cabin cruiser with several dark recesses, and pulled himself back onto the walkway.

Forget the coffee in the thermos. Forget the crossword puzzle. Go look!

The sixth boat was a small outboard. Mr. Thorne glanced at it but did not step onto it. The seventh was a low sailboat, mast folded down, canvas stretched across the cockpit. Mr. Thorne's knife slashed through the thick material. Blood-streaked hands pulled back the canvas like a shroud being torn away. He jumped back to the walkway.

Forget the coffee. Go look! Now!

Mr. Thorne stepped onto the bow of my boat. I felt it rock to his weight. There was nowhere to hide, only a tiny storage locker under the seat, much too small to squeeze into. I untied the canvas strips that held the seat cushion to the bench. The sound of my ragged breathing seemed to echo in the little space. I curled into a fetal position behind the cushion as Mr. Thorne's leg moved past the starboard port. *Now.* Suddenly his face filled the Plexiglas strip not a foot from my head. His impossibly wide grimace grew even wider. *Now.* He stepped into the cockpit.

Now. Now. Now.

Mr. Thorne crouched at the cabin door. I tried to brace the tiny louvered door with my legs, but my right leg would not obey. Mr. Thorne's fist slammed through the thin wooden strips and grabbed my ankle.

"Hey there!"

It was Mr. Hodges's shaky voice. His flashlight bobbed in our direction.

Mr. Thorne shoved against the door. My left leg folded painfully. Mr. Thorne's left hand firmly held my ankle through the shattered slats while the hand with the knife blade came through the opening hatch.

"Hey—" My mind shoved. Very hard. The old man stopped. He dropped the flashlight and unstrapped the buckle over the grip of his revolver.

Mr. Thorne slashed the knife back and forth. The cushion was almost knocked out of my hands as shreds of foam filled the cabin. The blade caught the tip of my little finger as the knife swung back again.

Do it. Now. Do it. Mr. Hodges gripped the revolver in both hands and fired. The shot went wide in the dark as the sound echoed off concrete and water. *Closer, you fool. Move!* Mr. Thorne shoved again and his body squeezed into the open hatch. He released my ankle to free his left arm, but almost instantly his hand was back in the cabin, grasping for me. I reached up and turned on the overhead light. Darkness stared at me from his empty eye socket. Light through the broken shutters spilled yellow strips across his ruined face. I slid to the left, but Mr. Thorne's hand, which had my coat, was pulling me off the bench. He was on his knees, freeing his right hand for the knife thrust.

Now! Mr. Hodges's second shot caught Mr. Thorne in the right hip. He grunted as the impact shoved him backward into a sitting position. My coat ripped, and buttons rattled on the deck.

The knife slashed the bulkhead near my ear before it pulled away.

Mr. Hodges stepped shakily onto the bow, almost fell, and inched his way around the starboard side. I pushed the hatch against Mr. Thorne's arm, but he continued to grip my coat and drag me toward him. I fell to my knees. The blade swung back, ripped through foam, and slashed at my coat. What was left of the cushion flew out of my hands. I had Mr. Hodges stop four feet away and brace the gun on the roof of the cabin.

Mr. Thorne pulled the blade back and poised it like a matador's sword. I could sense the silent scream of triumph that poured out over the stained teeth like a noxious vapor. The light of Nina's madness burned behind the single, staring eye.

Mr. Hodges fired. The bullet severed Mr. Thorne's spine and continued on into the port scupper. Mr. Thorne arched backward, splayed out his arms, and flopped onto the deck like a great fish that just been landed. The knife fell to the floor of the cabin, while stiff white fingers continued to slap nervelessly against the deck. I had Mr. Hodges step forward, brace the muzzle against Mr. Thorne's temple just above the remaining eye, and fire again. The sound was muted and hollow.

There was a first-aid kit in the office bathroom. I had the old man stand by the door while I bandaged my little finger and took three aspirin.

My coat was ruined, and blood had stained my print

dress. I had never cared very much for the dress—I thought it made me look dowdy—but the coat had been a favorite of mine. My hair was a mess. Small, moist bits of gray matter flecked it. I splashed water on my face and brushed my hair as best I could. Incredibly, my tattered purse had stayed with me although many of the contents had spilled out. I transferred keys, billfold, reading glasses, and Kleenex to my large coat pocket and dropped the purse behind the toilet. I no longer had father's walking stick, but I could not remember where I had dropped it.

Gingerly I removed the heavy revolver from Mr. Hodges's grip. The old man's arm remained extended, fingers curled around air. After fumbling for a few seconds I managed to click open the cylinder. Two cartridges remained unfired. The old fool had been walking around with all six chambers loaded! *Always leave an empty chamber under the hammer.* That is what Charles had taught me that gay and distant summer so long ago when such weapons were merely excuses for trips to the island for target practice punctuated by the shrill shrieks of our nervous laughter as Nina and I allowed ourselves to be held, arms supported, bodies shrinking back into the firm support of our so-serious tutors' arms. *One must always count the cartridges,* lectured Charles, as I half-swooned against him, smelling the sweet, masculine shaving soap and tobacco smell rising from him on that warm, bright day.

Mr. Hodges stirred slightly as my attention wandered. His mouth gaped, and his dentures hung loosely. I glanced at the worn leather belt, but there were no extra bullets there, and I had no idea where he kept any. I probed, but there was little left in the old man's jumble of thoughts except for a swirling tape-loop replay of the muzzle being laid against Mr. Thorne's temple, the explosion, the—

"Come," I said. I adjusted the glasses on Mr. Hodges's vacant face, returned the revolver to the holster, and let him lead me out of the building.

It was very dark out. We had gone six blocks before the old man's violent shivering reminded me that I had forgotten to have him put on his coat. I tightened my mental vise, and he stopped shaking.

The house looked just as it had . . . my God . . . only forty-five minutes earlier. There were no lights. I let us into the courtyard and searched my overstuffed coat pocket for the key. My coat hung loose and the cold night air nipped at me. From behind lighted windows across the courtyard came the laughter of little girls, and I hurried so that Kathleen would not see her grandfather entering my house.

Mr. Hodges went in first, with the revolver extended. I had him switch on the light before I entered.

The parlor was empty, undisturbed. The light from the chandelier in the dining room reflected off polished surfaces. I sat down for a minute on the Williamsburg reproduction chair in the hall to let my heart rate return to normal. I did not have Mr. Hodges lower the hammer on the still-raised pistol. His arm began to shake from the strain of holding it. Finally, I rose and we moved down the hall toward the conservatory.

Miss Kramer exploded out of the swinging door from the kitchen with the heavy iron poker already coming down in an arc. The gun fired harmlessly into the polished floor as the old man's arm snapped from the impact. The gun fell from limp fingers as Miss Kramer raised the poker for a second blow.

I turned and ran back down the hallway. Behind me I heard the crushed-melon sound of the poker contacting Mr. Hodges's skull. Rather than run into the courtyard I went up the stairway. A mistake. Miss Kramer bounded up the stairs and reached the bedroom door only a few seconds after me. I caught one glimpse of her widened, maddened eyes and of the upraised poker before I slammed and locked the heavy door. The latch clicked just as the brunette on the other side began to throw herself against the wood. The thick oak did not budge. Then I heard the concussion of metal against the door and frame. Again.

Cursing my stupidity, I turned to the familiar room, but there was nothing there to help me. There was not as much as a closet to hide in, only the antique wardrobe. I moved quickly to the window and threw up the sash. My screams would attract attention but not before that monstrosity had gained access. She was prying at the edges of the door now. I looked out, saw the shadows in the window across the way, and did what I had to do.

Two minutes later I was barely conscious of the wood giving away around the latch. I heard the distant grating of the poker as it pried at the recalcitrant metal plate. The door swung inward.

Miss Kramer was covered with sweat. Her mouth hung slack, and drool slid from her chin. Her eyes were not human. Neither she nor I heard the soft tread of sneakers on the stairs behind her.

Keep moving. Lift it. Pull it back—all the way back. Use both hands. Aim it.

Something warned Miss Kramer. Warned Nina, I should say; there was no more Miss Kramer. The brunette turned to see little Kathleen standing on the top stair, her grandfather's heavy weapon aimed and cocked. The other girl was in the courtyard shouting for her friend.

This time Nina knew she had to deal with the threat. Miss Kramer hefted the poker and turned into the hall just as the pistol fired. The recoil tumbled Kathleen backward down the stairs as a red corsage blossomed above Miss Kramer's left breast. She spun but grasped the railing with her left hand and lurched down the stairs after the child. I released the ten-year-old just as the poker fell, rose, fell again. I moved to the head of the stairway. I had to see.

Miss Kramer looked up from her grim work. Only the whites of her eyes were visible in her spattered face. Her masculine shirt was soaked with her own blood, but still she moved, functioned. She picked up the gun in her left hand. Her mouth opened wider, and a sound emerged like steam leaking from an old radiator.

"Melanie . . ." I closed my eyes as the thing started up the stairs for me.

Kathleen's friend came in through the open door, her small legs pumping. She took the stairs in six jumps and wrapped her thin, white arms around Miss Kramer's neck in a tight embrace.

The two went over backward, across Kathleen, all the way down the wide stairs to the polished wood below.

The girl appeared to be little more than bruised. I went down and moved her to one side. A blue stain was spreading along one cheekbone, and there were cuts on her arms and forehead. Her blue eyes blinked uncomprehendingly.

Miss Kramer's neck was broken. I picked up the pistol on the way to her and kicked the poker to one side. Her head was at an impossible angle, but she was still alive. Her body was paralyzed, urine already stained the wood, but her eyes still blinked and her teeth clicked together obscenely. I had to hurry. There were adult voices calling from the Hodgeses' town house. The door to the courtyard was wide open. I turned to the girl. "Get up." She blinked once and rose painfully to her feet.

I shut the door and lifted a tan raincoat from the coatrack.

It took only a minute to transfer the contents of my pockets to the raincoat and to discard my ruined spring coat. Voices were calling in the courtyard now.

I kneeled down next to Miss Kramer and seized her face in my hands, exerting pressure to keep the jaws still. Her eyes had rolled upward again, but I shook her head until the irises were visible. I leaned forward until our cheeks were touching. My whisper was louder than a shout.

"I'm coming for you, Nina."

I dropped her head onto the wood and walked quickly to the conservatory, my sewing room. I did not have time to get the key from upstairs; so I raised a Windsor side chair and smashed the glass of the cabinet. My coat pocket was barely large enough.

The girl remained standing in the hall. I handed her Mr. Hodges's pistol. Her left arm hung at a strange angle and I wondered if she had broken something after all. There was a knock at the door, and someone tried the knob.

"This way," I whispered, and led the girl into the dining room.

We stepped across Miss Kramer on the way, walked through the dark kitchen as the pounding grew louder, and then were out, into the alley, into the night.

There were three hotels in this part of the Old Section. One was a modern, expensive motor hotel some ten blocks away, comfortable but commercial. I rejected it immediately. The second was a small, homey lodging house only a block from my home. It was a pleasant but nonexclusive little place, exactly the type I would choose when visiting another town. I rejected it also. The third was two and a half blocks farther, an old Broad Street mansion done over into a small hotel, expensive antiques in every room, absurdly overpriced. I hurried there. The girl moved quickly at my side. The pistol was still in her hand, but I had her remove her sweater and carry it over the weapon. My leg ached, and I frequently leaned on the girl as we hurried down the street.

The manager of the Mansard House recognized me. His eyebrows went up a fraction of an inch as he noticed my disheveled appearance. The girl stood ten feet away in the foyer, half-hidden in the shadows.

"I'm looking for a friend of mine," I said brightly. "A Mrs. Drayton."

The manager started to speak, paused, frowned without being aware of it, and tried again. "I'm sorry. No one under that name is registered here."

"Perhaps she registered under her maiden name," I said. "Nina Hawkins. She's an older woman but very attractive. A few years younger than I. Long, gray hair. Her friend may have registered for her . . . an attractive, young, dark-haired lady named Barrett Kramer—"

"No, I'm sorry," said the manager in a strangely flat tone. "No one under that name has registered. Would you like to leave a message in case your party arrives later?"

"No," I said. "No message."

I brought the girl into the lobby, and we turned down a corridor leading to the restrooms and side stairs. "Excuse me, please," I said to a passing porter. "Perhaps you can help me."

"Yes, ma'am." He stopped, annoyed, and brushed back his long hair. It would be tricky. If I was not to lose the girl, I would have to act quickly.

"I'm looking for a friend," I said. "She's an older lady but quite attractive. Blue eyes. Long, gray hair. She travels with a young woman who has dark, curly hair."

"No, ma'am. No one like that is registered here."

I reached out and grabbed hold of his forearm tightly. I released the girl and focused on the boy. "Are you sure?"

"Mrs. Harrison," he said. His eyes looked past me. "Room 207. North front."

I smiled. *Mrs. Harrison.* Good God, what a fool Nina was. Suddenly the girl let out a small whimper and slumped against the wall. I made a quick decision. I like to think that it was compassion, but I sometimes remember that her left arm was useless.

"What's your name?" I asked the child, gently stroking her bangs. Her eyes moved left and right in confusion. "Your name!"

"Alicia." It was only a whisper.

"All right, Alicia. I want you to go home now. Hurry, but don't run."

"My *arm* hurts," she said. Her lips began to quiver. I touched her forehead again and *pushed.*

"You're going home," I said. "Your arm does not hurt. You won't remember anything. This is like a dream that you will forget. Go home. Hurry, but do not run." I took the pistol from her but left it wrapped in the sweater. "Bye-bye, Alicia."

She blinked and crossed the lobby to the doors. I handed the gun to the bellhop. "Put it under your vest," I said.

"Who is it?" Nina's voice was light.

"Albert, ma'am. The porter. Your car's out front, and I'll take your bags down."

e flowers growing between the tumbled stones ey, and I am content simply to be there and to sunlight and silence with them.

other days—cold, dark days when the clouds from the north—I remember the shark-silent submarine moving through the dark waters of and I wonder whether my self-imposed absti- be for nothing. I wonder whether those I dream solation will indulge in their own gigantic, final

arm today. I am happy. But I am also alone. And , very hungry.

There was the sound of a lock clicking and the door opened the width of a still-secured chain. Albert blinked in the glare, smiled shyly, and brushed his hair back. I pressed against the wall.

"Very well." She undid the chain and moved back. She had already turned and was latching her suitcase when I stepped into the room.

"Hello, Nina," I said softly. Her back straightened, but even that move was graceful. I could see the imprint on the bedspread where she had been lying. She turned slowly. She was wearing a pink dress I had never seen before.

"Hello, Melanie." She smiled. Her eyes were the softest, purest blue I had ever seen. I had the porter take Mr. Hodges's gun out and aim it. His arm was steady. He pulled back the hammer and held it with his thumb. Nina folded her hands in front of her. Her eyes never left mine.

"Why?" I asked.

Nina shrugged ever so slightly. For a second I thought she was going to laugh. I could not have borne it if she had laughed—that husky, childlike laugh that had touched me so many times. Instead she closed her eyes. Her smile remained.

"Why Mrs. Harrison?" I asked.

"Why, darling, I felt I owed him *something*. I mean, poor Roger. Did I ever tell you how he died? No, of course I didn't. And you never asked." Her eyes opened. I glanced at the porter, but his aim was steady. It only remained for him to exert a little more pressure on the trigger.

"He *drowned*, darling," said Nina. "Poor Roger threw himself from that steamship—what was its name?—the one that was taking him back to England. So strange. And he had just written me a letter promising marriage. Isn't that a *terribly* sad story, Melanie? Why do you think he did a thing like that? I guess we'll never know, will we?"

"I guess we never will," I said. I silently ordered the porter to pull the trigger.

Nothing.

I looked quickly to my right. The young man's head was turning toward me. *I had not made him do that.* The stiffly extended arm began to swing in my direction. The pistol moved smoothly like the tip of a weather vane swinging in the wind.

No! I strained until the cords in my neck stood out. The turning slowed but did not stop until the muzzle was pointing at my face. Nina laughed now. The sound was very loud in the little room.

"Good-bye, Melanie *dear,*" Nina said, and laughed again. She laughed and nodded at the porter. I stared into the black hole as the hammer fell. On an empty chamber. And another. And another.

"Good-bye, Nina," I said as I pulled Charles's long pistol from the raincoat pocket. The explosion jarred my wrist and filled the room with blue smoke. A small hole, smaller than a dime but as perfectly round, appeared in the precise center of Nina's forehead. For the briefest second she remained standing as if nothing had happened. Then she fell backward, recoiled from the high bed, and dropped face forward onto the floor.

I turned to the porter and replaced his useless weapon with the ancient but well-maintained revolver. For the first time I noticed that the boy was not much younger than Charles had been. His hair was almost exactly the same color. I leaned forward and kissed him lightly on the lips.

"Albert," I whispered, "there are four cartridges left. One must always count the cartridges, mustn't one? Go to the lobby. Kill the manager. Shoot one other person, the nearest. Put the barrel in your mouth and pull the trigger.

If it misfires, pull it again. Keep
you are in the lobby."

We emerged into general conf
"Call for an ambulance!" I c
accident. Someone call for an am
ple rushed to comply. I swoonec
white-haired gentleman. People
peering into the room and exclai
was the sound of three gunshots f
renewed confusion I slipped down
fire door, into the night.

Time has passed. I am very happy h
France now, between Cannes and T
happy to say, too near St. Tropez.

I rarely go out. Henri and Claude
the village. I never go to the beach.
the town house in Paris or to my pensi
Pescara, on the Adriatic. But even thos
less and less frequent.

There is an abandoned abbey in
go there to sit and think among the
ers. I think about isolation and absti
is so cruelly dependent upon the ot
I feel younger these days. I te
because of the climate and my freec
of that final Feeding. But sometin
familiar streets of Charleston and
are dreams of hunger.

On some days I rise to the soun
the village cycle by our place on t
those days the sun is marvelously

small wh
of the ab
share the
But o
move in
shape of
the bay,
nence w
of in my
Feeding.
It is w
I am ve

Permissions Acknowledgments

◆◆◆

Ray Bradbury: "The Man Upstairs" by Ray Bradbury, copyright © 1947 by *Harper's Magazine*, copyright renewed 1974 by Minneapolis Star and Tribune Co., Inc. Originally published in *Harper's Magazine*, March 1947. Reprinted by permission of Don Congdon Associates, Inc.

Fredric Brown: "Blood" by Fredric Brown, copyright © 1954 by Fredric Brown. Originally published in *The Magazine of Fantasy & Science Fiction*, February 1954. Reprinted by permission of Barry Malzberg for the Estate of Fredric Brown.

Hugh B. Cave: "Stragella" by Hugh B. Cave, copyright © 1932 by *Strange Tales*. Originally published in *Strange Tales of Mystery and Terror*, June 1932. Reprinted by permission of the Estate of Hugh B. Cave.

Carl Jacobi: "Revelations in Black" by Carl Jacobi, copyright © 1947 by Carl Jacobi, copyright renewed 1975. Originally published in *Weird Tales*, April 1933. Reprinted by permission of Arkham House Publishers Inc.

Garry Kilworth: "The Silver Collar" by Garry Kilworth. Copyright © 1989 by Garry Kilworth. Originally published in *Blood Is Not Enough*, edited by Ellen Datlow (New York: Morrow, 1989). Reprinted by permission of Garry Kilworth.

Stephen King: "Popsy" by Stephen King, copyright © 1987 by Stephen King. Originally published in *Masques II: All-New Stories of Horror and the Supernatural*, edited by J. N. Williamson (Baltimore: Maclay, 1987). All rights reserved. Reprinted by permission of Stephen King.

Tanith Lee: "Bite-Me-Not or, Fleur de Fur" by Tanith Lee, copyright © 1984 by Tanith Lee. Originally published in *Isaac Asimov's Science Fiction Magazine*, October 1984. Reprinted by permission of Tanith Lee.

Dan Simmons: "Carrion Comfort" by Dan Simmons, copyright © 1983 by Dan Simmons. Originally published in *Omni*, Sept./Oct. 1983. Reprinted by permission of Dan Simmons.

Clark Ashton Smith: "The Death of Ilalotha" by Clark Ashton Smith, copyright © 1937 by Clark Ashton Smith, copyright renewed 1965 by Caslana Literary Ent. Originally published in *Weird Tales*, Sept. 1937. Reprinted by permission of Arkham House Publishers Inc.

Mary A. Turzillo: "When Gretchen Was Human" by Mary A. Turzillo, copyright © 2001 by Mary A. Turzillo. Originally published in *The Mammoth Book of Vampire Stories by Women* (Carroll & Graf, 2001). Reprinted by permission of Mary A. Turzillo.

Lisa Tuttle: "Replacements" by Lisa Tuttle, copyright © 1992 by Lisa Tuttle. Reprinted by permission of Lisa Tuttle.

Manly Wade Wellman: "Chastel" by Manly Wade Wellman, copyright © 1979 by Manly Wade Wellman. Originally published in *The Year's Best Horror Stories, Series VII* (DAW Books, 1979). Reprinted by permission of David Drake.

Gahan Wilson: "When the Sea Was Wet as Wet Could Be" by Gahan Wilson, copyright © 1967 by Gahan Wilson. Originally published in *Playboy*, May 1967. Reprinted by permission of Gahan Wilson.

ALSO EDITED BY
OTTO PENZLER

THE VAMPIRE ARCHIVES

The Most Complete Volume of Vampire Tales Ever Published

The Vampire Archives is the biggest, hungriest, undeadliest collection of vampire stories, as well as the most comprehensive bibliography of vampire fiction ever assembled. Whether imagined by Bram Stoker or Anne Rice, vampires are part of the human lexicon and as old as blood itself. They are your neighbors, your friends, and they are always lurking. Now Otto Penzler has compiled the darkest, the scariest, and by far the most evil collection of vampire stories ever. With over eighty stories, including the works of Stephen King and D. H. Lawrence, alongside Lord Byron and Tanith Lee, not to mention Edgar Allan Poe and Harlan Ellison, it will drive a stake through the heart of any other collection out there.

Fiction/978-0-307-47389-9

ALSO AVAILABLE IN MASS-MARKET VOLUMES:

FANGS

The Vampire Archives, Volume 2

Including stories by Clive Barker, Anne Rice, and Arthur Conan Doyle

Fiction/978-0-307-74185-1

COFFINS

The Vampire Archives, Volume 3

Including stories by Harlan Ellison, Robert Bloch, and Edgar Allan Poe

Fiction/978-0-307-74223-0

Forthcoming from Vintage Books in Fall 2010 . . .

THE BLACK LIZARD BIG BOOK OF PULPS

The Best Crime Stories from the Pulps During Their Golden Age—The '20s, '30s & '40s

Weighing in at over a thousand pages, containing more than fifty stories and two novels, this book is big baby, bigger and more powerful than a freight train—a bullet couldn't pass through it. Here are the best stories and every major writer who ever appeared in celebrated pulps like *Black Mask*, *Dime Detective*, *Detective Fiction Weekly*, and more. These are the classic tales that created the genre and gave birth to hard-hitting detectives who smoke criminals like cheap cigars; sultry dames whose looks are as lethal as a dagger to the chest; and gin-soaked hideouts where conversations are just preludes to murder. This is crime fiction at its gritty best.

Crime Fiction/978-0-307-28048-0

THE BLACK LIZARD BIG BOOK OF *BLACK MASK* STORIES

An unstoppable anthology of crime stories culled from *Black Mask*, the magazine where the first hardboiled detective story, which was written by Carroll John Daly, appeared. It was the slum in which Dashiell Hammett, Raymond Chandler, Horace McCoy, Cornell Woolrich, John D. MacDonald all got their start. It was the home of stories with titles like "Murder *Is* Bad Luck," "Ten Carats of Lead," "Diamonds Mean Death," and "Drop Dead Twice." Also here is *The Maltese Falcon* as it originally appeared in the magazine. Delivered in the same trademark package as the New York Times bestselling *The Black Lizard Big Book of Pulps*, crime writing gets no better than this.

Crime Fiction/978-0-307-45543-7

Forthcoming from Vintage Books in Fall 2010 . . .

AGENTS OF TREACHERY

Never Before Published Spy Fiction from Today's Most Exciting Writers

For the first time ever, legendary editor Otto Penzler has handpicked some of the most respected and bestselling thriller writers working today for a riveting collection of spy fiction. From first to last, this stellar collection signals mission accomplished. Featuring: Lee Child with an incredible look at the formation of a special ops team; James Grady writing about an Arab undercover FBI agent with an active cell; Joseph Finder riffing on a Boston architect who's convinced that his Persian neighbors are up to no good; John Lawton concocting a Len Deighton-esque story about British intelligence; Stephen Hunter thrilling us with a tale about a WWII brigade; and much more.

Spy Fiction/978-0-307-47751-4